I needed time to at least talk to Simon and explain there was somebody else—but Spencer wouldn't listen…

I had mind blowing sex last night but I didn't remember making this official. I still needed to talk to Simon. At the very least he deserved—he deserved someone better than me. That was what this all boiled down to. I had turned into the one thing I used to despise, a careless, thoughtless, wishy-washy, Barbie and a slutty one at that. Everything had felt so good in the moment, but I was drunk and not thinking. *What am I going to say to Simon? Fuck, what am I going to say to Spencer?*

"Spencer I—"

"Don't," he said, sighing and holding his hand up. "Don't even start with the excuses. You chose to be here with me. Why the fuck do you keep doing this to me if you're in love with him?" he roared, slamming his fist into the mattress.

"I don't know if I'm in love with him—"

Cutting me off, he stood from the bed, and his deep voice shook the walls as he spoke. "Now!" he spit, as he moved closer to me. "Choose now!" he growled.

"I can't," I said back as sternly as I could.

"You can't or you won't?" Taking a step back, he turned from me shoving his hands through his tousled hair, the muscles in his back flexed, and I nearly went knees to the floor.

"You can't have us both, Elizabeth. You either stay with me, be with only me, love only me—or fucking leave."

His words were raw and savage as he turned back to face me. I couldn't talk, so I simply stared up at him. *This isn't happening, is it? Things were perfect five minutes ago, now everything is just wrong. It's all wrong.*

Coming quickly toward me, he grabbed my upper arms, taking me to lie down on the bed. He stared into my eyes before running his hand up the inside of my thigh. Two fingers slid deep inside me. Who was I kidding? Just seeing him made me aroused and arguing with him only made it worse.

A tale as old as time—a girl, tall and wispy, hair the color of the sun, eyes as blue as the sky, caught in a love triangle with the noblest of men…Not in this book, honey!

Okay so maybe I am caught up in a love triangle, but I'm sure as hell not running through a field of daisies in a sun dress. My name is Elizabeth and I've managed to avoid men for most of my life. I wasn't a nun by any means, but I know what the hot guys want—and it usually isn't me. How I got myself involved in a love triangle with one sexy photographer and a millionaire bachelor, who had women worshiping the ground he walked on, is beyond me. Yet, here I am, attempting to navigate waters that I've never expected to. Trying to figure out which man was right for me, dealing with my family—and have I told you about the paparazzi? Well, it's all really making me rethink the situation. Who do I trust? Who's being genuine? What should I do if both men are perfect for me in different ways? How the hell am I supposed to choose just one? Or better yet, do I *have* to choose just one?

KUDOS for *Torn Hearts*

In *Torn Hearts* by M. E. Gordon, Elizabeth Monroe is a slightly overweight beauty who isn't used to having men pursue her. Now all of a sudden two handsome and well to do bachelors want her for their own. Due to her insecurities, she pushes both of them away. But both men refuse to go, and Elizabeth finds herself in a quandary. Does she choose the one she really wants, or does she choose the one she thinks she deserves, or at least the one she thinks she can keep? I thought the book very credible, with realistic characters and true to life situations. It just goes to show how your own insecurities can mess up your life if you let them. As a steamy romance, there is plenty of sexual tension and some very hot love scenes. What's not to like? ~ *Taylor Jones, Reviewer*

Torn Hearts by M. E. Gordon is about a woman who's not a perfect size 6 and who is very self-conscious about her size. The last thing she expects is to have two men in hot pursuit. And I do mean hot. The one she wants is not the one she thinks she can have, so she settles. Never a good idea at the best of times and as Elizabeth discovers it can be disastrous. The story is very well written, with believable characters dealing with realistic problems. Okay, maybe not so realistic, as how many of us chunkies have two hunks after them, one a millionaire? But you know what I mean. It's also a thought-provoking treatise on how screwed up people can get when they don't fit what society thinks of as acceptable. ~ *Regan Murphy, Reviewer*

ACKNOWLEDGEMENTS

Writing the story was always easy for me. I have a mind that goes a mile a minute, thinking up characters and the crazy scenarios that they get themselves in, but if it wasn't for these people, there would be no M.E. Gordon.

I want to first off thank my husband Shaun for giving me the opportunity to be in my head and giving me the time I needed to put those characters on paper. I love you so much and I truly wouldn't be able to call myself an author if it wasn't for you.

I'd also like to thank my children Owen, Austin, Evan, and Natalie. Thank you for being my driving force. I want you all to be proud of me and, being a published author, I think that I'm doing just that. There is so much about being a stay at home mom that gets overlooked and underappreciated, but when I get to put on my author hat for those few hours and write, it makes all the messes and carpools worth it. I love you guys.

It's hard to find people that will give you their honest opinion about your story. Most want to inflate you with compliments to avoid hurting your feelings, but lucky me, I have a great group or women on my side. Dora, without you helping me along the way and encouraging me, I think I'd still be on chapter one! Aileen, thank you for being my spell check, wording, and grammar wiz because things would be a hot mess if you weren't there to help. Thank you to my sister-in-law Jessica. Together we changed and talked about things until we were blue in the face. Our meetings at the library when we got kicked out at closing and yelled at for having drinks and snacks (who can work without either is still beyond me) I'll cherish those fun nights with you.

To my development team...or person, Meaghan. I don't know what I'd do if I didn't have you to bounce my crazy ideas off of. Thank you for listening and jumping into my sometimes scattered brain to help navigate an outline with me.

My cover designer Melissa, you are so good at what you do. Lauri at Black Opal Books, thank you for giving me a chance. Faith my wonderful editor, I've learned a lot and will apply it to future books. All my fellow BOB authors that helped answer my sometimes silly questions.

Thank you to my parents, especially my mom for reading my crazy ideas before they were even a story. We were going through a rough time when I started this journey and I feel like this book brought us back together. Dad, I love you! Please, never read this book!

Lastly, I'd like to dedicate my first novel to my Grandmother, Irene. I used to ask her why she read so many books. I thought it was stupid, and a waste of time. I wish you were still here to read my first novel. I wish I would have known you even more than I did, because I think we could have been best friends. I think we were more alike than I would have liked to admit back when you were alive. I hope you can forgive me and are proud of me.

torn HEARTS

M. E. GORDON

A Black Opal Books Publication

GENRE: CONTEMPORARY ROMANCE/WOMEN'S FICTION

This is a work of fiction. Names, places, characters and incidents are either the product of the author's imagination or are used fictitiously, and any resemblance to any actual persons, living or dead, businesses, organizations, events or locales is entirely coincidental. All trademarks, service marks, registered trademarks, and registered service marks are the property of their respective owners and are used herein for identification purposes only. The publisher does not have any control over or assume any responsibility for author or third-party websites or their contents.

DEDICATION

To MomMom

Chapter 1

Beth

My heart rate accelerated as we pull up to the popular DC night club, Mood. I was currently sitting in a limo that my brothers sent over to retrieve my best friend Gia and me. Taking a steadying breath, I took a peek out the window. Of course, they had a small red carpet set out for celebrities and socialites like my brothers.

Let me make this a little clearer, I don't do this.

I didn't go out dressed up like I was right now. I glanced back at Gia who looked anything but anxious. She was in her element right now, and I...well, I was not!

I preferred sitting at home reading a good book. It was a passion of mine. My Gran was an avid reader. What could I say? I took after her and my mother, who happened to have been an editor in-chief for a big publishing company. I guess I could have followed in her footsteps, but I had a passion for History. With only a few classes left, I was well on my way to restoring books at the Library of Congress. Still, no matter how many books I'd read, nothing could prepare me for nights like tonight.

Sure limos, nice dresses, socialites, photographers, it all sounded like a great time, and maybe it was, but not for me. *Do you have any idea how difficult it is to find an appealing outfit for a size twelve, tall, curvy, twenty-three-year-old? Well I'll tell you, it's nearly impossible!*

Sure there were things in my size, but that wasn't the problem. The problem was feeling exposed, and not in a good way—the bad way, like every-inch-of-fat-had-been-magnified-by-tight-fabric way. Even Gia, the fashion stylist in training, had a hard time finding me something to wear. It' was mortifying.

I didn't know what I was more worried about, falling on my ass or getting my picture taken. Oh, right. It was falling on my ass *while* getting my picture taken. I tried my hardest to get Gia to go in the side entrance, but clearly, I lost that battle.

Gia stepped out first, thankfully. The cameras were snapping away like crazy, but why wouldn't they be? She looked like a movie star in her short gray dress and sparkling heels. Smiling at the cameras and swaying her long blonde hair, she posed like it was second nature to her.

Taking a deep breath, I closed my eyes. I could do this. *Just get out of the car and don't fall on your ass.* With one last, quick prayer, I scooted over and let my foot glide out of the limo. Holding on tight to the door handle, I exited the limo and cautiously made my way over toward the sea of cameras. I clung tight to the shawl that was covering most of the red dress that I had finally found, after hours of shopping with Gia.

I stopped moving when the photographers started snapping a few pictures. Maybe they thought I was a lighter haired Kardashian or something. It didn't take but a few seconds for them to find out I wasn't.

"She's nobody!" I heard one of the snakes say to his neighbor.

Knives, meet my heart...ouch! I wanted to run back to the limo or into the safety of the dark club, but I couldn't move. I glanced over in Gia's direction where she was using her hands to take off an invisible jacket. I guessed she was telling me to take my shawl off. I couldn't help but think that this was a very stupid idea. And, of course, against my better judgment, I did it anyway.

I quickly un-wrapped the fabric. My long, wavy, brown hair fell against my bare back and exposed cleavage. The unseasonably, cool air brushed against my arms, making a chill run up my spine. This dress was perfect, practically made for me. It hit all my curves and pushed my boobs and ass up too. But most importantly, it flattened my stomach—magic!

The wall of cameras turns back to me. I guess they think I might be someone worth photographing after all.

"Red Dress—Red dress, can we get a name?"

I turned in the direction of the warm voice and felt the heat rise to my cheeks. Embarrassment? Flattery? I tried to make out the person calling to me as I scanned the wall of photographers. My eyes were instantly drawn to a handsome man with shaggy, sandy hair and muscular build. Well, I'd like to think it was muscles under the sweat shirt he had on. I squinted to get a better look but lost sight of him as the flashes went off.

"A name?" another man called.

"Elizabeth Monroe," I answered back.

Chapter 2

We were sitting in the empty VIP area, sipping the drinks that the waitress had just dropped off. Gia and I scanned the room as more and more people entered and started dancing. My brothers both arrived with new girls. There was no doubt in my mind they'd only brought them to look good on their arms. *Beautiful people using beautiful people, such a vicious cycle. Glad I'm not involved.*

Getting up from one of the many white couches to greet my brothers, I was relieved when it wasn't as difficult as I imagined. *Tight dress, heels, me, I'm sure you get where I'm going with this.*

"Well, well, look who decided to grace us with her presence."

"Hello, Charles," I said smiling, while he cringed at his proper name.

"Will you ever just call me Chuck like everyone else?" he asked, giving me a big brother hug.

"Nope, I like watching you squirm."

Shaking his head, he took a step back to admire me from a distance. "Really Beth? You choose tonight, of all nights, not to look like a frumpy, housewife. We're meeting with an important business partner, and now I'm going to be distracted, trying to make sure guys don't try to...to...ugh, I don't even want to think about it," he said, pushing me away and into the arms of my beloved brother Teddy.

"Beth you look beautiful," he whispered in my ear because he knew I didn't like all the attention. "Unfortunately, I'm going to have to agree with Chuck on this one." He smiled down at me, kissing my forehead.

Out of the corner of my eye, I caught Gia hugging Charles a little bit too long. I couldn't help rolling my eyes. I knew she had a crush on him. She had for the past five years. I just thought that she would have gotten the memo. Charles was the playboy and Teddy was the keeper.

I'd been told by so called "friends" that my brothers were attractive. Sure, they both looked like Abercrombie and Fitch models—which, I thought, Charles did for a while. In all fairness, they possessed every beautiful feature my parents could have given them. *Tall, well built, perfect hair, perfect teeth, perfect eyes...do I have to go on? I'm getting more depressed just thinking about it. Why the hell did they have to get all the pretty genes? I'm the girl for Christ's sake.*

The more people started trickling into the VIP section, the more insignificant I felt. I didn't come to places like this ever. How Gia had wrangled me into this was still a mystery. One minute I was unpacking from summer break, then the next I was shopping for a dress.

I sat in a chair off to the back and people watched. As I glanced across the club, a man entered with two bodyguards. He caught my attention. My initial reaction was that it had to be someone famous. Who else would come into a club with bodyguards? I stood up to get a better look, but didn't recognize him at all—just another rich, attractive guy coming to the club to pick up a "Gia."

Okay fine, I guess you can say I'm jealous. Oh, for Christ's sake, I'm jealous, just because she can get picked up by a hot guy and I can't. Skinny bitches, I thought, as I looked down at the floor and shook my head.

When I looked back up, the Greek God was still making his way across the club and over towards the VIP area. I stared, openly gawking at him while his well-dressed body made its way through the crowd. The sea of people on the dance floor moved like he was Moses parting the Red Sea. *Wait a minute. Is he looking at me?* I couldn't take my eyes off of him as he ran his fingers through the dark hair atop his head. *Oh hell no,*

I'm dreaming or hallucinating. Someone must have put something in my drink.

Brought back to reality by the pain from the heels Gia let me borrow, I quickly sat back down. Leaning over, I rubbed the back of my ankle, basking in the relief. I wasn't even standing that long and I hadn't even started dancing yet. *See, this is why I don't wear heels.* Closing my eyes, I let my head fall onto my crossed knee, as I continued to relieve my aching foot.

Fingers grazed the side of my ankle, and I froze, because it wasn't my fingers doing the grazing. Something was happening to me. I'd never been so out of my own body. Although the mystery fingers stopped moving, the skin under them felt as if it was on fire.

What do I do? Scream? No, whose ever hand this was felt too good to scream. It would probably sound more like a moan. Instinct took over and I slowly lifted my eyes to follow the fingers. Mesmerizing was the only way I could describe the sea-blue eyes that met mine as a strand of dark hair fell on the forehead of the Greek God.

I could only imagine what my face looked like in that moment. A mouth gaping blow-up doll came to mind. *Why wouldn't it be the Greek God?* I glanced back down to where his hand was still around my ankle. Why the hell was he touching *my* ankle?

I perused his crouching body. No doubt he saw the confusion on my face because he let go and stood hastily before me. He was the most attractive man I had ever laid eyes on. I was finding it hard to focus on anything but his face. The loud music quieted and all the people around us disappeared, while I studied him.

"I'm sorry. I thought you might have hurt yourself."

Oh God, he sounds as good as he looks, he's definitely not human.

Say something Beth, tell him you're okay.

My throat was completely sealed. There were no words escaping any time soon. I smiled up at him and shrugged my shoulders with a little chuckle. I instantly wanted to melt into the chair and pray that this awkward situation would just end. Moving the hair from his forehead, he smiled back. *Oh my God, you could solve world peace with that megawatt smile.*

Before I could stand up and give a proper response, Charles came barreling over, making the Greek God turn away from me.

"Mr. Salvatore, it's great to finally meet you, please come with me and I'll introduce you to my brother Teddy."

Before I knew it, the ankle rubbing Greek God had a name and was taken away right before my eyes, not even a second glance back.

After gaining my composure, I watched as Charles ushered him away. He completely ignored me, in typical Charles fashion, not even bothering to introduce me. Well, now that I felt even more insignificant than usual, I thought it was time to go. I looked down at my phone. *New record, forty-five minutes.*

I looked back and saw Teddy shaking hands. My in-tune brother caught my gaze and mouthed "Are you okay?"

I nodded back, as a wave of guilt hit me. *I should stay.* Teddy was here and I didn't get to see him as often as I'd like to. So once again, against my usual better judgment, I pointed over to the restrooms. Turning on my six-inch heels, I made my way across the dance floor, all the while thinking about my chance encounter with a Greek God, or Mr. Salvatore as my brother had called him. *Why did that name sound so familiar?*

I reached the restrooms and, as always, there was a line. While waiting, I overheard two Bratz-looking dolls talking.

"Oh, my God did you see him, Courtney? Pictures do not do him justice!" one said.

"I know. I still can't believe we are in the same building as Spencer Salvatore, well worth the wait in line."

At the sound of his name, I found myself butting into their not so private, drunken conversation.

They clearly knew who he was and my curiosity was getting the better of me. I couldn't help myself but to ask, "Umm, excuse me, who is Spencer Salvatore?"

The two girls turned toward me and looked at me as if I'd just asked the dumbest question in the world.

"Uh, he's only one of the most attractive men in the universe. Not to mention one of the most eligible bachelors," the blonde doll said as she swooned over in the direction of the VIP area.

"He owns, like, every popular nightclub and bar on the east and west coast," the other added.

I suddenly felt stupid. I knew my brothers were meeting someone, in hopes of having them help open their own nightclub. I should have put two and two together.

"And most importantly, he's, like, top fifteen on the Forbes list. The man could buy an island if he wanted to," the first one said.

Well, I sure got all the information I needed from Thing One and Thing Two. Kind of weird that someone as exquisite as Spencer Salvatore was touching my feet. My cheeks flushed as my mind wandered back to the soft caress of his fingers on my ankle. A shiver ran through me and I shook my head to get the memory out, because that was all it was ever going to be, a memory.

Things like that didn't happen to girls like me. We didn't get swooped off our feet and carried away by the rich, attractive bachelor. Nope, we were the best friend of the girl who got swooped off her feet by the man who would never see us as sexy or alluring. Unfortunately, I knew this first hand.

On my way back to the VIP section, I did a quick Salvatore scan but he was nowhere to be found. He probably got what he came for and left. The dance floor was packed as I shimmied between people dancing. I got halfway when I ran into Gia and Charles dancing.

"Beth! There you are. Stay, dance with us!" Gia shouted over the loud music, while Charles held her around her waist. *Disgusting.*

"Let me go do a couple of shots and I will get the courage to come bust a move with you guys," I said before I walked away.

I saw some shots sitting on one of the tables and downed them one after another. I thought I stopped at four, but it very well could have been more. *Liquid courage*! I was ready to join them now. Feeling buzzed, I started swaying my hips to the music. These curves were good for something and, luckily, I had some rhythm to go with them. Gia and I took a few more shots and continued dancing, and singing at the top of our lungs. She leaned over, telling me that she was going to sit down. I nodded back, letting her know I heard her. Charles said something in my ear, but all I heard was, "Blah…Blah …Blah."

I lost myself in the music and felt free. *Maybe I should come out more often.* I felt so liberated. Alcohol could do that to a girl. My eyes got heavy and my movements became more drunkenly. I lost my balance, but two hands saved me as they gently landed on my hips and pulled me toward the mystery person they were attached to.

I turned around, wishfully thinking that it was that Salvatore God, but it wasn't. I looked at the man in front of me, sandy hair, good looks, and a nice thick body. It was the freaking photographer from outside and—damn, he smelled good, some kind of aftershave I guessed. And he was charming. But in that moment, right then, I didn't care who the hell he was.

I felt amazing as we danced together. I saw now why Gia came out all the time. *If guys did this every time, I might become a little more familiar with the night scene.* His hands were tight around me and his warm breath tickled my neck. I pushed back against him, wrapping my arm around his muscular shoulders. When I did, he sprawled his hand across my stomach. *Oh crap*! I instantly sucked my stomach in, but I wasn't sure how successful I was, since I was pretty much three sheets to the wind. I needed to stop this before he felt something not so attractive.

"Hey, do you want to come over and sit at the VIP with me?" I managed to say, turning to face him, the words slightly slurred. I expected him to say "No," and "Thanks for the feel up."

"Sure, lead the way, sexy."

He was mere centimeters from my lips. *Breathe, Beth*! *What the hell was going on around here tonight? Some rich, beautiful bachelor felt my legs up and now this gorgeous guy called me sexy.* I quickly squeezed my arm as we make our way through the crowd.

"Ouch!" I said loudly.

"Huh? Did you say something?" he asked as his breath warmed my neck again.

Nope, you are not dreaming.

The photographer helped me up the few steps. My dress's color popped on the stark, white couches as we sat down.

"So," I said looking at him.

Gorgeous, his eyes were a soft brown, his features...stunning. I couldn't believe he was a photographer. He could easily be a male model.

"So," he said back. "My name's Simon."

I had met men like him before, the ones that threw all the right lines and talked their way in and out of everything. I didn't know them personally, but I'd seen plenty of them try to pick Gia up.

He held out his hand and I put mine in his, still skeptical, but intrigued to see what he would do next. "Elizabeth."

"I know," he said. "Elizabeth Monroe. It's a pleasure to be in your beautiful presence."

Is this guy for real? Come on, really? I'm drunk, but this is a bit much to believe. I smiled back and lowered my head shaking it in disbelief. "You don't have to do that, act like you're interested in me just to get to the VIP section." I made sure he could hear the annoyance in my words.

With a raised brow and soft face, he looked me in the eyes, grabbing my hands that were resting in my lap. "Who said I wasn't interested?"

Wow, his hands are soft. Damn it! I'm not being that girl, not tonight.

"Come on, I know how this works. I see it all the time," I said coolly, sliding my hands out from his. I had to look toward the crowd as I spoke. *Stay strong.* "Be nice to the chubby girl and get in. I know how you paparazzi are."

"You really have no idea how beautiful you look tonight, do you? You're not chubby. Whoever told you that is just jealous, and I'm not with the paparazzi," he finished.

Heat rushed to my cheeks. Being flattered by men was something that just didn't happen to me. Insecurely, I lowered my head and rubbed my aching limbs. I couldn't look at him right now.

Catching a shadow, I looked up and saw Charles standing in front of me, all big-brother-to-the-rescue.

"Beth, can I have a word?" Charles's voice sounded annoyed.

I glanced over at picture boy, who seemed to be waiting patiently, and indicated I would be right back as I got up and walked away with Charles.

"What?" I spat at his face, annoyance dripping off me.

"Are you all right? Is this guy bothering you? Just give me the word and I'll make him go away. You know I will."

Still feeling tipsy, I almost lost my balance twice. I placed a hand on my brother's strong shoulder. "I'm F—F—Fine." I said, managing to stumble the words out.

"Really? I'm not so sure about that."

"Listen, Charles—"As I began to reprimand my brother, something stopped me and stilled every fiber in my body.

Across the way, that Salvatore God was staring over at us. I blinked my eyes to see if I was imagining it. *Nope*, he was still there. I stared back at him. There was no expression on his face.

He was just standing there like a beautiful sculpture. Slowly he turned, leaving from sight, but his image was burned into my mind.

"Elizabeth," Charles said, shaking me out of my God-knew-how-long trance.

"Huh?" I said, looking back at his worried face.

"Damn, Salvatore was right. You are done. I think it's time to go. You don't need hounds like this trying to take advantage of you." He nodded over in picture boy's direction.

"Wait—Salvatore was talking about me?" I asked.

"Yeah, we were finishing up when he saw you and douche bag over here. He thought it might be a good idea to come get you before something happened that you might regret in the morning."

Mr. Salvatore was concerned about little ole me? I was shocked. "Did he say anything else?" I asked, a little too hopeful.

"Nope, not really." Charles had a vicious, what-do-you-expect look on his face. The kind that I got all the time. It was even harder to have your own flesh and blood belittle you.

"Well, things are dying down and I'm not trying to close the place, so let's go, baby girl," Charles demanded.

"Whatever, Charles, I'm going to stay a little longer. Do you know where Gia's at?" I asked, scanning the crowd for her.

"No, you're not staying here by yourself and Gia is just as trashed as you. She's with Teddy getting the car. I was sent to get you," he said, crossing his arms and trying to sound intimidating.

"What if I don't want to go with you? I'm having a good time for once. Geez, you people are ridiculous. You bitch when I don't come out and, when I do, you make me leave when I'm actually having a good time." I folded my arms across my chest and pouted at the floor like a two-year-old.

While in my two-year-old pout, I saw two, well-polished shoes standing in front of me. I followed up the legs to the slender, fit waist and broad shoulders. *This isn't happening.* I blinked a few times, but Spencer Salvatore was standing in front of me and next to what I thought was my good-looking brother.

Spencer was by far the most attractive man in the universe, no joke. He kind of made my brother look ordinary. I liked the thought of Charles being average.

It made me chuckle inside.

"Spencer, I thought you left." Charles voice was high and he seemed taken off guard.

"I thought I forgot something. I saw you talking to your sister and figured I'd properly introduce myself." He smiled at me, his blue eyes absolutely breathtaking. Taking my hand in his, he brought it to his perfect lips and gently skimmed the top of my knuckles. The feeling of his lips on my skin went through my body like an electric shock, waking my insides with a spark of fire. "Miss Monroe, it's nice to meet you, my name is Spencer Salvatore."

A sad little, "Hello," was all I could muster out of my voice box. *Figures.*

"Well, it was a pleasure. I got what I came back for, and I'll see you two around." Just like that, he turned and walked away again.

"Okay, Beth, for real, let's get lost. It's two in the morning. I'm beat and your little friend got scared and ran away," he said, pointing to where picture boy had been sitting.

"Fine, my buzz is gone, anyway. Let me go grab my shawl and we can leave." As I reached down to the couch, I noticed a folded piece of paper where I was sitting. I grabbed the paper, hidden under my shawl, and walked out of the club with my brother. *Not how I pictured myself leaving twenty minutes ago, but at least someone possibly left me a note.*

Chapter 3

Light was shining through my window, which I had forgotten to close the night before as well as change my clothes. My head was pounding as I crawled out of bed. I stripped out of my new favorite dress and jumped in the shower.

The warm water ran over my face, washing away all the beautiful make-up and hair products until I was plain old Beth again. I stepped out of the shower and began drying myself off. Bending down, I dried my ankles and, in that simple action, everything from last night came rushing back—Spencer's gentle fingers on my leg and his soft lips on my hand. I stood abruptly and wrapped the towel around my body. Sitting on my bed, I tried to recall every little detail about him.

Falling back in a flush of bizarre giddiness—*because I don't do giddy*—my hand slid over a piece of paper. *The note!* I had totally forgotten that I even had it in my hand when I passed out last night. I held the note in my hands, opening it to see beautifully scripted handwriting.

You intrigue me. Miss Monroe. ~ S

Are you kidding me? Really? He couldn't just write his full name? My mind started racing. It could be from Spencer. He did say he left something behind. Maybe he placed the note on the couch. Or it could have been Simon. I thought that was his name.

Who am I kidding? I'll probably never find out. No name, no number, another mean joke at my expense.

There was a loud knock at the door, which nearly made me fall off the bed.

"Gia, you got that?" I waited for a response "Gia, I just got out of the shower," I called to her again, but all I heard from her room was a low grumble of what I thought was drunken English, saying no. *All right, I guess I'll just get it myself.*

I wrapped the towel even tighter around my voluptuous curves and went for the door. Looking through the peep hole, I saw a man standing with a vase full of red roses. I looked down at the towel around me and contemplated opening the door. Maybe he had the wrong condo number. When he didn't turn to leave and knocked again, I figured I'd better answer.

I opened the door just a crack.

"Are you Miss Monroe?" the delivery guy asked.

"Yes?" I answered, frowning.

"I have a delivery for you," he said sarcastically, holding the flowers up toward the door.

"Huh?" *Now I know why everyone hates my sarcasm.*

"Of course." He handed the big arraignment of flowers to me then turned, tipped his invisible hat, and exited down the hall.

I closed the door, rested on it, and took a deep breath. Gia came out of her room and perked up when she caught sight of them. "Oh, flowers for me? I wonder who they're from?" she said, skipping over.

"Actually, they were sent to me."

Her excitement dropped off and a depressed "Oh," left her mouth before she could stop it. "I didn't mean it like that," she said, making a quick recovery. "Well, open the card. I want to see who the hell sent you flowers," she demanded.

I pulled out the card and read.

Saw these beautiful flowers this morning
and thought of you ~ S

Nope, this can't be happening, there must be some mix up.

"Well, what does it say?" she asked, greedily taping her fingers together.

"Here," I said, handing it to her.

She read it and looked up with wide eyes. "Is it from that guy you were dancing with all night?"

Yeah, him or the ankle-touching Greek God. I made sure to keep that securely locked in my head, though.

ↈↈↈ

The next Saturday morning, I was drinking my tea and scanning the Internet for any interesting news. I clicked on the infamous gossip page, Fame, because they always had the latest scoop. I wasn't surprised to see a picture of my brothers, smiling and posing with Spencer Salvatore, the night outside of Mood.

Oh God, he even looks good on the gossip page. Unfortunately, my brothers looked just as handsome standing next to him. Disgusted by their good looks, I quickly clicked the over button to go to the next page.

Holy fuck! Was that me or just someone that kind of resembled a better looking me? Nope, that was, without a doubt, me, and that was clearly Spencer Salvatore on his knees, caressing my ankle.

The next picture was him kissing my hand. Some crazy paparazzi had sneaked a camera in and snapped the pictures. Some pretty good ones at that.

I stared, wide eyed. The memory made my stomach flutter as I thought back to the way his voice danced around my ears and how his soft lips felt on the back of my hand. Below one of the pictures, the caption read:

> *Spencer Salvatore, seen with beautiful vixen in sexy Ann Robin cocktail dress and vintage heels. Watch out, ladies, Mr. Salvatore might be off the market soon. He looks absolutely smitten, wouldn't you agree?*

I had to read and re-read the caption a couple of times to make sure I wasn't just willing the words on the page. Suddenly, it hit me, reality. Everyone who followed Fame, or even Spencer, would be looking at me as the vixen trying to weasel my way into his life. I could already see future posts in my head. *Who does this fat girl think she is? She can't steal the modern day sex symbol.* Ouch. I wasn't sure I could handle all that. Hopefully, no one would recognize me. I would be keeping my fingers, toes, arms, and legs crossed.

"What are you looking at, all face in the screen?" Gia asked, entering the kitchen.

I shot my head up from the computer and slammed it shut. "Nothing! Just the news," I said, as casually as possible.

"I find that hard to believe. Let's see it. What are you looking at?" she asked, trying to grab my laptop.

Thank God for good reflexes. I was able to move it before she could snatch it. "You were out late last night. I didn't even here you come in," I said, thinking fast on my feet to change the subject.

She held her hand to her head.

"I take it was a wild night," I said.

"It was so much fun. You should have come with me. Your brothers were even there," she said through a grin.

"I told you last week that it was a onetime thing?" I said, glaring at her.

"Well, you're going to wish you would have," she said teasingly.

What was she getting at? *Let's not play dumb with yourself, Beth. You know exactly what you want her to say and it involves a particular pair of beautiful, blue eyes.*

I watched as Gia walked back to the kitchen. She handed me a folded piece of paper. I took it with an anxious hand and saw the same beautiful script as the very first note.

Missed you tonight. ~ S

I stood there, bewildered again. "I give up, I must be cursed!" I said.

Snatching the paper from my hand, she read it out loud then sat down next to me.

"Who gave this to you?" I ask, frustrated.

"Just some random guy. I had never seen him before. He just told me to give it to Miss Monroe," Gia said, smelling the flowers.

Once again, Beth is getting the run around. It has to be some kind of joke. What can I say? I have experience in this area. Even though that was in middle school, I have learned my lesson. Trust no one, especially men.

I took the note back from Gia, stomped back to my room, and place it with the other two. I didn't have time to play silly games. I did have a life, and this wasn't middle school. I wasn't going to let this affect me. I walked over, pulled a random book off my shelf, and dove into it head first, not looking back.

Chapter 4

A h, the last first day of school. I walked up to the common area, taking in the fresh, fall air. What was with all these people just standing around? Students, teachers—and the closer I got I saw—

What the hell are the paparazzi doing here? God, I hope there not here for me.

"Hey, Tina," I called to a fellow History major. "What the heck is going on over there?" I asked, pointing to all the commotion.

"You didn't hear? It's been all over campus and the Internet."

Here we go—my demise.

"Danny Fenton, you know, the singer?" she continued. "He's starting his freshman year here."

Oh, thank God. I finally released the breath I had been holding for the whole conversation. "Just what we need our last year, Teeny Boppers." I glanced over in the direction of the building that I had to navigate toward. *Figures they would all be camped out at the building I have to go in.*

I was almost to the safety of the building. I just had to make it up the front stairs.

"Hey, red dress!"

I froze on the stairs as I recognized the voice calling. I immediately whipped around, but dropped my books in the process. Before I bent down to pick the books up, I scanned the crowd and saw people whispering as they looked me up and down. *Oh, shit, please don't let them recognize me in my regu-*

lar jeans and T-shirt. I quickly knelt down to retrieve my books while simultaneously hiding my face.

"Let me help you."

I looked up to see Simon kneel next to me. I'd thought that was his voice. "I'm sorry I startled you," he said. "I just wanted to get your attention."

Mission accomplished. Standing, I looked up into his warm brown eyes. He had his sandy hair tucked under a backward baseball hat and was even more handsome than I remembered. He definitely rivaled Salvatore with his boy-next-door good looks.

"How are you doing?" he asked.

Geez, I don't know…how about totally confused? "I'm doing well."

His lush lips turned up when I finally spoke.

"Did you get the flowers?"

Flowers? So he sent the mystery flowers. "Yes. They were beautiful. I wanted to tell whoever sent them thank you, but there was no name," I said, crossing my arms. *I can't wait to hear this excuse.*

"I'm sorry. I thought that guy was your boyfriend."

Boyfriend? My mind rewound back as fast as it could. *Charles.* "Oh, he's not my boyfriend. That's my brother, Charles." *The pain in the ass, that he is.* "Wait, how did you know where to send the flowers?" I asked.

"Well, I knew your name and the Internet did the rest," he said.

Okay, a little creepy that he knows where I live, but let's face it. He's, without a doubt, the most attractive man that has ever talked to me without being friends of my brothers.

"Hey, would you like to go get some coffee?" he asked.

Stay cool, Beth, act casual. Yeah, like guys this hot ask you out all the time. How the hell am I supposed to stay cool? I probably look like a bumbling fool.

"Yeah. That would be great!"

Oh, that came off a little overly enthusiastic. Bring it back a notch or two. "I mean, I have class now, but if you can wait till I'm done, I can." *Much better.*

"Sure, I can wait, I have to get my shots anyway," he said, holding up his camera.

Not paparazzi, huh? I find that hard to believe.

"Okay. I will see you after my class."

"Can't wait."

I turned and headed back up the stairs and into the building.

♥♥♥

After what seemed like an eternity, class had finally ended. As I rounded the corner of the building toward the benches, there sat a perfectly proportioned man, typing on his phone, a huge smile on his face. A dark gray T-shirt hugged his clearly worked-out arms, and the blue jeans he had on were just tight enough to not look girly.

"Hey, are you ready to head out?" I called as I walked over toward him.

Quickly putting his phone in his ratty old backpack, he looked over at me and stood to meet me halfway. "Yeah, where would you like to go?" he asked.

"There's a nice little café right off campus." I suggested this place because I knew it like the back of my hand. I had spent many a night cozying up with a book there. So just in case this guy was a psycho, I'd have home field advantage, plus I knew everyone that worked there.

"Sounds great, lead the way," he said, holding his arm out.

We got our drinks, which Simon very kindly paid for, and sat down in a cozy love seat at the back of the café.

"So," I said, taking a sip of my tea and placing it on the table next to me.

"So," he said back, a smile turning his lips up.

Déjà-vu much? "So, you *are* with the paparazzi?" I asked, getting straight to it.

"No," he said, sounding nervous, which clearly meant yes to me. "It's complicated," he continued.

"Try me," I said, taking another sip of my drink.

"Well, I work for celebrities and businesses. They contract me out to get good pictures of them and their businesses."

So he was using me. I should have guessed and he was probably using me now.

"Okay. Well, thanks for the coffee. I think it's best to just, ya know, move on." I stood from the couch, but didn't move as his hand held on to mine.

"Where are you going?" he asked, almost nervously.

"I get it, Simon, you just needed an 'in' to get pictures of my brothers or Spencer Salvatore. I'm not going to give you the chance to do that again."

Letting go of my arm, he stood, blocking my exit. "Elizabeth, please, I want to get to know you. Just give me a chance to prove myself."

I kept my eyes locked on his. *Maybe I should just give him the chance he's asking for. What's the worst that could happen?*

"Fine," I said, sitting back down and looking up at him. "Tell me about yourself."

I learned the essentials quickly—twenty-seven, only child, from California, and was an aspiring photographer. He told me he traveled a lot for his job, but he was contracted to the DC area until further notice. He didn't go in to too much detail, but he reassured me he was not the crazy, chasing paparazzi that I despised. He worked for a company who hired photographers to go out to events to help with good publicity. *I guess I have to take his word for it—until I get home and research it, thoroughly.*

He waited for me to start talking about myself. I hesitated, of course. The past wasn't something I liked to talk about with strangers, or anyone, so I tried to keep it light. "Well, I have two older brothers, Teddy and Charles. I'm twenty-three. I was born and raised in New York, and I came here five years ago to go to college. Not that exciting," I said, reaching for my drink.

"Five years? You on the long term college plan?" he asked, chuckling.

I couldn't help but smile. *Damn, he's charming.* "Ha, very funny! No, I had to take some time off to deal with some family issues."

"Oh, right, 'family issues.' That's what they're calling it. Give it up. Were you backpacking through Europe or were you spending all your time partying?" he said cockily.

I hit his shoulder, almost hurting my hand. *Fuck, this man is ripped.* "I wish I was backpacking in Europe. My grandfather passed away and we were really close. I just needed time off before getting back on track."

Simon froze, looking at me as if thoroughly embarrassed. "Elizabeth, I'm so sorry—I didn't—"

"It's okay, really." I knew he felt bad and I knew it was not really appropriate, but it was funny to see him taken off guard.

Hearing a buzzing sound from his bag, he bent down and pulled his phone out. Sending a quick message, he placed it back as fast as he took it out.

"Who was that?" *I can't help it. My mind instantly goes to a dark place, probably a girlfriend.*

"No one important."

Damn, he's good and that smile is contagious.

Our conversation then led to movies and music. Come to find out, we had a lot more in common than I thought imaginable. He was slowly captivating me, although my wall was still very securely up. There were times in the conversation when I could see him holding back, as if he was reeling in his personality, or trying to keep it business-like. It was weird, but he was hot, and I was a sucker for eye candy.

Standing up suddenly, he stretched his arms over his head and leaned to either side. His shirt rose when his arms did, and a sliver of flesh peeked out beneath. *Oh my God! Look at the floor, Beth. Look. At. The. Floor. Before you embarrass yourself. Too late.*

I could feel him smiling at me, as if he knew exactly what he was doing.

I wasn't going to let him win that easily. He didn't need to know that I was drooling on the inside. "Wow, didn't realize I was boring you," I said before he quickly looked down at me.

"Oh, you could never bore me, but my ass was starting to fall asleep from sitting and staring at you."

Well, my cheeks are officially red.

"You're blushing. You don't get compliments often do you?"

How embarrassing.

"Shut-up!" I said, hitting his arm.

"Well, you better get used to the compliments, because I'm going to be making a lot of them from now on."

Hold on a minute, time out. Did he just say that—to me? I scanned the room, expecting a camera crew to jump out. When no one in the café moved, I looked back up at his smiling face.

"Elizabeth, can I have your number?" he asked with a wicked grin.

"All right, I'll give you my number, but you have to promise me that you're not going to make me fall in love with you and then break my heart." I said it as a joke but the look on Simon's face had me worried. The smile left his eyes as he looked over at me. "I'm kidding," I said, nudging him. "I'm not going to fall in love with you."

"Don't be too sure about that," he said, chuckling back at me.

I checked the time on my phone as we exchanged numbers. *Holy crap!* We had been talking for nearly four hours.

"Well, I better get going. Photo ops await," he said, finally breaking the silence.

"Yeah, I have to get ready for my next class." I held on to my book a little tighter as he leaned down to kiss my cheek farewell.

"See ya around, Elizabeth," he said, before turning from me.

I hung there, momentarily dazed that my morning had gone so drastically different than I ever expected.

☙❦❧

I sat in class, staring at my un-open books, with the biggest smile on my face. Nothing could take it away.

Except for the jerk next to me.

"Are you going to get that?" he groaned.

I looked over to him, my smile replaced with a thin line.

"What are you talking about?" I snapped back.

"Your phone has been going off for the past five minutes, and I can't concentrate with the annoying buzzing in my ear."

I narrowed my eyes at him and reached down for my bag which was on the floor between us. I finally found my phone at the bottom of the black hole I called my purse. Two missed calls and two new texts. I hit the little envelope and saw that it was Simon who sent the messages. My grin returned as I read the first one.

Just making sure you didn't give me a bogus number ☺

I quickly read the next one.

I really enjoyed our morning 2gether. can't wait 2 see u again soon! ;)

This class could not end too soon. I had too much to tell Gia. I felt like a giddy little school girl waiting for the bell to chime. *I've been giddy a lot lately. Weird.*

Chapter 5

Gia and I sat on the couch while I gushed about Simon. This was so surreal. It was usually the other way around.

"Wow, he sounds great! I mean for what you know about him," Gia said warily.

"I know what you mean. He does seem too good to be true, for me at least."

"Don't sell yourself short like that. I hate it when you do that," Gia said.

God love her, she tried her hardest to make me feel better.

She talked over her shoulder while she headed toward her bedroom to grab her laptop. "Did he say anything about the other notes?" she asked, yelling from down the hall.

"No, he didn't mention it, but I never asked him about them either."

"I can't stand this damn thing. It's frozen again. Can I use yours for now?" she asked.

I could hear her slamming her laptop shut over and over again.

"Yeah, it's on my desk. It should be fully charged."

"Great! I'll be right back," she called from the hallway.

What the hell is taking so long? She's blonde but I don't think unplugging a laptop is rocket science.

"Oh my God, Elizabeth Monroe! Why the hell didn't you tell me that your picture was on Fame?"

Oh, crap. I hadn't turned on my computer since I saw the pictures of Spencer and me.

Gia was standing in front of me, shoving the computer in my face, as if I hadn't already seen them.

"I was going to tell you, I just got side tracked," I said, sinking onto the couch.

"Yeah, you got side tracked all right, reading a freaking book! You didn't feel the need to tell your best friend that The Spencer Salvatore is 'smitten' with you?"

Geez, you would have thought that I'd gotten married in an Elvis chapel and didn't invite her. I stood up, grabbed the computer from her, and quickly closed down the web page.

She sighed. "If you want my opinion, Salvatore's the way to go. I mean he's hot, rich, a gentleman. Did I already say hot?" A dreamy look washed across her face as she stared off, in another world.

"I don't think so, Gia. He's not my type," I said, shaking my head.

"Not your type. So your type doesn't involve hot, hot, and filthy dirty hot?" she said snidely, crossing her arms and tilting her head at me.

"Yeah, pretty much. Let's get real, Gia. I'm not his type."

I will not feel bad for myself over a man that I only said three words to in my life. I need to focus on other things.

"Are you kidding me? Beth you're gorgeous, I'd kill to have those curves," she said, looking me up and down as if I was a steak dinner and she hadn't eaten in months.

I ran my hands over my hips and shook my head fiercely.

"Don't you do that—don't start picking yourself apart." She eyed me up and I knew what was coming next. "If you'd come out more than once a year with me, you'd realize how hot you are. You always say your brothers got the good genes but they didn't, you did!"

"I appreciate that Gia, and I know that you're trying to be a nice friend but—"

"But what! If you wanted to, you could be the next Kate Upton."

I rolled my eyes at that similarity because it was absolutely absurd.

"I'm serious, stick some of your long, golden, obnoxiously

perfect hair, that takes me hours to even come close to, on her head and she'd look just like you."

"Even if that was true, it doesn't change the fact that Spencer Salvatore is way out of my league, if I even had a league—which I might. I'll be right back." I headed to my room, pulled out my cell phone, and finally sent Simon a message back.

Nope this is not a bogus #. u didn't trust me? My feelings r hurt.

Not five minutes after I sent the message and nodded in false agreement with Gia to get her off my back, my phone started buzzing on my desk. Jumping at the sound of it, I picked my phone up and scrolled to the new message.

I think I can trust you, but I know how you girls can be. when r u free? Id like 2 take u 2 dinner.

I was actually bouncing up and down in my chair. I could only imagine what that sight would have looked like. Luckily, the curtains were drawn and the door was locked.

Four messages later, we decided to go out Thursday night. Now I just had to get through two and a half days until I got to see if Simon could potentially be the man of my dreams. Well, one of them at least.

ᘓᘔᘓ

I decided to go for a jog to get the blood flowing and kill some very anxious time, since I had no classes. I might have been a size twelve, but I did try to take care of myself. And I might have been curvy, but at least they were smooth curves. Along with reading, jogging was one of my favorite pastimes. It really helped me to relax and clear my head.

With my black yoga pants and favorite work-out sports bra/tank top combination, I laced up my running shoes and headed down to the street. Popping my ear buds in, I set my jogging playlist. A few more last minute stretches and I was off.

Thirty minutes in, a light fall breeze cooled my reddening face. My pony tail bounced with each stride as I rocked out to the latest upbeat music. I was lost in the run. The street was unusually busy with people for a Thursday morning, but I guessed they were all taking advantage of the nice weather.

While weaving in and out of the crowd on the large sidewalk, I hit what felt like a brick wall and fell back, flat on my ass. Seeing what looked like white birds above my head, I soon realized that it was papers flying in every direction. I had tried to plow through a person, a large, hard person, who was also lying on the sidewalk, mirroring my exact position. . I watched the last of the flying papers fall to the ground, and that's when it happened. That's when I saw clearly who it was that I'd just tried to run through. There I was sprawled on my ass, staring straight into Spencer Salvatore's beautiful, blue eyes.

A wave of fear, excitement, and mortification came over me. Rushing to my knees, I started to pick up the papers which littered the side walk. Copying my position again, he started picking up the papers as well.

"I'm so sorry, I didn't even see you," I said apologetically, looking up at his face. Even though I was all red-faced from running, I could feel an embarrassing blush reach my cheeks.

"It's okay."

His cool voice danced around my ears and I had to shake my head to regain my senses, so I could go back to picking up the papers.

"You're hurt," he said, ignoring the scattered papers. Reaching over, he took hold of my wrist, turning it to see the cuts along my forearm and elbow.

Kneeling in front of this man while he looked at my arm, I took a second to look at his flawless face. I felt like I was looking down on a silly romantic comedy. *Good grief, here we go again. Another out of body experience with this man.* I jumped quickly back into my body and looked at the nasty scrapes on my arm. "Oh, it doesn't hurt. I'll be okay." *So true. I can't feel anything, except the ridiculous urge to have him never let go of my hand. Maybe sweep me off my feet, make dirty nasty love, but definitely not pain.*

"Come on," he said, helping me to my feet. "I think I saw a first aid kit inside. We should get this cleaned up."

Does that count for being swept off your feet? Because I'm totally ready for the dirty nasty love making.

"What about all this?" I said, holding up the few papers that I had managed to pick up. "Aren't they important?"

"No, not really. I have copies of everything on file. Jay can handle it," he said, gesturing at his assistant who was frantically running after the papers, which were blowing down the sidewalk.

I followed Spencer, stride for stride. His hand was still firmly around my wrist as we walked into the once-fine-dining restaurant. He took me back to where the bustling kitchen used to be. Finding the first aid kit, he snatched it off the wall and brought it over to where I was leaning against the large, industrial sink. Taking a damp paper towel, he dabbed the bloody scrapes. His touch felt like electricity coursing through me. I couldn't help it. Soon, I was imagining what it would be like to have his hand touch me in other places. *Oh my God, I need to think of something else before I combust in front of him.*

Finding my voice, I tried to engage him in conversation. "Are you planning on buying this place?"

He was paying careful attention to my scratched arm as he reached for a few bandages. Looking up to meet my eyes, he smiled that megawatt smile. "It would seem that way, wouldn't it?" he said, continuing to patch up my arm.

"Ah, a smart ass. I'm sure you get along great with Charles," I said, rolling my eyes.

"I do, actually."

What a jerk, a hot-ass jerk.

"It's one of the places I have in mind to buy." His voice was calm and confident.

Damn, he sounds good, too good.

"I like the area because it's close to the campus, but far enough away to still have the lure for high-profile clients."

Not sure why—like I even knew what I was talking about—I nodded my head in agreement.

"There," he said, applying the last of the band aids to my arm. "All better."

I looked down at my neatly bandaged arm, impressed with

his nursing skills. "Are you planning to turn this place into another restaurant?"

Nice one, Beth, engage him in business conversation. Men love talking about their businesses. I learned this one from watching girls with my brothers.

He was next to me, leaning against the sink. He turned his finely dressed frame parallel to mine.

Oh, and what a frame!

Tight-fitting dress pants, a vest layered over a crisp white shirt. And the top two buttons were undone, revealing the slightest glimpse of his stone chest. His sleeves were rolled up to his elbows, displaying his toned forearms which were currently crossed over his muscular chest.

"Come with me?" he asked, unfolding his arms and leaving his hand out in the open space between us.

Standing a little straighter, I tried my hardest not to take his hand as fast as I really wanted to. I reached my wounded arm out and gently put it into his. The spark was instantaneous, the moment my hand was in his. I wanted to catch his eye, see if he felt the same spark that I had, but I was too chicken because it was me and it was him, an attractive, sexy, man. I already knew the spark was clearly, only on my side, so I didn't look up. I didn't want to take that chance.

He led me to the middle of what was once the dining room and released my hand, standing before me.

Damn it, he let go.

"Picture this." Walking over to one side of the room, he held both hands up. "This is where the new bar will go, and over here will be the DJ booth, raised up about three feet, tables and chairs over there…"

As he kept enthusiastically describing his plans for the space, I couldn't take my eyes off of him. He was almost dancing around me with that megawatt smile on his face. He seemed carefree and young, not like the businessman I had met two weeks before. A small laugh escaped my lips while I spun in a circle to follow his every movement.

He walked back to the center and stood before me again. "Do I get the little sister's approval?"

Little sister? I knew I was imagining everything. It wouldn't be the first time that I've misinterpreted guys being nice to me just because of my brothers. "It sounds like it's going to be great!" I couldn't help the melancholy in my voice. "What about up there?" I pointed up to the second floor, which was guarded by a railing that encompassed the whole room.

"I haven't decided yet. This place is so big. Do you have any suggestions, Miss Monroe?"

How about a place to hang myself for thinking you like me? "It might be a nice place for dining or a VIP area," I said, shrugging my shoulders. I looked up at him to see confusion on his face. "Or don't do that. You asked for my opinion re-member." I crossed my arms and looked toward the exit, ready to bolt out of there.

"I know. I'm just trying to figure you out, Miss Monroe." His deep voice echoed off the barren walls, as his brows drew together while he studied me.

Okay, this is weird, right?

"So you live close to here?" he asked, running his hand through his dark hair and bringing out the business man side of himself that I had met two weeks ago.

"Yeah, a few blocks from the campus. I have a condo in the Vanderhall building." *Shit, I just told an almost complete stranger where I live! Who am I kidding? He could come snatch me out of bed anytime.*

"Oh, you are really close to here. This building gets better every second," he said, scanning the bare space one last time.

I felt the color rush to my cheeks and I instantly averted my eyes at the ground. He placed a hand on my shoulder. I pan-icked at the closeness.

"Are you okay?" he asked. "You're not going to pass out on me, are you?"

Ah, hell, I'm completely frozen by his touch. Speak, Beth. "No—I'm—I'm fine. I should get going." At this point, I tried really hard to bring back to mind that I had a date that night, and only half an hour ago, I was highly looking forward to it. But now I was slowly starting to forget all about it, and him! "I'm sure that you have tons of things to be doing."

Letting his hand fall from my shoulder, he simply stared at me.

"I'm just going to let myself out." I turned, taking two steps toward the door that I really wasn't ready to walk through just yet.

"Wait, I'll walk you out." He sounded annoyed as he walked over to meet me.

When his hand found my lower back, I felt my skin burn and I had to take the chance this time. The annoyance on his face was clear, but it melted the longer his hand touched me. *Legs, you better not to give out on me!*

We walked outside the building and that was when my subconscious reared her head for information—information that I'd wanted to know as soon as I realized who I had run into. But I suppressed it because I was too busy being a girl and gawking at his good looks. "Did you leave the notes?" I asked, once we were face to face.

Clearly shocked by my blunt question, he just stood there. I could see the gears turning in his head as he tried to come up with an answer.

Maybe deep down I didn't want him to answer, just in case I was fantasizing all of this.

Out of the corner of my eye, I saw an SUV pull up in front of the building. The window rolled down slowly and before Spencer could get a word out, Charles's annoyingly perfect face was hanging out the window.

"Hey, what the hell, Salvatore? You show our baby sister the place before your partners?"

Always the scene stealer, first with Simon and now, once I finally thought I was going to get some answers, Charles came barreling out of the SUV laughing, holding his hand out to shake Spencer's.

"Chuck," Spencer said, sounding irritated.

Seems I'm not the only one heated about this intrusion.

Teddy followed next out of the SUV and walked over to the three of us. Putting an arm around my neck, he kissed my head, like he always did. He then turned to greet Spencer with a disturbed look.

What was that for?

"What's going on here?" Charles asked, pointing to the both of us.

"Nothing, Charles, we just ran into each other."

There's no way I'm going to tell them that I actually ran in to him and knocked him on his ass and if Spencer knows what's good for him, he won't say anything either. I made sure to shoot him a warning look as I gave the false explanation to my brothers. Charles squinted his eyes at me. I knew exactly what he was getting at. The typical, if-you-screw-this-deal-up-I-swear-you-will-pay look.

I wasn't going to get any questions answered now, not with these two looming over me. "I have to go. Good luck on the project," I said, lifting Teddy's arm from around my neck. Before I turned to leave, I couldn't help but catch Spencer's eye. *Is he going to say something?*

He went to move in my direction, opening his lips, and getting ready to speak, just as Charles's voice flared up. "Bye, baby girl."

I need to leave now, before I kill my brother. I started walking away from the beautiful men, when I heard Teddy call to me. "Beth! Are you coming to Grans on Saturday?"

Turning, I glared at my brothers and Spencer, who looked just as annoyed as I felt. I made sure to speak loud and clear. "I'm not a baby, Charles Ferguson Monroe!" I caught Spencer raising a hand and covering his mouth as if to stifle a chuckle. Lowering my voice slightly, I addressed Teddy, who was also laughing. "Yes, I am going, and you and Fergi can pick me up at ten sharp!" I put my ear buds in, turned up the music, and jogged back to the condo.

I really hated the fact that Spencer had this strange pull to him. It was no wonder women couldn't get enough of him. I saw him and I wanted to be near him. I heard his voice and everything else went mute. But when he touched me, I felt like I could light all of Main Street with the electric charge I got from him. It was technically only the third time that I had ever spoken to him, but, damn, if each time, it didn't get more intense.

Through my jog, I tried to calm my body's sudden need for Spencer. So I made myself think of Simon, and the fact that I was going out on a date with him in less than seven hours. I had to be rid of any feelings for Spencer by the time Simon came to pick me up. It was pretty obvious that Spencer was a fantasy that I would never see come true, but Simon...Simon could be real.

Chapter 6

Satisfied with how I looked in my pencil skirt and sheer red blouse, I ripped the last tag off. Fluffing my curled hair one last time, I exited my room.

"Well, what do you think?" I spun in front of the TV where Gia was sitting. "Does the fashionista approve, or what?"

"Are you trying to get laid tonight? Because that's what that outfit says."

Grabbing a pillow off the chair closest to me, I chucked it at her face. "No! I just want to look nice, you freak!"

"Considering the last date you went on, where you wore jeans and a T-shirt, I would have to go out on a limb and say that you're really trying to impress this guy," she said, wiggling her eyebrows.

"No—fine—maybe a little," I confessed.

"I want to hear everything when I get home tonight," she said.

"Wait, when you get home? Where are you going?" I asked.

"Mood," she said, talking under her breath and not looking at me.

What the hell is she up to now?

"You're not going by yourself, are you?" I asked, sitting back on my hips and crossing my arms.

"No, not really. Chuck invited me," she said over her shoulder.

"When did you talk to him?"

"I was coming home for a lunch break today and he was

just standing outside some abandoned building with Teddy and Spencer Salvatore. Speaking of Mr. Hottie Salvatore, have you seen the Fame web page today?" she asked.

Damn, she's good at taking the heat off of herself and putting it elsewhere. "No, I try not to look at it on a daily basis. Why?"

Salvatore, plus me, plus Fame equals bad news. I can only imagine what she's going to tell me.

"Umm, there's another picture of you two up."

Great.

She turned her lap top so I could see. The scene on the screen was still very fresh in my mind. Spencer and I were standing outside the old restaurant when the photo was taken. I had just confronted him about the notes. His body was tense, his fingers in mid-run through his hair. *God, he looks good. Me, on the other hand? Not so much.* My face was red and splotchy, while my hair was falling out of the pony tail and, damn, did I look desperate. Scrolling down, I read the caption.

> *What's this? An intense, exchange of looks between Mr. Salvatore and his not-so-secret vixen. That's right. We know who you are, Elizabeth Monroe.*

What the hell? That's it. I'm convinced the world is out to get me.

"Spencer seemed to get more interested in our conversation when your name came up, in case you were curious."

As Gia spoke, I could feel the color drain from my face.

"You do have a thing for him, I knew it!" Gia clapped her hands happily and squealed. "Looks like you have a leg up on the competition, girly. I'm pretty sure no one else can say that he's kissed their hand or rubbed their feet, not in public, anyway. You know, he's, like, really private with his love life. I heard a rumor he pays woman to keep their mouths shut after he sleeps with them."

I rolled my eyes at her, not believing a word of it. "First off, I was jogging and ran in to him. Second off, I don't have a 'thing' for him. And thirdly, I don't believe he's 'private' with women. He's got to be linked to someone." I tried to say it like I didn't care, like he didn't make me go on the fritz.

"Okay. Fine, I'll let this go," she said smugly. "But eventually you are going to have to talk about it. I'm just letting you know I'm here when you need me to listen. And if you don't believe me about his love life, check for yourself. He's not linked to anyone, but you."

With that, the conversation ended as I marched to the kitchen to get a glass of wine, hoping to calm my nerves. I tried desperately not to think about Spencer or the fact that he "perked up" at the sound of my name. I took a sip of wine while I wrapped my head around the last ten minutes. I couldn't believe Fame rated me out. Now everyone would know it was me in all the pictures. *Lots of people had their pictures on that site, and they are all fine, right? I need more wine.*

There was a soft knock at the door. Gia and I quickly turned to one another, freaking out with excitement. I downed the last of the wine while Gia went over to let my date in. I straightened my skirt and fixed my hair, praying I didn't look a hot mess.

Gia ushered Simon in after a quick introduction and hello.
Damn, he looks good.

He had a light blue dress shirt on, which fit him perfectly. His biceps stretched against the fabric. The sleeves were rolled up to his elbows and, for a second, I forgot he was even here to pick me up. He had left his shirt un-tucked over a pair of light blue jeans that hugged his masculine hips. Looking around Gia's tiny frame, he found me standing near the kitchen. And that was when my brain registered that, yes, he was here to pick *me* up.

I chewed nervously on the inside of my lip, embarrassed by how long he stared at me. He finally walked around Gia. Practically brushing her aside and coming straight for me, he took my hand in his and kissed it softly.

"Wow, you look beautiful," he said, with a surprised inflection to his voice.

What the hell? Did he expect me to look like shit? Maybe this is a mistake.

"Are you ready to go? I got us a reservation," he said, clearing his throat, so his voice went back to normal.

"Yeah," I answered, inwardly wishing that I hadn't agreed to this date. "Let me just grab my shawl."

We took a cab downtown to a restaurant, where we were escorted to a private table at the back of the fine dining, Italian restaurant.

As he held my hand in his, I felt on edge. I could have sworn I could feel the tension in his hand as we made our way to the table.

"Can I offer you a glass of our house wine selection?" the waiter asked.

"Give us a bottle of your best," Simon said, smiling up at him.

When our wine arrived, I caught Simon watching me as I took a sip. "Did I spill some?" I asked, pulling my hand to my chin.

He laughed and shook his head.

"What then?" I asked, leaning over the table and resting my chin on my hands.

"I like looking at you. I really do," he said, almost as if he didn't even believe himself.

"Thanks?" I half-smiled back, arching an eyebrow at him. *I'm not imagining this, right?*

"Can I take a picture of you?" he asked, studying my face.

Damn you, cheeks. I know you're flushed! "Right now?" I asked, sitting back in my seat and looking around the crowded restaurant.

"Yes, right now. Can I?"

This is going to backfire. I just know it. I stared at him, still confused as to why he would want a picture of me right now.

"Please."

Oh, God, he's begging.

He pulled his cell phone out and smiled over at me.

Yup, this is going to bite me in the ass later, but I'm a gluten for punishment lately. May as well not stop now. "Fine, go head, but be quick about it," I said, glancing around at the room full of patrons.

"Okay, ready?" he asked.

I folded my hands back under my chin and gave a little smirk for the camera. He snapped the picture, checked to make sure it went off okay, then turned it for me to look at.

"Not too bad. If I didn't know any better, I would have thought Simon Sullivan, professional photographer to the stars, took it."

We both laughed, but as I thought of his picture, another came to mind, one with another man in it.

"Hey, Simon, I need to tell you something." I took a quick sip of wine before I continued.

"What is it?" he asked, looking at the picture on his phone again.

"Do you ever look at Fame's web page?"

He tensed and placed his phone back in his pocket before answering my question. "No, not really my thing. Why do you ask?" His whole demeanor had changed. His cheerful personality was gone as he waited for me to answer.

"Well, there have been some pictures of me with Spencer Salvatore. I don't know if you know him—"

"I know him," he said, cutting me off abruptly.

"I think they're trying to say we're romantically involved, but it's not true. They're just digging for a story." *Ew, that tasted so bitter. Hopefully, he'll believe me.*

"It's no big deal. Like I said, I don't follow that stuff. I'm sure they'll stop soon." He said it as if he knew for sure.

Any tension that was brewing just a few seconds before was gone and Simon's cheerful personality returned.

I still had my doubts. Sometimes he seemed uninterested, and other times, he was fawning all over me, complementing me, reaching for my hand. One minute, we'd be talking like we were old friends, which was great but, the next, he'd act like he didn't want to be there. It was almost as if he was fighting with himself. Sometimes, it seemed like *he* didn't even believe that he could actually be having a good time with me.

"So, you haven't told me about your family. All I know is that you're an only child," I asked, after the whole Fame nonsense.

"Not much to tell. My mom stays at home and volunteers her time, and my father is a hot shot lawyer in LA."

Okay so his family has money, explains the career choice.

"My parents expected me to be a lawyer or football player," he continued. "I played all through college. I could have gone pro, but decided against it. I got a degree in sports medicine, but I never really got into it. I did it more for my parents."

Football player, eh? I should have known he played sports, with that physic.

Taking another sip of his wine, he caught me in a day dream. "Am I boring you now?" he asked.

Snap out of it, Beth! I was stuck with a cheerleader-quarterback fantasy, fresh in my mind, and couldn't help the wicked grin on my face. "No, not at all." I quickly held up the menu to hide my embarrassment.

"What about your parents? You conveniently skipped over them," he said, looking over his own menu.

Crap! Can't hide now. He used my own line to dig for information. Here goes nothing. "They died when I was two." *Wait for it. There it is. The look everyone gives me when they find out my parents are dead.* I hated when people acted as if I was still that fragile two-year-old I was when they were taken from me.

"I'm so sorry, Elizabeth. What happened?" he asked, placing his menu down on the table.

"They died in a car accident." I kept it short and simple, Simon didn't need all the baggage in one night.

"I'm…wow, Elizabeth."

Poor thing is fumbling his words. Better save him. "It's okay. It was a long time ago." I caught him doing that internal struggle thing again. "You know, I'd love to know what's going on in there," I asked, pointing to his head.

He laughed nervously and took a sip of wine. "Me, too. All I know is that, I'm really enjoying tonight."

I looked at him questioningly. *Did he expect tonight to be a total bust or what*? "That's good. So stop looking like you're shocked that I'm so cool," I said with a grin.

He shook his head and laughed. He seemed to relax at that and acted like the Simon that I was finding to be pretty irresistible.

The restaurant was emptying and I figured it was getting late. *Holy cow, almost eleven*! I slid my phone back into my purse just as Simon's went off.

He checked the screen then looked up at me apologetically. "I'm sorry. I have to take this. It's my boss."

I motioned for him to go ahead and take the call. I sat back in my chair for the first time and tried not to listen to the conversation going on across the table.

"Right now?...I can't...This isn't right...No, I'm not..." Simon turned away from the table when he spoke, making it hard to hear anymore. His boss must have said something very convincing because the next words out of his mouth were, "Fine, I'll have the package there within the hour." He didn't even say bye, just hung up in frustration.

"I guess you have to go?" I asked.

"Yeah. The guy that was going to cover for me got sick, so I got caught." He placed his cloth napkin on the table. His expression was torn, as if he didn't want to do something. Calling the waiter over, he asked for the check. Not even bothering to look, he placed his credit card in the binder and handed it back.

"I can help. How much do I owe?" I asked, grabbing for my purse.

"I think I can pay for your dinner, Elizabeth. I might be a struggling photographer but I'm not poor."

Leaving my bag in my lap, I smiled back at him and shook my head. *Men and their chivalry. Can we say sexy?* "Okay, but next time you let me pay or at least tip."

"Fine," he said. "I guess I can do that."

This stupid grin on my face is actually hurting.

The waiter came back and handed Simon the small black binder with his card and receipt.

"So where do you have to go?" I asked while he signed his name.

"Mood, actually. Will you come with me?"

I frowned at him. "You want me to go to Mood, while you work? I don't know. I should probably get home," I said as we both stood from the table.

"Come on, we had fun the last time we were there together."

What's he getting at? "Well—" I paused, considering.

"Great! You're coming with me," he said, not even giving me a chance to say no. "A birdie told me your brothers and friend are there. You can hang out with them, until I'm done."

I couldn't help the eye roll that came when I thought about sitting in a crowded club. "Fine. I'll go, but you better never ask me to do this again."

Crossing his heart, he held up his hand like a boy scout. "Promise, this is the one and only time," he said with a warm smile.

e/೨e/೨

Before I knew it, I was entering through the back door of Mood. Simon was able to get me in without causing a fuss. Not that I couldn't just walk up and tell them my brothers were here, but I didn't want to hurt his ego. The music was loud and the place was packed. Simon walked me to the bar where we were able to share a drink before he had to leave.

I scanned the place for my brothers or Gia. I should have guessed. VIP. I walked over.

A man dressed all in back stopped me just before the VIP area. "Sorry, miss, this is the VIP area. You can't come in unless you have an invite."

No shit, it's the VIP. With my hands firmly planted on my hips, I set fire to him ranting and raving that I was Elizabeth Monroe and that my brothers probably paid for him to stand there. I went on, yelling at him that he should let me through before he lost his job. "Go over there and get them. They will tell you who I am. They just can't hear or see me over all these people and this loud fucking music—" In mid-sentence, I saw the bodyguard abruptly turn from me and hold his ear piece closer.

What an asshole. Now he's ignoring me!

"Yes, sir, I understand," he said, before facing me again.

I was confused, and a bit scared, when he leaned in closer to me.

"I'm sorry about this. Mr. Salvatore was sure to straighten everything out. Please," he said, holding his hand out to help me up the few stairs.

Why can't I move? Move, Beth. It was no use. My eyes wandered around the crowded club. I was on the hunt for blue eyes and a beautiful face.

"Miss Monroe? Are you okay?"

I looked back at the man standing before me. "Yes—yes I'm fine."

I took hold of his helping hand and walked up the steps. Spencer was there, somewhere, watching me. I didn't know if I should feel flattered or petrified. In that moment, it was a nice combination of both.

The beautiful people saw me as I was coming down from a Spencer high. "Beth, what the hell are you doing here?" Gia asked, rushing over to me.

She's drunk. "Simon had to come here to work and persuaded me to come with him."

Gia hugged me tightly, swaying me side to side.

Yup, she's done.

"Baby girl, you are just everywhere today," Charles said from beside me.

"Charles, always a pleasure—not," I said, shooting him a look.

"Oh, whatever. We're actually here for a good time, so don't ruin it." He slurred his words as he grabbed Gia around the waist and kissed her neck.

That's pretty gross. I tried to hide my disgust because Gia clearly loved all the attention she was getting from him. I saw Teddy stride over, drink in hand. Placing his brotherly arm around my neck, he gave me my usual kiss on the head.

"Don't you dare let him take her home," I said, looking threateningly up at him.

"I won't, baby girl. I won't let him hurt her."

I got the feeling that he wished it was him she was wrapping her arms around. Stifling the urge to pry, I decided that this was neither the place nor time.

I danced to a couple of songs with Gia, then I finally saw Simon walking over. I wrapped my arms around his neck, talking into his ear so he could hear me over the music. "I thought you would never be done."

Okay maybe I had a few too many drinks. Do you blame me?

"I'm not, just on a little break."

I held him tight as we swayed to the music. This felt good, he felt good. I'd never felt this comfortable with a man. His strong arms held me securely and I melted into him.

Simon's hands moved over my backside and around either hip. Dropping a hand, he pulled out his phone, checking the time I assumed.

"Do you have to leave already?" I asked. *Please say no, please say no.*

"No, not yet, one more dance." He pulled me even tighter and I let my tired head lean against his chest. It was happening whether he liked it or not. I felt him tense up when I did, but the alcohol was making it easy to ignore.

When the song changed to another, he pulled his phone out again. "I have to go now. Will you be okay to go home with your brothers and friend? I have to do some more work."

"Yeah that's fine." I was relieved he had to go. I still didn't get him. He was so back and forth all night and, with me so tipsy, I didn't trust myself to "walk away" if things got intense. *Slow and steady—there is still so much I don't get about him. Now, if I could only remember that when I'm around Spencer, I'd be good.*

With one last hug, he casually kissed my cheek. I watched him walk back into the crowd and eventually disappear.

I didn't see Simon again after our two, short dances. I wanted to believe that we could take things farther, but I was skeptical. Spencer was MIA the whole time I was there, but I could feel him, like a dark, sexy, looming shadow in the corner. It kept me on edge the entire night. The only time I was able to relax was when I was in Simon's arms. Unfortunately, the moment I was left alone, I was back on that thin ledge, waiting for Spencer to pop out of the shadows or sneak up next to me like he did that first night at Mood. *Vampire*? No way this wasn't *Twilight* and I sure as hell wasn't Bella.

I spent the rest of the night sitting on a couch, watching, waiting for something that never came, something that I imagined up in my head.

Chapter 7

I slept soundly, waking up when my alarm went off at eight. A huge smile appeared on my face as I stretched. I'd categorized last night as a nice first date, or a great start to a friendship. Either way, it was fun. I made my way to the shower and, as I took my shirt off, the fabric caught on the bandages that were still on my arm. Blue eyes were all I could see when I closed mine. My heart raced at the memory of Spencer Salvatore. *This calls for a very, very cold shower.*

My hair was still damp when I went to the kitchen for tea. I had time before class, so I decided to leave early. I needed a nice long walk. I had hoped the fresh air would help clear my mind of the fact that I was infatuated with two men—two men who were so different.

I walked by the front desk on my way out, saying "Hi" to Derrick before leaving. "How's it going Derrick?" I asked as I walk by.

"Miss Monroe, things are wonderful. It's Friday and I have an exciting weekend planned for the misses."

Derrick was my favorite desk operator. An older man, probably the same age my father would be if he were alive. His salt-and-pepper hair was combed back off his face. He was some kind of handsome for an older man.

"Oolala,"I sing-songed back. *I love talking to him.*

"Speaking of oolala, someone dropped these off for you very early this morning."

He held a bouquet of red flowers out in my direction. They were beautiful.

Reaching for them, I wondered who could have left them.

"Looks like someone is going to have an exciting weekend as well," he said, winking over at me.

"Oh, I don't know about that. I'm scared to ask, Derrick, but was there a note left with them?"

"How did you know?" he asked, raising an eyebrow.

"Fourth time's a charm," I said, shrugging my shoulders as I smelled the beautiful flowers.

Without missing a beat, he pulled a small note from under the desk and handed it over.

I took it with a shaking hand. "Thanks, Derrick, see you after school." I held the flowers in one hand and shoved the note into my pocket. *This is going to have to wait until after class. I need to concentrate. Lord knows, I need to graduate this year.*

Ugh I can't stand it! That didn't last long. I tried to submerge the urge to read the note before class. *Be strong, you can do this. It's only an hour class. You can wait that long.* Chewing anxiously on the inside of my cheek, I felt my stomach doing summersaults. I couldn't decide who I wanted the flowers to be from, and the fact that the answer could be in my pocket was royally killing me.

I managed to make it all the way to campus. I was outside of the English building when I couldn't take it any longer. *Fuck it, I don't care.* I quickly sat on a bench, placing the flowers next to me. I reached in my pocket, took a deep breath, and opened the note slowly. When I saw the signature handwriting that I knew was Spencer Salvatore's perfect penmanship, I panicked.

You're killing me... lose the surfer. ~ S

Once again, this man had totally confused the hell out of me. If he meant that I was "killing" him, then why the hell didn't he do something about it?

I'm not doing anything to him. Where does he get the right to say that? And who the hell is he to tell me to "lose the surfer"? What a jerk! At least Simon had made an effort, even if he was a bit wishy washy. *You know what? I like the fact that I affect Spencer but, come on, all these little double meaning notes are getting old, and a bit creepy.*

In class, the teacher and a few straggling students arrived a few minutes after class was scheduled to begin. One late comer sat next to me—a girl definitely in her freshman year. *Great, another leggy blonde to add to the army of them walking around campus. What is this girl's problem?* She kept leaning forward on her desk, trying to take stolen glances up at me. I tried to ignore it as the teacher organized herself up at the front of the room. *Okay, for real, what is this girl's deal? Maybe she's into girls. Who knows?*

"Can I help you with something?" I asked with a frown, making sure to keep my voice quiet so I didn't draw attention. She paused while looking over at me. *She's got five seconds before I lay in to her.*

"I'm sorry. You just really look like Elizabeth Monroe. Ya know, the girl that has been linked to Spencer Salvatore," she said, studying my face.

My vision became blurry and the room began to spin. I closed my eyes, hoping that my body would right itself. When I opened them back up, I prayed that I hadn't given myself away. *Goddamn Fame!*

"I guess you're not though," she said, a little disappointed.

The teacher started calling out people's names for attendance. I looked up toward the front, ready to make a run for it, but I couldn't move fast enough, because the next name she called was mine.

"Elizabeth Monroe? Is there an Elizabeth Monroe in attendance?"

Fuck! I've been had. When I raised my hand, about fifteen women turned around in their seats to get a good look at the "vixen" who had Spencer Salvatore smitten.

"I knew it!" the skipper doll next to me said.

"Do you think you could just—umm—keep it to yourself? There's nothing going on between us."

My nonchalant statement was more than overlooked as she stared at me in awe.

"Well, yeah, I saw the pictures from last night," she said. "I can't believe you left him for whoever that guy is. I mean he's cute too, but Spencer, come on, you must be crazy."

Just then the skipper doll turned her computer screen around and there I was on the pages of *Fame* again.

A picture of Simon and me dancing was the first one up, and you could clearly see Spencer looking on in the background. The next few pictures read like a movie in stills, as Spencer watched while I held on to Simon and rested my head on his shoulder. In the last picture, he had turned and was out of the frame. I stared at the pictures and couldn't get over how angry he looked in the photos.

The flowers and note finally made sense. *Wait a minute, why do I feel bad? Like I betrayed him? I don't owe him an explanation. I don't even know him. Well—No! I don't know him!* If he was really as mad as he looked, why didn't he do anything about it? I was alone most of the night and he knew I was there. *Oh, right, I know why. Hot, attractive, sexy men like that don't like girls like me, that's why! This must be his idea of a sick joke.*

"Well, if you're not interested, would you mind giving him my number?"

Who the hell does this Mattel doll think she is, handing me her number? Goddamn skinny bitches always feel they are entitled to men like Spencer.

"Ooo, sorry I can't. He specifically told me he doesn't like the 'Barbie doll look.'" I held a straight face as I watched skipper melt into a puddle of plastic.

After her rejection, she didn't say a word to me for the rest of class.

I closed my books and packed up, grabbing the bouquet from the chair next to me. I approached the door, noticing that there were a number of people standing around in the hallway. I ducked my head and pushed through the waiting bodies. The sun was so strong when I opened the door, I was momentarily blinded. Blinking, I raised my hand with the flowers to help shield my eyes. As I found my sight again, I heard the familiar click of a camera or two or three. *What the hell? Who is taking pictures? Wait a minute, are they taking pictures of me?*

My nightmare was confirmed when I saw three men with cameras. "Who are the flowers from?" one yelled.

"Are you dating the new guy?" another asked.

"Why did you leave Spencer?"

I didn't know what else to do, so I just covered my face with the flowers and kept walking, giving them nothing but the middle finger. *Take that, Fame!*

"Ahh, come on, Elizabeth," one man said as I walked past.

Shit, they really know who I am now, no more hiding for me. They followed me for a while, still asking questions, before the campus police stopped them, but they couldn't stop my fellow students from snapping pictures with their cell phones. *Great, now my face is going to be plastered over every gossip site known to man.*

I reached my building and ducked inside. Thankfully no one followed me home. Heading into the condo, I placed my bag on the table and got a vase for the flowers. *Why did they have to smell so good? What is your deal Salvatore?* Pulling my laptop out, I expected to see my face but so far nothing had been posted yet. I jumped when my phone started buzzing from within my bag. Dumping it out frantically on the table I found it and a new message from Simon.

I had a great time last night. For some reason I can't get you off my mind.

How cute was that? Not creepy, but thoughtful. So, why was I still getting the feeling that this was all too good to be true? These love-story scenes never happened to me, yet there I was, getting secret notes and thoughtful texts.

I couldn't tell if Spencer was for real or not. It seemed a bit out of character for a multi-millionaire bachelor, and all that. The number of women that must throw themselves at him had to be through the roof. *Maybe he's watching out for me like my brothers do. On second thought, I don't want or need another over-protective brother telling me what to do and who to date.*

Now I had to deal with the freaking paparazzi following me, too. I was finally at a point in my life where I was happy with myself, my body image, which now I was more than paranoid about. My career choices were…well, I could only imagine what the media was going to say when they found out I was going to school to become a librarian—double embarrassment. I couldn't go back to the way I was, a yearlong depression, anger management, and countless hours of therapy sessions. That was something I wouldn't wish on anyone.

I think I'll take the lesser of the two evils.

I texted back, *It's because I'm awesome.*

That's not too weird, right? Too late, I already sent it. The scent of the flowers drifted past my nose and, with that, Spencer was back at the forefront of my mind. I didn't want to cast him out just yet. I wanted to believe that someone like Spencer Salvatore could really like me, even love me maybe?

R u free tomorrow?

At least I didn't have to lie about that. I was leaving early to go visit Gran with my brothers and we usually ended up staying all day if not overnight. Since the boys had taken over all of our father's companies we did these weekends at Grans less and less.

I'm out of town for the weekend. Rain check for Monday?

He responded. *Okay, is it sad that I wish it was Monday already? Have a great weekend.*

Even with all the crazy emotions, I couldn't help but smile at the fact that this man seemed to like me. His warm browneyed smile came to mind and I soon found myself wishing it was Monday, too.

∽✸∽

The ride to Grans started off quiet. Teddy drove, Charles sat in the passenger's seat looking at his phone, and I was banished to the back as usual. We endured the three-and- half hour ride to the eastern shore where Gran spent her springs, summers, and falls. I had stayed with her all summer at the beach house, lapping up the sun and enjoying the quiet that was Fenwick Island.

Not able to stand the quiet any longer, I decided to get answers from Charles about Gia. "So what are your intentions for my friend?" I asked.

Turning in his seat, he looked back at me with a frown. "Gia?" he asked, as if it was a stupid question.

"Yes, Gia. Why do you keep asking her to go out with you?" Turning back to look out the front window, I heard him chuckle. "Charles, I'm not messing around. Don't lead her on," I barked at him.

"I'm not leading her anywhere. I didn't sleep with her— wait, did I?" he said as a smirk appeared on his face.

I had been friends with Gia ever since I went to college. We were roommates our first year. A bit of an odd couple at first, we had become fast friends. She didn't put up with my stubbornness, and I didn't treat her like she was a super model. So it was not like Gia just came into my life. She'd been to plenty of Christmases and vacations with my family. Of course, I had always known she thought Charles was attractive, but she never did anything about it. Not until lately. Now, she had been sure to put herself in places where he was going to be.

"Charles, this is not funny!" I yelled, smacking his shoulder.

"Geez, Beth, I get it. You don't want me to mess with her. That's fine, but I can't help it if she can't resist all of this," he said, gesturing to his body with his hand from his head to his toes.

"You are so full of yourself!" I huffed, sitting back in my seat. "You're going to get an STD if you don't knock it off with all the women."

"What the hell, Beth? Why are you giving me such a hard time? Teddy does the same shit. I don't see you yelling at him."

He pointed over at Teddy, who adjusted himself in the driver's seat at the sound of his name.

Looking away from the road and over at Charles, Teddy defended himself. "I might take out different girls, but I'm not bringing them home with me, and Beth is right. You should cool it. Maybe focus on one girl, instead of leaving a trail of carnage behind you."

"God, you both are out-of-your-minds cryptic today. You think I'm going to get some deadly case of syphilis and you think I'm leaving a trail of dead bodies behind me."

"Chuck, we just care about you. I know you are so much more than a stupid one night stand," I said from the back seat.

"She's got a point. We just want the best for you," Teddy added, placing a hand on our brother's shoulder.

"You guys are talking like I'm dying, but if it will give you both peace of mind, I will cool it with the women, and I promise to stay away from Gia." He turned while he talked to me His face softened and my loving brother smiled back at me.

We arrived at Gran's in the afternoon. Even though I had just left the beach house, I was so happy to be back. There were so many good memories made here, it was hard not to look around and think of one. Gran had decorated in classic beach fashion—blues, whites, and lots of nautical-themed …well everything.

As usual, we found Gran on the back deck in her rocking chair, reading. Hearing the footsteps from behind her, she turned to greet us. Her bobbed white hair was blowing in the warm sea breeze. A smile appeared on her face as she saw us. She looked timeless, like an old Hollywood actress. Her eyes were a brilliant blue like Teddy's and her hair had once been dark brown like Charles.

"Gran!" Charles yelled. Running to greet her, he picked her up, spinning her around.

"Oh, Chuck my dear, I'm getting a bit old to me tossed around like this," she said through a laugh.

"Never," he replied as he placed her firmly back on the ground.

Teddy walked over next giving her a hug and kiss on the cheek.

"Where's my little muffin?" she asked, looking between my brothers.

I had stayed inside, looking out the window from the kitchen.

"You two broods didn't forget her, did you?"

"Nah, we tried but she just kept following us," Charles said, shrugging his shoulders.

"That's because she looks up to you boys. How many times

do I have to tell you that? It's like you're ten years old again, the way you complain about her following you."

Thank you, Gran. She was always getting on Charles's case about being nice to me.

"She's coming," Teddy said. "I think she stopped off in the bathroom."

"Come on, Teddy," Charles said. "Let's get our suits on and check out the water."

It was an exceptionally warm September day, and my brothers never let a beach day go to waste. They ran back into the house, sounding like a herd of cattle going up the stairs. I made my way outside and sat down next to Gran in Pop's rocking chair.

"Oh, there you are, muffin. I was starting to worry," she said, picking her book back up from the table.

"Hey, Gran," I groaned.

"Oh, I don't like the sound of that hello," she said, looking over at me.

Just when I was ready to tell Gran everything about Spencer and Simon, the herd of cattle came back down the stairs and out on the deck.

"Come on, sis, let's go," Charles demanded, standing in front of me.

"Umm, I don't know. I think I'm just going to sit up here with Gran."

"Well, you have no choice in the matter. Teddy and I couldn't make it down all summer so we are getting it all in now!"

A wicked grin appeared on Charles's face and I knew I was in for it. I stood to run away, but he grabbed my hand tightly and held me under my arms. Teddy came over and grabbed my feet, lifting me completely off the deck. It was no use. I was no match for their strong, overpowering bodies. They started to carry me down the back stairs, as I screamed for them to put me down.

"You boys be careful with her," Gran scolded, like they were teenagers taunting me just like they did years ago.

"Don't worry. We will take good care of your little muffin," Charles said as he rubbed his knuckles into my scalp.

"Will you stop that? And put me down, you creep!" I yelled, trying to flail my body, hoping that they would either drop me or put me down. But, of course, it only made them hold on tighter. Lucky me, there were only a few people to witness the pathetic excuse of an escape.

"Come on, guys, put me down." *Maybe if I'm nice, they'll let me go, since sheer physical flailing is not working.*

"Hold still, will you? It will be over soon," Charles said, cackling so hard he almost dropped me in the sand.

"Hold her, Chuck, we're almost there. If you drop her, she's going to run." Teddy's upper body was shaking from laughter, too, but he recovered by scooting up my legs to hold me tighter around my thighs. I made sure to shoot him a death glare.

They finally made it down to the water. "Ooo, that's a little chilly," Charles said, sucking in air.

"Please don't throw me in. These are my favorite jeans. I promise I will get in. Just let me change into my suit," I begged.

"Too late," Charles said, nodding up at Teddy.

"One...two..."

I didn't hear three because I was under the water. Jumping to my feet, I pushed the hair from my face, just in time to see the next wave coming straight for me. We all dove under, and it wasn't as cold as I thought it was going to be. The rays of the sun helped make it feel warmer.

Coming up from the wave, I screamed at my brothers and swam over to them, jumping on their heads and pushing them under the water. Looking back at the house, I saw Gran standing at the railing, laughing at us. Seeing her happy made my brothers and me very pleased. We were all that was left of our shrinking family, and I'd do anything for them, even Charles.

Dinner was delicious—like I expected anything less with Gran's cooking. The boys were telling Gran about all their business deals. Charles got extra excited when he started talking about the club. "I think we have decided to call it 21, what do you think, Gran?"

She smiled at her eager grandson.

I couldn't help myself. "Why are you calling it 21? So you know how old you have to be to get in?"

"No, Beth, that's not why. Well, it's not final but we like it because it has sentimental value, you know, Mom and Dad. Teddy and I want it to have a meaning, and what better meaning then the love shared by two people. Makes for a romantic setting. We plan on running it by Spencer, our business partner this week."

Oh, God. My fork stilled in my mouth and I almost choked on a piece of meat. Coughing, I placed my hand around my throat, trying to catch my breath. Again, the mere sound of Spencer's name took me by surprise.

"Geez, Beth, I only said his name. I know you women are all crazy about him, but damn."

I do not need this right now. "It's not like that, Charles," I snapped, a little too fast, and felt the redness in my cheeks.

"Beth, we have all seen the pictures of you guys on Fame," Charles said, taking another bite of food.

"I—I—"*There goes my college vocabulary again.*

"I think it would be best if you stayed away from Spencer," Teddy said, placing his fork down on his plate.

"Thanks for the warning, but there is nothing going on between us and, even if there was, I think I could handle it on my own, thank you."

"I'm sure that you could, but I would just feel a lot better if you kept your distance."

Why does he do this? He's not my father. "You're not my father, Teddy. I can talk to whoever I want." I narrowed my eyes at him, ready for the next warning.

"Now, children, let's please have a pleasant dinner. No more of this talk. Do you understand?" Gran always had a way of pulling us back from an imploding argument.

"Sorry, Gran," a chorus of voices said.

That evening, I grabbed a blanket and joined Gran outside on one of the couches.

"Ahh, my little muffin, come sit with your Gran tell me what's going on in there?"

I sat next to her, laying my head on her shoulder while she played with my hair. I took the quiet time, while my brothers were out, to spill my heart. I told her everything, from the first night at Mood to all the crazy notes, the run-ins with Spencer, my date with Simon. "Do you see why I'm so confused now? It's not like I have ever had *one*, let alone *two*, guys knocking down my door. What am I going to do?" I sat up to look at Gran, praying that she'd have the magic answer.

"Well, muffin, I think that you need to just have fun. Don't worry about anyone but yourself. Do what makes you happy, not what will make others happy. If you want to go out with both of these guys, then I think you should. We don't live in the stone ages anymore. Get to know them both, see what happens, and who you find you can't be without," she said matter-of-factly.

I kept thinking that I had to make a decision on who to concentrate on, but here was my grandmother telling me to just go with it, which I was more than ready and willing to do.

"I saw those photos of you on that web site. I may be old but I keep up with the gossip like everyone else, especially if my grandchildren are involved. I think you are one lucky girl to have these two hunky men pursuing you."

"Thanks, Gran, but I'm not so sure Spencer will be coming around any time soon after seeing those pictures of me and Simon online, if he even looks at them. He's so confusing, and he's too good looking. My eyes actually hurt when I stare at him too long. It can't be healthy."

"A man like that does not back down so easily. Your father was one—a young, self-made man. They don't usually take no for an answer. Look how long it took for your mother to come around, but once she finally did, they were the happiest couple I had ever met." Gran had always told me stories about my parents. How my father pursued my mother for over a year before she finally gave in, then six months later they were married. My parents were twenty one when they got married and they had twenty-one great years together.

"Spencer and I are nothing like Mom and Dad. He's perfect, like I think he was called the sexiest man alive in a magazine once, and I'm—well, it took me a long while to be happy with who I am. And perfect and me don't go together." It was the truth. It was what I thought and I was sure the entire world thought that same thing about Spencer and me. "Ouch!" I shouted, rubbing a spot where my gran had pinched my arm.

"If I ever catch you talking like that, a pinched arm is going to be the least of your worries. You understand, young lady? You are perfect. You are someone's perfect. You just have to find them. It might be this Simon guy or it could totally surprise you and be Spencer Salvatore, or it could be the garbage man. You have to stay optimistic and let things fall where they may." She sat me up and held my shoulders as she spoke.

Her words hit me. I was *someone's* perfect, though I highly doubted I was Spencer's. But I wouldn't tell her that. I didn't want another bruise.

Chapter 8

My weekend at Gran's went by so fast and, before I knew it, it was Monday morning. After my revelation over the weekend, I now had a new attitude on my situation. I knew Gran told me to just let things fall into place as they would, but I liked to be in control, especially with my so-called love life, which had been nonexistent until a few weeks ago.

Spencer was a fantasy—one that I planned on keeping locked tight in my mind. I knew, deep down, I was simply imagining everything with him. The stupid gossip about us was good enough to make even me believe I had something with him when I clearly was imagining it all.

Simon was reality and a pretty hot reality at that, no Greek God, but I was definitely attracted to the boy next door. I wasn't going to sabotage my chances at a real relationship with a great guy just because I had some school girl crush on the popular guy. I sent Simon a text. *It's Monday, what u doing 2nite?*

It didn't take long before I got a response to that little text. *U ;)*

That was the smallest and sexiest text I had ever received in my life. *What a smartass.* I was sure I looked like a crazy person, laughing out loud in the library.

But I could play that game too. *Sorry your boss called. You have to work tonight.*

Don't mess with the queen of sarcasm, you will lose every time. I placed my phone back in my bag and continued walking home. I was a few steps farther before my pocket starting buzzing.

"Hello?" I answered after seeing it was Simon calling.

"Elizabeth, it's Simon."

No shit. "Yeah. I know. Caller ID," I said.

"I—umm, my boss called you?"

I stopped walking and look down at the phone. *What?* "I'm not at liberty to say," I said, exaggerating.

"I'm so sorry."

He sounded strange and I couldn't help but laugh at him. I saved him before he embarrassed himself anymore. "Simon, I was joking. Why would your boss call me? If you're going to be a smartass, then you're going to get it right back."

The sigh of relief through the receiver made me chuckle again. "Right, I knew that," he said.

I could practically see the relief on his face. "Secret's safe with me," I said. "So tonight. My place? Movie?"

Gia had a late class and was going out after. We would have the place to ourselves. See if it was friendship or who knew what else?

"I'll be over around seven," he said, amused.

"See you then," I replied.

"Hey, Elizabeth?"

"What?" I asked.

"I wasn't being a smartass."

I couldn't reply before I heard the phone click dead. I hung up my end, beaming with delight. If it wasn't sunny out, I was sure the glow off of me would have lit the whole street. Soon, the glow dimmed as I thought about what he was really implying. I was not a virgin, by any means, but sex with a guy like Simon was new territory for me. Having a horrible body-image problem could do that to your sex life. The shield that I had built up since getting to know Simon was slowly falling down. Maybe it could be more than a friendship.

∽∾∽

I sat on the couch, nervously waiting for Simon to arrive. I jumped up and out of my skin when I heard a knock at the door.

When I opened the door Simon stood casually on the other side. "Hey."

Upon entering, he didn't waste one second. I was wrapped in his arms tightly as his lips found mine. Releasing me, he coolly walked over and placed his tattered bag on the kitchen table. I stood, shell shocked as I watched him.

Something had changed in him. Maybe he had let his guard down, too. Closing the door behind me, I took a second to re- cover. God, did he look good in a hoody and jeans, and he smelled even better. Turning back to me, he stopped to admire the flowers that were on the counter. *Crap! I forgot to get rid of them. Please don't ask about the flowers. I could always say they were Gia's.*

"You look wonderful tonight," he said, turning from the flowers and walking over to me.

Thank you. Having my silent prayer answered, I exhaled with relief. My eyes met his just as his complement registered. My cheeks instantly flushed with color. *If I had a dollar for every time this man made me blush.*

"I told you to get use to the compliments."

He had warned me earlier.

I shook my head as I lead him to the couch. "Come on, Casanova, let's find a movie."

I went to turn the TV on but Simon took the remote from me and placed it back on the coffee table. He took my hand in his, running his fingers softly over the tops of them.

"What's this about?" I asked, looking down at our hands.

"I'm just grateful to be here, getting to know you," he said, as if he hadn't been all the other times we'd been together.

"I'm glad you're here, too. Did you see the pictures from our date?" I asked, squeezing his hand a little, figuring this was why he was acting weird.

"No," he said, looking a little scared. "Did you take a pic- ture of us that I don't know about? I thought I was the photog- rapher…Speaking of pictures, this light is perfect. You don't mind if I take yours right now do you?"

His eyes seemed to sparkle as he asked.

"Seriously, Simon, some paparazzi snuck in and took a picture of us. It's actually a good picture, but it's still annoying."

Letting my hand go, he went over to his bag on the table. "I told you, I don't care about that stuff. I don't look at it and, frankly, neither should you. Now, more importantly, perfect light, camera, you."

How did he do that? Be so confident and unbiased? People were going out of their way to take candid, intimate pictures of us in front of Spencer. *Okay, so I left that little detail out but still, he should be flipping out .Hell, I've been flipping out since the first camera clicked.* I'd had enough with the pictures and paparazzi. Going from a nobody to a mysterious vixen had me ready to move to Siberia.

"You don't want to take a picture of me. I look awful," I said, running my fingers through my hair.

"Never, that's impossible. You're perfect." He walked back over as I covered up my face. "Come on, I know you're not shy." Sitting back down, he started snapping away. "Perfect," He said it without hesitation. *It couldn't be that easy, could it?* Could I be his perfect match? Was he mine? Sure, the times we had spent together felt right, but were they perfect? All I knew was it was way too early to give in so fast, especially with the weird way he acted on our date. He was battling something and—*God damn it, that was like thirty clicks of the camera*!

"Okay, that's enough," I said, peeking through my fingers before letting them down all the way. Looking at him through the camera lens, I couldn't help the stupid smile on my face. I was sure I looked like a goof ball, but I couldn't hide my smile, even if I'd wanted to.

Moving the camera, he looked down at me. "Has anyone ever told you that you should model?"

Ha! He's joking, right? Me, a model? That's rich! I chuckled. "Umm, no, I don't think I have ever heard that one before—oh wait, Gia's tried to tell me I look like Kate Upton. I told her she was crazy and, frankly, so are you."

"She's right you know, only, you're more beautiful. You

photograph really well. It's so easy to take a good picture of you."

Apparently it was, and apparently he was not the only one that had been. He was telling me all this while he walked back over to his bag. Pulling out his laptop, he placed the memory card from the camera into the computer.

"That's very nice of you to say, but I'm not the modeling type," I said firmly, shaking my head.

"I'd beg to differ," he challenged, turning back and winking at me from the table.

"It's true. I'm more of a book worm than a flashy butterfly."

Rejoining me on the couch, he placed his laptop on the coffee table. "Look," he said, messing with the computer some more.

I glanced at the screen and ended up doing a double take. *Shit, it's stunning.* Turning the pictures to black and white made such an artistic difference. These photographs were gorgeous, and they were of me. *His camera must be magical. That's the only logical answer here.*

"I told you, Belle, you are a beauty."

Taking my eyes from the computer, I studied him.

"Belle, huh? Does that make you the Beast? Simon, I can't believe you just did this. You really are good at what you do."

"It wasn't me, it's all you. And yeah, I like the name Belle. You love books and you're beautiful. I would be honored to be your Beast, so long as I turn into the prince at the end," he said as his warm eyes met mine.

I smiled over at him. "Okay, Beast it is."

I loved his sense of humor and his witty one liners. He seemed to always know exactly what to say, in a good way. So the real question was, what was the catch? *My doubting mind can't help itself. It knows guys like this don't just magically pop into my life.*

Just like that, the little piece of my shield I lost earlier was replaced. I was safe, at least for tonight. We never even turned on the TV, nor did he let my hand go the entire night.

The front door rattled then swung open as Gia came barreling in with shopping and school bags. "Oh, God," She jumped back when she saw us sitting. "Sorry I just barged in like that." She looked just as shocked as I felt. "I'm just going to go back to my room, lots of work to do!" she said, holding up her bags and heading out of the room backward.

"Well, I think that's my cue. I'd love to stay all night and talk, but I have an event I have to get to." He stood from the couch, but kept a hold of my hand, pulling me up to join him. Letting go only to pack his bag, he quickly took back possession of my hand. I grabbed onto his large biceps, not even able to wrap my hand half way around it. Our eyes met as he pulled me even closer. My heart raced faster at his closeness. His lips only an inch from mine, I was in a trance as I watched his tongue dart out and wet his full lips.

"I'd like to make this a new habit of mine."

It took me a moment to focus on what he was saying, because all I could seem to concentrate on was his hand moving slowly up and down my back. Once again, I was glad he had to go. My shield had so many cracks in it after sitting with him all night.

"I'd like that. I mean, I have class and need to study. I'm a pretty busy person, but I think I can make some time for you." I said, rolling my eyes.

"You better," he challenged.

"Oh really, is that a threat?" I asked, smiling up at him.

I could feel his body tense as he began to lean closer. His soft lips were millimeters away now.

"Yes," he said, nodding once and wetting his lips again.

I closed the miniscule space that separated our lips. I took the chance and was wholly rewarded.

I felt so comfortable in his arms. I didn't mind his hands running over my hips. He wasn't judging me or my size. I couldn't help but think that this was how it was supposed to feel when you started to fall for someone. That feeling when it was just the two of you and nothing else mattered. *I hate to admit it, but I like this feeling, a lot.*

Breaking the kiss, he whispered softly into my neck, "You are making me do things I didn't think were possible. I'm completely under your enchantment, Belle."

That's it. My knees are going to give out. He was still holding me tightly and I relished the moment as his warm breath danced across my ear and down my neck.

With one last kiss, he stepped back and made his way out the door and to the elevator down the hall. "I'll call you tomorrow," were the last words I heard him say as the elevator swallowed him up.

I rested on the back of the door, taking deep breaths. He was under a spell I wasn't even trying to cast.

Chapter 9

I waited lazily on the couch for Simon to arrive. We had spent every free second we had together. We'd meet at the café. He'd help me study, and I had to succumb to him taking pictures of me. I'd protest, but eventually give in. The past two weeks had been out of a story book. With no word from Spencer, I felt liberated. I concentrated all my efforts on Simon. Fame seemed to have dropped their relentless attack on Spencer and me, and even though I knew it was for the best, a little part of me missed it.

I was usually excited when Simon came over, but tonight I was all nerves. Gia was away for the weekend and she was always my go to for stopping things before they got too far. I knew that he knew that she was gone. He was here earlier in the week when she told me about it.

Simon was a man. I shouldn't expect anything less than the next step. Not that I didn't want him to be on top of me, I just didn't want him on top me with me naked.

Tonight, I had made sure my armor was polished and welded as strong as I could get it. I wasn't ready yet. Three weeks might be all right for others, but I needed more time. *I'm not ready for him to see me naked and vulnerable.*

The knock at my door set my heart racing. I knew that tonight was going to be the hardest night. It was like everything had been leading up to it. The kissing and touching had become deeper and more sensual. Simon might have had it in his head that he was going to have sex with me tonight, but I had other plans.

He stood in the doorway, smoldering as usual. "Hey, baby." Simon's voice always warmed me.

"Hey, come on in."

Closing the door, he sat on the couch in our usual spot. Walking over, I had to stop in front of him. Otherwise I was going to jump on his lap and run my fingers through that perfect, sandy hair of his. "How was your day? Do you want something to drink?" I asked.

"Sure, whatever you're having is fine, and you should know by now that my day always gets better when I'm over here."

Shit, the first notch in my armor. Too fast. At this rate he's going to have me sprawled on my back in ten minutes flat.

I headed to the kitchen to get some wine. I took my time pouring, needing a minute to recover. I handed Simon his drink and sat farther away from him than I ever had. He eyed me skeptically. I took a big gulp of my wine.

"What's going on with you? Do I smell or something?" he asked, sniffing his arms.

Not a chance. You could never smell bad. I need more wine. "No, I…umm…I think I might be catching a cold. Don't want to spread it," I said with a very fake cough.

"You don't look sick to me, let me check you out. Come here. Dr. Sullivan is in the building."

There's no getting out of this one, is there? I gave his gorgeous body a once over and found myself unintentionally moving closer to him. *Why am I so nervous about this? Simon has given me no reason to be even the least bit insecure.*

He patted his lap. I laid my head on his thick thighs and looked up into his concerned face.

Gently, he brushed my hair so it fell over his leg. "Now, let's see here."

My mouth instantly went dry and I was finding it very hard not to close my eyes in pleasure as he brushed his fingers through my hair. He felt my forehead, cocking his head in concern. "You feel a little hot and your cheeks are pretty flushed. I think I need to keep checking you out. Don't want to miss anything."

I can't take it anymore. My eyes closed as his hand moved down my neck and shoulders.

"How does that feel? Any pain?" he asked.

I opened my eyes to look up at him, shaking my head no to his question.

"Good."

Shifting down over me, Simon's lips found mine, kissing them tenderly. I reached up, curling a hand around the back of his neck. The thin strap of my tank top slid down and off my shoulder as Simon's warm hand ran over the top of my chest. I arched into his hand, wanting more. I was sure he could feel my heart pounding against my chest. He had to, because, to me, it felt as if it was going to explode from my body. I dug my fingers into the back of his neck as I raised my head off his lap to kiss him deeper.

I want it bad! Really bad! And I want it now! I want his hands all over me. I can't believe I was even considering shooting him down. There is no way my body is ever going to let that happen. I just needed to shut my stupid, doubting head up. It was obvious Simon was into this. I could feel it on the back of my head for Christ sake.

The gentle hand on my collar bone took a slow plunge down the center of my chest. Thank God I didn't have a bra on, because his hand on my skin felt too good.

"Your heart rate is a little elevated."

I opened my eyes to see his smiling face. "I wonder why that is, Doctor."

Smiling back at him, I let a soft murmur escape as his hand ran over my breasts. I arched off his lap again, grabbing him around his neck, pulling him closer to me. *That's it. No more shield, I need this. I need* him, *now!*

I pushed him off of me and sat up.

"Feeling better?" he asked smugly.

He knew what he was doing. I stood from the couch, looking down at him, grabbed his hands, and led him back to my room. If I was going to do this, it needed to be now before I chickened out or started thinking logically.

The seductive come-hither look I gave him was all he

needed to move his ass off the couch. Ushering him over to my bed, I laced my arms around his neck, nervously biting my bottom lip. I watched in awe as he raked his eyes hungrily over me. *Shit, this man is so sexy.*

His strong arms grabbed me, pulling me closer to his hard body. The heat radiating between us was something I had never felt with anyone before, except—*Nope, don't even go there, Monroe.*

His breathing was just as labored as mine as we panted between kisses and fell on the bed. His sturdy body straddled mine, his eager hands pushed up my tank top to reveal my stomach and bare chest. *God, this feels good.*

He sat up and unzipped his sweat shirt, taking it off with urgency. My hands seemed to have had a mind of their own as I slipped them under the hem of his shirt. My fingers moved slowly over the ripples of muscle. I had never felt a stomach as toned as his before, or arms as ripped as his. *Yes, I want this! I'm so ready for this. I don't even care if he's just using me because I'm not far from using him in the same way.*

Grabbing my jaw, he turned my head slowly, gaining access to my neck and leaving deep kisses along it. My eyes rolled to the back of my head as his tongue made my body spring to life with a sexual desire I had deprived it of for so long. The muscles in his back flexed and moved under my hands. Lost in the moment, I regrettably heard the familiar buzzing in his pocket. Of all the nights for him to get a call, it would be tonight, right in this moment. Stilling over me, he pushed himself up, pulled the phone from his pocket, and stared at the front screen. *He's joking right? He won't answer it, will he?*

I looked up at him, suddenly questioning everything. His expression was not what I wanted to see right then. What I wanted to see was him tossing the phone against the wall and finishing what he'd started.

Maybe I can persuade him. "Come on, don't answer it."

I tugged at the belt on his jeans, hoping to make him forget about whoever was on the other side of his ringing phone.

"Elizabeth, I'm sorry, I have to."

Clearly he wasn't desperate enough or I wasn't seductive enough. *What a blow to the ego.* I let my hands fall from his belt. *This is why I need armor.*

He moved off of me, leaving me on the bed in a fit of raw sexual frustration. I felt like hiding under the covers or making a beeline for the bathroom. Tugging at my shirt, I covered my exposed chest.

What is wrong with me? Am I that repulsive? I mean, hello, I'm basically laying here saying take me and he just gets up and leaves me—for a phone call! Here it comes. My mind was fully awake. That was not what a girl like me needed. Well, it wouldn't be the first time I got left alone in a bed. I should be used to it by now. I just thought Simon was going to be the exception. Wrong again.

As much as I wanted to turn away from him, I couldn't. My gaze was fixated on him as he pulled the phone up to his ear. His right hand rested on his hip just above the belt I'd been trying to relieve him of a few moments ago. Too busy admiring his body and the naughty things I wanted to do to it, I didn't hear much of his side of the conversation. Although, I did make out a few phrases in-between the long list of fantasies that were piling up in my head.

"Can't you get someone else?"

Work, it was always work. I really wanted to give his boss a piece of my mind.

"Fine…whatever…I'll be there soon," he said, clearly aggravated.

All the delicious things that were just running through my head suddenly fell to the depths of the floor. I glanced up at Simon as he placed the phone back in his pocket and turned his attention to me. With a wicked grin on his face, he ran over and jumped on the bed, making me lose my balance. I giggled and squirmed in protest. Simon had gone right for the tender spot just under my ribcage and tickled. Finally, he let me breathe. I sighed with contentment as he pulled me closer to his body.

Face to face with me, he ran a tender hand over my cheek. "I have to go," he said

"No, stay with me."

That was pretty damn desperate. I hoped he would fall for it. I made sure to bat my eyelashes a few extra times. *It worked in the movies.*

"You are making it very hard to leave, but I have no choice in the matter. Trust me, it's better if I go."

What? He has no choice. Something isn't right here.

"Better if you go? You don't want this—me?"

Great, I must have freaked him out, or grossed him out. Sitting up in my bed, I drew my legs in close. I knew I should have waited. He didn't want this, or me.

"Belle, that's not what I meant at all. I want to stay here so badly, but I'm stuck in this job and I can't tell them no. There is nothing wrong with you. You are perfect and beautiful. Maybe it's just the universe telling us to take this slow. I want you, Elizabeth Monroe, and nothing is going to stand in my way."

Taking my chin between his fingers, he turned my head up so I was forced to look into his eyes—soft brown eyes that warmed me whenever I stared into them. *I'm so screwed.*

I opened the front door for him while he slid his sweatshirt back on and zipped it up half way. Pulling the straps of his backpack over his broad shoulders, he stood in front of me, wrapping his hands around my hips, swaying me slightly. I smiled up at him.

"I promise you, next time, I'm not going to answer the phone."

"You better not or I might chuck it out the window, but not before I tell your boss off."

As he laughed down at me, I took in the deep resonance of his voice. He kissed me one last time then I pushed him out the door and leaned on the frame.

"Ooo a little hostile. I think I like it," he said with a smirk.

"Ha, not even close, more like sexually frustrated. Get out of here, Doctor, before I sue for malpractice."

Holding his hands up, he backed away from the door. "I'm gone. I'll call you tomorrow, bye, Belle," he said, before turning down the hallway.

Several hours later, I called it quits on school and changed gears to check my neglected e-mails. Scrolling down the screen and skipping over all the junk, I saw a message from Gran, not uncommon, so I opened it.

> *My Dear Muffin,*
> *It's your gran. I have been thinking about you, and how things have been going with the new men in your life. You seemed so excited when you visited the other weekend. I hope that these words find you well. Call your old gran more often. I miss the sound of your laughter. I'm very excited about the charity event. Theodor called me today to make travel arrangements. I'm looking forward to seeing all my beautiful grandbabies. Love you, Muffin.*
> *Gran*

Crap, I totally forgot about the charity event. With all the excitement in my new found love life, it completely slipped my mind.

Since we had been old enough, my brothers and I gave back every year to the program that helped us cope with the loss of both our parents. Over the years, the event had become bigger and bigger. I was sure my brothers being in the spotlight helped out, too. Anything we could do to raise a little money to help those in need. We hadn't even started planning anything yet. I mean, I knew that Teddy usually took care of everything, but we always met up to discuss costumes and activities for the kids.

Grabbing my cell phone, I got ready to call Teddy. On second thought, it was nearly two in the morning. I decided to just wait until later to bug him. Before closing my laptop, I decided to check out Fame's webpage. *Yeah, I like punishing myself, so what?*

There were new pictures of Spencer up. *Shit, that man looks good in a suit.* They'd been loaded only a few hours ago. I clicked through all of them. He didn't look pleased at all to be getting his picture taken. He looked pissed and irritated, and

I couldn't blame him. Scrolling down, I read the caption.

> *Spencer Salvatore, highly private but sought after bachelor, caught leaving the night time, hot spot, Mood in DC. Why look so glum, Spencer? Are you missing your vixen? Were you hoping to see her to-night? So sad, I'm sure there are plenty of ladies, waiting to make you number one on their list.*

My heart froze as I drew my hand up to my mouth in disbelief. *Could any of this be true? Oh God, do I want it to be true? Yes—No*! He hadn't tried to contact me and I knew that he knew where I lived. I'd told him for Christ's sake. Not to mention, he sent flowers. *Shit, I guess I can be blamed, too. It's not like I couldn't ask my brothers for his number or where he's staying.* I didn't want to admit how much seeing him or hearing his name affected me, but it wasn't a good thing. It was not right to be so affected by someone you knew nothing about. *Nope, that definitely can't be healthy. God, why do I feel bad for him? Shit, it's not like we were ever dating. We will never be dating.* I wanted to punch the little devil and angel on my shoulders, just so they'd shut up and stop arguing back and forth.

Slamming my computer closed, I flopped down on my bed, waiting for sleep to come. I was stuck wrestling with the fact that I barely knew Spencer, yet the minute I saw him or heard his voice, all the crazy things I thought I felt for him came to the surface.

Crap! Then there was Simon, and his compliments that made me hold onto his every word. I really thought I was starting to fall for him. How could someone not fall for that? Sure, it started off rocky, but he hadn't acted shady or distant since those first few nights. *You'd have to be deaf, dumb, and blind not to fall for him.*

Chapter 10

I sluggishly opened my eyes, then rolled onto my back and stared up at the ceiling. My face was flushed with the memory of a naughty dream, and I couldn't help the grin that spread across my face as I tried to remember it. Tossing the covers off, I skipped into the shower and let the scalding water fall against my chest. Steam rolled up and out of the shower, filling the room with a foggy haze. Leaning against the wall of the shower, I let my hands roam my body as I fantasized that they weren't my hands at all, but the strong hands of a man. But which one? *Both*? *Yes, please—*

What am I doing? *I don't do this*! My eyes flew open and my hands dropped from my sensitized body. I placed them on the shower wall, as if I was getting arrested for touching myself while thinking about two different men. I quickly turned the shower to spout out cold water. *Come on, Beth, snap out of it. It was just a fantasy for Christ's sake.*

Rushing across the room, wrapped in a towel, I snatched my cell phone off my desk as it rang loudly. Grinning widely when I saw it was Simon calling, I wasted no time answering. "Hey, you!" I said happily.

"Hey, how did you sleep?" he asked.

"Good, how about you? Were you out late?"

"A little…Umm…Elizabeth, I need to tell you something."

The sudden silence on his side of the phone was starting to scare me. If he was going to end things, he needed to just get it over with. *Damn it, I knew he was too good to be true.* I guessed he figured out last night that I wasn't what he wanted after all. I waited for him to talk but there was just silence on his end. *Oh, for Pete's sake, if he's not going to say anything, I guess I should just get it over with.* "I get it, Simon, I had a blast spending time with you, and thanks for making me feel special for a while. Good luck with your photography career," I said, trying to sound just as happy as I was when I answered.

"Wait, Elizabeth, are you breaking up with me?" he asked.

I can't believe he's still trying to string me along. Way to rub salt in it. "Weren't you going to break up with me? I mean, usually 'I need to tell you something' equals we're done in my book," I said, getting pissed off that I was still on the phone with him.

"Well, not in mine. How could you think that? I'd be stupid to let you go."

He seemed shocked and possibly hurt. *Shit! I always over-react.*

"If you weren't ending things, then what were you going to tell me that made your voice all weird and stressed?" I asked.

"I have to leave town for work for the next week. My flight is leaving in an hour. I found out as soon as I woke up. Not exactly the wakeup call I was expecting."

I didn't know whether to be relieved or upset at this news. "Oh, well, where do you have to go?"

"I think they're sending me to Seattle. Hopefully, I'll be back by next weekend," he said.

Just a week, I can handle that. "Will you call me?" I asked. *Shit! That sounded desperate and clingy. I am so off this morning. Damn you, sexy dreams!*

"Of course, I'll call you, every morning and every night. Elizabeth, I'm going to miss you."

How sweet is that! I needed to let my guard down and accept that good things could happen to me. Enough with the doom and gloom. I'd had an adequate amount of sadness and heartache, to last a lifetime.

I was tired of never letting anyone get close to me and, even if I was trying to fight it, I was letting Simon get close to me.

"I'm going to miss you, too." I said, smiling into the phone.

❧❦❧

The week Simon was gone went by faster than I expected. He kept to his promise and called every day, sometime twice a day. He ended up having to stay out on the road for longer than he'd thought, some special project that his boss wanted in only his hands.

I took the time I had alone to study and catch up on school work. I couldn't afford to let my classes slip out from underneath me. After hitting the books all morning, I took a break and made myself a quick lunch. Just as I was getting ready to indulge in the masterpiece of a sandwich I had made, my phone started buzzing from in my room. I ran down the hall, snatching it from its charger. *Simon*! Fumbling with excitement, I finally slid the unlock button and accepted the call.

"Hello," I said, a little too excited to speak with him.

"Hey there." His voice was instantly calming.

"How are you?" I asked, almost sighing into the phone.

"I'm doing better now that I hear your voice."

The raspiness of his voice sent a shiver down my spine. *Thank God, he can't see me because I know my cheeks are pink.*

"You're not blushing, are you?"

Damn, how did he know that? "Wouldn't you like to know?" *That should shut him up.*

"You're damn right, I would like to know. I miss you. It's so boring here."

"Don't be so beastly. I miss you, too. When are you coming home?" I asked.

"Don't be mad, but they are making me stay for the rest of the week," he said.

"Really? They already made you stay one week, now they get two! I think you should find a new job." *If I didn't like his boss before, I really despise him now*!

"I'm sorry. I'm kind of stuck between a rock and a hard place. Don't have too much fun without me."

His voice sounded jealous, as if I would ever go out with someone else. *Well—No*! *What am I thinking*? *Spencer has*

*been MIA for almost three and half weeks. I'm pretty sure he's
not going to show up to touch my ankles, anytime soon.*

"You're not the angry, jealous type, are you?" I asked curiously.

"They don't call me the Beast for nothing," he said, practically growling into the receiver.

"Maybe I should go out with someone else. Will it bring you home faster?"

"Don't even joke about that! You know I'd be on the first flight home, but I'd also be living in a van down by the river if I didn't have this job."

Huh. Good to know.

Our conversation continued for the next hour. He told me that he was going from Seattle to Vegas, for some restaurant opening, and then coming home Friday.

"I wish I could come with you. I've never been to Vegas."

"Next time, baby. When you're done with school. Speaking of such things, I don't want to keep you from your work, so get back to it."

Looking down at my now-hour-old sandwich, I sighed, knowing that he was right. "I miss you. Call me later on when you have free time between jobs."

"I miss you too, Belle. I'm counting down until Friday!"

"Me too!" I said, smiling into the phone.

"Bye, babe."

"Bye."

ოჯოჯ

Two days later, I decided to go pay my brothers a visit at their office. Most of the time they were in New York at my father's building, but since taking over, they had expanded to DC and LA. Their office was located in the tallest building in DC. It oozed New York sky scraper among all the older, more historic-looking buildings. To be honest, I wasn't sure why they moved some business down here. Probably to keep an eye on me.

Walking into the lobby of the building through the revolving doors, I was still proud to know that my brothers had accomplished so much in such a short time.

"Hey, Danielle. How's it going?" I asked, nodding over at the long-haired model-looking receptionist.

"Hump day!" she said, smiling back. "Oh hey, can you give Chuck a message for me? I've been trying to catch him, but we keep missing each other."

I rolled my eyes, disgusted that she was interested in Charles. "Really, Danielle? Charles? You are so much better than that."

"Oh, come on, he's your brother. He can't be that bad. Can he?" she asked, leaning over the desk and watching as I entered the elevator.

"You should know by now," I yelled out the elevator as the doors closed.

Hitting the number seven on the panel, I leaned against the back wall as the elevator began ascending up to my brothers' floor. Two other business men took the ride up with me. Smiling to myself about how crazy women acted when my brothers were involved, I let out a little chuckle. Both men turned to stare at me—another classically, embarrassing moment.

The numbers highlighted as the elevator kept making its way up, stopping at the third floor. One of the men exited. Hearing my phone buzz, I dived into my black hole of a purse in search of it. The other rider got off next and I continued ascending to the seventh floor. I was left alone in the elevator and finally found my phone at the bottom of the black hole. I leaned back against the wall again. It was Simon who had called. I made a mental note then to call him back as soon as my meeting with my brothers was over.

Just as the elevator came to a stop, I could feel a charge of anticipation and excitement coursing through my veins. I usually got excited to hear from Simon, but this was a new sensation all together.

The doors opened and, as I looked up from my phone, I was confronted by a man in a stunning three-piece midnight blue suit. The man stood there staring at me from the opposite side of the elevator doors.

My heart fell from my chest into the pit of my stomach with a thud that echoed in my ears. My phone slipped from my hand when I realized who it was that had just made my heart thump into my abdomen. Spencer Salvatore's blue eyes were locked tight on mine. Coming out of my momentary paralysis, I dropped to my knees to retrieve my phone and, of course, my bag fell off my arm. All of its contents spilled over the floor. *Perfect!*

"Oh my God." I said aloud. *What is it about this man that makes me so, on edge?*

"Here, let me help you," he said, stepping onto the elevator with me.

Fear gripped me as he knelt down to help pick up all my scattered belongings. *I am so cleaning this purse out when I get home. Honest. Only I would have candy wrappers and an empty box of Gas-X fall out of my purse in front of the most gorgeous creature alive.* I snatched up the incriminating evidence before he even had a chance to see it. Or at least I hoped he hadn't seen it. Nothing turned a man off more than a girl with gas. *I can only imagine how red my face is right now.*

When we stood back up, he held a lip gloss and a pen that he'd managed to grab before I could. *Thank God, it wasn't a tampon.*

"Here," he said, holding them out for me to take.

Ugh, he even sounds hot. This is not my day. As I took the objects from him, our fingers grazed against each other's. The charge was instantaneous. I glanced into his blue eyes and felt dizzy. He ran his hand through his thick, black hair that had fallen perfectly onto his face while he was helping me. My heart again thumped loudly in my ear. *Sexiest man alive. I totally get it now. Maybe he doesn't have a trail of ex-girlfriends because they are all dead from having heart attacks. It's a theory I'm seriously willing to consider.*

With my chest rising and falling faster the longer I stared at him, I felt the elevator begin to descend. *When the hell did the doors close?* The sudden movement jarred me to look down and see that our hands were still touching.

"Thank you," I said, moving my hand from his.

I tossed the lip gloss and pen back into my purse, not caring which pocket they fell into at all. *Okay, breathe. What do I do now? What do I say? This Greek God of a man leaves me strange notes and flowers and then disappears for three weeks. How do you start that conversation?* "Hey, asshole, what's with the notes? *Or maybe are you playing a sick joke by getting my hopes up that you have any kind of interest in me?*"

The silence in the elevator was chilling, but the tension was searing. Standing next to him in the tight confines of that small space, I could feel my skin tingling. I knew he had to feel something too. There was no way that I was imagining all of this.

"Sorry you missed your stop." His deep voice broke the heavy silence, and my knees nearly gave out.

"Oh, it's okay. I can just take the ride back up again." I *needed* the ride back up, to calm myself down.

"I was just meeting with your brothers. We decided to open on New Year's Eve," he said, very businesslike.

Peeking up at him, I knew my face was screaming confusion. How the hell could he just start talking to me as if nothing weird had happened in the last month and a half? *I guess if he's going to act like nothing is strange, then I will, too.*

"That's great. I'll have to let my boyfriend know to save the date."

Oh shit! I didn't mean that. Damn it, I need to start thinking before I speak. I took a chance and glanced over at him. The sexy little smirk he had on earlier was gone, replaced by a hard thin line while his hands went into his pockets.

Gran's advice rang in my ears, something about having fun and getting to know both guys. I shouldn't want to get to know Spencer. I was happy with Simon—I thought. *Damn, he looks really upset. Curse me and my sardonic mouth.* If I ever wanted a chance to get to know him, I needed to bring him back from the edge of annoyance before the elevator came to a stop. "Did my brothers tell you about the charity event that we host?" I raised my eyes to gage his reaction. *Thank God, the tension is fading away. At least he's not scowling at me anymore.*

"No, they didn't mention it. We usually just keep to business during meetings."

Leaning back against the cage of tension we were stuck in, he crossed his arms over his solid chest. I swallowed the dry lump in my throat and attempted to shake the image of him rushing across the distance and crushing his lips to mine.

God, I need to get laid. "My brothers and I host a charity event. It's a costume thing since it's around Halloween," I said, still trying to shake that earlier image.

The doors to the elevator opened and we both turned, not expecting the ride to be over yet. "This is my stop, good luck with the event," he said, stepping out of the elevator and turning back toward me. His eyes roamed over me from head to toe.

Holy fuck! He just eye fucked me!

Rubbing the stubble under his chin, he turned and headed toward the exit. *Okay, I didn't just imagine that because Danielle is staring at us with her jaw practically on the floor.* There was no way I was letting him walk away after that little stunt. Taking a quick step out of the elevator, I stopped the automatic doors from closing. Standing half in and half out of the elevator, I yelled across the lobby. "Come to the charity event, for me?"

The tall, six-foot, god-only-knows-how-many-inches of pure, sexy male eye candy stopped in his tracks and turned back toward me. His blue eyes fixed on mine, and I was all sorts of messed up.

"Please," I pleaded, when he didn't answer.

I can't believe I'm begging. What am I saying? Yes, I can. Anyone in their right mind would beg to those blue eyes. I dragged my suddenly heavy leg back into the elevator. *Come on, doors, any time now. Why are these freaking doors not closing? Any other time they close too fast, but not today when I want them to.* I hesitantly looked up, expecting to see the empty lobby. But as my eyes rose up from the floor, they latched onto Spencer, now only standing a few steps away. *Any time now, doors.*

Finally, they began to close, but the last thing I saw was

that megawatt smile, and I knew that I hadn't been imagining anything.

Slumping back against the wall, I stood there in a shocked awe. My hands went to my mouth as I covered the stupid grin that was actually hurting my face. It only took twenty-three years but I was as giddy as a twelve-year-old.

I finally reached the seventh floor again. Walking past the reception area, I nodded over at Adam, a friend of my brothers from college.

"Hey, Miss Monroe, did you see that Salvatore God?" he asked, fanning himself.

"Yeah, I did," I said, trying to stifle the effects of my intense elevator ride.

Adam was a gossip queen and I didn't need my brothers knowing I had a thing for their business partner.

"Oh, the things I would like to do to that man! You know, I heard a rumor he swings my way."

I couldn't help but laugh. There was no doubt in my mind that Spencer was *not* hitting for Adam's team.

"I guess anything is possible," I said, laughing and walking past him as I headed back to Teddy's office.

On my way, I stopped by Charles's office. He was sitting at his desk with his feet propped up as he talked on the phone. *I can't not take advantage—*

I banged loudly on his door with my fists, adding some extra oomph with both feet. Charles jumped so hard that he fell off his chair. For my own safety, I booked it down to Teddy's office and hastily closed the door behind me.

Crouching over, I held my stomach tightly as tears ran down my cheeks from laughing so hard. Teddy was sitting at his desk, going through the mounds of papers in front of him.

"What the hell is going on?" he asked, freezing, the papers still in his hands.

"Elizabeth!"

We both turned toward the door to hear Charles storming down the hall. I ran behind Teddy's chair for safety. The door swung open. Charles was on a mission—to kill me. We ended up running around Teddy's desk like a cat and mouse.

"You're going to get it, you little twerp. Come here, baby girl," he sang devilishly.

"I'm not a baby. Stop saying that, jerk," I yelled back.

"Oh no, not that, anything but 'jerk.' You know it's my kryptonite," he said, standing still and clutching at his heart, while falling to his knees.

"You two need to grow up!"

Charles and I looked at each other before throwing our heads back in laughter.

"Lighten up, Teddy," Charles said, sitting in one of the two large leather chairs in front of his desk.

"We were just messing around," I said.

"Well, do it somewhere else, not in my office. Some people have to work."

Shit, now I feel bad. I knew Teddy worked hard and I felt bad that he couldn't put work down to have a good time, even for a minute. I backed off and got to the point of why I was there.

"I wanted to talk to you about the charity event," I said, sitting in the other leather chair.

"I have everything done, invitations have already been sent out. It looks like it's going to be nice turn out this year," Teddy said matter-of-factly, all business.

"Oh? Do you think you can send out one more invitation?" I asked.

"I just need the name and address," Teddy said, his face still in all his papers.

"I—umm—I have a name, but I don't know the address. It's for Spencer Salvatore."

Teddy jerked his face up to me with a look that could kill. "Why the hell would I send him one?" he asked, almost crumpling the papers in his hand.

"I kind of invited him. I ran into him on the elevator and brought it up. I thought you guys would have already invited him since he's your business partner and all." *What is Teddy's deal with him? I swear, I see steam coming out of his ears.*

"Well, we didn't invite him and I don't think he should come."

I turned to Charles for help on this one. "Come on, Teddy, it's charity," he said. "He's got a lot of money. May as well take advantage and let him put it to good use to help the kids out. What's it going to hurt, anyway?"

At least Charles is good for something.

"Fine, but if I see anything out of the ordinary, he's gone. I'm not going to ruin what the three of us have worked so hard on because you feel bad about not inviting him." Teddy pointed to me and his eyes showed just how serious he was about kicking Spencer out.

Thank God that's over. Talk about overreacting. "Anyway, on to more important things," I said. "What are we going to dress up as?" After shooting down blue body paint for Avatar people and unattractive, angry bird costumes, I finally couldn't hold my tongue any longer. "You two suck at picking out costumes. Must I do everything around here?" I said, shaking my head.

"Pray tell, Queen Elizabeth. What do you want to wear this year?" Charles asked, looking over at me from his chair.

"Ha, very funny, Charles. I was actually thinking about a Mad Men theme." I waited as the idea slowly sunk in before I elaborated.

"Mad Men, huh? I like it. We can get some vintage suits. Nice idea, Beth," Teddy said.

"Thank you!" I took the small victory because there was no way I was going to strut around a party in blue body paint.

"Since that's settled, get the hell out of my office," Teddy demanded.

Charles got up to leave first, pointing over at me with two fingers once he got to the door. "You better watch it, baby girl. I got my eyes on you."

"Yeah, yeah, I love you too, Chuck."

Once the door closed behind him, I stood from my chair and approached Teddy's desk. *Call me nosy or intrusive, but I have to know why he is so against me having anything to do with Spencer. He did agree to be his business partner, after all. It must be bad. Maybe he hates kids or is involved in an underground kinky, sex ring—head out of the gutter, Beth.*

"What, Beth?" Teddy asked, looking up at me as I quickly pulled my mind out of the underground sex ring.

"I—I was—umm. What's your deal with Spencer?"

His full attention was on me the second he heard my question. "You're my little sister. I feel the need to protect you. It's what I do, what I've always done. I just think you should stay away from him, that's all." Teddy's posture and the command in his voice screamed father figure.

I still don't get it. "But why should I stay away from him? What did he do that was so horrible or unworthy of your respect for him as a person rather than just another business partner?" My need to know any and everything about Spencer was starting to become a nasty little habit.

"Beth, drop it. I said he could come to the charity event."

Hearing the anger rise in my brother's voice, I decided to let it go—for now. "Okay." I sighed. "I guess I'll see you on the plane. We're leaving Saturday, right?"

"Yes, everything has been booked. I'm going to have a car pick Gran up."

Walking around my brother's desk, I leaned over and gave him a hug and kiss on the cheek. "Thanks, Teddy."

"Bye, Beth. Please stay out of trouble, no pictures on Fame. We don't need any more stress for the week."

"You trying to tell me I'm a trouble maker? Have you met our brother Charles? I'll be an angel, promise," I said with a grin.

⌀⌀⌀

Thank God, Wednesday was my light day, only one class, which I sat through thinking about Spencer and his gorgeous hair falling over those brilliant, blue eyes. *That man does something spectacular to a three piece suit.*

Knowing full well there was nothing to eat at home, I decided to take my chances in the cafeteria. Hours later, I was through eating and my research for my impending paper was practically done. Needing a break from ancient China, I went to my home page to catch up on the latest news. Scrolling down, my eye was automatically drawn to a small picture of Spencer with the word "Caught" under it.

Clicking on the picture took me to Fame's web page. There, in black and white, was a picture of Spencer and a beautiful woman holding his arm. *I think I'm going into cardiac arrest.* My first instinct was to slam the computer shut, but I liked to cause myself unnecessary heartache. I tried to look away, but instantly started to size myself up to this chick. *You know what makes this even better? That fact that she's a fucking Barbie doll! Tall, thin, and blonde.* Now I knew I was just imagining everything between us. *Us? Like there ever was an "us" to begin with.* Nope, it was just a man taking advantage of a woman who became mush when spoken to. *I am officially delusional.*

The rock-star Barbie was wrapped so tightly around Spencer's arm, his face looked like he was in pain. At least he wasn't passionately looking into her eyes. Maybe he was pulling a Chuck? *Why am I trying to convince myself otherwise?* This was the same man that a month ago was never even photographed with a woman. *Now, he has one hanging on him like a freaking scarf!* I pulled my ear buds out and closed up my computer, throwing everything into my bag. I needed to get home before I broke down in public over a man who was never mine to begin with. *Jealousy is such a bitch.*

It was dark by the time I made it home. "Hey, Derrick. You're here late tonight?" I asked stopping in front of the desk.

"Getting some overtime, the new guy is running late," he replied, shrugging his shoulders.

"Sorry, hopefully he will be here soon." My feeble attempt to sound encouraging was dismal.

"Oh, Elizabeth, before you go, up a package was dropped off earlier for you." Bending below the counter, he reappeared with a very small child size shoe box looking package.

The box was wrapped in brown shipping paper, I recognized the handwriting instantly. Salvatore. I took the box from Derrick's hand cautiously, like it might explode if handled the wrong way.

"Are you okay?" Derrick asked, looking over at me curiously.

"I'm fine. I just have to sit down and figure out if I want to open this or toss it in the trash." Sitting in the lobby, I dropped my bag next to me and sat, placing the box on my lap.

I weighed my options. On one hand, he was a freaking Greek God, and if a Greek God sent you something, you should probably open it. On the other hand, Salvatore was absolutely baffling. *Who goes around grabbing random people's ankles? And who sends someone flowers and love notes, and then goes out to be publicly photographed with another woman? What, he didn't think I'd see it? Maybe he is into kinky, underground, multiple partner sex/relationships. Yuck! I think I need to bow out before I find myself chained to a bed.*

I started to think that maybe Teddy was right. I needed to stop day dreaming about someone who wasn't at all who I was pretending they were, and focus on the man I was getting to know and really like. Taking to my feet, I grabbed my bag and put the box under my arm as I started to head toward the elevator.

Standing outside my door, I could hear talking. *Damn, Gia must have the TV up loud.* Turning the knob, I opened it slowly, taking one last breath to clear my head of anything having to do with Spencer Salvatore. I looked down at the box in my hand before covering it with my jacket and placing it on our entry way table.

"Hello, Belle."

Spinning with sonic force, I whirled around to see Simon standing at my kitchen island next to Gia.

"What are you doing here? I thought you weren't coming home until Friday?" Dropping the rest of my belongings, I did a double take to make sure the box was securely concealed from Gia's prying eyes.

I met Simon halfway in the living room. He grabbed me in a tight embrace. I had almost forgotten how strong he was and what it felt like to be wrapped in his gentle arms. Guilt hit me hard as I realized I hadn't thought about him since I was trapped in the elevator with Spencer.

"I've missed you so much, Belle."

His voice was deep as his eyes raked over me. The hunger in them was so real, I thought he might throw me over his shoulder and take me to my room right then and there.

"I missed you, too," I said a little less enthusiastically.

I didn't mean it to sound as bad as it did. *It's just been one hell of a confusing day.*

"Where have you been? I've been waiting for you all day. I tried calling, but you never answered. Your phone just kept going straight to voice mail."

Crap, my phone! Everything before Spencer came rushing back to me. I remembered getting a call from him and missing it. I was going to call him back, but Spencer happened. I never even looked at my phone the rest of the day.

Did I even have it on me? I think I would have heard it ring. Taking a step back from Simon, I held my hands up to his chest.

"Hold on a minute, let me check my bag." I dived head first into my bag, searching through the black hole. *Nothing.* "I must have left it at my brothers' office, God I hope I didn't lose it."

I looked up at Simon. He smiled back at me, holding his hand out for me to take.

"I'm sure you just left it with your brothers," he said confidently.

"I hope so." Placing my hand in his, I came toe to toe with him. I almost forgot how wonderful he smelled too. *Stupid Salvatore.*

"Did I tell you how beautiful you are?"

The warm breath that escaped his lips ran over my ear. The sensation sent a chill through my body, waking it up from its Spencer slumber. I pulled back to look deep into his warm, brown eyes. *This is the man I should be thinking about. This is the man who treats me the way I deserve to be treated. It took long enough, but I think I finally found him.*

I draped my arms around his neck and pushed up on my tip toes to kiss his waiting lips. As he pulled me closer, I forgot where I was and concentrated solely on the hand that was running from the middle of my back and over the curve of my bottom.

"Ahem, I'm still standing in the room."

Gia's voice brought me back. Breaking our kiss, I smiled up at Simon who still had a firm grip on me.

"Sorry," I said apologetically.

"It's fine. Just take it to your room. Otherwise, sit your ass down, Survivor's about to start," Gia said on her way to sit on the couch.

Looking up at Simon, I pleaded with my eyes. I wasn't really in the mood to go to my room. Unfortunately, Spencer was still clawing at the corners of my mind, evidently not wanting me to have any fun with Simon.

We sat on the couch with Gia and I tried to focus on the show, but I wasn't even in the same room as them. I heard Gia talking and felt Simon rubbing my arm, but as much as I hated to admit it, I was stuck in a small elevator with Spencer Salvatore.

I found myself making a dumb excuse about being tired and needing to sleep after the show was over. Not even arguing with me, Simon simply kissed me goodnight. *How much more perfect could he possibly be?* The guilt of thinking about another man while being in the arms of this one was gnawing at my insides. *I don't deserve Simon.* I found it hard to believe Simon was so laid back and easy going.

Chapter 11

Grabbing my jacket with the box tightly concealed under it, I made a break for my room. "I've got a lot of work to get done, so I'm just going to call it a night," I said, keeping my head down and heading for my room.

"Hey, are you all right? Did something happen today?" Straining her neck before I slipped into the hall, Gia shot a concerned look my way.

I can't get into this with her right now.

"Nah, I'm fine, just a lot on my mind with the charity event and school." *Hopefully that will keep her off my back until I'm ready to bring another person into my twisted love life.*

Turning back to the TV, she called down the hall, "Well, I'm here if you need me."

"Thanks, Gia," I said, before closing my door.

That night my head was moving at warp speed. How could someone I barely knew, have such an effect on me? I should have been knee deep into Simon, yet I was lying in bed, alone, watching the clock tick as my mind kept throwing ridiculous fantasies of Spencer at me.

It was a good thing I didn't have classes tomorrow because, before I knew it, it was two in the morning and I hadn't even closed my eyes yet. *Oh, this is ridiculous!* I ripped the covers off and went to sit at my desk. I turned the computer on and waited for it to start up.

Fame's website stared back at me. It wasn't a good idea. I shouldn't be interested in anything on this web page. *Oh, what the hell*? I moved the cursor to search and typed in Spencer

Salvatore. The page went black while it loaded. *Lovely.* His beautiful face was staring back at me when I looked up. Scrolling down, I read the little biography they had on him.

> *Spencer Salvatore, young, determined, and sexy as hell! This thirty-year-old has taken the night, bar, and restaurant scene by storm. Having over twenty hot spots all over the world, this newcomer has plans to expand even more. Did I mention he's single, ladies? Although Mr. Salvatore is rarely seen with a woman by his side, it seems times are changing. Recently spotted with Elizabeth Monroe—the mysterious sister to Theodore and Charles Monroe—it seems there is still hope for those of us waiting for this very eligible bachelor to pick the perfect woman. We'll all be on the edge of our seats, waiting to see what happens.*

Bad idea, very bad. I slammed the computer shut and threw myself into bed, thankful that sleep finally came, but not before I imagined what it would be like to be with Spencer, to be his "perfect woman."

I woke up in a haze, not sure how to deal with the day that was ahead of me. I still hadn't opened that stupid box and I had to find a way to get excited about Simon, since Spencer pretty much made me forget about him with one look. I needed to shower. *Maybe I can wash Spencer out of my mind.*

With my thoughts back together, I called Simon on the house phone.

"Hey, babe," he answered.

"Good morning."

"You just get up?" he asked with concern in his voice.

"Kind of, I was up later than I expected catching up on school stuff." *Well, not all of it was a lie.*

"Oh, well, do you want me to come over and pick you up? I'd like to spend my whole day looking at you."

Damn he knows how to make me feel good. "Yes, please. I wouldn't mind looking at you all day, either."

"I'm on my way," he said, before hanging up.

I was watching TV when the doorbell chimed. There on the other side of the open door stood Simon, arms crossed and the devil in his smoldering brown eyes, not saying a word. I had to back up to give him room as he walked in. Smiling at me, he moved quickly. His strong arms lifted me up and spun me around.

My first reaction was to wiggle free. Not one to be picked up like a rag doll, I was petrified he was going to drop me. *How embarrassing would that be, my fat ass landing on top of him.*

"Oh my God! Simon, put me down." My half-laughing, half-shrieking protest was high-pitched and not normal coming from my mouth.

"I've never heard that sound before. I like it," he said, nuzzling his head in my neck, as he let me slide down his solid body.

Blushing—I know I am.

"There it is, that beautiful pink hue on your cheeks."

I took a moment to look up into his warm, brown eyes, his smile, his…hair? "You cut your hair!" I ruffled his shorter hair. *Man I can't curl it around my finger anymore. What the hell?*

"What? You don't like it? It was getting a little long. I don't want to look like a girl, or worse, Fabio."

Fantasies started taking over. Simon with long, shoulder length, sandy hair leaning over me as it gently fell around his face. *Add that one to my ever-growing list.*

"It's okay for now, but I kind of like the idea of Fabio," I said, while running a hand back through his shorter hair.

"Well, if Fabio is what you want, Fabio is what you'll get. I'm never cutting it again," he said, grinning. "I was thinking that we could go over to your brothers' office, see if anyone has found your phone, and then possibly get lunch? What do you think?" he asked, holding me tight around the waist.

Humph, the two of us riding in the elevator hand-in-hand? Of course, Spencer would be standing right outside the doors as they opened. I'd drop Simon's hand and rush into Spencer's arms, because that's what I do in my fantasies. I always choose the wrong guy. Not today! I'd hold onto Simon's hand. Who cares if Spencer sees me with someone else? It's not like we are, ever were, or ever are going to be dating.

"That's a great idea and you can officially meet my brothers."

"Wow, this just got serious, meeting your family. Maybe I should have thought this out a little more. I'm a little nervous all of a sudden."

Stretching up on my toes, I touched my lips to the corner of his mouth. His hold on me tightened, as he turned to kiss me full on. His now-familiar taste was welcome on my lips.

"If you do that in front of them, there might be a little tension, so make sure to keep your beastly paws to yourself while were there."

Smiling down at me, he rested his head on mine. "Dually noted, no groping in front of your brothers. It will be challenging, but I think I can manage for an hour," he said, smiling against my cheek.

When we arrived at my brothers' office, we went straight for the elevators. I waved over to Danielle as we waited for the doors to open. She gave me a big thumbs up and smiled over at me. I smiled back, not really sure what the thumbs up was for. *Did she finally get to sleep with Charles? Who knows with that one?* She then pointed next to her, nodding her head as she looked Simon up and down. I peeked over at Simon who was oblivious to the whole silent conversation. The sun caught his light-colored hair and his muscular frame was perfectly dressed.

I instinctively grabbed a hold of his hand, claiming him as my own. Such an insecure thing to do, but who was I kidding? It wasn't every day a hot guy like Simon was with a girl like me.

"What's this about?" he asked, holding our hands up. "Nervous?"

I couldn't help but chuckle up at him. "See the girl over at the reception desk?"

He tried his best to nonchalantly look over, but he was a man and incapable of that.

"Yeah?" he said, turning back to me.

"Let's just say she's a bit of a man hoarder. She was checking you out and I wanted to make sure she knows you're not available."

"Oh really, a man hoarder?" he asked, looking over at her again.

"She collects them. She's currently trying to get Charles, as of yesterday, that is. Who knows about today?"

I could hear the elevator approaching. It couldn't have gotten there fast enough. It was an awkward feeling, having to claim someone so they didn't get snatched out from under you. Glancing up, I saw Simon smile over at Danielle, only to see her send a seductive one back. The next thing I knew, my cheeks were warm and covered by large hands that weren't mine. Lips found mine as Simon kissed me. Pulling away when the door opened, I blinked my eyes open to see a wicked grin spread across Simon's face. Taking my hand in his again, he pulled me into the elevator, spinning me so my back was to his front. As the doors closed, I saw Danielle's, mouth hanging open.

"What was that for?" I asked, chuckling and squeezing his arms around my waist.

"Just making sure she knew I was taken. That's all," he said into my neck before kissing it.

I chuckled. "I think that definitely did the trick."

As we ascended, the tension turned more serious with every floor we passed. The nerves seemed to be getting to Simon. He wasn't joking around anymore and he became still. Just as we reached our destination, I pulled away from his embrace, because...*Ugh, who am I kidding? I know why I pulled away. The scenario of Spencer standing on the other side of the doors terrifies me and, if by some chance it does come true, I don't want Simon to feel my body tense up at the sight of Spencer.* When they did open, I was extremely relieved that no one was standing on the other side. I walked over to Adam, Simon hot on my heels.

"Hey, Adam," I said, leaning on his desk.

"Hey, girl, you miss me that much?" he asked, while he primped his slicked back, blond hair.

"Obviously! But in all seriousness, I lost my phone yesterday. I was wondering if anyone has seen it."

"No, honey, I'm sorry, no one has said anything."

"Great," I said, rolling my eyes. "If you see it or hear anything about a found phone, please let me know or give it to my brothers."

"Sure thing, I can do that. Hey, did you ask Danielle downstairs?"

I shook my head, smiling inwardly. "I'll ask her on the way out. Are the boys busy?" I asked, pointing down the hall, silently sending a prayer up that they were alone and not meeting with a certain someone.

"Nope, they're just in their offices. They only had one meeting today, which was early this morning. You can go ahead on back. Not like you need my permission."

I smiled across to him.

"Umm, who's this?" Adam asked, resting his elbows on the desk to hold his head up, a seductive smile spread across his face.

What is with people today? Doesn't anyone have any self-restraint? "This is Simon. Simon, this is Adam, my brother's very nosy receptionist."

Adam held his hand out femininely toward Simon. Taking Simon's hand in his, Adam shook it daintily. "And Simon is..." he asked, gazing into Simon's eyes.

"Umm...he's umm..." I stumbled with my words like a child.

"I'm a good friend," Simon said for me.

We hadn't discussed anything about how I was going to introduce him to, well, anyone. Were we dating, hanging out? The idea of casual dating made me feel a little less like a crazy, horny woman with her sights set on two different men.

"Well, I'm Adam, as Beth so nicely put it before, and if you need anything, you just let me know," he said, winking at Simon as he finished introducing himself.

Still holding onto Adam's hand Simon leaned a little closer to him. "Oh, I will do that, thank you."

I was pretty sure if Simon hadn't been holding Adam's hand, Adam would have fallen off his chair.

Shaking my head, I grabbed Simon's free hand. "Come on, you savage beast, let's go find my brothers." I dragged him down the hall, all the while Adam was practically leaning over his desk to watch us walk away. "You sure do know how to leave people speechless," I said to Simon.

"I can't help it. I have that effect on people. After all, that's how I got you."

I shook my head as I peeked into Charles' office. "You are something else. Should I be worried if you have this 'effect' on everyone? They must be in Teddy's office, come on." I started walking the rest of the way down the hall, but was pulled back toward Simon.

"No," he said.

Confused, I frowned, not sure what we were actually talking about anymore.

"You don't have to worry about anything or anyone. You are it for me. There's no one else."

"Oh, that's good to know," I said, smiling up at him.

"Belle, listen, you're not my good friend." He held tighter onto my hands. "You're more than that, but if that's what you're comfortable with right now, then that's what I'll be for you, but I want you to know I'm ready for more. I'm ready for all of it, all of you."

Is this happening right now? Is he asking me to be exclusive with him? All the years I spent as a lonely teenager, only wanting one thing—to have a boy ask me out. And now, I can't even be sure I can say yes without thinking I'm making a mistake. God damn, Salvatore, why did I have to meet him?

I was so mad at myself for not being able to just say yes. Simon was searching my face for an answer, a smile, something to show him that I was in it with him. When I didn't answer him, he did.

"I can be whatever you want me to be, just know that it's not going to turn me away, or stop me from doing this," he said, pulling me closer to his body. Caressing my cheek, he ran his thumb across my lower lip then down the side of my jaw before he kissed my lips tenderly.

"Thank you, Simon, thank you for being patient with me. I don't deserve it, but I'm so new at this I—I know that's not an excuse, but I still have a few walls up. I'm working on them, I promise."

Giving him one last comforting hug, I walked to Teddy's door. I knocked gently before opening it, walking in, and checking the surroundings. The boys were sitting at a table filled with papers and their lunch.

"Hey, guys," I said, walking all the way in, but taking a glance back to nod Simon in after me.

"Hey, baby girl," Charles said, spinning around in his chair like a child. He quickly slammed his feet on the ground to stop the spinning the moment he saw Simon walk in behind me. Teddy simultaneously looked up to see Simon mid-bite into his sandwich. He placed it back on the wrapping paper.

"Who's this?" Charles asked rudely.

My usual, jovial brothers were nowhere to be found, as they eyed Simon up.

"This is Simon, my umm…"*God here we go again. Why can't I just say it?*

I turned to Simon for help. Taking a step closer, he took my hand in his, and I was thankful for the support.

"I'm dating your sister."

As if the tension in the room wasn't already on high, my over-protective brothers both stood, looking at one another.

Teddy was the first to move toward us. I didn't know if he was going to shake Simon's hand or punch him in the face. Fortunately, no one was punched in the face. Teddy held out his hand and introduced himself. My brother was taller than Simon and had a more slender build. Charles soon followed suit and introduced himself. Although he was the shortest of the three men, he had a certain air about him which I was sure was why women flocked to him.

I took a second to admire all three of them. I felt really out of place. Put Simon in a suit like my brothers and, if someone would have walked by, they would have thought it was a photo shoot for Ralph Lauren. Then there was me, standing between them in jeans and sweatshirt, my hair in a messy bun, and no makeup. *Just plain, ordinary, and frumpy.* I shook myself out of my self-pity to give my brothers a better introduction to Simon.

"So you're sleeping with my baby sister?" Charles asked, going totally off topic in the middle of my intro about Simon being from California. "Well, are you?" he asked again.

Simon laughed nervously, running a hand through his hair. "Umm—no?" Simon said nervously.

"Are you asking me or telling me?" Charles replied.

"Charles! Are you kidding me right now?" I shouted, letting go of Simon's hand to hit Charles in the arm.

"What? I'm just getting the facts," Charles said, rubbing his arm.

"You don't need any facts, you jerk. It's none of your business," I snapped back at him.

Finally, Teddy stepped into help with this very awkward and embarrassing conversation. "I think what my no-filter brother is trying to say is, are you treating our sister the way she deserves to be treated?"

"I believe that I am, but you'd have to ask her."

All three heads turned toward me, waiting for my response. I stood there opened mouth, stunned that this was really happening.

"Yes! Of course he is. Good God, you people are making this way more stressful than it has to be."

"Just checking hiney holes, baby girl. You never know—"

"Charles, stop now. Just stop talking," I said, holding my hand up to him.

Everyone laughed as we took seats at the table filled with papers and half eaten lunches. Simon began explaining what his company did and how it worked.

"If you don't mind, I'd love to get a business card. We might need some good publicity for the opening night of 21," Teddy asked.

"Here you go," Simon said, pulling his wallet out of his back pocket and handing a card to Teddy.

We had been sitting and talking about this and that when my stomach rumbled loud enough for all to hear. I felt my face instantly flush.

"Geez, Beth, hungry much?" Charles asked.

I held my stomach in embarrassment. "Ha, ha, Charles. I haven't had anything to eat today. We were going to get lunch after coming here," I replied, relaxing a little.

"Well, don't act too much like a pig at a trough. Don't want to lose this good guy here," Charles finished with a haughty laugh.

You know, for someone who says he wants to protect me, take care of me, and would never hurt me, he sure knows how to make me feel like scum.

"Damn it, Chuck, you are such an ass sometimes," Teddy said, coming to my rescue like always.

"What's wrong with a healthy appetite?" Simon chimed in, placing his hand on my knee under the table.

Charles looked between us all, a bewildered expression on his face as if he didn't just say something cruel. "Whatever, you guys. Beth, you know I'm just messing with you."

"It still hurts my feelings, regardless if you're 'joking' or not," I said as calmly as I could, since I was doing my damnedest to hold back the tears that were moments from flowing.

"I'm sorry, baby girl, come here," he said, as he stood and walked around to me. Tugging me up and out of my chair, he wrapped his arms around me. "I love you and I won't talk to you like that again. I promise."

He spoke softly in my ear, and a smile spread across my face whether I wanted it to or not. My brother could be the biggest jerk to me, but he was one important part of my life. Jerk or not, I loved him.

"I think Simon and I should get going. You guys look like you have a lot of work," I said, gesturing to all the papers on the table.

Standing, Simon shook Teddy's hand once more. "It was nice to meet you guys."

"Same here, Simon," Teddy replied.

"I guess we'll be seeing you next Friday?" Charles said, while taking his turn to shake his hand. Simon looked quizzically from my brothers to me.

"What's next Friday?" he asked.

"Oh, I was under the impression that—umm." Charles raised his brows in my direction not sure if he should continue.

Shit, I had forgotten to invite, let alone even tell, Simon about the charity event.

"I'll fill you in at lunch," I said to Simon, taking his hand and leading him out of the office, as my brothers looked dubiously at one another.

Just before the doors to the elevator closed, Adam made his way back to his desk. I waved bye to him and caught Simon giving him a little wave and wink.

"You are trouble!" I said, hitting his arm and laughing.

"So I've been told. I like keeping people on their toes. Now come here," he said, pulling me into his arms and kissing me.

Before we left the building, I asked Danielle if anyone had found a lost cell phone, but there was no luck there either. Danielle was usually a very confident person. Not many people, men in particular, could get her all twitchy and anxious. Simon was standing behind me, holding onto me around the waist, which still made me cringe a little, knowing that he was touching parts of me I wasn't even comfortable with. I could only imagine what he was doing back there because the expression on Danielle's face was priceless. I turned to see what all the fuss was about only to catch Simon grinning down at me, all innocent and hot.

We decided to get a sandwich from around the corner. I filled Simon in on the charity event, not expecting him to be able to come.

"So, you're leaving on Saturday?" he asked with a tinge of sadness to his voice.

"Yeah, I've got to get there early to set up and organize all the activities."

"I wish you would have told me so I could have made arrangements to be with you. Wait one second, I'll be right back."

I watched as he stood from the table, pulling his phone out of his pocket, and walking out of the sandwich shop. I sat there, not thinking anything of it.

"I've got good news!" he said when he came back. "I just talked with my boss and I can make it out there Thursday night, which gives you the whole week to get things together without me being there to distract you."

I sat staring at him with a stupid look on my face—that, I was sure of. "Wait. You're going to come?" I asked in disbelief.

"Of course, I am. If it's important to you, then I want to be there. Where am I going for this event?"

I explained to Simon that it was at our family's house outside of New York City. My parents bought it, to get us out of the city. It was the house they were going to grow old in, see their kids grow up in, and have their grandchildren come visit. The house was huge, something you'd see on the life styles of the rich and famous. It had its own staff to keep the massive space clean. Gran and Pop lived there with us after my parents died. Now Gran lived there during the winter until she could go back to her beach house.

We hosted the event at the house every year, it was more room than needed with a massive hall for parties and tons of rooms for guests, Gia was even able to claim a room for herself. My brothers and I couldn't bear to sell it. It was the last thing our parents had given us and there wasn't a chance in hell we were getting rid of it. Mixed emotions went rushing around my head. I was glad he was going to come, but the more I thought about it, the more I was hoping he wasn't going to be able to make it. I wanted to get answers from Spencer, if he even showed up. Subconsciously, I knew that was why I didn't tell Simon in the first place. I wanted to have all my attention on Spencer, find out what his deal was, or if I was seriously imagining it all. I didn't need Simon breathing down my neck while I was trying to get answers out of Spencer.

Just then a fabulous idea popped into my head, an idea where I could win all around. "You need to bring your camera with you. I'm officially putting you to work. We could use the pictures you take at the party to put on the site and send to magazines." *God, you are so smart, Elizabeth Monroe. While he's taking pictures, you can question Mr. Salvatore.*

Feeling pleased with my plan, I smiled devilishly at him.

Chapter 12

The week leading up to the charity event blew by and before I knew it, Thursday night had arrived.

"That was so yummy, Gran. I've really missed your cooking," I said as I cleared the table of dirty dishes.

"You know, I love cooking for my grandbabies, even if it is just one of you tonight," she replied.

"So remember, tonight Simon should be getting in late."

"I remember, muffin, you've told me every night since you got here and I even spoke with him yesterday. I may be getting old but perhaps you should have your memory checked?"

Witty old bat.

"I'll send him up to you when he arrives," she continued, winking up at me as I took the plate from in front of her.

My brothers were out for the night and staying in the city, so it was just Gran and I. Thankfully, she was a night owl. Me, not so much.

With my brothers gone for the night, I felt it safe to have Gran send Simon to my room, not that I would listen to them, anyway. Even though our house was huge with lots of spare bedrooms, I still wanted Simon with me. *No distractions.*

After cleaning up the kitchen, I retired up to my room. I got comfy in my bed and began perusing the local TV channels. I stopped on a pop-culture news station while I waited for the Thursday night line up to begin. The screen flashed to a picture of Spencer and all at once, my stomach started doing summersaults. *Shit, the ultimate distraction.*

"…we have just been informed by an irrefutable source that

Spencer Salvatore is here, in New York, for a charity event. It seems the multi-millionaire has been inspired to publicly do some donating to a charitable cause. Our sources say that he will be attending an event, conveniently hosted by once thought to be lover, Elizabeth Monroe. Is this a chance to get back together? Our sources say yes. It seems as though he is taking all opportunities given to win her back. But like everyone else, we will have to wait and see what happens. In other news, lead singer from ONS, Kane Lawson has been..."

I quickly turned off the TV. The picture of Spencer was still burned into my mind even though the TV had been shut off. My thoughts turned to the box he left me. I had packed it, along with all the little notes. They were all sitting at the bottom of my suitcase in the closet.

Why would he choose my family's charity event to make a big stink about?

I chewed nervously on the inside of my cheek. My eyes burned a hole through my closet door. *Should I look in his package*? *Ahh, hell, I can't take it anymore*. I had put it off since I'd gotten it and I couldn't ignore it any longer. I needed to know what was inside.

I rushed over, slung open the door, and kneeled down. I quickly unzipped the bag and there, at the bottom of my suitcase, was the still perfectly wrapped box. My fingers grazed lightly across his perfect penmanship. I ripped the paper on the side. My chest became heavier with every rip. Setting the paper aside, I lifted the lid.

The first thing I saw was my phone on a bed of browning rose petals with a post it stuck to it.

Sorry. Picked this up thinking it was mine.

I picked it up, pushing the on button, but it was completely dead. Glancing back down at the box, I notice a folded piece of paper amongst the petals.

I was almost positive that I was going to pass out. I unfolded the paper and read.

Miss Monroe,
It seems as though I can't shake you. I will come
to your event if that is what you want, but I do not
share. I will not be made a fool. ~ Spencer Salvatore

Oh God, I didn't need this right now. Why did he keep doing this? I was so confused. If he wanted me, why hadn't he
just told me in the elevator or outside the club? Clearly, he had
come by my building—twice! Why not just call up for me or
wait for me to come out? I really needed some answers now.
This was getting borderline stalker. He'd better show his face
tomorrow night because, I had a mouthful for him.

ༀ

As I lay in bed, sleeping, I was awoken by the rustle of
clothes and a warm body cozying up to me. My eyes flew
open, and I scooted back in bed, kicking my legs at the warm
body.

I screamed when a hand wrapped around my ankle, totally
forgetting that Simon was even staying with me. My first
thought was that somehow Spencer had broken into my house
and was trying to do god knew what to my ankles.

I reached over and flipped on the light on my nightstand
and grabbed my alarm clock, ready to hit someone in the head.

"Hey, babe," Simon said sheepishly.

I clutched at my chest as my adrenaline slowly began to
subside once I realized it was Simon and not Spencer or a bur-
glar. "Jesus Christ, Simon."

He had a devilish smile on his lips and a twinkle in his eye.
"Sorry I didn't mean to scare you. Your grandmother told me
you were expecting me. FYI, I see where you get your good
looks."

I pushed his shoulder as he laughed at me. "You scared the
begeezus out of me!" At that point, I was so far away from
him, I was almost falling out of my queen-sized bed.

"That wasn't my intention, believe me." He scooted closer,
rested his head on the edge of the pillow, batted his eyelashes

like a girl, and stuck his bottom lip out. "Can you find it in that big ole heart of yours to forgive me?"

I rolled my eyes before I lay back down next to him. "I guess."

"Good, now come here." He pulled me against his warm shirtless body. "I'm beat and although I might kick myself later, I'm very content just holding you and passing out. That all right?" he asked.

I nodded "Yeah."

I was glad to have him close again. I hadn't realized that I missed him as much as I did. But with Spencer still fresh in my mind I was thankful he only wanted to sleep and not "sleep" with me.

ↄ⌣ↄ⌣ↄ

The morning light came through the window sooner than I wished. Simon's arm was still holding onto me tightly, as I listened to the many voices bustling around downstairs. I needed to get up and get helping, but the comfort of my bed with a man in it sure was tempting. Turning to face Simon, I reluctantly opened my eyes to stare at him.

"Hey," I said, letting my fingers glide down his stubbly jaw line.

He stirred beneath my touch, his warm brown eyes opened and found me. He kissed the tip of my nose. "Hey, back."

"I have to get up and get my butt in gear. It's going to be a busy day."

Lying back on his pillow, he rubbed his eyes with the backs of his hands. I took that as my opportunity to get out of bed. I was a second away from throwing the covers off when I found myself pinned down.

"I don't think so," he said with a seductive grin.

"Simon! I have to get up." I smiled up at him, but he didn't budge. Using both hands, I pushed hard on his chest to get him off me. No luck, I was stuck, and not going anywhere. "Move, you beast!"

"Nope, not a chance, sweetheart. I was a nice guy last

night. This morning is a whole different story. I haven't seen you in a week," he said, kissing either cheek. "Belle, you're not going anywhere until I say so."

"Simon, I get—"

"Shhhh. No talking." He trailed kisses up and down my neck. "You. Taste. So. Sweet."

My body took over, and I lost the fight. Arching up to him, I pulled him down closer to me. A warm hand brushed against the skin under my night shirt. His hand continued to move over my stomach and ribs, stilling under my chest. It felt so good, I didn't want to him to stop.

This was it. All this time, and I was finally going to sleep with Simon, in my childhood bed no less. The bed that I had spent every evening praying for a boyfriend, praying for someone to love me the way I was. *How ironic.*

Breaking the kiss, he sat up, kneeling between my legs. Instinct took over. I reached out for him, dying to feel his bare skin under my hands. The tips of my fingers rippled over his abs. Covering my hand with his, he pulled me up toward him. Taking the bottom of my shirt in his hands, he pulled it off and tossed it on the floor, laying me back down. I prayed that I looked at least half as hot as I was picturing myself.

Swallowing hard, I tried to wet my dry mouth. I stared up into his warm brown eyes. I felt safe with him, comfortable. We had come a long way and I was ready to get and give more.

"You are so beautiful."

I watched his eyes dance over me. All the self-deprecating thoughts left my mind because I knew that he was attracted to me, the same way that I was to him. Not able to wait any longer, I swiftly wrapped my arms around his neck, pulled him down over me, and kissed him.

"Elizabeth," he said, pulling back slightly from my kiss, "I need to tell you the truth before we go any farther." Taking a breath, he started again only getting a syllable out before all hell broke loose.

With what felt like a tornado, my door flew open.

"Baby girl, time to wake up and work—"

And just like that our sensual moment was ruined as we watched Charles barrel through my door. The word "work" still lingered in the air as his shocked saucer eyes stared at my bed.

Simon quickly moved off of me as I simultaneously pulled the covers over my head. "Charles!" I screamed from under the covers, letting only my eyes look over the top. "Can't you freaking knock before coming in to someone's room?"

Charles stood in the middle of my room, looking as if he wanted the image out of his mind as badly as I did.

"Jesus Christ, Beth…" he said, turning back toward the door. "Hurry the hell up and put some clothes on. Next time do me and everyone else a favor and lock your door!"

He slammed the door closed as I pulled the covers back over my head.

This would *happen. The Gods have it in for Simon and me. I'm definitely convinced.* I felt the covers start to slide down my face. Simon's bright smile met me on the other side.

"Can you believe that?" I asked. "If it's not your boss calling you to work, it's one of my brothers."

"Ah, come on. It will happen when it's supposed to happen. Don't worry too much about it. This is only going to make it all the better," he said, kissing my forehead.

God, this man is perfect. Who says stuff like that? Simon Sullivan, that's who.

He chuckled. "Well, I guess breakfast is going to be interesting."

I put a pillow over my face. "Oh my God, I don't want to get out of this bed. Kill me now!"

"Come on, it's not that bad. Go take a nice cold shower. I'm sure Chuck won't run his mouth. He looked just as embarrassed as you did."

"You must not know my brother. He lives to rile me."

Grabbing the extra cover at the bottom of the bed, I wrapped it tightly to my body. It was one thing to be lying under a hot guy, but to stand in front of them, in only my panties, in the light of day, was something that I had no intention of doing—ever.

I stood up, wrapped safely, or so I thought. Simon ripped it away from my body. Right away, I covered whatever I could with my arms.

"Nope, not a chance, baby. Now walk your sweet ass in that bathroom."

Really? Jerk! Backing up, my feet grazed his T-shirt on the floor. I bent down, grabbed it, covering my ass with it as I hightailed it into the safety of the bathroom. I could hear him laughing through the door, which I made sure was locked.

"You better be careful. Paybacks are a bitch," I yelled from behind the door, before turning the shower on.

After my shower, I reached for my towel on the hook. Dread nearly stopped my heart. *Where's my towel? In my closet of course, on the other side of the room.* Holding his shirt over my chest, I opened the door slowly, praying it wouldn't creak, and peeked out. I was safe. He was sound asleep. I tiptoed across the room, but stopped to watch him for a moment.

Perfect. This guy was everything I could have ever wished, dreamed, or prayed for. And I did all of the above. Why couldn't I just be happy, content?

Fucking Salvatore.

છળળ

Closing the door behind me, I made my way downstairs. A dozen or so people ran frantically around the first floor. Turning into the kitchen, I was pleased to see Gran sipping tea and reading the morning paper. Looking up, she smiled over to me.

"Good morning, muffin. Where's Simon?" she asked.

"Still sleeping," I said while getting myself a glass of orange juice and sitting next to her. "Thanks for waiting up for him."

"Not a problem, muffin. Your brothers came home early this morning. Have you told them yet that Simon is staying here?"

"They'll figure it out." *Chuck already did, and I'm sure he's going to rat me out to Teddy.* "I'm not a little girl. I can have man sleep in my bed," I said, holding my head up high.

My brothers had never had to deal with me and a guy before, but they were going to have to get over themselves because Simon wasn't going anywhere.

"I know that, and I respect it, but your brothers—"

"They'll deal with it, Gran." A look of concern was all over her face. "Spit it out," I said. "I know that look."

She wasn't very good at hiding her feelings. I guess I got that from her.

"I was reading the paper this morning and it seems we've made the *Times*," she said, casually handing me the paper.

I saw not only my brothers and me, but a picture of Spencer off to the side. There it was in black and white.

Spencer Salvatore to Attend Monroe Fundraising Event.

"I just lost all respect for journalism."

"Have you talked with him to see what his intentions are?" she asked, sipping her tea as if it was no big deal and there wasn't another man laying up in my bed.

These were the times I wished my Gran wasn't so liberal.

"No, but as you can see, I guess he's coming tonight." My thoughts drifted to last night with Simon, and then to Spencer's notes. The emotions I'd squashed when Simon wrapped his arm around me crept their way back to the forefront of my mind.

Teddy and Charles came in the kitchen, papers in hand. *Great, here it comes. Is it weird that I can sense when I'm about to be ridiculed?*

"Good morning, Beth," Teddy said, kissing the top of my head as he made his way to the coffee pot.

"Hey," I replied.

Taking a chance, I glanced at Charles as he turned my way. Closing his eyes, he shook his head and body as if a chill went down his spine. *Go figure. I should really revel in this. I've never known what it's like to have the upper hand on him. This feels good. No wonder he messes with me so much. It's a great feeling.*

I busied myself the rest of the morning, checking on all the activities we had set up for the children that were attending this year's event. On my way back to the house, I spotted Simon sitting on the porch steps, talking on his phone. And, from the looks of it, he wasn't having a very pleasant conversation. Once he spotted me, he quickly got off the phone, ending the conversation abruptly.

Strange, but you know what? These days, not much surprises me.

"Hey, sleepy head," I yelled over at him.

Shoving his phone in his pocket, he stood, walked in my direction, took my hand, and kissed my cheek. "It looks great out here."

"It looks okay," I said, smiling up at him. "Who were you talking to? Looked serious. You don't have to leave, do you?"

He shook his head. "No."

I gripped his arm tightly. He smiled down at me. I didn't buy it. It wasn't his usual carefree smile. There was something else going on that he wasn't telling me.

"Your brother, Chuck, came to see me," he said, squeezing my hand.

"Oh God, what did he say to you? He couldn't even look at me this morning. Which was kind of nice actually."

Pulling me even closer, he laughed softly. "It wasn't bad. He just wants to make sure I'm treating you good. Very big brother of him. I didn't get the father sitting on the front porch with a shot gun vibe from him."

I chuckled at his analogy of my brother. Simon had it dead on. "He's much more laid back. Teddy, on the other hand, is definitely a shot-gun-wielding father figure."

"Well, for my sake, I'm glad it was Chuck and not Teddy this morning."

We made our way back to my room to get into our costumes. The kid part of the party was less than an hour away. As Simon took a shower, I got ready. The door to the hallway opened slowly and Charles stepped in, looking around—no doubt making sure no one was naked.

We stood there not saying anything for a while.

"All right, let's get this over with," he said. "I'm sorry I barged in. I never thought that—I mean, I wouldn't have—I'm sorry."

Charles apologizing? I couldn't help but snicker. Of course, he wouldn't think I'd be sleeping with anyone. *Ouch, that hurts a little.*

"Thanks, I think. I'm sorry you had to see that, trust me."

Shaking his head and body like he did at breakfast, he finally made eye contact with me. "Don't worry, my lips are sealed, especially to Teddy. If it would have been him, I think Simon would be on the next flight home."

Even though they were fourteen months apart, my brothers were decades from each other in the way they treated me. I loved that we both got how old school Teddy was. It was the one thing that we could agree on. I walked over to my brother, who was already in his vintage suit and fedora hat, and gave him a hug.

Pulling away from each other, we turned in unison as the bathroom door opened. Simon came walking out. His muscular body was glistening from his recent shower. His hand ran through his sandy hair as droplets of water fell onto his face. *And the best part*? *Only a small, white towel was sitting low on his hips.* If my brother wasn't standing right in front of me, I think I would have jumped him or taken a picture.

Glancing up, Simon realized that it was more than just me in the room. Quickly, he covered his body with his arms. *Funny, I believe he made fun of me for that this morning—two words, pay back*!

"Dude, for real, the next time I see you in my sister's room without clothes on, you're sleeping on the front lawn," Charles roared. Rolling his eyes at us, he adjusted his hat and exited my room, stopping at the door. "And remember to lock this please," he said, slamming it closed.

I glared over at Simon.

"What?" he demanded, shrugging his bare shoulders. "I forgot to take my clothes into the bathroom with me."

Chapter 13

The big night had finally arrived. We were all standing in the kitchen when Simon entered in his *other* costume. He'd thought his Superman spandex might be a bit much for the more upscale party. Although I was sad to see the spandex go, I loved the "Newsies" look. Wool cap turned backward and newspaper in his back pocket, he truly looked like he'd stepped out of the 1920s. Gia arrived just in time for the main event. Donned in our retro dresses, we were waiting for our hair and make-up artists to arrive. If we were going to do this, we were going all out!

Later, just before people started arriving, I took one last look to admire the amazing job the ladies did on my hair and make-up. My hair was in perfect, honeycomb waves, half of it pulled back, and the rest falling over my shoulders and back. I felt beautiful and confident—that was, until I glanced at the box sitting at the bottom of my closet.

All the confusion from the past few months was going to be resolved once I was able to confront Spencer. I needed this little infatuation to be over. I needed to move on. It was the right thing to do. I grabbed all the notes, shoving them into my clutch, and left the safety of my room. I wasn't sure what to expect tonight, but I knew I was ready to get it all over with and move on. I hoped.

❦❧❦

Standing with my brothers, monotonously saying hello to

everyone as they arrived was making me more anxious, for with every car that arrived it was one more closer to having to confront Spencer.

Before I knew it, I was being escorted into the ballroom in our house. No Spencer. A wave of relief/sadness engulfed me. I knew this was all a joke, that someone like him would never be interested in someone like me. *What was I thinking? I should know by now.* He was just being nice to me because he was in business with my brothers, simple as that. *I'm not going to feel bad for myself!*

I took a moment to scan the room. People were happily mingling with each other. Waiters were serving drinks and hors-d'oeuvres on shiny silver trays. It seemed like everything was going great. In my scan around the room, I saw Gia open-ly gawking at Charles. Although he was giving her a little bit of the cold shoulder, I still caught him checking out her ass when she walked by him. Charles was still Charles and I guessed he couldn't completely ignore a beautiful woman.

On the opposite side of the room, Simon was hard at work taking pictures of all the guests. When I caught his eye for a second, he gave a cute little wave and wink. I waved back, blowing him a kiss. This was how I wanted my life to be. I was so grateful he was here to share this with me. I couldn't think of anyone else—

Suddenly a sharp chill ran down my spine. Rubbing my arms, I felt the hair on them rise as goose bumps covered my flesh. I turned around, expecting to see someone. When I found no one remotely close to me and the doors securely closed, I turned around again, trying to locate where the chill had come from. *Weird, must be a draft above me.* Rotating away from the crowd of people again, I looked up at the vent-free ceiling. I had no clue what that chill was. In mid-spin back to the filled ballroom, I jumped back when I realized there was a man standing in front of me. *How the hell? Jesus Christ, I think I'm having a heart attack.* I clutched at my chest and I tried to steady my frighten heart.

I bent over, putting my hands on my knees, while I took a few deep breaths. Straightening, I focused in on the mystery man. It took me less than a second to figure it out. Salvatore. I narrowed my eyes up at him as he removed his dark sunglasses and placed them on the inside of his jacket pocket. Those cool, sea-blue eyes found their way to mine, and I felt like a pubescent, pimpled-faced, pre-teen getting caught looking at naughty pictures.

"Good evening, I hope I didn't catch you too off guard," he said in that sweet, seductive tone as he held his hand out.

Not even thinking, I placed mine in his and watched as his lips brushed across my knuckles. *Frozen, who knows how long, a second, a minute, an hour?* Everything came back to real time, as I looked down at my hand in his. I instantly ripped it away and held it tightly to my stomach.

"Hello," I said boldly, as if my world hadn't just literally gone into slow motion when he touched me.

Placing his hands in his pockets, he turned his head, trying to hide a chuckle, but I saw it. *Jerk.*

"Looks like a nice turn out. Hope I'm not too late."

Oh no, don't do it. Please. Dammit, he's running his hand through those dark, Greek God locks of his. Focus, Beth!

"Yes—I mean no, not at all, you're not late. It's a wonderful turn out." *Ugh, someone shoot me.*

"I was—"

The pure sound of his voice was like a melody I could have listened to all day. *That's it, I can't let him talk. He's a jerk, just remember, he's a jerk.*

"So," I said cutting him off rather rudely. "Who are you supposed to be dressed up as? Yourself?" *Jerk, he would come to a costume party dressed as himself. What a conceited* jerk!

Maybe that wasn't the best idea. A seductive grin turned up his lips as he chuckled softly to himself. "You have a bit of an edge tonight. You can't tell?"

He stood there, fixing his jacket and looking all sexy. *Stay strong!* I shook my head and popped my hip out, as if I was bored by him.

"I'm an agent from Men in Black," he said, pulling his sunglasses out of the jacket and putting them on for a second before taking them off again.

"Humph. Very clever."

He made me so on edge, but I sure as hell wouldn't admit I was so affected by him. *I'm only talking to him right now to get to the bottom of whatever he wants with me.*

I should have stayed planted right where I was, asked the questions I needed answered right there. But I didn't I want an audience. I looked around and saw a few people pointing in our direction, no doubt trying to decipher what was being said between us.

"Will you come with me?" I asked, pointing with my clutch at the door.

"Of course," he replied without delay.

No one followed us as I led the way down the hall and around the corner to my father's office. The large window behind my father's desk let the moon light shine in, which danced off the glass book shelves. It always reminded me of a disco ball and tonight was no exception.

Setting my clutch on the desk, I reached in and grabbed the notes, holding them tightly in my hand for strength. Looking up, I watched as Spencer closed the door behind him. The notorious click of the lock made my heart quicken. *Why the hell is he locking the door? Great he probably locks all his girls up then kills them or something. That'd be my luck.* Fear and excitement coursed through my veins. I prayed that I hadn't missed the article that said he was an axe murderer.

Smoothly turning back, he strode toward the desk, all Greek God like. The tips of his fingers slid across his bottom lip. *Oh my goodness, I want to touch those lips—Beth*! I snapped myself back to reality, which looked pretty damn good right then, but I needed to get serious. Checking that I had what I needed still clutched in my hand, I took a deep breath and began my interrogation.

"What is all this?" I demanded, walking from behind the safety of the desk—which was the only thing keeping him from me and me from him. He calmly undid the buttons on his jacket. I could only watch, motionless for the second time tonight. He shrugged his shoulders, and the jacket fell easily down his arms. A sliver of jet black hair slipped out of place as he laid the jacket on the chair next to him. His crisp, white shirt was tight enough to see the outline of his muscular body but loose enough to bunch together.

Looking up at me, he raked the stray hair back in place. "I think you know damn well what they are, Miss Monroe," he said evenly.

"My name is Elizabeth," I replied, annoyed that he was trying to make this funny or jovial. "I know what they are, jer—" I held back what I really want to say. "I want to know what they mean, what any of this means."

"They mean exactly what they say. What else would they mean?" he responded matter-of-factly.

All right, that's it. No more ms. nice girl! "Fine, you need it spelled out for you? Stop being a confusing, note dropping, word twisting, sexy-ass man and tell me what you want from me! You leave me notes and act all nice then disappear. I don't know if you're messing with my head, if you're an escaped mental patient, or—craziest of all—if you're actually into me. Jesus, I don't know how much more of this back and forth, here today gone tomorrow, stay with this guy, give that one a chance, he likes you, he doesn't like you, I can take," I ranted until I had to suck in a breath of air.

Closing my eyes, I rested my hands on the top of my head in frustration. I realized I had called him a "sexy-ass man," during my five minute rant. *Incredible. I* would *say something like that*! I took a second to breathe and collect my thoughts.

Within that second of retreat, strong arms wrapped around my torso and plush lips crushed mine with a sensual force I had never felt before. The feeling of being weightless came next as I was lifted off the ground. Instinct took over as I dropped all the papers that were clutched in my hand. I wrapped my arms tightly around Spencer's strong neck, then wrapped my legs around his waist, and gave in fully, kissing him back, like I had done so many times in my dreams.

All the frustration I had built for Spencer went right out the window the minute his mouth touched mine. The only thing I could concentrate on was his lips—and the fact that they felt so good against my own. Every single stolen moment, the catch of an eye, the graze of a hand, it had all led up to this.

With one hand firmly under my ass and the other on the small of my back, he took the two steps to the desk and set me down, his lips still on mine. Our movements were as choreo-graphed as a dance—how perfect that moment was. Taking only a second to look him in the eye, I stared back in amaze-ment before he kissed me again. His hand rested against my waist and I wondered if he could feel the slight roll under the fabric of my dress. I did my best to sit up straighter, all the while praying that he didn't notice. The worst thing that could happen was that he'd realize I wasn't one of his typical, fa-mous arm candies. *Fuck! I don't know what I'm going to do, because now that I've had a taste of him, I'm not sure anything will ever be as good.*

Breathing heavily, he slowed all his movements. *Oh God, he felt it, the pudge roll. Please don't leave me sitting here alone.* He rested his forehead on mine, and I was so thankful that he didn't turn and leave because that was by far the best first kiss I had ever had.

"Oh, so you are crazy," I said, finding my voice.

We smiled at one another as I played with the collar of his shirt. Surprisingly, it didn't feel weird or forced—no silent awkwardness. It just felt right. Being in his arms felt right.

"No, I'm not crazy or so my doctor says, and I'm not mess-ing with you either."

I arched an eyebrow at him. "Really? Then why all the notes and awkward run-ins? Why didn't you just talk to me, ask me on a date? I don't understand." I sat back from him, wanting my answers *now*.

"I don't know. I mean, I know—it's just that you make me feel things, things I don't—I haven't let myself—you were always leaving or with someone. It was just never the right time," he said brushing it off as if that was an acceptable ex-cuse.

Is he kidding me right now? Come on, he can't be serious. How lame an excuse. I played back all of our little run-ins and he was kind of right, then there was Simon—*oh God, Simon. Shoot me now. I'm a horrible person.* Apparently, seeing my sudden change in body language, he took my hand in his.

"I tried to keep my distance," he noted, turning my chin with his fingers so that I was forced to look into those beautiful blue eyes of his. "I tried not thinking of you. Be the gentleman I was raised to be. But you were always there when I least expected it, even if you didn't see me, I saw you, everywhere. At night, I'd close my eyes and you'd be there. I had to do something, so the notes were my way of dealing."

He held his head down as if he was ashamed of thinking about me. *Well, that makes me feel peachy*!

I snatched my hands from his. "Dealing, so you're dealing with me?" *Oh, I am right.* To him, I was just the annoying little sister of his business partners. "All right I've heard enough, I'll make sure to stay out of your way since you don't want to think about me, see me, or be in the same room with me. Like I said before, and what I honestly thought all along, you're crazy and I'm even crazier for thinking that—"*What was I thinking? That we'd end up together? Ha! Joke's on me.*

With my hands on his strong chest, I tried to push him away.

"What are you doing?" he asked, planting himself farther against me so I couldn't move.

"I'm trying to get off the desk so I can leave."

"I don't want you to leave."

"Too bad, playboy, I'm leaving."

"No, you're not."

"Yes, I am," I replied, standing my ground.

Just like before, he took me by surprise, only this time I saw it coming and I didn't do shit about it. I saw him lean in that extra inch. I watched as his eyes closed, and his hand reached up to cup my cheek before his lips caressed mine for the second time.

I ran my hands over his chest, feeling his stone-like muscles. *Does this mean I haven't been imagining everything and this is really happening?* It really was *his* chest rising and falling beneath my hand, and it was his hand that was gripping my neck and drawing me in for more.

Spencer pulled back and studied my face. Those were really his eyes looking back at me. I didn't know what to say. He had me pinned there and, lord help me, I didn't want him to let me leave.

"Not leaving," he said on a sigh.

I nodded my head, agreeing with him, loosened his black tie, and unbuttoned the top few buttons of his shirt. My fingers sneaked inside, and I had to remember to act cool. If this was my one chance to do this, I wasn't going to waste it. His chest was firm and solid. No doubt he worked hard to stay fit, but his skin was surprisingly smooth. I didn't know if any of this was real. I could have woken up at any moment, but I knew right then that I didn't want it to end. All thoughts of anything but Spencer Salvatore left my mind.

I watched him as his eyes closed at my touch. I thought of what we had been missing out on for so long. If only he would have talked to me, told me.

"You should have told me," I said, stubbornly pulling my hand away from him as I sat back and crossed my arms in frustration at how things could have been so different.

Taking a calming breath, he pulled back, too, removing his hands from me to rest them on either side of my hips on the desk. "I told you, I was trying to stay away. I thought it was better that way. I thought you were happy. I tried to find someone else, but something kept pulling me toward you. I know you feel it, too."

His voice turned raspy, almost needy as he rushed forward, grabbing the back of my nape. His possessive kiss took my breath away for a third time.

His warm hand found my knee and moved up and under my dress. With his thumb latched tightly in my underwear, I sat up straighter trying to hide whatever imperfections I could. They were my tricks of feeling toned and I had a whole library of them. Inside, I was thanking myself for wearing lacy boy shorts rather than spanks. *How embarrassing would that be if he couldn't find my underwear because they were hiked up under my boobs? Thank God for small miracles.*

His hand moved painfully slow until it reached my core. Before I could even comprehend, his hand was on me. I felt my underwear being ripped away and I watched as he discarded them on the floor. *That's not fair! He's too sexy.* He quickly slipped his hand back under my dress. I moaned as his warm fingers moved back and forth, petting me, before one sank deep inside me.

I dropped my head back in pleasure and clutched the edge of the desk for dear life. I'd been touched my men or—should I say—boys before but, Spencer must have taken extra sex education courses, because he knew every stop and the exact amount of pressure to apply.

Not much was going through my head at that moment, but the one thought that kept popping back up was that I couldn't believe I was letting this man make mush out of me. Up until tonight, I had never been so ready so fast, or given it up so fast. It was like he knew exactly what I wanted and when I wanted it. *Every man should enroll in whatever sex education courses he's had.* Within minutes of his hand being under my dress, I was on the verge of exploding.

My hands left the sides of the desk, needing something else to grab onto. I clutched his shoulders, bringing my forehead to meet his while I rode his hand.

"Come for me," he said in a deep, seductive whisper.

Ah hell, that's it, I'm done for. Those three words had me clawing at his shoulders as I grinded into his hand harder. My sheath squeezed around him. Leaving his hand under my dress, he kissed my lips softly. I realized then that I wanted even more—more of him, more notes, more anything Spencer.

Thinking I heard someone jiggle the door handle, I quickly came back to my senses. "I think someone is trying to come in," I breathed. "Did you hear that?"

Turning to look over at the door, I felt his arousal graze the inside of my thigh. The sudden urge to touch, see, even have that particular appendage inside me made me erupt with excitement. *What is happening to me? I don't think or talk like that. What the hell has Spencer Salvatore done to me? I've got sex on the brain!*

Praying my eyes had gone back into their sockets before he turned back, I was saved by the obvious knock at the door.

"Okay, I heard it that time," he whispered, stepping back. Grabbing me around the waist, he helped me off the desk.

"Hey, who the hell is in here?" It was Teddy's distinct voice from the other side as he tried to turn the handle.

Spencer and I looked frantically at one another. He began buttoning his shirt and fixing his tie, while I fell to the ground to pick up the pieces of paper. I stood, straightening my dress, then ran behind the desk and grabbed my clutch, shoving the papers inside.

"I said, who's in here?" Teddy's voice got noticeably louder.

Striding over to the door, I put my hand on the knob. Glancing back at Spencer, I nodded, letting him know I was going to open it.

Crap! *My underwear*! I quickly looked on the floor, but didn't see them. Hopefully Spencer had gotten them. Turning back to the door, I undid the lock and opened it, looking up at Teddy who appeared to be on the verge of kicking in the door. He took a half step back, startled to see me. Taking a second to look me up and down, he then shot a look over my head at the man looming beside our father's desk. I could actually see the blood rush to my once-calm-and-controlled brother's face.

"What the hell is this?" he asked, looking across the room at Spencer then back down at me.

"I was just showing Spencer dad's old office. I always thought it looked so cool in here at night. Remember, like a disco ball when we were kids?"

I knew Teddy wasn't buying anything I was trying to sell.

"Okay, Elizabeth, would you mind giving me a moment alone with Spencer?"

Not knowing if I should stay by his side or leave him for Teddy, I looked apprehensively over at the man that I was ready to fight with my brother over. But Spencer simply nodded his head.

"Fine, whatever," I said, not giving either man a second glance.

I strode out of the room and down the hall, feeling like a fool. Stopping at the end, I turned back to catch my brother's other foot enter the room. Inching back up the hall, I saw that he'd left the door cracked. I moved close enough so I could hear what was being said.

Not even starting with small talk, Teddy just got right to the point. "What are you doing with my little sister locked in a room?"

"Nothing. She was just showing me around," Spencer replied.

"Don't play dumb with me, Spencer. I will not have you treating my sister the way you treat other women."

My heart dropped, questions popping in my head. The biggest one—other women?

"She's not a little girl. You can't—" I heard Spencer take a deep breath, as if trying to calm himself. "Listen, it's not what you think. She's not like any other woman I've been with. I care for her and she cares for me."

"Oh that's rich, Salvatore. Glad to know you *care* for her. That makes it all better. Now cut the crap. You're nothing to her and don't you dare tell me what she is or isn't. You don't even know her. You've met her, what, two times?" Teddy paused and drew in a deep breath. "Let's just finish this club. It's a little more than two months away and, once it's done, you can get the hell out of town and leave my family alone."

"And what if I choose to stay?" Spencer asked challengingly.

"Fine, do what you want, stay, go. But if I see you near my sister again, I'm going to unleash a reign of fire on your perfect little persona. I'm not naïve. I do my research on people before doing business. I found some pretty incriminating stuff that you made sure to keep out of the public's eye. You see, it's actually rather simple, stay away and I keep quiet. Keep your troubled life away from my little sister. She's seeing someone else, anyway. Have a little respect."

I waited to hear what Spencer said in response. I expected him to fight, call Teddy's bluff, but I heard nothing, only the sound of Teddy walking out of the room. I leaned up against the wall as my brother stormed out, not even noticing me on the other side.

A defeated looking Spencer followed, his jacket hanging over his arm. He stopped just outside the doorway. Stepping away from the wall, I stared at him, wrapping my arms tightly around my waist. The look in his eyes told me I was never going to be in his embrace again, and I was crushed.

"You're not going to listen to him are you?" I asked, desperation in my voice.

"Miss Monroe, I'm very sorry. Your brother is right. I'm no good for you, and you're with someone else." He sounded all business and not like the Spencer I had just spent the last hour with.

"I told you, my name is Elizabeth! And who the hell is he to say what I want or don't want? I know you. I know enough to make a decision to get to know more of you. Spencer, I can't function—in a good way, the butterflies and fireworks kind of way—when you're around."

I was getting little, if any, reaction out of him, not even a smile, nothing. He was straight, poker faced.

"I'll leave him," I continued in a rush. "I'm not even technically with him. I'm willing to take this chance with you." I took a step closer.

He smiled back! *That's a start.* "Everything I told you or that you have heard is true," he said. "Tonight wasn't a mistake. It just made me realize I'm not as lost as I thought I was. I think I'm falling for you. But it's safe to say you've changed me, woke me up. Thank you." Placing his hand in his pants pockets, he turned to leave.

What the hell? Here we go with Confusion 101 again. I thought for sure we'd passed this class already.

"No! No," I yelled, making him turn back around. "You can't say that and then just expect to leave. I won't let you! Jesus, you can't keep doing this to me. Please, I'm begging you."

Sighing, Spencer finally walked back over to me. Running the back of his hand down my cheek, he ran it along my jaw as he kissed my forehead. "You are a stubborn woman. You make it hard to walk away, but—"

Now, I'm pissed. I stepped back from him, pushing on his

chest in frustration. "But what? You can't tell someone you're falling for them and then—nothing, you're not even willing to try, give it a chance? Nothing?"

Closing the distance between us, he dropped his jacket and pulled me tight against him, his hands firmly on my cheeks. I was taken aback by the fierceness in his voice when he spoke.

"Damn it, Elizabeth. Just—" He crushed his lips to mine, his hand pressed firmly on the small of my back, pulling me painfully close, before letting me go and stepping back. He reached down and picked up his jacket, slinging it over his arm. "I have to leave."

As fast as it all started, it was over. Not saying another word, he turned and walked down the hall. I stood for a second until he rounded the corner. I made a mad dash for the stairs, taking them two at a time. Rushing into my childhood room, where I spent most of it crying over being teased or boys using me, I slammed the door shut behind me, leaning against it. My legs gave out from under me. I slid to the floor and sat sobbing like a baby. Spencer's last words echoed in my head. *How bitter sweet. He finally says my name, and it could very well be the last time I ever hear him say it.*

Chapter 14

I lay on my bed for what seemed like hours, staring at the ceiling. I was able to get all my questions answered, but now there was a brand new set of them. *It shouldn't be this hard or complicated, right?*

Hearing a gentle tap on my door, I gave my eyes a final wipe.

"Belle? Are you in here?" Simon's voice was coming sweetly from the other side and the only thing I could think about was how I'd just royally screwed this up.

"I'm here." *How am I going to do this? Should I even tell him about Spencer? Clearly anything with him was going nowhere, so why bring it up? It was done, I was done.*

"Can I come in? Your brother told me you usually slip to your room during these events."

It must have been Chuck that sent him because I knew Teddy was fuming somewhere and the last thing he would do would be to send a man to my room.

Jumping off the bed, I checked my make-up. I made my way to the door when I realized—*Shit! I don't have underwear on!* I was one leg in, one leg out, when the door handle started turning. *Shit, shit, shit!* I jumped on one leg into my closet just as the door opened all the way. I thrust the other leg in and shimmied them up as fast as I could. *Only me!*

I walked out the closet to see Simon closing the door behind him. I went to sit on my bed as Simon twisted toward me. He undoubtedly noticed my puffy face and red eyes.

"Hey, what's the matter?" he asked as he walked over to me.

Pulling me to my feet, he engulfed me in his strong arms. I couldn't very well tell him that another man had just fingered the heck out of me and then confessed he was falling for me, only to leave me on the side of the road for vultures to pick over. *Not happening.*

How can I feel so strongly for such different men? Is there something wrong with me? I couldn't deny the lust I felt for Spencer, yet I felt safe, protected, and cared for standing there engulfed in Simon's arms. *I'm really screwed up. No wonder men usually stay away from me, and here I thought it was my size.*

"Are you thinking about your parents?"

Oh thank God, he said that. I can totally run with that topic.

"It gets to me every once in a while, especially during nights like tonight." I made sure to give a little smile to show I was okay.

"I'm here for you if you need to talk." Real concern etched his face, as if he had just been told really bad news. His body tensed around me, and his eyes drifted elsewhere.

It almost felt like he wanted me to say no, that I wasn't upset about my parents. *He couldn't know about Spencer, could he?* I reached for his cheek, turning his face back to me.

"Are you okay?" I asked.

"Huh? Yeah, I'm good, just concerned about you."

You know, I think he's an even worse liar than I am. I don't buy it. "Really? Because you kind of went blank a second ago."

Looking into my eyes a little more seriously than needed, he held my hand in his. "I'm just glad that I'm the one that's here to comfort you," he said, caressing my cheek.

I smiled up at him, still not totally convinced that it was just about me being upset about my parents. Honestly, I was too tired to try to figure anything else out right then. All I knew was that in the short time that I had gotten to know Simon, I knew he would never leave me if he didn't have to and, for that, I was thankful.

The soft kiss Simon put on my lips quickly turned deeper. He ran his hands up and down my back. Finding my zipper, he hooked a finger between my skin and the dress, letting it seductively unzip. He flattened his hand against my back, until I was flush against him, and unhooked my bra with ease. With the release of fabric around my chest, I took a much-needed breath.

Panic set in. *What if he can somehow smell or sense I was with someone else? That would be devastatingly embarrassing. Do men have a sixth sense about that kind of stuff?*

"Simon—I—" I tried to concentrate between his kisses. "I'm not sure if right now is—"

I was quickly cut off when his hand covered my mouth and a wicked grin spread across his face. "Elizabeth, it's been a long, sexually frustrating day for both of us. Now is perfect and much needed."

Crap, how do I say no to that? I knew it was wrong and, in some sick way the universe would get pay back, but maybe this was where I was meant to be. Held safely in Simon's arms and not Spencer's. After all, he did say he was no good and I shouldn't be with him. *Fucking jerk! He was just playing me. Screw Spencer, I hope he gets crabs!*

I slid his suspender straps off and pulled his tucked shirt out. He ripped his shirt off the rest of the way and brought himself back to me. I freely explored his broad chest and gently planted kisses along his collar bone.

It was a different feeling with Simon, slow and gentle, whereas my earlier escapades with Spencer probably left bruises. The raw intensity to be as close to Spencer as possible was exhausting, if only for the brief time we spent together. I wasn't sure which was better, but right then I needed Simon and his gentle touch to help suppress the crazy girl inside me who still wanted any part of Spencer she could get her hands on. Watching my dress fall the rest of the way to the floor, I stood in front of Simon as vulnerable as I had ever let myself be.

"You are beautiful, every single inch of you. I'm going to take such better care of you, I'm not leaving—"

I looked up at him and felt the color drain from my face. *He knows, he has to.*

"—until I kiss every inch of your body."

The familiar flush of embarrassment filled my cheeks. *Maybe I'm just paranoid.*

A caressing hand ran down the middle of my chest, grazing against my breasts. Closing my eyes in pleasure, I made sure to keep breathing. His soft hand made its way down to my stomach. I sucked it in—habit of mine—took his hand, and walked back to the bed.

"I think you still have too many clothes on," I said, being in only my underwear, while I eyed up his fully clothed bottom half. I undid his pants, letting them fall to his ankles. Only his black boxers stood between me and the lust I saw beneath them. "I hope that you turned your phone off. I'd really hate to have to throw it out the window."

We both laughed, thinking about all the times we had been interrupted before.

"Don't worry; no one will be calling me tonight. I'm done with work for now," he said, smirking down at me.

Stepping out of his shoes and pants, he laid me down on the bed, covering me with his solid body. Cupping a breast in his hand, he rubbed his thumb back and forth. Leaving kisses down my neck and chest, he brought his gaze back up to me.

Feeling brave, I kept my eyes locked on his while I felt my way down his chest and over his abdomen. Jealously sank in as I realized he didn't have to "suck it in." I grabbed him through his boxers, tugging on him roughly, because I was still irritated that he had never had to worry about a flabby stomach. *Damn gym rat.*

Adjusting himself in between my legs, he moved my hand and pulled it off of him. He shook his head and took my underwear off. Lifting my hips off the bed, I helped move it along faster. His hand slid back up my leg, giving me chills as I could only guess where he was headed next. Simon's fingers ran softly over the joint of my leg and inner thigh. I let my eyes roll back in my head as his thumb circled my raw flesh. Thank God he was so gentle with me. I hadn't realized how sore I was.

I opened my eyes to watch him but was a little disappointed that I wasn't met with dark hair and cool, blue eyes. Instead, I saw the warmest, caring, brown eyes staring back at me.

Reaching over the bed, he pulled out a condom from his pants and glided it over himself. *This is it. We're actually doing this.*

So many nights of being interrupted and thinking that maybe he wasn't into me were gone. The only thing I was left with was the fact that he wanted me. I could feel it between my legs. There was no faking that.

I took a deep breath, preparing myself because after we did it everything would change. There was no going back to just playing around and having fun. Things were going to get serious. So all excuses about Spencer would be worthless. I would be in the wrong.

Seeing the fear in my face, Simon leaned down and whispered in my ear. "I won't hurt you."

Those four, simple words meant more to me than he could ever know, to me they told me he wouldn't run or leave me stranded in a cold hallway.

As he entered, I inhaled sharply, hissing through my clenched teeth. It had been a while since the last time, or maybe all the other, two, men I'd been with were just no comparison to Simon.

"Are you okay? If you don't want to, we can stop," he said, halting over me.

"No," I said hastily. "It's just, been a while since, you know…I'm fine," I said, trying to move under him to keep going.

"Wait a minute. You're not a virgin, are you?"

Is he kidding me right now? A virgin? Am I that bad?

"No!" I snapped at him, irritation oozing from my pores. I sat up as much as I could and leaned back on my elbows to glare at him.

"Okay, okay. Calm down. We never really gave a list or

number or anything, not that I care," he said, with a crooked smile.

"Well, I'm not, so whatever." I flopped back down and crossed my arms over my chest. My bravado was officially popped.

Leaning over me, he kissed my cheek while I was looking at anything but him. "You're so hot when you throw these little tantrums."

I tried to stifle the growing smile on my face. I punched his chest then quickly grabbed him around the neck pulling him closer for a kiss.

Filling me, he rocked slowly, taking his time while I got used to him. It was sensual and special. He didn't take his eyes off of mine. At times, I wanted to look away, hide my face, but I couldn't. I melted into him, letting pleasure take over. Time once again stood still as we moved together. A deep growl came from his lips, as if he'd been holding back, but wasn't able to any longer. His body turned rigid as he slammed into me a few more times, clearly finding his release.

Collapsing on top of me briefly, he withdrew and rolled over to lay his head on my torso. "I'm so sorry. I tried to hold on longer but, damn, you just took any will power I had away with these hips."

I sat up on my elbows, smiled down at him, and squeezed his cheeks like an annoying aunt on holiday. "It was perfect, Simon. Don't worry. We have plenty of time to build up your stamina. Are you sure you aren't the virgin?"

"Give me twenty minutes and I'll show you stamina," he said, squeezing my ass.

&&&

As I lay in bed, with Simon sleeping soundly behind me after our night of working on his stamina, I tried desperately to fall asleep. I stared blankly across the dark room, trying to put my mind to rest. Five hours ago, I was willing to give up on the man who was next to me, all because of a feeling, a chance meeting, and a few passionate moments. *What was I thinking?*

That someone like Spencer, a powerful, handsome man, would even consider being with me? I was a charity case. His partners' little sister.

I found myself arguing with my own reasoning. Why couldn't I just shut up and see what was right in front of me? Simon was perfect, a gentleman, caring, and funny. Spencer? Spencer was dangerous.

His words echoed in my mind. '*Everything I say is true.*'

And the little girl inside me, who dreamed of love at first sight and fireworks when you kissed, wanted to believe him, but I how could I? He'd just left me standing there.

Chapter 15

The next morning, Simon and I made our way down to the kitchen. My brothers were sitting at the table, going through all the donations. As Charles was unfolding one, he choked on his coffee.

"Holy crap!" he managed to say between coughs.

"What?" we all said in unison.

"Here, look at this!"

Charles handed me the check. Looking at the number, I had to take a double take to make sure I was reading it right. Usually people would donate a thousand or, if they needed a good tax write off, maybe five thousand. The number that appeared on this check nearly took my breath away. *One million dollars*! Someone had donated one million dollars to our little cause. I quickly scanned the check to see who this generous person was. Spencer Salvatore. The info at the bottom of the check said nothing but *For Elizabeth*.

Snatching it back from me, Charles gave it to Teddy to look over. I glanced up at him, praying that he didn't call attention to the fact that Spencer gave that much, for me.

"I told you it would be all right to invite him," Charles said, proud of himself. "He only came for what, an hour? He dropped this massive check off, then left."

"Yeah, well let's just keep it strictly business with him from now on." Teddy's voice was deep and stern.

I knew for damn sure that was directed at me.

I caught Simon looking at the check over Teddy's shoulder. Shaking his head with a half-smile, half-sneer, he turned away from us and headed for the coffee pot. I immediately got up and followed him.

"Nice sized check, huh?" I said, bumping the side of him.

"Yeah, I'm sure all that money will go to a better cause than he could ever do with it."

I frowned up at him. "Got beef?" I asked only half-jokingly. *Why would he have a beef with Spencer? They don't even know each other.*

"Nope," he said, smiling back down at me and kissing the tip of my nose. "Not anymore."

I was speechless. *Oh God, they know each other? I feel faint. Someone get ready to catch me.*

"Hey, you okay? I'm kidding. I don't even know the guy. Just jealous he has so much money, that's all."

Oh, thank God. I have enough issues without them knowing each other. Geeze, could you imagine if they were betting on who would sleep with me first? Disgusting.

We all hung out at the house before we boarded the family plane for home. I let Simon know that I finally found my phone, some random excuse about finding it in my luggage.

As we touched down and exited the plane, Simon got that infamous call from work, so off he went. To be honest, I was glad. I needed a night by myself to really figure things out, not that there was any figuring out to do. Spencer was gone and Simon was here. The choice was clear. But I had to get it all off my chest. I couldn't carry it on my own any more.

☙❧

"Why the hell didn't you tell me?"

I ducked quickly as a pillow flew over my head. *Okay she's only a little mad at me.*

"I wanted to, really I did, I just—" I side stepped as a half empty water bottle landed on the floor next to me. "Shit, Gia. I forgot," I said as a pitiful excuse.

"You forgot? You forgot to tell me Spencer Salvatore, the number one sexiest man in the world, was leaving you secret, love notes!"

Okay, maybe she's really *pissed.* "Don't be so dramatic, Gia. It's over. No more notes or run-ins," I said, slumping down on the couch.

She slammed a pillow at my head and connected that time. *I deserve that.* After explaining everything to her, all the suppressed emotions I'd been holding in the past twenty-four hours finally crashed through. I tried to hold it together but, she could tell. That was what best friends did. They just knew.

"I don't know, Gia. What should I do? Keep pretending Spencer never happened? Do I tell Simon I can't be with him? Oh crap, I should have never have slept with him. Shit, I might be in love with someone that I have only talked to four times. That makes me sound crazy. I'm clinically crazy and losing my mind, aren't I?" Covering my face with my hands, I turned on the couch and curled up in the fetal position.

"Aww, Beth," Gia said, comforting me. She sat next to me as I sat back up on the couch. "I can't believe you've been keeping this to yourself," she continued. "I mean, obviously I knew about Simon, but Spencer—I thought that was all fabricated by the press. I had no clue you actually felt anything for him."

"Ha, neither did I until Friday night," I said, shaking my head in disbelief.

"You really feel that strongly for him that you were willing to leave Simon?" she asked skeptically.

"Yeah, I know it's stupid, but I just had a feeling that…I don't know how to describe it. He makes me nervous, excited, and hot in all the right ways."

The physical ache I'd felt in my father's office, the need to be as close to him as I could, was making my heart race like it had that very night.

I was brought back by the sound of Gia's voice. "I can't say that I have ever had that happen to me, but I do know Simon, and I know that he wouldn't leave you like you said Spencer did. Maybe what your brother said about him being bad news is good. I'd hate to see you get hurt and ruin something good with Simon over someone like Spencer."

Instantly, I wanted to defend Spencer, but I didn't. I knew there was logic behind her words.

"Beth, you might have this heat-in-the-moment feeling for Spencer, but Simon has been here, putting in the time, the effort, to get to know you. I know you care about him. You seem happy when you're with him."

I took in all that she'd said and filed it away." So, your advice to me is to stay with Simon and forget about Spencer?" I snapped, irritated because, deep down, I wanted her to tell me to go after Spencer, go with that butterfly feeling, but she didn't. She suggested I forget it all like a good dream and get back to reality.

"Yeah, I think that's what I'm saying—kind of. I'm just trying to play devil's advocate here, get you to see both sides because you sound like you're only thinking about one side."

Slumping back, I raised my arms in the air all dramatically. "God! Why me?" I screamed. *He couldn't just send me one hot guy. He had to send two, at the exact same time!*

"Well, it's not like you have to make a decision right now. You're not marrying the guy. You're not marrying him, are you?" she asked, looking quizzically at me.

"No! I'm not marrying anyone."

"Good, so you slept with Simon. Big deal. Guys do that shit all the time to girls. They sleep with someone then move on. Doesn't mean you can't do the same to them. If hottie Salvatore wants you bad enough, he shouldn't care what Teddy or anyone else says. He should just come after you full force."

Maybe she was right. Maybe if Spencer really believed what he told me, he shouldn't walk away because of Teddy's threats. There was just one small problem. He'd already walked away from me once.

That night I didn't sleep a wink. I simply kept replaying everything over and over in my mind. My phone started to buzz on my night stand. I didn't recognize the number and decided to let it go to voice mail. If it was important, they'd leave a message.

A few seconds later it buzzed again, indicating a new voice message. *I guess they did want to talk.*

"Elizabeth, it's Simon. My phone's dead so I'm calling from the hotel. I have to get this off my chest. I can't rest until I do. I wish this was in person, but I need to say it now. I'm falling in love with you. I know you've been a skeptic about me, but I need you to know that I'm serious and I want us to be serious. Call me in the morning. Night, Belle."

As if things couldn't get worse, Simon just poured his heart out in a voicemail.

ᘓᗢᘓᗢ

Good grief, it was morning already. I squinted, trying to block the bright sunlight coming through the window. My head felt like it had been stuck in a washing machine on spin dry. I stumbled out of bed and into the bathroom and immediately took medicine to stop the pounding in my head.

Lying back in bed, I pulled the covers over my head, hoping I could get some more sleep. Twenty minutes later, I realized it was not happening. I reached over, grabbing my phone off the night stand. I listened to the message Simon left me one more time. His voice seemed to calm me down. I relaxed and, for the first time, came to terms that things with Spencer were not going to happen. Simon was here, making an effort. I needed to give him more of me and put Spencer to rest. I redial the number he called me from waiting to hear his genuine voice on the other line, and I didn't have to wait long, by the end of the first ring he picked up.

"Hey," he answered.

"Hey, so I got your message." I replied.

"You did, did you?" A cocky air came across in his voice.

"Yup."

"And what do you think about it?"

Not wasting any time, this one. I cleared my throat, making sure to word what I wanted to say the right way. "I think it's very nice of you to tell me how you feel." I wanted to be able to tell him that I was falling for him too, but something was holding me back, something that I still needed to deal with. Salvatore.

"Really, that's all?" he asked, deflated.

Here I go. I'm going to ruin this. Spencer doesn't want to give us a shot and here I am about to lose Simon because I can't tell him how I really feel. My life is officially a soap opera.

"Umm—well—"*I'm stuttering, literally stuttering.*

"Babe, you don't have to say anything, say it when you feel it. I do, so that's why I said it. I said that I'm falling in love with you because I am."

Damn he always knows the right thing to say, like he has some love guru whispering in his ear.

"Okay," was all I could say back. *Pathetic, I know*.

"Can you meet me at the café in a little while?"

We usually found ourselves there at least once a week, so I didn't find it odd at all. "Sure. Can you give me half hour to get showered and I'll meet you?"

"That's fine; I'll see you in a few."

ℯↄℯↄ

I walked into the café, looking over to our little couch, and saw Simon sitting on the edge fidgeting nervously with his hands. He was dressed up, which was not his usual style. The carefree Simon that I usually saw was not there. He was tense and anxious.

As I walked over, I called out to him, "Hey, Simon."

Standing, he took the two steps to meet me halfway, wrapping his arms tightly around me.

I knew without a doubt, something was up. "What's going on?" I asked still in his embrace. "Simon, you're starting to scare me. What's going on?" I repeated, pulling back from him.

"I'm sorry," he said, leaning down giving me a quick kiss on the lips. "Can you sit down?" he asked, gesturing towards the couch.

I instantly went on edge as he prepared to talk.

"Beth—"

Oh shit, he used my real name. This is going to be serious.

"I'm leaving," he said, taking my hands in his.

It took me a second to register what he had just said. But once it did, I pulled my hands away from his. "What?"

I felt the blood drain from my face. *Again*? I clenched my jaw to keep from screaming. I fisted my hands until they hurt, my nails were digging into my palms, but I kept on squeezing them.

"I've been contracted overseas until late December. I tried to get out of it, but I can't. I need the opportunity and the money. Something like this might never happen again for me. I have to go."

Taking a deep breath, I steadied myself. "How long have you known about this 'opportunity'?" I asked, still fisting both hands at my sides.

"I had a meeting with a few people today and they informed me that I need to be there by tomorrow evening." Holding his head down, he rubbed his eyes as if he hadn't slept since we got back, either.

"Well, if you have to go, then—it won't be that bad," I said, trying to sound encouraging. Sitting back, I saw his eyes glisten over. My defenses came down the moment I saw how much this was paining him. I relaxed my hand and reached for his, giving it a reassuring squeeze.

I suddenly felt horrible for even thinking about Spencer. Here Simon was saying and showing me how much he loved me, and where was Spencer? *Who knows and who cares*? *I'm done. Decision made, I'm Simon's.*

Spending the rest of the day and night with Simon was exactly what I needed. *Spencer who*? Lying in Simon's bed, stuffed from all the room service we ordered, we simply lay in each other's arms, sometimes talking, sometimes in silence.

I turned in his arms so I could look at him. "I'm going to miss this."

"Yeah, me, too. It's too bad that once people stop interrupting us, we become separated by an ocean."

Smiling at him, I already missed his humor and he wasn't

even gone yet. *How am I going to do this*? "I can't believe this is happening." I turned to check the clock. I only had five hours to be with him until I had to drop him off at the airport.

"Ugh," I whined, hitting the bed with my arms.

"What?" he asked.

Sitting up, I straddled him in only my bra and underwear. I was thankful the only light was from the glow of the silent TV behind me. I didn't need him picturing my rolls for the next month while he was gone. I glanced down at him, watching as he took in every inch of my body; burning my image into his mind. I grabbed a pillow and placed it over my stomach, my insecurities getting the better of me.

"We only have five hours left," I whined again. A low, deep growl escaped his lips as he reached for the pillow. I struggled to keep it in place but failed miserably as he ripped it out of my grip and tossed it on the floor.

"Five hours, huh?" he asked.

I nodded back, crossing my arms and pouting.

"What am I going to do without you?" he asked, sitting up and holding onto my hips.

"I don't know. What are you going to do *with* me?" I asked teasingly.

"Wouldn't you like to know?"

"Yes, I would like to know, now, preferably before you have to get ready to go."

"Is that so? What if I just want to lay here and stare at you?" he asked, resting his hands behind his head.

"You know, you're on your way to spending the rest of this night alone, buddy. You're leaving me tomorrow, you're teasing me, and you tossed my security pillow on the floor." I said, pointing to the pillow on the ground. "Plus, you're testing my patience.

"Well, we both know your little 'tude is a turn on, so. how about I show you, instead?"

Yes, please!

Unclasping my bra and tossing it aside, he ran his hand up my chest. His stubbly face met my neck. The rough five o'clock shadow scrapped my skin in the most delectable way as he inhaled my scent before leaving soft kisses along my body. His hot breath sent a shiver to my core like it had done many times before tonight. I pushed him back, needing more. I pulled his shirt off, flinging it to meet my bra. I took my time to drink in his image as he did mine. I scooted back off his lap to get the full view before I went for the goods. I ripped his boxers off while he lay back on his elbows, watching intently. The need to please him took over and I couldn't help but get a little anxious as I wrapped my slightly shaking fingers around him.

I moved with a seductive rhythm, glancing up to see him still attentively watching. Knowing that this was it before he was gone for six weeks, I leaned down over him, teasing him with kisses everywhere except for the one place I was sure he wanted my lips.

"Jesus Christ, are you trying to kill me?"

I looked up flirtatiously at him, before I gave him what he wanted. The salty taste of him on my tongue was a welcome surprise.

"Oh my God, Belle, that feels so freaking good."

That was all I needed to hear. His rough breathing made me work even harder.

Minutes later his voice cracked. "Stop!" he said abruptly through gritted teeth.

I quickly released him, before he moved away. *Great, I must have grazed him with my teeth or worse he doesn't like it.*

"You have to stop," he said, panting and holding his hand up toward me.

All my nightmares are coming true in less than forty-eight hours. You know, typical Beth Monroe.

"You have to stop because I'm not going to be able to make it another minute if you keep doing that."

Oh, well then. A sexy grin spread across his lips and before I knew it, I was up on my knees as he slid my panties down, only to take them tight in his hand.

"You don't need these do you?" he asked through a wicked grin.

"You are a beast. I guess I can let them go."

"You don't have a choice because I'm taking them with me, even if you say no," he said, spinning them around on his finger.

I wrapped my legs around him, bringing his body closer to mine. I raised my hips, rubbing up against him. I couldn't take it anymore so I took him inside me, rocking my hips into his, needing him to push deeper. Kissing my neck, he gave me what I needed and flipped us over so he was on top of me.

Everything was perfect. We rolled around, not wasting a single second of the time we had left together.

"Shit!" he yelled, almost biting my shoulder.

He moaned so loud, I thought the neighbors might call the front desk because someone was getting murdered in the room next-door. *What the hell was that for?* I suddenly got it as I felt him pour inside me.

He pulled out and sat back on his knees. "I'm so sorry, I totally forgot a condom. I swear, I didn't do it on purpose." Simon moved his hands off me, holding them up like he had just committed a crime.

"Simon, it's okay," I tried to say, but the panic in him was too funny.

"I can't believe I—I didn't, I swear—we are going to the pharmacy to get the 'Plan B Pill' as soon as they open. I'm not getting on that plane until you take it."

I couldn't help it. The chuckles I had been holding in finally came pouring out as I started laughing hysterically. Catching his questioning face, I felt tears of laughter start running down my cheeks.

"What the hell is so funny? This is serious."

Covering my face, I took a deep breath to calm down.

"What?" he demanded.

"I'm on the pill, you nut! I'm not stupid. You think I'd let you do that without protection? I might not get around, but I do protect myself from hounds like you." I tickled his stomach and burst out laughing again as the words I said started to sink in. Smiling down at me, he shook his head. I giggled. "Oh God, you should have seen your face, it was priceless. Plan B Pill? You're killing me here."

I tossed my head back and laughed even harder.

"Come on, it's not that funny. Well, I guess..." He smiled back and tickled my side in retaliation.

He held me that night until we finally fell asleep, but all too soon the alarm was going off.

"I have to get ready," he said, moving the hair from my neck to kiss it.

"I know," I grumbled back.

With one last kiss, he left the bed and went into the shower.

I got out of bed and dressed in the clothes I had on yesterday, all but my underwear which I slipped into one of his suitcases. *I think he'll truly enjoy that little surprise in eight hours.*

ᴄ/ᴈᴄ/ᴈ

Standing in the airport just before the security checkpoint, I held on as tightly as I could to him. Simon's large, muscular frame held me just as tight. I was trying to be strong and stay positive, but it was just not happening.

I felt the sting of tears run down my face. At least I wasn't sobbing. That could get ugly, and the last thing I wanted was for this hot man to have the image of my blotchy, sobbing face in his mind. Looking at his watch, he pulled me back.

His warm eyes locked in on mine. "I have to get heading back there. I can't miss this flight."

Taking a breath, I nodded in agreement.

"Elizabeth, I need you to do something for me. I need you to know that I love you, I truly do. Don't pay any attention to Fame or the paparazzi. I wouldn't be able to stand it if you were hurt and I'm not here to hold you."

He knew it upset me to see myself on the Internet, and I knew he didn't follow any of it but, after that request, I couldn't help but think that maybe he did.

He held on to my upper arms, slightly shaking me. "Promise me, Belle. Promise me you won't look at it. I need you to promise me, no matter what, you will not look at it."

"I—I promise."

Giving me one last hug and kiss, he walked down the hall

toward the stupid plane that was going to take my perfect man away.

I stood holding my arms tightly around my chest. I wasn't sure why, but it felt more like a "goodbye" than a "see you in a month." I had a sinking feeling that things were changing, and I wasn't sure that they're going to change for the better. What part of him leaving was for the better?

None of it. I had chosen Simon and I'd be Goddamned if anything, even Spencer Salvatore, was going to ruin this for me.

Chapter 16

My first day with Simon gone...*How do I put this? It sucks!*

I decided to take my frustration out on a nice run around the park. Clearing my head and getting some much needed vitamin D was just what the doctor ordered. I was going to run the whole five miles around the park, kill as much time as I could.

Halfway into my five miles, I was seriously reconsidering. Red faced and sweaty, I dug deep to keep going. Over on the open grass, I saw someone in a serious workout regime. The whole shebang—crunches, lunges, push-ups. *Damn it, now I feel like I should be doing some sit-ups. I hate it when I see someone working out.* The sudden urge to keep up with the stranger in the field wouldn't be the first time I'd done a little extra to try to look fit. Of course, it usually ended with me laying down sore for the next week.

The closer I got to the over-enthusiastic health freak, the more I tried to make sure I kept things sucked in. I adjusted my tank top to make sure it wasn't riding up and did my best to smooth out what I knew was a frizzy pony tail. When I glanced back over, I barely kept myself from tripping over my own feet. *Oh my*! *His health regimen is clearly working.* He was facing away from me, as I watched in totally guilty pleasure. Taking his hat off, he held it in his hand as he reached behind him to pull off his sweat-soaked shirt. *Jesus*! *If the front of him looks as good as the back—*

Running a hand through his hair, he turned in my direction.

I was hit with brilliant, blue eyes and a perfect physic. *Holy fuck, it's Salvatore, and he's sexy—ahhh. This is just my luck*!

I was slightly satisfied to see him working out. It would be too much if he was just blessed with a perfect body along with a chiseled face. My jog had slowly turned into a pathetic walk the closer I got. At least I had someone looking out for me, because he was too into his workout to even notice anyone else. Taking a second, I gave myself a treat and perused his sweat-glistened body. His shorts hung low but securely around his waist, the band of his boxers above that. *If this would have been last week, I think I would be running over toward him, but now I can't trust myself around him.* I cared too much for Simon to do that, let alone on the first day he was away.

Even though Spencer had left me, I could still feel it. Whatever "it" was. It was really messing with my head. I needed to get away fast. Turning back toward the trail, I picked up speed and turned my slow walk into a full-out sprint. I honestly didn't think I would ever see him again, except for in a magazine or on the Internet. *I can handle that, but in person, half naked—*

Bam! All I could see was ground, then sky, ground, sky, and finally mud. I landed face down, my head smashed into a huge mud puddle. I checked my surroundings and saw a woman covered by a bike. A kind passerby was helping her up. Pushing my upper body out of the mud, I sensed someone around me as well. Hands held me under my arms as I sat bottom-down just out of the mud. Checking my hands, I wasn't surprised they were all scraped up and bleeding. My knees poked through my ripped pants, bleeding as well.

I tasted dirt and immediately spit to the side of me, then wiped my eyes free of the mud.

"Are you okay?"

Oh that familiar, deep voice, I'd know it anywhere. Spencer knelt down next to me, clearly not recognizing me.

"I'm fine," I said quickly over my shoulder, and in a deeper voice to keep my identity hidden.

Checking the lady that I clearly ran into, I watched as she mounted her bike.

"I'm so sorry, I didn't even see you. Are you okay?" I asked, getting to my feet and away from Spencer.

"I'm okay, just a few scrapes. I'll live." And, without another word, she set off down the trail. The few people who'd stopped to help turned and went back to their own activities.

I stood shell shocked, mud dripping off my face and clothes. Sensing Spencer take a step in my direction, I froze, praying that he'd just walk away.

"Elizabeth—Elizabeth Monroe is that you?"

I should run, shouldn't I? My legs betrayed me as I turned around. *I guess I should be polite and thank him for helping me up.*

"Hey," I said, making sure I didn't make eye contact with him.

"It *is* you. I thought it was. Are you all right? I watched the whole thing, I'm pretty sure you flipped, like, three times. Do you want me to call someone?"

Perfect, he watched the whole thing. With a deep breath, I placed my bloodied hands on my hips. "I'm fine, thank you," I snapped at him, finally making eye contact. I saw the sting my tone had on him, and I didn't feel bad about it at all. *What is he doing, looking at me all poor, pitiful Spencer? I'm the one that got left behind and I'm the one that just somersaulted through the air.*

His whole demeanor quickly turned business like. "I'm glad I ran into you. I've had a lot on my mind and I need to talk to you about what happened."

"You do, do you? You really want to talk to me or are you just going to play me for a fool? Because I'm not falling for it again."

Lowering his head, he moved it slowly from side to side. "I deserve that. Although I believe you need to hear me out." He stood a little straighter, looking as if he wanted to reach out for my hand.

"You're kidding me, right? I don't think so, Spencer. You're a little late, buddy."

I turned quickly on my heel to walk away from the messed up situation. I was stopped before I could even take two steps.

A strong hand wrapped tightly around my arm and I was whipped back around to him. "You need to wait a minute," he said, pulling me closer. His raw scent hit me like a ton of bricks. "I had a lapse in judgment that night," he continued. "People don't threaten me, period. When I want something, I do my damnedest to get it."

He was demanding and possessive. His body was tense. The testosterone was through the roof. My body was clearly in a war with my head. My knees felt rubbery as I stood before him. But my head was telling me to get the hell away, that this wasn't healthy. Now my heart—my heart was twisted. Sickly twisted. Thankfully, my head had taken over. I searched his eyes and realized this was insane.

I glanced down at his tight hold on my arm and jerked from his grip. "Is this the real Spencer?" I asked, rubbing the arm he had held. "No wonder you're never seen with women, you probably beat them!" I slightly regretted it the second it left my lips.

Steam seemed to escape from his ears, as his temper got the better of him. "Don't you ever say that to me. I told you I was falling for you, I would never hurt you," he roared in his defense.

I wanted to believe him but…"You're joking, right? You said that and then walked away! You don't think that hurt me? If you do like me, you sure have a sick way of showing it. Goodbye, Spencer."

Before he had the chance to reciprocate, I turned and ran toward the exit of the park. My five-mile run had turned into a two-mile blood bath.

Later, showered and mud free, I rushed over to make it to class and sat through the two-hour lecture slumped over on the desk in the back row, rerunning this morning over and over in my head. *I can't get over how he acted or how he looked. I'm only human and it was so hard not to look at his body. What am I thinking? He's a jerk. A rude, aggressive, sexy-as-hell jerk! This is ridiculous. He's like a drug and I am fully addicted.* The only way that I was going to be able to kick this Spencer habit was cold turkey, plus staying far, far away from him.

e❀❀

"What are you looking at?" I asked, coming into the room to see Gia sitting on the couch with her laptop in front of her, clearly examining something very interesting. Tossing my bags on the floor, I slumped down on the couch next to her. "Geez, what are you looking at that you have to slam it shut. Looking at naughty pictures?" I asked, relaxing into the couch.

"No!" she clipped.

It was way too fast for me to believe her. "Come on, is it Charles? Has he been caught on Fame with another slut? You know Teddy and I told him to scale it back some, but I guess he just has a social media death wish." Sighing heavily, I opened my eyes and sat up a little to look at her.

"It's not Chuck that I was looking at," she confessed.

Now she's got my full attention. "So, who's the mystery man? Teddy?" I asked, hopeful.

"No, it's not Teddy."

What is going on here? If it's not one of my brothers, then I don't have a clue who she's talking about. She hadn't shown interest in anyone except Charles in forever.

"Come on, Gia, out with it. Who's the new guy who has caught your eye?"

Taking a breath, she opened her computer and turned it in my direction. *Check my pulse please, because I know I've just died.* Ripping the computer from her lap, I moved in closer and instantly felt nauseous. Staring back at me on the screen was a picture of Spencer and me on my father's desk! *This can't be happening.* My arms were wrapped tightly around his neck as he kissed me. His palm flat on my back, his other hand invisible, but I knew exactly where it was. A warm tingle ran through my body as I relived that night through the image on the screen. I shoved the computer back in Gia's lap as I ran to the bathroom. The nausea took over, and I buried my head in the toilet.

Regaining my composure, I sat back down next to Gia. "How long has that been up?" *And how did I not know about this?*

"It says it's been up since this morning," she responded.

"How long have you known?" *And why did you wait until now to show me,* I wanted to ask angrily.

"I just saw it before you got in. Julie told me she had seen it," Gia said over the screen.

How the hell am I going to show my face outside of this condo? Who would do something like this? Hide in the bushes outside my family home just to get a picture? Disgusting.

I wonder if Spencer—Oh shit, Simon! He said he didn't follow social media, but fuck, if he saw this, I was done for.

"Beth," Gia said, bringing me back. "Just call your brothers and see if they can pull some strings and get it removed."

She said it like it was no big deal, like my brothers were super famous and could get favors like that. They might be well off and known a little around town, but they didn't have those kinds of connections. Besides, that would involve them having to see it first!

A cheery tune came from the heap of bags I'd dropped on the floor. I was too scared to see who it was, so Gia took the hint and got my phone out of the bag for me.

"It's Simon," she said, handing me the phone.

It would be. This is the universe getting back at me. I knew it would. Better to get this over with. He'll dump me and I can hopefully move on quickly.

Sliding my finger to answer, I take one last deep breath. "Hello." I waited for an angry voice on the other line.

"God, it feels good to hear your voice," Simon said, his sweet voice coming through the phone.

I couldn't say anything, my vocal cords were severed.

"Hello? Are you there?" he called.

I could hear the concern in his voice as I stayed silent. "Yeah, I'm here," I said as normally as I could.

"What's wrong? You sound like you're getting ready to cry."

Oh no, I am, I really am about to cry. "I just really miss you." *Wimp.*

"Baby, it's only been a day. We've been apart for longer than this before. I know now were official and everything, and it's a little different, but is something else going on?"

He knows, he has to. He's poking at something. I can't do this right now. I need to think about how to say it before I tell him anything. I promised him that I wouldn't look at Fame and I did in the first twenty-four hours.

"No, just missing you."

I glanced over at Gia as she rolled her eyes. I hit her shoulder and got up to go in my room. I didn't need to have her next to me, judging my conversation. I was positive the whole world was doing that as they commented on the photo.

We made small talk for a few minutes before he said he had to go. He said he'd call me tomorrow and I was relieved that he hadn't brought up the picture. Hanging up with him, I felt like crap. Sitting at my desk, I brought up the photo. *God, I hate Salvatore for looking so goddamn sexy.* He was totally engulfed in me, like a vampire going for the jugular. I stared at the picture, until it updated by itself.

Oh, this is just getting ridiculous now. The latest gossip was seriously lacking if they had nothing better to do than take pictures of Spencer and me. Now it was the scene from earlier today that popped up on the screen.

> *Helping his damsel in distress? We think it's safe to say the heartbreaking Spencer Salvatore is indeed romantically involved. You can officially start hating, ladies.*

ϾჂϾჂ

I talked to all my teachers and explained my situation. Thankfully all of them loved me and gave me all my work to do outside of the classroom. I was not leaving this condo anytime soon.

As the week went on, more and more people were hovering around, trying to see God only knew what. *It's not like Spencer lives here, and who would want just a picture of me?* Apparently, every paparazzi within a fifty-mile radius.

By the time Friday came around, my brothers had each

come over once to try to coax me out. Tonight they both came. I was securely locked in my room, not wanting to face either of them.

"Beth, please come out. We just want to talk," Teddy said through my door.

"Save it, Teddy. I know you're disappointed. You already told me earlier this week."

He had come by and sat on the other side of my door, ranting and raving about how I was better than this and Spencer was a dirt bag. I didn't need to hear it all over again.

"Beth! You open this fucking door now or I'm going to knock it the fuck down!" Charles yelled from the other side, hitting it for added effect.

Clearly, Charles had a different approach. Early in the week, he tried bribing me out with food, not the best idea for a girl with body issues.

I told him to fuck off and he did.

"Cut the little woe-is-me act, Beth, I'm not playing around. You have to three to open this door or I am going to kick it in! One…two…"

I ran from my bed and opened the door, because I knew he wasn't bluffing. I'd had plenty of doors kicked in when I was a sulking teenager. Standing in the doorway, I looked up at my handsome brothers and caught Gia standing behind them.

"Goddamn, Beth you look like shit."

I scowled up at Charles. "Oh, thanks. You know if I wanted to get shit on, I could have just stayed in my room and kept reading all the comments on the fucking web page."

I couldn't help myself. Once I read one, it was simply a chain reaction. Everything from, being called a gold digger to a fat unworthy whore.

"Shut up and get out here, twerp," Charles said, wrapping his arm around my neck, dragging me out and into the hallway to finally sit down at the kitchen table.

"I'm sorry that this is happening to you, but I'm pretty sure that it's going to calm down now." Teddy was confident as he talked, which made me suspicious of the whole thing.

"Really and what makes you think it's going to 'calm' down?" I snapped.

"Well, we had a meeting with Spencer today and he has his people working on getting it removed. They've been working all week on it. We tried on our own but Fame is a very secure site and we couldn't do it."

Spencer was the last person I expected to help me after our little incident.

"See, Beth? It's going to be fine. Everyone is going to go right back to forgetting you," Gia said as I glared across the table at her. "I mean—umm—"

"I get it, Gia, relax. I'm sorry for being so snappy lately, I'll try to keep it together better," I said as I looked into the faces of the people who meant the most to me.

I couldn't imagine why Spencer would fix it after our fight in the park. If the roles were reversed, I'd have been just fine leaving it up. I could be rather harsh when I wanted to.

Curiosity got the better of me. "Did Spencer say anything else?" I watched intently as my brothers exchanged glances.

"Nothing important," Teddy said, cutting Charles off before he had a chance to speak.

"That's pretty shifty, bro," Chuck said.

"Drop it, Chuck, it's irrelevant," Teddy snapped back.

"The hell it is. She deserves to know."

They had pushed back in their chairs, turning to face one another, looking like they were ready to go blow for blow.

"Enough!" I stood from my chair, anger raising my voice. "What should I know? Just spit it out, already. I'm not a little girl anymore you don't have to protect me."

They turned to me, forgetting about what ever beef was going on between them.

"Really?" Teddy said, sounding more like a parent than a brother. "You can handle everything on your own? I don't think so, Beth. We just had to literally threaten you out of your room."

"I was dealing with it, in my own way." *So what if I was just going to wait out the storm?*

"Okay, okay. Fine go right ahead tell her everything. Clearly, she has her life in order and doesn't need us," Teddy said, getting up from the table.

Great guilt trip, just what I need right now. "I didn't mean it like that, Teddy, I do need you guys, but you don't have to keep me sheltered like I'm that scared kid whose mommy and daddy never came home. I grew up. I'm tough. I've been through a lot and I just need you to support me rather than keeping things from me."

I turned back to Charles, hoping he would continue with whatever he was going to say earlier. "So this is what went down..." Charles began.

I sat back down, ready for whatever he was going to tell me.

"So after Teddy yelled at him for fifteen minutes for defiling you," he said, arching an eyebrow in Teddy's direction. "He stood up from the meeting and declared his love for you. He told Teddy that he could do whatever he wanted, but he was going to win you over and he didn't care if he had our blessing or not. Of course, your cool brother—me—told him to give it his best shot. Mr. old school over here, didn't," he finished, pointing at Teddy.

I followed Charles's thumb to see Teddy shake his head in disappointment. "Beth, I'm not going to tell you what to do. I just don't have a good feeling about all of this. I'll keep my opinions to myself if that's what you want, but I will, under no circumstances, let him hurt you. I will not hesitate to do what I think is necessary if he, in any way, upsets you."

Little did he know that that had already happened. *And see? I dealt with that just fine.* Or so I liked to tell myself. The fact that Spencer would go to my brothers and say all that had my head spinning. This just clarified to me that Spencer wasn't playing me, that he was telling me the truth. As fucked up as it was, I guess he liked me. The embers that I felt for him had sparked again. *Not that I'm going to go running into his arms. I mean, he's still a jerk, but I don't loathe him as much as I did ten minutes ago.*

The four of us sat around the condo for the rest of the night. The boys went out and got some wine and takeout. The smell of the food was intoxicating. I had been so caught up in every-thing, I had stopped eating. A nice proper meal was a great way to end my week of granola bars and tea.

The wine didn't last long, between Gia's frustrations with Charles and…well, me. Feeling fuzzy was just what the doctor ordered, an excuse to let everything go and just dance! In typi-cal Monroe fashion, we moved all the furniture and made a dance floor.

Five songs in, I plopped down on the couch with Teddy. Conveniently for Gia the next song was a slow one. I watched as Charles, who may have had a few too many beers, grabbed Gia's hand and pulled her closer to him. *Nothing new—until it was.* Charles buried his face in her neck as they swayed to the music.

I shouldn't be watching this. I turned to talk to Teddy. The look on his face was almost worse, as the two of them kept dancing. He was obviously as uncomfortable as I was.

Thankfully, it was a short song. Charles took a step back from Gia but still kept his hands on her hips as they simply stared at each other. In the background, the upbeat music start-ed again, but still they didn't move. *Oh, fuck! I know that look. It was the same look I got when I was with Spencer—the I'll-do-anything-to-keep-this-moment-frozen-in-time look.*

I got up and broke through their eye contact by taking Charles hands off of Gia and dancing with him.

"Come on, Teddy," I yelled over my shoulder. "You can't bow out on us. You only danced to two songs." Taking matters into my own hands, I pushed Gia in to Teddy's lap. As she fell in his lap, her arms wrapped around his neck. He held her tightly so she wouldn't fall off his lap. Well, he couldn't say I never tried to help him.

I would have much rather seen Gia with Teddy, if I got to pick that was. Charles was great but, face it, he was not dating material, and I didn't want my friend to get hurt or have Charles come between us because he couldn't keep it in his pants.

ତ৵৩৵৩

Sunlight was not my friend the next morning. I grumbled into my pillow, pulling the covers up and over my spinning head. The sound of people talking in the family room got my attention. I stumbled out of bed and around the corner to see the door close quickly and Gia whip around to lean up against it. *Okay, my curiosity is peeked.*

"Who was that?" I asked, crossing my arms.

"No one," she said, all high-pitched and walking quickly by me to get to her room.

I followed her, holding the door open, making it impossible for her to close it.

"Bullshit. It wasn't no one. Spit it out. Oh God, did you sleep with Chuck? That little bastard, I told him to keep his paws off you. He would—"

"Beth, it was no one. I just thought I heard someone at the door, that's all."

I frowned at her, questioning her story. "I've got my eye on you. Something fishy is going on around here," I said, eyeing my friend up and down.

"It's nothing, Beth. Don't worry about it," she said, trying to sooth me.

"Okay," I said, holding my hands up as I walked back out to the kitchen to get some hot tea.

Chapter 17

Spencer had managed to get the photo taken off the Internet by Saturday morning. I guessed my brothers were right, because as soon as it was taken off about half the photographers were gone.

With only a few paparazzi camped outside, I attempted to head to the café to do some reading. I needed to get out of the condo and the café was the safest place I knew.

Walking up to the counter, I ordered my usual.

"Beth is that you?" Karen, one of the baristas, asked.

Taking my hood off slightly, I nodded, holding my finger to my mouth. "Yeah, it's me," I said quietly. "I'm trying to, ya' know, lay low, stay incognito."

Nodding in agreement, she rang me up. Taking my tea and muffin, I went and sat on my cozy couch minus one perfect man.

The first few days, Simon was calling me every night, but as the week went on his calls became every other day, and the last three days I hadn't heard from him. He had texted me, but no calls.

Relaxing back, I set in and opened my new book. It didn't take long before I was totally lost in it. I was 200 pages in to the 400 page book when I caught a chill from the door being opened for an unusual amount of time. Closing the book, but leaving my finger to hold the page, I looked up at the commotion toward the front of the store.

A bull of a man, who looked really out of place in this small café, walked in my direction. A slightly smaller man followed behind him, holding his head down. A flash of light from the window put everything in perspective. This man who was dressed casually in jeans, a sweat shirt with black blazer over top and lowered baseball cap was clearly in hiding. I knew the exact feeling. *Holy crap! I can't shake this man. He is literally everywhere!*

I watched from just above the book that now covered my face as Spencer went to the counter to order a drink. Karen was lost in his good looks, just like every other girl, as she fumbled her words in front of him. Leaning around him very obviously, she tried to get my attention to let me know who was currently ordering a large coffee. *Like I don't already know who it is?*

I shook my head at her, mouthing "Don't make a scene."

Spencer was looking confused as she appeared to be talking to an invisible man beside him. He turned to see who she was talking to. I tried as quickly as possible to cover my face with the book, but he saw me. *I really need to work on my reaction time.*

Thankfully, Karen quickly recovered. "Would you like anything else, sir?" she asked, getting his attention again.

"No that's all," he said, handing her some cash. "Keep the change."

As his back was toward, me I reached down to grab my bag, I needed to get the hell out before he could say anything. Pulling my hood over my head, I planned to walk the outskirts of the café to make sure I kept my distance from him. It was no use.

He caught me by the arm—again, before I was able to even take two full steps.

Damn it, why do my knees get weak when he touches me?

Holding my arm just above my elbow, he turned me toward him. As he did, a chorus of flashes went off on the other side of the window. "Elizabeth," he said.

I looked nervously around the café. It was obvious that everyone had stopped their conversations to watch us. *Great now we have an audience.*

Moving my arm from his warm grip, I took the two steps

back and sat down on the couch. Looking up into Spencer's face, I nodded my head at the empty seat next to me.

He paused momentarily before joining me. *I hope he thinks I'm going to belittle him in public.* Turning toward him, I got my first good look at him since the park incident. He was still handsome as hell, but it looked like he hadn't slept in a week. Dark circles were under his beautiful blue eyes. When he took his hat off, his hair was a disheveled and unkempt mess.

I decided that right now wasn't the time to get nasty. "So I guess I owe you some thanks," I said, adjusting my bag on my lap so I had something to keep my nervous hands busy.

"You don't owe me anything. I'm sorry the picture got out, but I'm not going to apologize for what happened that night."

Well, I guess we're going to do this again. "Spencer, listen. That night was a mistake. I'm with—" I needed to say this to him so why wouldn't the words come?

"I know you're with another man, but you and I both know that night you weren't. You were with me."

Technically, but that's irrelevant now. This was not how I pictured this going at all. "Spencer, what do you want from me? This was never going to work. It's for the best."

His expression was unchanging. His strong presence kept me on my toes. I felt as if I never knew what was going to come out of his mouth. And I hated that that excited the hell out of me.

"I know you're with someone else. What I want from you is—" He stopped, as if he was calming himself down, trying to rein in his temper. "I don't believe in fate, but I can't help but think that I'm supposed to be near you. Look at this," he said, glancing around the café. "You can't keep calling these little run-ins coincidence."

There was desperation in his voice for me to agree with him, but I just couldn't get on board.

"Well, maybe if you stop stalking me, we'd stop running in to each other."

Sitting back on the love seat he looked back at me, stunned. "You think I have nothing better to do with my day but sit around and figure out where you are going to be and what you are going to be doing. I'm fucking Spencer Salvatore. I don't have time to figure that shit out!"

Just when I think that maybe he's a decent guy, he goes and says some shit like that.

"That's not what I meant," he said, trying to reel me back in along with his temper. "I try to stay away from you. Honestly I do, but you have to believe me, I'm not stalking you. I stay away from relationships and women. The feelings that I have for you, I haven't had in a long time. It got me in trouble once and, ever since, I have been very careful to not let it happen again. But when I'm with you, I find myself wandering back down that road and it fucking scares me to death."

I stared at him, silently wishing that he would have told me all that earlier, but I was with Simon now and I wasn't going to ruin that.

"Excuse me, your coffee's ready," Karen called from the counter.

Standing abruptly, he looked over at her. "Thank you," he said, before turning back to me. "Believe what you want, Elizabeth, but I believe something else entirely is going on here— fate, destiny, call it whatever you want. I'm not going to fight it anymore. Like I told your brothers, I don't care if they approve or not, and I don't care if you're seeing someone else. End it with him, don't end it with him, but you can damn well count on me not giving up."

Without another word, he walked over, got his coffee, and left the café.

I stayed seated, crippled by his words. *How can he do this to me? Make me want to strangle him one minute, and the next throw everything away just to be in his arms again?*

I needed to know more. I needed to figure him out, and the only way I was going to do that was if I had a conversation that was longer than ten minutes with him.

Just as I got ready to call after him, my phone began vibrating then ringing from within my bag. Glancing at the phone, I saw Simons name light up. I almost threw it back in my bag and ran after Spencer—almost.

I heard the crazy questions from the paparazzi as he opened the door to leave and decided to keep quiet.

"Do you love her?"

"Is she the one?"

"Why Elizabeth Monroe?"

I'd like to know the answer to that question, too. Why me? What did he see in me that made him have these feeling that he hasn't had in years? Why am I so special?

The ringing of my phone brought me out of my questioning mind. I was with Simon, and I owed him my attention. "Hello," I said, trying to sound cheery. I found myself having to do that a lot when I answered his calls.

"My beautiful Belle, I didn't think you were going to answer. You had me a little worried there for a minute," he said, but the background noise was making it hard to hear him.

"Sorry, I was studying. Where are you at? It's really loud."

It went quiet before he spoke again. "Better? I'm at a café for a shoot."

I smiled, thinking that even though we were thousands of miles apart, we were still kind of in the same place.

"Funny you say that. I'm at our café."

"How's Karen doing? You keeping my seat warm for me?" he asked.

Thankfully he was thousands of miles away so he wouldn't know that someone else had been in his seat if only for a few minutes. Settling back on the couch, I caught up with him.

He was truly a jet setter. This week he was in England, next he was going to the south of France, then on to Spain. "Well, like I said, this week is going to be tough, but I will call you when I can. I miss you."

Umm Spencer who? I loved talking to Simon. I really wished he was here with me, then none of this would be happening right now.

"I miss you too, you have no idea how much," I said back.

"I think I do," Simon responded, before saying bye and hanging up.

‹›‹›

"He really said that? Like legit, he told you he didn't care about the other guy? That he was going to just keep at it?" Gia asked, getting a little too excited over my chance meeting with Spencer.

"Not in so many words, but that's creepy, right?" I asked, taking a bite of the Chinese food we'd ordered.

"Umm, it's only creepy if the guy saying it is a total weirdo. I've met Spencer. He's not a weirdo. A sexy beast? Yes. Weirdo? I don't think so. You did say you wanted to get to know him better"

Great, Gia was jumping on the Salvatore train now.

"I mean, come on, the man is sexy as hell. Look at that," she said, holding a *Forbs Magazine* with Spencer on it in front of my face. "Jesus, how do you not do whatever he says with those eyes looking at you? You got some will power, sister."

I took the magazine from her and looked at it before tossing in on the coffee table. "You know, not too long ago, you were telling me to forget about Spencer and focus on Simon. What's with the sudden change of heart," I asked, bumping her shoulder.

"I didn't say that—exactly. I merely told you that you should wait and see if he makes an effort, which I think he has. I mean, he did talk to your brothers."

Damn, she's right. I hate it when she's right.

"Wait a minute. This doesn't count. He is just running in to me. It's not like he's chasing me down or calling me or knocking on my door."

Grabbing the magazine again, she leaned back on the couch and stared at Spencer's picture. A wave of jealousy ripped through me and I hated it. I hated that I felt so possessive over him.

"Well, call it my inner slut coming out, but when your not-even-boyfriend-at-the-time leaves for a month and the hottest man in the world confesses his undying love to you, I say, jump that ship see how it rides."

I tore the magazine from her. "Ugh, Gia, that's dirty even for you. Tell your inner slut to calm down over there."

Our attention was suddenly turned toward the television, as we heard my name come through the speakers.

"Turn it up," I said, hitting her arm, while the blood drained from my face.

"...Spencer Salvatore used to be a very private person—that is, until he took on a business adventure with DC locals, and playboys in their own right, Theodore and Charles Monroe, better known as Teddy and Chuck to their growing fan base. But it's not these handsome playboys the world is obsessed with. It's their little sister Elizabeth Monroe, who started off as a nobody. We've all watched as the two strangers met and soon a relationship unfolded on the pages of Fames website. A modern day love story. The world simply can't get enough of them. The very private sister to the Monroe brothers has been in hiding since the racy picture leaked over a week ago. The world wants to know more about the voluptuous Elizabeth Monroe. She is a nice image change to the typical slender model figure that most famous playboys sport. It seems as though things aren't as perfect as we once thought. A recent photo of the duo taken in a local café is raising eyebrows. Witnesses say there was tension between the thought-to-be-lovers. We will all be watching to see how this—what some people are calling fairy tale story—ends..."

What did I do to deserve this? I must have been a horrible person in another life. I probably threw kittens in a river.

"Well, they didn't say anything bad about you. They said nice things actually."

I shot Gia a warning look to shut up. "Yeah? Well, if people didn't know who I was then, they sure as hell do now. Shit, even I'm buying into the whole 'love story, how will it end' bullcrap. My life is a freaking soap opera," I said in frustration.

"Well—"

"Shut up, Gia, you're not helping here."

Chapter 18

The weeks flew by. My school work started piling up, which helped to keep my mind off other things. Simon's calls became even more infrequent, but when he did call, the conversations we had were great. Long distance was not fun, especially when everything was still so new.

Spencer had been MIA as usual—no flowers with creepy notes and no accidental run-ins. I only hoped that maybe this was all over and he was over whatever little infatuation he had with me. *I am ready to be Spencer and paparazzi free, I think. No, I definitely am.*

Checking out the window one last time, I shook my head at the nonsense that was going on. These people, if you could even call them that, were relentless at trying to get a picture of me. I couldn't wait any longer. I needed to get home. So, against my better judgment, I stood from the quiet sanctuary of the library and pulled my sweatshirt over my head.

My flip-flop-clad toes caught a chill from the mid-November air. I thought I was going to be safe going out the back. Obviously not. I'd been seen. Within seconds, more photographers were hot on my ass. Jogging, I tried to get away faster. The fear of being chased made my heart pound. *Nothing like running for your life.*

Getting frustrated that I wasn't giving them anything, the hounds turned nasty. "Hey, chunks, wait up."

"Haters are going to love this action shot."

"You're not hot enough for him. What's he thinking?"

Well, it worked. *Good job.* "You all are heartless assholes.

I'm sure you're parents are so proud of you," I yelled over my shoulder.

Which, of course, only made things worse. It was like they multiplied before my eyes. I turned and ran even faster as I slipped back into nightmares of being chased and teased as a child. Only, this time, my brothers weren't here to take the heat off me. I had learned to handle idiots like this by the time I got to high school, but I really didn't want an assault charge filed against me.

I held in the anger and tears for another block, but soon a tsunami of tears and emotions had taken over and fell from my eyes. It was hard to tell what was in front of me as I ran, the tears making my vision blurry. My flip flop got caught on a section of the sidewalk that had jutted up. I braced myself for the fall and the flashes of light that I was sure were going to follow. And they did. I was surrounded by cameras. I couldn't see anyone's face, just their unforgiving cameras.

Quickly, I tried to stand, but I stumbled back to the ground. My ankle was not having it. I held my head down, hoping that everyone would magically just disappear when I looked back up, but they didn't.

I registered that some people were yelling at the swarm around me, telling them to back off and leave me alone. One voice stood out against the rest. "Back the fuck up, if you know what's good for you."

Grasping my ankle, I could tell that something was not right. There was a huge knot on the side and it was changing colors before my eyes. *I cannot handle this right now.* The lingering tears made it hard to focus on anything other than the figures surrounding me. Sensing someone walk up behind me, I pulled my body into a tighter ball, praying silently that they wouldn't resort to kicking me. *This was enough public shaming for one day, without adding being stomped.*

I felt the weight of a hand rest gently on my shoulder, as the person knelt before me. Whipping my head up and almost getting whiplash, I stared into Spencer's beautiful face.

"I'm going to get you out of here," he said.

I froze. The distinct noise of clicks going off was all I could concentrate on.

"Elizabeth, look at me. I'm getting you out of here."

I nodded up at him, absolutely relieved. The tears start rolling again. Effortlessly, he picked me up off the ground. I wrapped my arms tightly around his neck and buried my face in his shoulder. Damn, he smelled good.

He took a step then stopped. "I said back off!"

The roar of his voice would have scared the shit out of me if he had yelled at me like that. He walked the rest of the way to the large SUV parked on the side of the road. I scooted over, giving him room to hop in and slam the door to all the chaos outside.

The driver pulled away and we started down the road.

"Are you okay?" he asked, turning to look at me. "Let me see it," he said, pointing to my ankle.

Wiping my eyes, I fixed my hair and clothes. "I'm fine," I said, holding the edge of the seat, white knuckled. I kept my eyes fixed on the window and clenched my jaw every time the pain shot up from my ankle.

"I'll be—Goddamn, your ankle is huge. Just let me look at it," he demanded, sounding exactly the same as he had in the park.

Checking my swollen ankle for myself, I winced as the adrenalin started wearing off.

I felt another sharp pain shoot from the swollen knot that resided on my once petite ankle—clearly, the only petite part of me.

"I think I broke it. I should just—"*Wait a minute. How the hell did he know it was me*? "How did you know it was me out there? You are stalking me. You are. I knew it!"

I scooted farther away from him. *This is how movies on* Lifetime *start.* I was not trying to be a Saturday-night-movie special.

"Jesus, I'm not stalking you. You really are full of yourself."

I went to open my mouth to tell him off, but he stopped me before I could.

"I was on my way to oversee some changes for the club when my driver saw you running down the sidewalk being chased by paparazzi. When I saw you fall, I wanted to make sure you were okay, and it's a fucking good thing that I did. Now let me see it!" he said, tapping his lap and talking to me like a child.

I am not a child! I glared at him. "I don't think so."

He shook his head angrily. "Damn it, Elizabeth, you can be so fucking stubborn."

He leaned down, gently wrapping his strong hand around the back of my ankle and placing his other hand on my shin. He lifted my leg smoothly, resting it softly on his lap. He let his fingers run up the back of my foot and I had to squeeze my thighs together. *Damn, body, control yourself. This is happening right now. One touch and I am on the fritz. Simon, think Simon.* But I couldn't. All thoughts of him were squashed as the throbbing pain in my ankle took over.

"Well, I don't think it's broken," he said, looking it over again.

"Right, I think I'll get a doctor's opinion. Playboys don't have that great a track record, so I'll get a second opinion. Thanks." *There that should shut him up.*

"Actually, Miss. Monroe, I am, or was."

Huh? Did he just say he was a doctor? "Yeah, right, and I'm the queen of England. Nice try."

He held his body still and just studied me. "God, you really get to me woman," he said through a clenched jaw. "Here, I am thinking I'm being nice, saving you from the crazies, and you keep looking at me like I'm going to kidnap you and lock you in a cellar."

Lifetime movie, I'm telling you. But in all honestly I was grateful. "Listen, I'm sorry, I didn't mean to act ungrateful. I am, believe me, but all those people have made me fly over the coo coo's nest. I'm usually not a crying, emotional, rambling—well, I guess I do kind of ramble. My brothers are always telling me—"

"Elizabeth," he said, cutting me off. "Shut up, it's fine. I'd do it again, even if you didn't want me to."

I sat up a little, adjusting myself on the seat. *Okay, I think it's time to put egos aside and just talk to him.* "You said you 'were' a doctor. What is that all about?"

Looking over at me he shook his head again. "Oh, so now you want to talk, get to know me?"

Well, that was the idea, but obviously he can't put his ego aside. He crossed his arms on his chest but left my leg on his lap. *This man is sooo confusing!*

"Fine, whatever, Spencer, I'm trying here. If you want to keep being an ass, go ahead and just take me home."

Turning as far as I could without moving my foot, I looked out the window. As much as my stubbornness made him angry, his mood swings made me furious. The silence filled the car as we both refused to give in to one another.

A few minutes passed, yet the silence remained. I turned toward him when I felt his fingers gently running over my leg—a mindless touch. I watched as he tenderly rubbed it.

"I'm sorry. I'll stop," he said coolly when he registered what he was doing and that I was intently watching.

"No, don't. It feels good, helps take the pain away." I smiled up at him and was rewarded with a smirk. "Okay, for real. Tell me how you were almost a doctor?"

A full on smile made its way onto his face, and I knew that the calm Spencer was back.

"Well, before all this—" he said, looking around the SUV, "I was in school to be a doctor. I quit a few years in. It wasn't for me. My parents wanted it more than I did. My father's a doctor. My mother was a nurse. They thought that I was just going to follow in their footsteps."

I remembered reading that his family was big in the healthcare profession, mother father, even his two sisters. *Okay, so I stalked his family. I was bored one night.* "So you just dropped out and decided to open night clubs?" I asked, not really getting it.

"Pretty much. I have a knack for throwing parties. A talent I found while I was in school. So what better way to showcase it, than opening night clubs and bars?"

Makes sense. "I bet your parents were a little upset. Doctors and night clubs are on completely different sides of the spectrum."

A shot of pain raced from my ankle and a hiss escaped my lips, I braced myself as the pain throbbed harder.

He checked out my foot again, his warm breath tickling my skin as he leaned closer. "Maybe we should go to the hospital to get an X-ray."

Not fair! I'm a cripple. I can't get away from him. Because if I could, I'd open this door and roll out before I do something stupid. "You're the doctor, Mr. Salvatore, you make the call," I said, laughing nervously. There it was—the smile that could bring a woman to her knees.

"It's up to you. I'll take you wherever you want me, too."

Oh those are loaded words, Salvatore. I took a deep breath and tried to relax. "I guess you should just take me home. I can make an appointment tomorrow. Sitting in the ER sucks on its own, add the paparazzi, and you pretty much have hell."

"I couldn't agree more," he said, still caressing my foot.

Silence filled the car again as we drove to my home. My thoughts consumed me. Maybe Spencer was on to something. Maybe this was fate bringing us together all the time. He was pissed at me and I was…well, pissed at him. Yet, he couldn't help but rub my leg, and I was more than happy to let him. *Let's face it. I try so hard not to think of him. I put on a good front, but I wouldn't have wanted anyone else saving me today. Partly because it was his fault, of course.*

I let a chuckle out breaking the silence and gaining his attention.

"What?" he asked.

I hesitated, making sure I said it right, and didn't mess it up. "I'm glad it was you." At his frown, I continued. "I'm glad that you were the one that saved me from the crazies. I mean it was your fault—"*I love his smile. Ooo, it makes me melt.* "For real though, maybe I need to rethink things because I wouldn't want anyone el—"

My phone, my stupid phone is going off. I reached into my bag, rather than finishing my thought. *Simon.* It was Simon. I felt all the color drain from my face as I looked up at Spencer, who was watching my every move with an uneasy look on his face. "I—I—umm—have to get this." I slid over to answer and prepared to sound happy. "Hey."

"Baby, are you all right?"

Confused by his question, I frowned. "Yes. Well, no, not really," I said, adjusting my answer as I looked down at my swollen ankle.

"Are you hurt?" he asked, terror coming through his voice.

"I—umm—I tripped and I think I sprained my ankle—wait a minute. Where are you? How do you know I'm hurt?" I demanded.

I glanced over at Spencer, who was listening in on the conversation. Real suspicion played out on his face as I was sure it did on mine, too.

I waited for an answer that I felt was taking too long to come.

"Don't be mad at me," he said. "I just happened to be on the Internet and there is a picture of you being carried off by someone. I closed the computer and called you immediately."

It's already on the Internet. What was that, like fifteen minutes max?

"Did it say anything else?" I asked, praying that he hadn't seen that it was Spencer who carried me off.

"I don't know, baby. I told you I was just checking my e-mail and there you were. How many times do I have to tell you? I don't read into that stuff, and neither should you."

Great, a lecture from overseas from my absent boyfriend.

"I don't!" I snapped at him, gaining a chuckle from Spencer.

No doubt Spencer was amused that I was snapping at someone other than him for once.

"Okay, calm down there. Don't get all heated. I'm not there to benefit from it."

Now that had me chuckling. *The man always has me laughing.* "Funny. I'm fine. I'm going to make a doctor's appointment tomorrow. I'll call you when I find out."

"Well, who are you with now?"

I looked nervously up at Spencer and, by the expression on his face, I knew he was hearing everything.

"Umm, a friend is giving me a lift home."

He shook his head in disappointment and I shouldn't have, but I felt horrible. I ended my conversation with Simon and put my phone back in my bag. *Can you say tension you can definitely cut it with a knife?* Blue eyes shot laser beams at me.

"I'm sorry you had to—"

"So that was him?" he asked, making the words run ice cold over my skin.

Crap, moody Spencer is back.

"How can you do that? Say what you said to me then talk to him like I'm not sitting here listening. Why do you protect him?" he asked.

I should have just called Simon back. *Why did I answer? I hate you, universe! Shit this is exhausting.* "It's complicated, and I don't protect him," I said, getting aggravated.

"No. You really do. And it's really not complicated at all. Do you even know him?"

Oh, it's on Salvatore. "Do I even know you?" I said, crossing my arms.

"I think you know me better than him," he challenged.

Oh, he's fallen off the wagon one too many times, clearly.

"Really? That's what you think? Because every second I'm with you I feel like I'm with three different people!" *Take that!*

"He left you Elizabeth." His tone was malicious.

"No. No way, Spencer. You don't get to say that about him. He's working. He didn't leave me, that's what you did! You didn't even turn around. You just left me standing there!"

"And I hate myself every fucking day for it!" he yelled. The passion in his voice bounced off the confines of the SUV.

I can't believe this is happening now, in a car, where I can't get away—or can I?

We pulled up to the back of my building, avoiding all the gawking people who had flocked out front. As the car came to a stop, I lifted my foot off his lap and swung it around. Pain seared in my ankle but I pushed through it and opened the door. He followed suit and got out on his side. Coming around, he stood in front of me as I balanced on one foot. As always, I failed miserably and fell back onto the SUV.

"Damn it, Elizabeth," he said, placing his arms under me helping me gain my balance.

His hold on me was tight and I wanted to hate it but I didn't. I got back on my good foot and balanced myself. "I've got it," I said, looking up into his unbelievable blue eyes.

It took only a millisecond to register as his hands grabbed my face and he kissed me hard. The passion and power behind that kiss was more than I had ever felt before. I didn't want it to end. In that moment, I didn't want reality to come crashing down on us again like it had in my father's office. But it couldn't last forever.

"You are going to ruin me, woman," he said with a smile, pulling back while running his thumb over my flushed lips.

I smiled back. "Not if you ruin me, first."

"Come on, let me help you up to your room."

We turned, and I expected to wrap an arm around his shoulder for balance so I could hop inside, but he didn't even give me the chance. Lifting me up, he carried me all the way to my door.

He set me down and I rummaged in my bag for my keys. I may have taken a little longer than necessary to find them, and maybe I just moved my hand around aimlessly so that his hand would stay securely on my hips. Maybe. When I finally opened the door, he lifted me back up, carried me to the couch, and placed a few pillows under my foot to elevate it.

"Do you have an ice pack?" he asked, sitting on the coffee table.

"Yeah, there should be one in the freezer."

Standing, he walked over and retrieved one. Walking back over with the ice pack in his hand, he smiled down at me. "So you're going to want to keep the ice on it. Twenty minutes on ten off. And keep it elevated to help with the swelling."

Placing the ice pack on my ankle, I winced at the coldness hit my skin. "Okay, Dr. Salvatore, ice and elevation. Got it!"

We turned in unison as the door flew open. Not only did it scare me to death, but it made me jump, which made the ice fall off. Picking the ice back up, Spencer placed it back on my foot.

Gia's familiar laugh bounced off the walls. "Oh, come on, it wasn't that bad," she said, coming fully into the room from the door way.

I was utterly shocked to see Teddy follow her in to the condo. Once he saw Teddy, Spencer turned away from the door. And once my brother and Gia saw me laid up with a bum foot, they flipped out.

"What the hell is going on here, Beth?" Teddy asked, rushing over to my side.

Spencer rose from the coffee table that he was sitting on and kept his head down as he backed away.

"I fell, Teddy. We think it's just a sprain," I said, trying to gauge my brother's response.

"Who the hell is we?" Gia asked, looking over at the mystery man.

Spencer turned slowly to show his face. Not the cocky Spencer I was used to seeing, that was for sure.

"Hey, Teddy, Gia," he said, giving then a curt nod.

They looked between us two times, me then Spencer then me.

"Well, I'm going to head out," Spencer said, all business like, and moved toward the door. "I have some work that I need to tend to,"

"Spencer!" I called to him.

He froze in his tracks and turned back to me.

"Thank you for helping me. I'm glad it was you. I'll have to thank fate for having you there in the right place and time."

I wanted to run to him, hug him, thank him again, kiss him again. But I was stuck on the couch with a bum foot and an extremely overprotective brother in my way.

"Me, too." It was all he said, and it was all he needed to say, as he walked out the door.

Chapter 19

Gia and I sat in bed, eating ice cream and gushing over this and that. "So, what's with you and Teddy?" I asked, wiggling my eyebrows.

"Nothing. We just ran in to each other and he offered to give me a ride home."

Frowning, I ate another scoop of ice cream.

"You know, Charles isn't as bad as you make him out to be," she said quickly, putting her spoon in her mouth.

I knew that. I knew he could be a good guy but, I wasn't going to tell her that. She didn't need a confusing relationship. I needed her sane to help me with all my issues. *I'm only being a little selfish.*

❧❧❧

Hobbling in the back entrance on crutches, I followed as Gia headed toward the elevators.

"Elizabeth," Derrick called as he walked over from the front desk. "I heard that you hurt yourself. Are you okay?"

Derrick is the best. What can I say? We have the best front desk man in town.

"Yeah, those crazy people outside were harassing me and I tripped. It's a bad sprain, so I'm stuck with a boot and crutches for the next week."

He gave a look that could kill at the front doors, and I could have sworn I heard him growl. "I'm so sorry. Please let me know if you need anything," he said, turning back to Gia and me.

"Can you just make sure that they leave the back entrance open for me so I can keep sneaking in and out? I don't think they've figured it out yet," I said, pointing my crutch in the direction of the very tinted front windows and door.

"Will do, and, Gia, you take care of her and yourself. I can't have my two favorite girls getting hurt," he said, smiling at us before making his way back to the front desk.

༄༅༄

Getting to class wasn't as bad as I expected it to be. Derrick had called a high-class cab company and had them pull around the back with complete discretion as to who they were driving around. Once we pulled onto campus, I was safe. The campus police was beefed up, thanks to its two famous students. No one without a badge was let on campus. It was truly a God-send.

As my last class let out, I waited until everyone had left before I hobbled across the room. The sun had begun to set and darkness was quickly approaching. Even with all the security, I still hated walking around here at night. *Lifetime Movie network has me really paranoid lately.*

With my bag around my shoulders and crutches under my arms, I headed for the door. "Hey hold the door."

Thanks, buddy, for holding the door for a cripple person. I steadied myself and reached down to open the heavy door. I kicked one of the crutches so that it held the door open and I could weasel my way out. The door slammed behind me as I removed the crutch. "I'm going to kill myself on these," I said out loud to no one.

"I think that's a very accurate observation."

I turned to my right and found a fine-looking figure leaning up against the wall. "Spencer Salvatore, you sure do know what to say to charm the ladies," I said, watching as he walked toward me.

His casual attire let him easily pass for a student. The dark blue jeans hugged his hips just enough that I found myself imagining things just below the belt, before I looked up at his black leather jacket complete with hoodie underneath. He looked good enough to eat.

"What are you doing here?" I asked, realizing that he even went through the trouble of getting a campus badge to walk around freely. *Clearly this was not a "run-in."*

"I went by your place to check on you and…well, let's just say after much negotiation with your door man, he told me you were at school. So what did the real non-playboy doctor have to say about your foot?"

Ha, ha, I see what he did there. I shuffled closer to the wall to get out of the way of people walking by. "Funny, Salvatore. The real doctor said it was just a bad sprain."

"Seems my playboy doctor skills are still intact. I should start charging."

Cocky as shit this man is. We stood there smiling at one another, until I shifted on my crutches. *Damn these things make your armpits hurt.*

"You all right there? Let me give you a ride home." His blue eyes bore into me, waiting for my response.

"I guess," I said, turning to walk out the building.

I heard him chuckle to himself then follow me to the exit. *This isn't going to be good. I should have said no. Hey, at least it beats calling a cab.* I sat down in the front seat of his SUV while he took my crutches and placed them in the back.

"What? No scoffer tonight? You're really slumming it," I said, as he sat in the driver's seat and turned the car on.

"I know, but sometimes I like to pretend I'm a commoner. Spice things up, throw off the paparazzi. Someone's got to keep them on their toes. I mean, some people are just asking for it, running down the street"

"Hey, not cool," I said, hitting his arm.

Oh my God, he has huge muscular arms. I wish I hadn't done that. Damn it! I squeezed the tension between my legs. *Calm down, Beth. He's just a guy giving a crippled girl a ride home, and he should, because it was his fault that I was hurt in the first place.*

Our laughter became silent as we both heard my phone buzz from the inside of my bag. *Oh God.* I looked up to see a scowl on his face rather than the jovial smile that was there only seconds before.

"Are you going to get that?" he asked, jealousy clearly in his voice.

I looked up at him and smiled. "Nope."

This was good. After last night, we needed to talk, figure this out. This was my chance to get to know him even more.

"So do you have plans for Thanksgiving?" I asked, settling into my seat as he drove off campus and toward my home. This was the perfect question, simple, non-sexual, which was a big plus, and it was happening next week. *So perfect. Go, Beth.*

"I do," he said, leaving it at that.

"Care to elaborate there, playboy?"

He looked over at me, a cocky smile in the corner of his mouth. *I think I'm melting into the car. This question was not meant to be sexual!*

"Playboy, huh?" he asked. I smiled over at him, nodding. "I hate to break it to you," he said, "but I'm not a playboy."

"Well, that's not what the Internet says, and everything on the Internet is true, so you are. Now, you were telling me your plans for Thanksgiving."

He ran his hand over his five o'clock shadow and I had to look at my feet to keep from swooning.

"The Internet also says that we're in some kind of romantic modern-day fairy tale. Is that true?"

Well that back fired. Damn my smart mouth. "Umm..." I racked my brain for a fast recovery but couldn't find any.

"I'm going home for the week to spend time with my family. I do it every year," he said, saving me.

"That's really nice that you can do that. Go home for a week."

This was the way I saw this conversation going.

"Yeah, my family put up with a lot of my shit when I was younger. It's the least I can do," he said, glancing over to me. Do you have plans?"

"Yeah, my brothers and I go to my grandmother's beach

house and help her winterize it, and of course, we have dinner."

"Sounds fun," he commented.

"Not really, I mean the food is good. My Grandmother is the best cook—" *Oh shit, am I really talking about food in front of him? I have completely lost my mind. It's not safe for me to be around him. Quickly change the subject.* "So your family lives, where?"

"Las Vegas, well, just outside"

We had reached the back entrance of my building, and he put the car in park, turning fully toward me, his arm resting on the steering wheel.

Leaning back against the window, I got a better look at him. "Vegas? You know, I would have pegged you for a Manhattan boy."

"Well, I'm kind of."

His whole demeanor changed as he said that. I watched him as he seemed to be reliving a bad memory.

"What do you mean kind of? You can't kind of be a New Yorker."

He refused to look at me which was weird. I didn't get it.

"I was born there, lived there for a while, then some bad shit happened, and I moved." His tone was even and he had no expression on his face as he spoke.

I blatantly ignored the standoffish vibe he was putting out. "What happened? You make one too many little girls go weak in the knees?"

I gave his arm a playful nudge. But quickly realized that might not have been the best idea.

"Horrible things," he said.

He can't leave me hanging like that. "Like what?" I asked, clearly pushing him, but he had my interest perked.

He stared straight out the front window. "Bad things, Elizabeth. Now fucking drop it, okay?" he yelled, whipping his head in my direction, almost making me pee my pants.

I had managed to push too far, which I may have had a tendency of doing when it came to Salvatore. His eyes were hard but there was obviously something else going on, pain, regret.

"Geeze, I'm sorry. You don't have go all Dr. Jekyll on me."
If he didn't want to talk about it, why even bring it up?

Slumping down, he ran his hands through his hair. "I just don't talk about it. I don't talk to anyone about my past. Congratulations. You're one of six people that even know I lived in New York as a child."

Sitting up, I realized that this conversation was done. I reached for the door handle to let myself out. "Well, your secret is safe with me. Thanks for the ride home." I opened the door to get out. Suddenly remembering I had a bum ankle, I sat trying to figure out which foot to put down first.

"Hold on, I'll help you," he said, getting out.

Reaching into the back, he grabbed my crutches, placing them in front of me. Letting my good foot touch the ground, I took hold of the crutches and propped myself up on them. I leaned back into the car and reached down for my bag. One of the crutches lost its grip and fell out from under my arm. I frantically reached for something to hold myself up. The first thing I grabbed was Spencer's jacket clad chest. I clawed at him, gripping the fabric as the other crutch fell from under my arm to the ground.

I swear I'm not this klutzy. It's the bum foot and the hot guy. I can't keep my shit together. Reacting quickly, Spencer wrapped his arms around me. I pushed back off of him but the damage was already done. Being in his embrace had my heart racing and body aching.

"Whoa, careful." He steadied me and then retrieved my crutches again. He also grabbed my bag from the floor of the SUV. "Why don't you just let me carry this?" I reached out trying to snatch it from him, but he was too fast. He kept teasing me like a little kid, and my patience was quickly getting away from me. "I don't think so. I said I'd carry it," he said.

I hate when people treat me like a child. "Please hand me my bag," I asked him as calmly as I could.

"You can't carry this and use those," he said, pointing to my crutches.

Well, I definitely can't stand when people tell me what I can and can't do. Another reason why this will never work.

We're both too hard headed. "I'm not asking," I said through clenched teeth.

I watched as he smiled at me then turned and walked across the short distance to stand before the door. "Well, come on, stop being so damn stubborn and waddle your ass over here and take it."

What? Did he just say waddle? I do not waddle! Pregnant woman waddle and I sure as hell am not pregnant.

"No!" I yelled over at him, crossing my arms.

"Get over here," he growled.

"No! You come back here and give me my bag. I'm not an invalid. I did just fine earlier before you came along." *There was no way I was going to budge.*

"Really?" he questioned.

"Really, I did fine all day until just then."

Small lie, I might have tripped three or ten times, but he doesn't know that.

"Okay, I guess I'm just going to have to come over there and really embarrass you. I have no shame. I'll throw you over my shoulder. Because you are not carrying the bag and attempting to walk with those while I'm around."

Shut the front door, what a jerk! "Fine!" I said, slamming the door behind me then hopping—not wobbling—my way to the door.

"See how easy that was to let me help you?"

A sly smile crept across his face as my knees went weak. *Good thing I have the crutches.* "Yeah, yeah, you win. Give the playboy a medal for making the cripple walk across the parking lot," I said as I hobbled past him and into the building.

Ↄ∽ↄↄↄ

"Which one?" he asked, holding up my keys.

"Why, you going to make a copy?" I said snidely.

"Don't tempt me, woman," he said in all seriousness.

I shook my head at him and wrinkled my face, but deep down the little slut in me was hoping he would. "The silver one," I informed him.

Unlocking the door, he held it open so I could get through. The intoxicating smell of man and expensive cologne was enough to make me move a lot slower than necessary when I passed by him.

Pivoting on my crutches, I watched him place my bag on the table next to the door and my keys on top of that. He looked torn, like he wanted to come in but was waiting for me to invite him. *What is he, secretly a vampire?*

"Would you like something to drink?" *There, I can be polite.* He did help me home.

"No I'm fine."

Okay. I looked around the room nervously. Things were getting awkward fast.

He walked closer and took me by surprise. I found myself toe to toe with him. The familiar electricity stared to course through my body as he grazed my chin with his finger. He made me look at him, whether I wanted to or not. His hand snaked around my waist and pulled me even closer. I let the crutches fall gently as I held on to him for balance.

He looked down at me, moving a stray piece of hair behind my ear. "Why are you so perfect?"

Perfect? Me? Okay, one of two things is happening right now. One, he's been drugged, or two, he's been abducted by aliens. As of right now, it might be both. "Spencer, I am nowhere near perfect."

My voice went low as I pulled back from him. All sorts of insecurities rushed to the forefront of my mind as I stared up at him, and that was when I realized for a third time tonight why we would never work.

Grabbing my wrist, he pulled me back to him. It didn't hurt, but the passion behind it was insufferable. My knees wobbled and my mouth went dry as I watched his eyes dance over my face.

"You are beautiful, and challenging, and stubborn. You push all my buttons."

Wow what a charmer.

"You make me angry and happy all at the same time. And this—" he said, letting go of my wrists to slide his fingers so they interlocked with mine. "Every time I touch you, I feel alive, and I haven't felt alive since I left New York."

New York? He said he left when he was a kid. *He's telling me he hasn't felt anything since he was a child*? I stared into his eyes, shaking my head in disbelief.

I watched in slow motion as his tongue ran over his lips, wetting them before leaning over to kiss mine. I was floating, as our lips move against one another's. Slow and soft, his tongue brushed mine. Before I woke up from the dream I was positive I was in, I fisted my hand in the back of his hair, pulling him down closer to me, needing him more than ever before. Just as I began to truly believe that maybe I was perfect, perfect for him. That I should be with—

I heard my phone calling me from across the room. Pulling away from me, Spencer looked down at me and I couldn't turn away from him. The ringing stopped and relief came over me, but not for long. Finally breaking eye contact with him, I glanced over at my bag. I knew it was Simon, I just had this feeling. My stomach felt sick as I retuned my gaze to Spencer. He also looked over at my bag then back at me. Dropping his hands, he clenched his jaw. The muscles hardened and I knew he was furious.

"Go," he said, gesturing toward my bag.

I stood there frozen not sure if I should answer or let it ring.

"Go!" he yelled thunderously.

Taking a step back from me, he shoved his hands through his hair.

There's my answer. He was pissed, but he knew I was with Simon. He knew I was someone else's, when he started.

I was right. It was Simon. I hobbled back over in Spencer's direction.

"I have to answer it," I said, looking in his eyes for forgiveness.

"Oh, by all means. Don't let me stop you."

What an ass! *He knows I have a boyfriend.*

"I will be right back," I said, before limping back to my room. Taking a breath I calmed my nerves and answered. "Hello?"

"Hey, you were starting to scare me there for a minute. Thought you might be with another guy."

I knew he only said that to be funny, but it wasn't. It tore at my heart. *I can't do this to him over the phone.* I didn't know when, but between the time we came into the condo and Simon called, I'd had a change of heart. I wasn't going to keep pretending with either guy, but I also wasn't going to tell Simon over the phone. Spencer was going to have to wait and I just had to get through until Simon came home. I had to stay neutral. No more passionate kisses or staring dreamily into Spencer's eyes. My plan was to tell Spencer I wanted to try it with him but I needed to wait until Simon got back. The moment I got off the phone with Simon, I was running right back to Spencer's arms.

"I was studying and had my phone on vibrate," I said, cringing from lying so easily to him.

"Well, how did the doctor's visit turn out," he asked. "You never called."

"Oh, sorry. I had to get to class. It's fine, just sprained."

Hearing him sigh through the phone, clearly relived that I was okay, stung pretty bad.

"I wish that I had been there to help you," he stated.

"Yeah me, too." *Liar*! my conscious yelled, calling me out.

"All right, well I don't want to keep you too long. I know you're studying like crazy."

Perfect, this man was perfect. *What is wrong with me? A short three minute conversation and I'm...I'm so confused.* Thoughts of running to Spencer were shattered as I was drowned in guilt.

"All right. Well, I love you and I'll call you tomorrow."

"I love you too, bye." I hung up quickly so I could go talk to Spencer and tell him that I wanted to try it with him, no more fighting fate. The sound of the door slamming, hit me like a hard right hook to the face as I saw that the door to my room was wide open. Spencer had heard the whole conversation, and it was then that I realized that I told Simon I loved him.

Dropping my phone, I moved as fast as I could, grimacing

in pain every time my foot made contact with the floor. I got out around the hall and—

He's gone. Curse my big mouth!

Chapter 20

*S*hould I just ask Charles to give me Spencer's number? *Should I call him and beg for him to listen to what I have to say? How would I even explain it to him without sounding like a total whore?* I had screwed up royally. Whatever chance I thought we might have had had been washed down the soap scum, hair-filled drain that I was looking at. I didn't want to admit it out loud, but maybe it was time to just let it go—for good. Spencer clearly had issues and I could be…well, people had let on that I could be rather stubborn. We would be a disaster together.

I needed to put it all behind me. I had a great, understanding guy. *So what if he's overseas, and not around? That doesn't mean he wants to be away from me. I should be happy. Why am I not happy? And why can't I get the smell of Spencer's cologne off of my skin?* I scrubbed even harder, making my arm turn red.

芝芝芝

Hours turned to days and I hadn't heard from either guy.

"Maybe I'm getting what I deserve for messing around with two guys. Opportunities like this don't usually present themselves to me. I didn't know what the hell I was doing." I shoved another spoon full of soup in my mouth, but almost spit it out as the doorbell rang.

Gia dropped her utensils and looked across the table at me.

"Who the hell is that?" she asked, looking at the door almost as frightened as I was.

Something was up with her, but honestly I didn't have time to try to figure it out. I was too busy trying to keep my pounding heart from jumping out of my chest. I so badly wanted it to be Spencer on the other side of that door.

Rising from the table, I went to answer the door. I opened it slowly to see a man standing with a bouquet of long stem red roses. I took the flowers from him and slammed the door in his face. Cringing as it closed, I quickly opened it back up.

"I'm sorry for slamming the door in your face...Thank you!" I smiled as I closed the door, softly, this time.

Placing the flowers on the table, Gia grabbed the card before I could even look for it. "It's for you," she said, relief showing on her face.

Something's just not right with her. I took the card from her and opened it, but it wasn't the handwriting I was hoping for.

> *Elizabeth,*
> *I'm sorry I can't be there to make you feel better. It's killing me that I'm not the one there to help you. I love you. Don't forget about me.*
> *Simon*

I saw the water splotch on the card before I even realized that it was coming from my eyes. *What am I doing? I was doing the one thing Simon just asked me not to do. I was forgetting him.* Handing the paper to Gia, I sat back down at the table, suddenly feeling queasy. "Gia, I need to stop this. It's literally making me sick." I held my head in my hands and kept taking deep, calming breaths.

"I know what you mean," she said, looking a little green in the face, too.

࿇

Gia and I decided to focus on school. She was going to help me stay on the straight and narrow and I was going to make sure she stayed home and studied. I needed to get back to who I was at the core. I wasn't a love sick, playboy-chasing, Internet sensation. I was just Beth, a regular, determined, soon to be college graduate. My acceptance letter had finally arrived, and I was officially an intern at the Library of Congress. Things were looking up.

The paparazzi had disappeared as fast as they arrived. Since it was public knowledge that Spencer was in Vegas. They caught him at the airport and he had confronted them for the first time, letting them know he was leaving town for the week to go home—alone. As of then or at least the next week, I didn't have to stress about running into Spencer.

Simon and I had talked a few times after my epic "I love you" but he never brought it up. Until he did. "Why haven't you said it?" His voice turned questioning.

I cringed on the other end of the phone as I punched the bed that I was lying in. *Fuck, how do I explain this? Here goes nothing.* "Simon, I really care about you—"

"But—" he said, taking the word right out of my mouth.

"But I'm not sure. You've been gone for so long, and I love talking to you and I do miss you. I just—it kind of just flowed out rhetorically." I hoped that that made sense. Lord knew, I couldn't tell him some other man had totally shaken me to the point where I didn't know what color the sky was when I was with him.

"I kind of figured that's what happened. But I want you to know that my feelings haven't wavered. If anything, they have only grown. I wish I didn't have to be away, but I don't have a choice. You have to trust me. It's for the best."

Hearing him sigh through the phone made me feel horrible. "I do, I do trust you."

I just don't trust myself. The only thing I could say for sure was that every day I didn't talk to or see Spencer, I found myself taking another step toward Simon. I knew that I had to tell him everything once he got home, then the decision was up to him. As for right now, I didn't see the harm in talking to him.

Some people might call me a slut, but I refused to tell him over the phone or in an e-mail. He deserved more. And even if Spencer had fallen off the face of the earth and I never saw him again, I was still going to tell Simon everything.

The conversation came back around to a lighter note and I was thoroughly relieved. We discussed that I would be picking him up the Sunday evening he returned. We had eight days to get through, but the real question was, was he going to want to stick around once he found out about everything.

"Hey, I gotta head out. I love you—Don't say it back. I want to see your face the first time you say it for real. I'm officially calling a do over," he said, and I knew he was smiling on the other end.

"Deal. I'll talk to you tomorrow," I said, smiling from my side as well.

Chapter 21

I watched as Gia ran back in her room to get just one more shirt to add to her already over stuffed overnight bag for a two day trip. "Gia, come on, we're going to be late, and you know how Teddy hates being late."

Running back out of her room she carried at least three more shirts. "Calm down, they're not going to leave without us."

"I don't know why you pack so much. You know you're going to go shopping and buy a new outfit anyway."

We were on our way to New York to celebrate getting through our exams. My brothers were nice enough to go with us, so we had our own escorts for the weekend.

സ്ദ്രേ

Walking into our Manhattan apartment, which we inherited from our parents, I took a second to look around. The boys had lived here for a while, but once I decided to move to go to college, they followed. It had been a few years since I had been here. Not much had changed. It was a bachelor pad, and probably always would be. It was masculine and didn't have a throw pillow in sight.

"So where are we going tonight, people?" I asked, ready to release some pent-up energy. I was anxious about going out, but I felt protected having my brothers there to keep an eye out.

They had promised me they wouldn't leave my side, that tonight was about Gia and me. Not them.

"Only the best for you two," Charles said, looking between Gia and me. He took a second too long looking over Gia. She really was beautiful in her black cocktail dress and stunning high heels. Me, on the other hand, I went for old trusty—the red dress that played a wicked part in all my recent issues.

"Where might that be?" Gia asked, flipping her long blonde hair in Charles's direction.

Chuckling inwardly at the way Charles obviously sniffed the air, I had to look away before I let a laugh out. I glanced at Teddy who seemed to do the same thing. We watched Charles straighten his tie and clear his throat.

"Ummm, we're going to Blue"

Blue? I know that. How do I know that? Wait a minute. "Is that—" I was cut off by an overly excited Gia.

"Oh my God, you got us into Blue?"

"The number one night time spot on the east coast. Well, that is, until ours opens up, but yes I did," Charles said with a cocky smile.

Teddy stood up from the couch and walked toward me, seeing the concern on my face.

"Yes, it's Spencer's club," Teddy said, confirming what I had suspected.

I want to throttle them! Why would they take me there knowing all the shit that was going on with Spencer?

"He won't be there. We had a meeting with him earlier in the week and he informed us that he was going to be on the west coast this weekend," Teddy said, rubbing my arm.

"What did you do to him, Beth? He's been a real ass the past couple weeks, flipping out over the smallest details."

Charles just has to rub my nose in it.

"Knock it off, Chuck," Teddy said, taking a step away from me and toward Charles.

"What?" Charles demanded. "It's not like this is new news. We all know but no one talks about it."

"Chuck, just shut your face. The club is almost done, and we won't have to deal with him on a daily basis anymore.

Leave Beth alone. This weekend is supposed to make her feel good, not like shit."

My hero. Teddy was my hero. He might be over protective but he was such a good man. He was going to make some girl so happy.

"Okay, well, now that we have all that awkward tension out of the way, let's get the hell out of here," Gia sang. "I've got my dancing shoes on and I'm ready to mingle with celebrities!"

Thank you, Gia.

✂✌✂

I saw why this place was so popular. It was right in the middle of everything—restaurants hotels, businesses, other bars. It was sleek and modern, under a luxurious hotel. The music was great and everything looked expensive. I was afraid to touch anything. Simply put, it was breathtaking, not unlike the man who owned it. Our dinks were ready for us as soon as we sat down. *Thank you, Spencer, for getting me drunk so I can hopefully forget about you*, I said toasting to myself before downing the first of many drinks.

Our night was going perfectly, no sign of Spencer or photographers. I was well on my way to not remembering anything in the morning. No surprise, Gia was not too far behind me. Charles was being Charles, dancing and talking to anything that had legs. Teddy was being the sensible adult and keeping tabs on all three of us.

"It is so much fun out there!" I called to Teddy as we all sat down at our reserved table.

The music took a sultry jazzy turn as people paired up on the floor swaying seductively to the music.

Standing abruptly, Teddy walked over, taking Gia's hand in his. "May I have this Dance?" he asked, kissing her hand.

Not taking her eyes off of his, she walked with him to the dance floor. He pulled her close to him as they moved to the music. I saw my brother's hand slide down her slender back. At the same time, I heard Charles hiss and grumble under his breath. Jealousy had turned Charles's usually cocky demeanor sour.

"Ha!" I laughed loudly, gaining his attention. "I guess she finally listened to me," I said, looking back at them on the dance floor.

"What the hell is that supposed to mean?" Charles asked, downing the rest of his drink.

"Charles," I said, feeling the alcohol go to my head. "Gia has been obsessed with you since the day I introduced you guys. And well—let's just face facts here—you don't have a great track record with women, so I may have pushed her in another direction," I said, slurring a few words but still managing to smile wickedly at him.

"Jesus Christ, Beth, you told me to leave her alone." He looked back at the dance floor, then back at me. "So you push her toward Teddy? You really think that little of me? That I'm just going to use her? I would never...What the hell has happened to you?" He grabbed Teddy's half empty drink and downed that before getting up from the table and leaving me sitting there—alone.

"Well, damn, look who's sitting alone at a club—again. This chick," I said, pointing to myself and talking too loudly. *Damn, I have to pee.*

Walking back out from the bathroom, I covered my ears. *I swear they turned the volume up.* I started to make my way back to the table when I was stopped. Feeling a heavy hand on my shoulder, I turned around to see a man behind me. Taller than me with a bald head and wide shoulders, he looked like a WWF wrestler. "Hey, baby, you want to come dance with me?"

Do I know this guy? Hell, I don't even know what day it is right now.

"Sure, why the hell not?"

Seductively, I ran my hand up and over his arm, gaining a smile from him. Taking my hand, he led me toward the back of the club and into a more private area.

Once at our destination, he pulled me close to him, running his hands up and down my curves as I moved to the music.

"You are one sexy bitch," he said, talking in my ear so I could hear him over the music.

I looked up at him as the room spun slightly and grabbed his neck to keep from tipping over before turning around to, for lack of better words, grind on him. *Right now, I have no shame.* My hair fell over my face as we moved to the beat of the music. It felt good to be seductive and sexy. I hadn't realized how much I missed it until this moment.

Opening my eyes, I registered that someone was standing in front of us but I brushed it off and continued dancing. Moments later, I still sensed someone in front of us. My hair flew back sending the smell of my shampoo through the air as I tried to see who was in front of us. My eyes focused on the figure and I fell back into the large bald man as Spencer took a step closer.

"Dude, back the fuck up, I got this," the man behind me said, holding on tighter around my waist.

"No, you don't. Now take your hands off her," Spencer said, looking solely at the man behind me as if I wasn't even there.

"Who the fuck are you? Get a life man, she's with me."

Laughing at the man, Spencer rubbed the stubble on his face as he took another step closer, pinning me between the two of them. My face was just under his neck and I was hit with his scent. *Oh God, come on knees hold it together.*

"She's not with you, she's with me."

The way he said it, so possessively, sent a chill up my spine. I quickly sobered up. Not waiting for another word to leave the bald man's mouth, Spencer grabbed my arm roughly. The familiar jolt of electricity made my heart jump to life. It had been over two weeks since he'd touched me but it didn't change the way my body reacted to him. My heart raced and heat pooled between my legs.

He turned abruptly, leading me out of the main area and into what I could only guess was his office, hence the big desk and computer. He tossed me in, slamming the door behind him. I stood there, not really sure what was going on. I watched as he walked around the back of the desk running his hands roughly through his dark hair, his three-piece gray suit hiding his perfect body from sight. He turned abruptly to look at me.

I stared back at him, not giving into his obvious disappointment in me. *Like I've said before, I don't need another good-looking disapproving brother.* "I was fine out there. You didn't have to rescue me. Why the hell are you here, anyway? Aren't you supposed to be on the west coast?" I said, crossing my arms.

"Elizabeth, don't do this right now," he said, almost yelling.

"Don't do what? I was dancing. Trying to forget everything, ya know, like these past two weeks for instance," I yelled back, louder than necessary.

"Well, they haven't been a fucking picnic for me either," he roared. "Why would you let someone touch you like that?"

I held my ground, making sure that I kept my wits about me. "What does it matter to you? You come and go as you please. Why can't someone else? Stop acting like you care, because clearly you don't."

"You have no idea what I'm going through, or what I'm giving up. But you, little miss-be-nice-to-everyone-but-Spencer, you can't even be bothered to do the same for me. You always cater to him. Why do you keep holding on to him? He's not even here. Look around, Elizabeth. It's just us. It's always been just us. Stop pretending he's standing in the room, judging you, he's not. He's not here." His voice was harsh and desperate.

"This is all about Simon, isn't it? It has nothing to do with tonight, does it?"

His eyes were on fire as he yelled at me. "Of course, it's about him! It's about him, and us, and this whole fucked up situation!"

Jealously is a bitch. I had done this to him. I had made this strong, determined man, question himself.

He paced back and forth, as if having an internal battle in his mind. "Fuck it, I don't care." The words weren't even off his lips before his mouth landed on mine. Wrapping his long fingers on either side of my head, he kissed as if like he wasn't going to be able to do it again.

Deep down, that was what I had wanted since the beginning. I had tried to push it down, keep it from the forefront of my mind, but I had lost that battle the moment he looked at me that first night at Mood. It was only now that I realized it.

Pulling back from me, he rested his forehead on mine. "Not here, not like this. Come with me?"

Hell, yes! I would go anywhere with him right now. I nodded, not moving my face from his, feeling his smile rather than seeing it. Taking my hand in his, he pulled me out of the office and through a door that led to an elevator.

When the doors opened, I didn't even have time to fully look around. I saw an impressive wall of windows, looking out over the New York City skyline. He rushed me down the hall and in to a room. We stood before a huge bed, its crisp white sheets catching the light from the city below us.

"Shut up and just listen to me, please," he said, holding my hands in his.

I scowled at him. *He can't talk to me like that.* I tried to open my mouth but his hand quickly covered it.

"Nope, no talking, just listen."

I exhaled and shrugged my shoulders, seeing as I couldn't say anything else.

"I need you," he said removing his hand from my mouth. "I haven't been myself since I met you and it scares the shit out of me that I feel this way."

Shit, I was thinking the exact same thing about him.

"I'm done trying to compete. I'm taking what I know is mine, what has always been mine," he confessed.

"Am I allowed to talk now?" I asked smartly.

"No," he said pulling me closer.

I heard the fabric of my dress rip down the seams before I felt it. *Damn it, that was an expensive dress!* Hastily he pulled it off, discarding the scraps on the floor. *Not fair.* Breathing heavily, I reached up yanking his jacket off angrily. I fumbled with the buttons on his vest before he just ripped them off. *I can take a hint.* I grabbed either side of his un-tucked shirt and ripped it open to reveal his bare chest. The buttons hit the floor, going in different directions.

Nothing mattered then, not my brothers, Gia, or what the media would say, not even Simon. The only thing that mattered to me right then was getting as much of Spencer Salvatore as I could. And I didn't care if the whole world saw me.

I watched his jaw tense up as my hands ran up his chest. His mouth crashed down on mine and our tongues danced back and forth. I noted the way his hand ran over my body, leaving my skin tingling underneath his touch and begging for more.

Moving me closer to the bed, he ran his hand up my neck then pushed my shoulders down so I sat on the edge of the bed. I scooted back, grabbing a pillow and placing it in front of my stomach. I needed to have a safety blanket in front of me. I was afraid he'd get a look at me without clothes and change his mind.

With a sly smile across his face, he leaned down kissing me again, I released the pillow, my hands going to either side of his face. The pillow that was protecting me was moved from my lap and hit the floor with a thud. *Damn it! My safety blanket!*

"No hiding, I want to see everything. I want to see all of you," he said, kissing just below my ear, sending a chill down my spine and heat between my legs. I leaned back from him, looking closely into his beautiful cool eyes. *Shit, they are actually sparkling.*

I watched, open mouthed, as Spencer did the most erotic thing I had ever seen in my life. Backing away from the bed, he lowered his head. His black hair fell from its slicked back position. The few strands swept over his eyes, but that didn't stop him from looking through them and down at me. I was going to put a hole through my own lip at this rate. He wasn't even touching me and I was on the verge of an orgasm. *How the hell am I ever going to make it through sex? Oh my God, I'm going to have sex with him.*

Reality hit and I began to panic. I tried to look everywhere but in his eyes.

Clearing his throat, he gained my attention again, but the

whole situation was so hard to believe that I found my eyes wondering away from him again.

"Eyes on me, Monroe."

I looked at him, dazed and terrified. But I turned away again, as shyness crept in. I was not a shy person. *Why can't I look at him? I know why. I'm afraid that I'll never be able to look away.*

He leaned back over the bed and took my chin between his fingers, forcing me to look at him. "Take them off me again and you're going to regret it," he said, half smiling and half sneering at me.

Standing up, he raised his hands and loosened the tie that was still around his neck, but left it so it hung loosely. Unbuttoning the few buttons that I wasn't able to rip open, he slid his shirt apart. And that's when I got my first glimpse of his hard muscular body up close. The moon light from the window made his tan skin glow. Dark hair was lightly dusted across his chest and down his abdomen and continued teasingly under his—

I can't take it anymore. I rushed from the bed to stand before him as my hand went up his chest and around his shoulders. Pushing the fabric of his shirt down and off his shoulders, my fingers traveled up his defined arms. My mouth went dry as I touched his chest. I stopped over an angry scar that went down right over his heart. The raised skin was the only imperfection I could find on his body. He inhaled deeply, hissing as I left kisses up and down the scar.

The clasp of my bra released, and we both watched as it fell to the floor. His hand made contact and cupped my breast. My head fell back, and the moan I had been holding in escaped my lips.

He took me back over to the bed, stepping away from me again. *Doesn't he realize I appreciate the whole strip tease, but let's face it, it's a tease and I need more—now.*

"Get on the bed and lay down." There was no sound of jovialness in his voice. His expression was stone cold and serious.

I stood there slightly confused, questioning his request.

"I said get on the bed and lay down."

Really? He's bossing me around? Doesn't he know yet that that doesn't work for me, the whole being told what to do and all?

I shook my head and I crossed my arms defiantly. "No."

"Stubborn woman, you really don't know what's good for you. You see, I do. I know exactly what's good for you and do you know what that is, Miss Monroe?" He paused as I shook my head no at his question. "It's you lying down on that bed so I can fuck you all the way to tomorrow."

Without even realizing it, I backed up and got on the bed.

"Good Choice," he said, moving to crawl over top of me.

His large frame made me feel small beneath him. Taking my hands, he pinned them above my head. Letting go of control wasn't hard anymore, I quickly embraced the way he took control of me, silently praying he made good on his previous statement.

Good God, I was going to lose it. I watched as he took each of my nipples tenderly between his lips. Involuntarily my hips moved up to meet his. *How is it possible that he still has pants on?* He was going to torture me all night. I could see it already, *but I think I'm going to like it.*

I kept watching as he kissed his way down my stomach. Automatically, I sucked it in, not wanting to appear flabby against his rock hard body. Stilling, he looked up at me. A sly smile turned his lips up at me before continuing on.

Tracing my lacey boy shorts with his fingers he slipped them off smoothly, down my hips, past my thighs, around my knees, and finally over my ankles and off my feet. Kissing the tips of my big toes, his hands slid slowly down the inside of my legs, pushing them apart. Warm fingers ran over my core. *Oh my God!*

Arching off the bed and closing my eyes the moment his fingers entered me, I instantly felt a tightness building up. The unexpected velvety feeling circling my core was an amazing surprise. *Damn, if he doesn't know exactly what is good for me.*

His tongue slid between my folds slowly, his fingers still

moving rhythmically inside of me. I couldn't help what came next even if I'd wanted to. Heat radiated from my core, release was just around the corner.

"Come for me, give me what I want." Spencer's deep voice vibrated through me as he beckoned for my release.

I lost it, everything. Self-control, self-awareness, it all went out the window as I called his name begging him not to stop. Moving with me as my hips flexed off the bed, he continued until he felt the last ripple run through my body. I lay there, panting, as I watched him stand from the bed. *He still had his pants on?* Not for long.

The first glimpse of him was everything I had hoped it would be. I watched as he slid a condom over himself. Heat pooled between my legs again and I was ready for more. Crawling back on the bed, not taking his eyes off mine, he slowly made his way over me and finally in me. *Oh, this shouldn't feel this good.* I was tight around him, the perfect mixture of pain and pleasure.

Kissing my chin, he pushed even deeper. I reached up and grabbed a fist full of black hair from the back of his head and pulled him down over me. My hands ran up and down his back, feeling the curve of his body as he moved above me. Again my insides burned with the promise of a sweet release.

Once my eyes locked on to his, I couldn't tear them away. I tried to wait longer because I didn't want him to move off of me. Heaven help me, I didn't want him to go anywhere. Gripping on tighter to his arms, my fingers dug into his skin as I came undone for a second time. Taking my cries in a kiss, he growled back seconds later as he moved faster in me.

He supported himself on his elbows, his weight pressing me down into the mattress. And I loved it. I loved the way it felt to have him on top of me. I didn't want him to move, not for anything. Kissing my lips softly, he pulled out and moved from over top of me. I curled into the pocket of his arm and ran my fingers over his damp chest.

"Stay with me," he asked, kissing my forehead.

Well I certainly wasn't going to say no to him after all that. Reaching up, I gave my answer with a kiss.

I took advantage of the quiet moment between us and caressed his face, making sure to take in every inch of it. Examining him for the first time, no secret notes, stolen glances, I didn't have to worry about getting caught so I took my time and really studied him.

I started at his forehead, ran my fingers through his hair. It was soft and thick. My fingers got lost in it and it smelled as good as it looked, all messy and wild. My thumb ran over his thick eyebrow and down his strong cheek bones. The bridge of his nose had a slight curve to it like it had been broken once before. His eye lashes were thick and black as night. He had a small scar on his right eye, hidden conveniently in his smile lines. You wouldn't know it was there unless you were close up on it. Another small scar lay on the left side of his upper lip. I wanted to know what happened to him, why each scar was there. I wanted to learn everything I could about the mystery man that was Spencer Salvatore. But for now, I was content with the silence. The way we argued back and forth, silence was golden.

My finger stilled over the small scar on his lip. Parting them, he caught my finger between his lips. His tongue licked the underside of my finger seductively. Releasing it, he tugged me up off the bed and, before I knew it, he had moved under me. Laying his hands on either hip, he stared up at me. I leaned over him, kissing him deeper as his hands ran down my thighs and back up to my hips.

This could be trouble. I wasn't good on top. *Please don't let me mess this up with all my insecurities.* His hands moved from my hips, spread across my stomach, and up between my chest. The instant he did it, I sucked in and sat as straight as I could. *The longer I make my body, the less frumpy it will appear.* Taking his hands off me the minute I did, he placed them casually behind his head. He cocked a smile at me and I felt a heat rush to my face.

What is he doing? I averted my eyes from him. *I don't want to see his face. I'm sure he's disgusted at how I look on top of him.*

I waited for him to move me off but he didn't.

"Elizabeth, eyes," he said in a deep seductive voice.

I looked back down at him, feeling insignificant.

"Why do you do that?" he asked, adjusting the hands that were behind his head. The muscles flexed in his arm with each move he made and I was finding it hard to do anything but stare down at him, until I realized what he had just asked me.

No shit, he is calling me out!

"Do what?" I responded, trying to sound clueless.

"You know what. Don't do it again."

His voice was stern and sexy as hell but—

"Excuse me?" I said, crossing my arms defiantly. *I hate being told what to do! When will he catch on to that?*

"Don't do it again. You wouldn't be here right now if I didn't think every inch of you was perfect. Do you understand me?"

No I don't. My doubting self would probably never understand what he saw in me. I stared down at the perfect specimen below me, and it was ridiculous how much it was messing with my head. I didn't understand why he would want me, so I shook my head and buried my hands in my hair, hiding my face from him.

Sitting up abruptly, he engulfed me in his long arms. His hands moved mine, pulling my hair together and letting it fall over my back. He held a hand to my cheek as he spoke. "You are perfect to me, and you better not forget it."

I stared in his eyes, in true disbelief. "I—I'm not—"I stuttered.

"Shut up, Monroe, just shut up. Don't fight me on this because I'm right tonight and you're wrong. Get over it."

He kissed my lips then lay back down on the bed, his hands going behind his head again. I was really speechless. *This rarely happens to me.* So I did what felt like the natural thing to do after someone tells you that. I adjusted myself over him, rolling my hips to take him in fully. *Who knew? Spencer without a condom is even better.*

I relaxed on him. Moving on him, without worrying what I looked like, gave me a chance to enjoy being on top. Previously I had avoided it like the plague but with Spencer I was able to put my insecurities aside for the first time and just be in the moment with him, or moments in our case.

Chapter 22

I woke up not sure of my surroundings. Taking a second to look around I felt an arm pull me closer, and a very hard erection push against my back. *Holy Shit, I slept with Spencer. I slept with him and it was everything that I had ever imagined—and more.*

The clock on the nightstand read eleven-forty-eight a.m. We had fallen into a deep sleep. Hell, we needed it after the night we just had. Keeping still so as not to wake him, I took the chance I didn't get last night to really examine the room around me.

There were no pictures hanging on the walls or anything personal. Except for the one and only picture frame that sat on the night stand. A young woman hugged a dark-haired, blue-eyed little boy. Spencer and his mother had the same blue eyes and tan skin. They looked truly happy in the photo.

Was this the last time he was truly happy? The picture was taken in New York. I'd know that backdrop anywhere. Turning my head slightly in the other direction, I saw the bathroom across the room. Once I saw it, I magically had to pee. *Damn, I don't want to move, but if I don't get up, I might really embarrass myself.*

I held up his arm, feeling the true weight of it as he continued to sleep. I wiggled out from his grasp and watched as he rolled over to lie on his back. Sitting up, I took the sheet off my legs and let my feet find the hardwood floor beneath them. Giving Spencer one last look, I giggled like a school girl as I watched him adjust himself under the covers. The simple action of him touching himself had me heating up again. Grabbing his shirt from the floor, I slipped it on. Attempting to button it, I quickly remembered that I couldn't because all the buttons were all over the floor. *Oh well.*

Quietly, I closed the door to the bathroom and turned the light on. When I finished, I took the time to snoop around. There was the usual toothbrush, comb, soap, and that intoxicating cologne he always wore.

Hearing Spencer stir in the bed, I made my way out of the bathroom. He was sitting up, his back leaning on the head board, his arms crossed over his bare chest, the sheet loosely over his waist.

"Hey," I said, holding the cuffs of his shirt in my hands.

"Nice shirt. I think you're missing a few buttons there," he said, eyeing me up and down.

"Well this crazy, wanna be playboy stalker ripped my favorite dress, I had to do something in retaliation." I said tilting my head innocently.

"Well, that crazy, wanna be playboy stalker thinks it looks better ripped up on his floor."

I crossed my arms and pouted at that. "Jokes aside, that really was my favorite dress you ripped."

"Like I said, it looks better on the floor."

Walking over to the bed, I hit his shoulder. "So you didn't like my dress?" I asked, straddling his waist.

"I like you naked. Besides, doesn't it look good down there?" He leaned over to get a look at the scraps of my dress.

"It was expensive. I would have liked to at least gotten my money's worth, before it went to rags," I said, placing my hands on my hips.

Running his fingers over the collar of his shirt, he smirked up at me. "I'm pretty sure you got your money's worth last night," he said, pulling me closer to kiss my neck.

Last night was—I abruptly came out of my little fantasy as reality once again ruined things between us. *Shit my brothers and Gia probably think I'm dead.* Sitting back from him, and taking him off guard, I went to move from his lap.

"I have to go," I said, panicking.

"What? Why?" he asked, gripping my waist so I couldn't move off of him.

"My brothers and Gia. I have to call them. They're probably looking for me."

I tried to wiggle but it was pointless.

"Elizabeth. They know you're with me."

A wave of relief washed over me. "Wait. How did you—"

"I sent a message to Charles while we were in the elevator." He rubbed my hips seductively and licked his lips.

That was a panty-wetting look if I ever saw one! Good thing I don't have any on.

"Well, don't you just think of everything?"

"I do, and now that you're with me, I can concentrate on even more."

Wait a minute. With him.

I had mind blowing sex last night but I didn't remember making this official. I still needed to talk to Simon. At the very least he deserved—he deserved someone better than me. That was what this all boiled down to. I had turned into the one thing I used to despise, a careless, thoughtless, wishy-washy, Barbie and a slutty one at that. Everything had felt so good in the moment, but I was drunk and not thinking. *What am I going to say to Simon? Fuck, what am I going to say to Spencer?*

Go figure, at that exact moment my phone started ringing from my clutch bag, which was somewhere on the floor. Spencer shot death rays at me as I got off of him and went to search for my bag. Once I found it, it began ringing again. Pulling it out I nearly cried. It was Simon. I wasn't going to answer, but I needed to get out of there. I shoved it back in my bag and looked over at Spencer who was shaking his head and laughing. He looked a little crazy, as if he had missed a couple of shock treatments at the mental institute. Needless to say, I was terrified at what had yet to come.

"Spencer I—"

"Don't," he said, sighing and holding his hand up. "Don't even start with the excuses. You chose to be here with me. Why the fuck do you keep doing this to me if you're in love with him?" he roared, slamming his fist into the mattress.

"I don't know if I'm in love with him—"

Cutting me off, he stood from the bed, and his deep voice shook the walls as he spoke. "Now!" he spit, as he moved closer to me. "Choose now!" he growled.

"I can't," I said back as sternly as I could.

"You can't or you won't?" Taking a step back, he turned from me shoving his hands through his tousled hair, the muscles in his back flexed, and I nearly went knees to the floor.

"You can't have us both, Elizabeth. You either stay with me, be with only me, love only me—or fucking leave."

His words were raw and savage as he turned back to face me. I couldn't talk, so I simply stared up at him. *This isn't happening, is it? Things were perfect five minutes ago, now everything is just wrong. It's all wrong.*

Coming quickly toward me, he grabbed my upper arms, taking me to lie down on the bed. He stared into my eyes before running his hand up the inside of my thigh. Two fingers slid deep inside me. Who was I kidding? Just seeing him made me aroused and arguing with him only made it worse.

"Can you honestly tell me you feel this when you're with him?" he asked, talking hoarsely in my ear.

My heart raced and my body betrayed me as I softened at his touch. Forcing his fingers in and out of me, he rubbed his thumb magically over me as he kissed my neck, breasts, and finally my lips. Crying out from the pleasure that I couldn't fight, I grasped at his arm and called out his name. He knew exactly what he was doing and what my body craved. Abruptly taking his fingers from within me he showed them to me, glistening in the mid-morning light. Then he ran his glistening fingers over my lips, before taking it all back in a kiss.

I held his face in my hands and stared into his eyes. Rage and passion filled my veins, and I didn't know whether to slap him or kiss him back. *Not like this.* He wasn't going to force me to pick him. Simon would be home in one day. He was going to have to wait one day.

"Can't you just give me one day to make this right—to make a decision?" I said, letting him go and pushing him off of me.

"You still need to make a decision? Elizabeth!" Standing from the bed, he set his fiery gaze upon me. "You are so stubborn. And fuck, I don't trust him. He's up to something. He's not good for you. He's going to hurt you. He already has. You just don't know it yet." he ranted.

I was totally confused by that. "What are you talking about Spencer? You don't know him," I said in Simon's defense.

"I know a lot more than I want to. If you stay with him, you're never going to be happy, you're never going to feel with him what you feel with me. There's no fucking way. I'm always going to be there in the back of your mind, just like you are for me," he said, pacing the room before coming to stand powerfully before me and hitting his own chest with his fist.

"You're one to talk, Salvatore," I yelled up at him.

I wanted to punch his chest but I dared not touch him. I needed to stay strong, and touching him would most likely do the complete opposite. "I've heard you've got skeletons in your closet too, hell we all do. You even told me I wasn't good for you, that being with me scared you to death. What are you scared of? That you're going to hurt me? Too late, yet here I am, against my better judgment, arguing with you. You don't know what Simon and I have, and it sure as hell doesn't involve him being so damn confusing."

He sat back on the bed, my last statement silencing him.

Defeated, he looked up at me. "Make a choice, Monroe."

I backed away from him and the bed. "Spencer, don't make me choose. I'm asking for one day. Give me one day," I begged

"Why? Why should I give you one day?"

I got down on my knees in front of him, begging for him to see the absurdness in all this. "Spencer, please don't make me do this." I took his hands in mine.

"Why? Because you'll choose him? Tell me I'm wrong."

Standing I let go of his hands, took a random pair of sweat pants off a chair, and put them on. I knew that I was delaying the inevitable.

"Fucking choose, Elizabeth!" he shouted from the bed, his face turned red with anger.

"I can't!" I yelled back.

"Why?" he asked, standing.

"Because—"*Here we go.* "Because if I choose you, I get hurt. You'll get tired of me and break my heart, if the media doesn't do it first. If I don't choose you, I get hurt because I'm not with you. This—whatever this is between us—might work. Hell, it might be amazing, but you're a hot head and I'm stubborn as hell. Look at us, Spencer. We're not even together and we're fighting about being together. We're going to lose either way." That was the truth. I didn't want it to be, but it was kind of hard to ignore. "If you make me choose now, I'm going to walk, and that will be on you, not me. If you give me the time I need, then maybe we can work it out. I'm asking for one day." I stared over at him desperately.

"One day shouldn't matter, Elizabeth. Choose."

I wanted to stay, I wanted to stay forever. But I needed to see Simon first. I needed to see if it was real with him or was it just convenient because Spencer was so here one moment and gone the next. I couldn't live with myself if I didn't at least give Simon a chance.

"Fine, Spencer. I'm not going to fight you anymore. I'm tired and confused." I grabbed my clutch and head for the door. Turning before I passed through it, I looked over at him.

He stood across the room naked, not even bothering to put his boxers on. I'd never be able to get that image out of my mind for as long as I lived. I wanted to run into his thick arms and forget about the rest of the world, but that was not the reality of it. We couldn't stay hidden in his room forever. If he wasn't willing to give me one day, how was I going to be able to give him all of mine?

"I get lost in you," I said, gaining his attention. "And I might get lost without you. You made this choice on your own. I don't know what else to tell you, Spencer. You'll always have a piece of me, and I'll never forget this night."

I turned away as a hot tear rolled down my cheek. Standing in the elevator, I pulled my phone out, slumped down on the floor, and made a call. "Gia—can you come get me?"

Chapter 23

I felt naked, standing in the upscale lobby of Spencer's place. No bra, no panties, I was wearing a men's dress shirt with no buttons and baggy sweat pants. If this wasn't the walk of shame, I didn't know what was.

Finally, Gia walked across the lobby, a large bag hung on her arm. I grabbed it and ran in the bathroom. I had given Gia strict instructions—come save me and make sure my brothers were nowhere in sight. The walk of shame was hard enough. I didn't need Teddy's disapproving looks or Charles's laughter.

Feeling more like myself in a fresh pair of jeans and T-shirt, I walked out of the bathroom toward Gia. "I need to get out of here. Let's go," I said, grabbing her arm, and headed for the door.

We sat in a café a few blocks away from my brother's place. I told Gia everything, no detail was spared. She got the good, the bad, and the sexy.

"I can't believe he called you at that exact moment," she said, sipping her coffee.

"It's weird, right?"

"Yeah it is. But how could he know? There is no way for him to know that if he's half way around the world. Are you going to tell Simon?"

I looked across the table at her trying to gage her thoughts. "I think I should. I can't keep going on like this. Maybe I need to just end it or tell him I need some time to figure things out." I stared out the window, my thoughts drifting back to my argument with Spencer. *How can we go from perfect to cata-*

strophic in less than five minutes? "Damn, that man is so frustrating. Hot then cold. I can't keep track of all his mood swings. It's exhausting."

Smiling across the table, Gia chuckled to herself.

"What's so funny about that?" I asked crossing my arms.

"You're not the most even tempered either. You can be a real stubborn ass when you want to."

She had a point but I wasn't going to let her know I agreed. "At least I have a little more finesse when I do it. So what happened after I was so rudely taken away last night?"

"Sure let's go with that," she said, taking another sip of her drink. "Chuck told me he wanted to date me, after I got done dancing with Teddy. I think he had too much to drink so I told him there wasn't a chance in hell I'd be caught dead with someone who sleeps around as much as he does. He didn't take that too well and disappeared for the rest of the night. Thank God, Teddy was there."

I watched as a dreamy look washed over her face. "You like him, don't you?"

Her pale cheeks went a crimson red. "Beth, come on. Teddy would never go out with me. He thinks I'm his little sister, not dating material."

Sneering across at her, I did a happy dance in my head. Finally, she was getting the right idea. "I wouldn't be so sure about that. Teddy definitely doesn't think of you like a sister."

Her mouth nearly hit the table in shock. "Shut up, that's not funny to joke about," she said, closing her gaping mouth.

"I'm not joking," I said through a Cheshire grin. "We need to get out of here. I need a shower and I think you need to have a talk with Teddy."

e/ഉc/ഉ

"Hello?" I said, walking through the door.

"We're in the kitchen" Charles said.

Coming around the corner, Gia and I were greeted with the sight of my brothers in only their boxers sitting on stools drinking coffee. I'm sure Gia appreciated the view.

"Well?" Charles said speaking to me.

"Well, what?" I asked back, throwing my bag over the couch.

"Was it everything you thought it was going to be, baby sis. I mean sleeping with the 'worlds sexiest man' is a big deal. He didn't disappoint, did he?"

I wanted to slap the smug smile off his face. Lucky for him I didn't have the energy. I walked to the sink and got a long drink of water to replenish my dehydrated body. "I'm going to pretend that I didn't just hear that."

"What? You can give me crap for sleeping around on women, yet you can't take it when it's you who is leading two men on."

What a jerk.

"Chuck," Gia said, gaining all our attention. "Drop it. Why are you so mean to her?"

Charles immediately stopped his attack on me. Maybe he was trying to show her he could behave. He was going to fail miserably but I wasn't going to let that stop me from watching.

"Beth, you can't keep seeing Spencer and Simon. It's not healthy," Teddy said very calmly.

I couldn't help it. I snapped at him for, once again, trying to tell me what to do. "I know, Teddy. Simon comes home tomorrow and I'm going to tell him everything and leave the ball in his court. Spencer—ugh that man is a fucking hot head!" I said, turning to fill my water up again.

"Did he hurt you? I told you to stay away from him. Goddamn that mother fucker—" Teddy looked like he was going to punch something. His disapproval for Spencer had hit an all-time high.

"He didn't hurt me. He wanted me choose right then and there, and I couldn't. I needed to talk to Simon first, and Spencer wasn't willing to wait for me to do that, so he kicked me out."

"Well, I'm glad you left. Simon is a great guy. Maybe it was a blessing in disguise," Teddy said, coming over to wrap his bare arm around me.

"Eww, Teddy put some clothes on before you touch me. I love you but not that much."

I watched as my brothers looked between one another and I knew exactly what was coming my way. Standing, Charles came closer. I tried to run, but Teddy caught my arm and full on hugged me. Charles of course joined in, too. They held tight to me and jumped up and down shouting "Elizabeth sandwich."

Why are brothers so gross?

ⓔⓢⓔⓢ

During the flight home, I noticed the change between Gia and Teddy. He held her hand as she rested her head on his shoulder. They were watching a movie and I was so happy. It seemed like they were going to give it a shot.

Charles sat across from me, sulking in his seat as he watched the two of them. "Why did you do it?" he asked.

"What are you talking about? What did I do now to ruin your life?"

He always found a way to blame everything on me. "Gia, why didn't you tell me she liked me?"

Really he's going to ask this right now? "Charles, she's my best friend, the only one I've got. I didn't want her to get hurt. You know how you are."

"If I had known—whatever, it's too late now. Looks like she's hopped on the Teddy ban-wagon."

"You only want her because you can't have her, Charles. You didn't even notice she was throwing herself at you for the past five years. I think it's for the best. And I think deep down you know that." I reached over and squeezed his hand reassuringly.

"I hope your right, because the way I feel right now, in this moment, I want to run over there and rip her away from him."

"Oh, don't be so dramatic. That's my job," I said, smiling across at him. "You know Danielle from your office has a thing for you. She's a sweet girl. You should ask her out. Like really ask her out. Don't just have sex with her."

Sitting up in his seat he appeared to think about what I just suggested. "She does have a tight ass little body."

"Okay, too much info there, but I guess that's a good start," I said, cringing.

"Thanks, baby girl."

"No problem, bro."

 презентация

I hung back at the airport, waiting anxiously for Simon's flight to arrive. I ran all possible scenarios through my head. And every single one of them ended with me—alone. I sat on the floor, checking e-mails while I waited. *Damn Fame doesn't miss a beat!* There on the front page was a photo of Spencer dragging me behind him and into his office. Our fight resonated in my mind for the millionth time that day.

Fames website is going to be the death of me. They managed to get a picture of my walk of shame through Spencer's lobby. *Great, icing on this already rotten cake.* The world had all the proof it needed to figure out that Spencer and I had slept together.

Why couldn't he just have given me one day? None of this would be happening right now. *Hell, I'd probably still be in his bed!* After I told Simon what had happened while he was gone, he was going to leave me, and I would have been free to choose Spencer. But no, he had to let his ego take over. He had his chance. He could have run after me. He could have chased me down on the street, but he didn't.

"Belle!"

I heard my pet name coming from behind me. Turning, I saw Simon jogging toward me. Getting up fast, I put my phone back in my bag. He looked the same, handsome, and his hair—he cut all his hair off. His warm smile was a sight for sore eyes.

Dropping his bags, he lifted me in his arms, spinning me around and kissing me. I didn't hesitate to kiss him back. I had missed him, but I hadn't realized how much until I was wrapped in his safe, warm arms.

"Damn, I missed you," he said, holding either side of my face. "Come on, we have to get out of here before I rip your clothes off."

I couldn't help but laugh. "Calm down there, cowboy." I grabbed my bag off the floor, as he led me quickly to the exit of the airport.

The ride in the elevator up to his hotel room was torturous. All I could think about was that he was so happy right now. But in five or ten minutes, he was going to hate me. Only letting go of my hand to pull his bags, he led me into his hotel room.

I stood in the door way, frozen. My stomach was doing flips and I thought I was going to throw up at any moment. I watched as he threw his suit cases in the closet. I couldn't step over the threshold of the door. Gripping my purse, I watched as he registered my appearance.

"What's wrong?" he asked, standing a few feet in front of me. Concern washed across his face.

Here we go...

Chapter 24

I watched Simon's smile fade from his face as he realized something was wrong. I stood my ground, standing in the door way. I couldn't go in. I somehow felt stronger standing outside the room. Taking a calming breath, I began. "Simon, I have to tell you something. Why don't you sit down?"

The room was small with a chair right as you walked in at a desk.

"I'm fine standing. What's going on?" he asked, taking a step closer to me.

Instantly, I held up my hands, making him stop dead in his tracks. If he held my hand or brought me inside, I wasn't sure if I would have the strength to tell him what I needed to.

"Baby," he said, confusion on his face. He went to reach for my hand.

"Simon! Stop, just stop. There's someone else." I spit it out in frustration to get him to stay put. I didn't want to say it like that but, there it was.

His concerned face turned sour as bewilderment crept up. One step, then two, he backed away from me cursing to himself and hitting the table with his fist.

"Simon, I'm sorry, it just happened. I tried to stop it but—"

"Do you love him?" he asked, cutting me off.

"I—I don't know," I answered honestly.

I watched him pace back and forth, talking to himself. "I knew it. I knew deep down—fuck, why did I even do this for her?" He continued to mumble, but low so I couldn't hear him.

"I swear I didn't want it, I didn't want any of it," I said in my defense.

Hearing my voice made him come back and walk straight at me. "I'm not leaving you. I was gone but now I'm back and I will fight like hell to win you."

What is going on here? I just told him I like someone else and he's not running for the hills. He's not kicking me out or telling me to drop dead?

This wasn't at all how I expected this to go. I wanted him—needed him—to be mad at me. I wanted him to yell in frustration for deceiving him, tricking him. But he just stood there, holding my hands begging me to give him a chance. *No.* He needed to understand that I was a horrible person.

I needed him to punish me, yell at me for Christ sake. Letting go of his hands, I dug in my purse for my phone and brought up Fame's page. I brought up all the incriminating pictures and shoved them in his face. "This is what I've been doing while you were gone." I did it hoping to spark some anger in him.

He looked at them then, as I swiped my finger from picture to picture. "Stop," he yelled, pushing my phone away. "I don't care what happened. What I care about is right now, and right now I'm here and I want you. We can start over, pretend this never happened."

That wasn't what I wanted, either. Annoyance took over as I shoved my phone back into my bag. Now I was downright furious that he wasn't more upset that I had betrayed him.

"I slept with Spencer Salvatore!" I yelled. "Simon, I slept with him two days ago and I didn't even think about you."

Instantly, I knew that I had gone too far. Pulling my hands up to cover my mouth, I wished that I could take it back. Unfortunately for him, it was the truth. Maybe the truth was what he needed to hear, to realize who I really was—a severely messed up chick.

He finally stepped back and silently leaned up against the chair for support. His expression was blank, no emotion at all. He stayed there for a few minutes, staring at the floor. The silence in the room was deafening.

"Say something, Simon. Just say something," I yelled at him, still needing him to punish me for what I had done to him, to us.

"What do you want me to say, Elizabeth?" he asked, looking up from his now-sitting position in the chair.

His elbows rested on his knees, his hands clasps together. I could finally see some anger tensing up his forearms as he spoke to me. I braced myself for what came next, what he should have said the moment I told him I was with someone else.

"You want me to call you a slut?"

Yes. I closed my eyes waiting to hear the rest.

"Well, you're not."

Huh? What the hell?

"You want me to hate you? I can't."

I stood there, dumfounded.

"Am I hurt? Of course, I am. I'm fucking human, Elizabeth, but how can I blame this solely on you? I was the one who left. I left you with him. God help me, I just left. I saw it all happening, even before you did. I tried to ignore it, because you were telling me you cared for me. I—I was naive in thinking that the media was blowing things out of proportion."

My jumbled mind tried to process all he'd said, but the one thing that stuck out was that he saw everything, or better yet that he saw everything happening.

"You saw everything happening?" I thought back to all the photos that were taken, the ones on my father's desk sticking out over the rest.

"Yes, I saw everything," he said, exaggerating the word everything.

God, I feel dirty. How did I get myself into this mess? Blue eyes and a chance at a fairy-tale ending, that's how.

"Why aren't you with him now?" Simon asked, standing from his chair.

"He made me choose, stay with him or leave."

Something I'd said made Simon hesitate. "So he's known about me the whole time. He knows who I am? You told him about me." He sounded crazy as he asked me questions, like he was a secret agent who might be about to have his cover blown. "He knew and still pursued you?" he asked.

"Simon, he didn't pursue me. He—we just kept running into each other. It was innocent, until it wasn't." Rubbing my face, I took a moment to rein in my thoughts.

"So let me get this straight. He made you choose him or leave?"

"Yes," I replied.

"You left him? So you chose to be with me?" he asked hopefully.

Shit, how do I say this? "I did leave, but I left because I needed to tell you everything before I made a decision. Spencer wasn't willing to give me time to tell you and figure out where my heart belonged." I lowered my head and ran my hands through my hair, trying to relieve whatever stress I could.

"So you left him, to come tell me with the chance that I might leave you, too."

Nodding in agreement

I glanced back up at him.

"Well, that was his loss. I'm not leaving and I want you to take as much time as you need to figure it out," he said.

I stood there mesmerized by his maturity—the fact that he could put his ego aside and give me a chance to figure out how I felt. *Why was he doing this? I don't deserve this. Him.* He was so caring and compassionate and the complete opposite of Spencer Salvatore.

I walked over to him, finally crossing the threshold of the room. The door closed behind me as I made my way to stand before him.

"I'm so sorry, Simon."

Reaching his hand up, he brushed a tear off my cheek, which I hadn't even realized was there. I couldn't help leaning into his warm hand.

"You're beautiful and a major pain in the ass, you know that?"

I laughed against his hand and nodded in agreement.

"Elizabeth, please just let us start over," he begged, leaning over and leaving a soft kiss on my lips.

He pulled me into him. Holding on tightly around my waist, he rested his head on my shoulder.

I had to fight to gain control over my body and eventually I did. Pulling back, I held my hands up to his chest. "I think I should go," I said against him.

"Yeah. Okay," he said reluctantly.

Taking a step back I turned toward the door.

"Belle" he called, making me smile and turn back to him. "I want this, I want you. Call me when you make your choice."

I smiled back at him before opening the door and leaving. Standing on the other side of the door, I sighed in relief. That wasn't what I expected but at least everyone knew. There was no more secrets, no more burdens on my shoulders, except for the fact I had to decide what I was going to do. *Wait around to see if Spencer…well, I guess see if Spencer even cares that I'm alive, or start over with Simon.* I had a huge choice to make and, either way, someone was getting hurt.

If I choose Spencer, I would crush Simon. If I started over with Simon, then I finally had to put Spencer to rest for good, forever.

⁂

I woke up praying that the past four months had been a dream, but they weren't. I thought that once I told Simon everything, he would leave. Deep down, I kind of hoped he would, just so I wouldn't have to go through this anymore.

I was ready to go back to normal. The media was being so harsh. I wanted to stay barricaded in my room, *for eternity.* How could people be so cruel to another human being?

Against my better judgment, I'd sat up all night reading any and everything that had my name attached to it. Like I said, bad idea. Just because I wasn't a size two, people hated me. They hated the fact that an attractive man like Spencer would even give me the time of day. It was bad enough that they were attacking me, but they were also attacking him. With every good compliment, there were at least five to go against it. Spencer and I had taken over social media, and I hated it. I hated all of it.

It wasn't even worth it, anymore. All the baggage that came along with Spencer was just too much. The way he acted wasn't worth me throwing my whole life's work away. *Was it? I'm not made for the media. I've always left that to my brothers.*

I needed to do something. Slamming shut the computer, that still showed all the mean comments, I walked in my closet to grab my suitcase. Throwing it on the bed, I unzipped it and begin unpacking. Back to normal. I needed to keep my mind occupied and unpacking was going to be my distraction.

Throwing the dirty clothes on the floor and laying the clean ones on the bed to re hang, I quickly realized that it wasn't the best idea. Staring at me from the bottom of my suite case was Spencer's white shirt.

That shirt represented the best and worst night I had ever had with him, and just in general. Some of the strings from the buttons I had ripped off lay flat against the white fabric. Closing my eyes, I had a flash of the memory of how strong his chest felt under my hands. It took me right back and that's when I smelled it. Spencer's scent drifted under my nose, making the memory even sweeter.

This is insane. A shirt shouldn't have this much of an effect on me. It's a fucking shirt! A really good smelling shirt, but a shirt nonetheless. Grabbing the shirt and sweatpants that lay underneath, I walked them over and into my closet. I granted myself one more sniff before tossing them into the black abyss that was the back of my closet, never to be seen again, or at least not until spring when I cleaned it out.

There, that wasn't so hard. Pulling my hair back off my face, I cringed when I smelled it on my hands. Running into the bathroom, I quickly got a glob of soap and washed them. Content that they didn't smell anymore, I smiled up at myself in the mirror. "Beth, you are a strong independent woman. You don't need someone like Spencer Salvatore telling you what to do and who to be with."

I nodded back at my reflection and really took a moment to look at myself. Maybe I was beautiful. I might have flaws, but everyone did. I wasn't going to let Spencer or the media ruin me, anymore. He hadn't thought of anyone but himself when he'd made me choose and I wasn't going to let the paparazzi or people's nasty comments affect me, or get me down. It took all this bullshit, but I knew then that I was perfect for me, and that was all that I should be worried about. I was going to concentrate on me, like I should have been doing all along.

I missed my easy-going life. I missed hanging out with Gia. I missed sitting at home watching TV, and I couldn't do all that if I was with Spencer. If I would have stayed with him, my life would have changed. I'd have to be that girl I used to hate. I'd be followed by paparazzi. I'd have to go with Spencer to fancy clubs and red carpets. That was not what I wanted out of life. I wanted a family. I wanted to stay in one place and, most importantly, I wanted to stay out of the spot light.

I could have that life with Simon. I could be happy with him. But the doubt that Spencer had planted in my mind was slowly taking over. Like a disease, it kept coming back to the forefront of my mind. "You'll never feel for him the way you feel for me."

He was right. I might not, but it was better than having nothing at all. *And let's face it, I'm terrified that I'll never find someone as good hearted and kind as Simon.*

Chapter 25

The week went by, and my life had slowly gotten back to normal. It was a Friday night and I was doing something normal—sitting around the house watching a movie. There was one thing that was different. Gia and Teddy lay cozily on the couch, holding each other as we all watched a TV movie.

Since they had made it official, Teddy had been over every day and night for the past week. One night, I needed Gia's approval for an orientation outfit for my internship. So not thinking anything of it, I walked into her bathroom while she was in the shower and started babbling about my clothes. When she didn't answer me, I got concerned and pulled the curtain aside—not one of the better images I have of my brother. Then I walked in on them having a little too much fun on our kitchen table which made me take new precautions around the house. I had made it imperative to announce very loudly whenever I was entering a room.

When the show went to a commercial, Gia turned to me, serious and expecting answers that I had been withholding for the past week. I had been avoiding all questions involving my love life, and it was obvious that she was getting anxious for information.

"Are you ready to talk?" she asked, totally out of the blue.

I made my eyes large and nodded over at Teddy. There was no way I was going to spill my guts, especially in front of my over-protective brother. He'd probably have a hit out for both men, even if Simon didn't do anything wrong.

Just as I said "No," Teddy's phone went off on the coffee table, vibrating so much it almost fell to the floor.

Sitting up with him, Gia moved over so he could reach for the phone.

"Theodore Monroe, talk to me."

I watched as his expression hardened when he heard the voice on the other end. I knew immediately it was Spencer. I'd know that voice, muffled or not.

"Spencer, how can I help you? I told you to contact Chuck with any questions this week."

I tried not to listen, but I couldn't help it. I caught a few things. Something about a mistake and it was imperative that he spoke with Teddy, now. Typical Spencer, thinking the world revolved around him. Not Teddy, not my brother. He wouldn't get up and—

"Hold on," Teddy said into the phone.

Well, I guessed Teddy was victim to his demands as well. Kissing Gia's cheek, he covered the phone. "I have to deal with this. I'll be right back." Getting up from the couch, he went to the door and walked outside in the hallway.

Starring at the door, I tried to listen but the soundproof walls and door were too thick to hear anything.

"Well?" Gia asked. "You finally going to tell me what happened with Simon?"

Better to get it over with because she wasn't going to stop pestering me.

"Short story—he still wants to make it work. He told me he wanted to start over."

Gawking back at me, Gia shook her head in disbelief. "You've got a fucking horseshoe up your ass! He wasn't even mad?"

"Trust me, I don't and, of course, he was mad. But he blames himself for leaving. He told me to take my time to figure out what I want."

The wheels clearly turned in Gia's head. "Do you think he cheated, too? And that's why he's not upset. That would make so much sense," she suggested.

Damn it, she's got a point. I am a fucking door mat for

men. He was messing around with someone, too, and here I thought he was a good guy. "I have to ask him. It would almost be better if he did, right? I mean, he is a good-looking guy. You know Danielle at the boys' office? She was drooling all over him."

Nodding in agreement, Gia took a sip of her drink. Placing it back down she got this really serious look on her face, and I knew the next question before it was out of her mouth. "What about Spencer?" Sitting back on the couch, she got comfortable and waited for my response.

"What about him? He's a fucking jerk!" I white-knuckled the pillow in my lap as I spoke.

"Calm down there, hulk. Don't rip the pillow apart."

I looked down and released my tight grip on the pillow. "He did this, not me. It's on him," I said, smoothing the crinkled pillow.

"You are so stubborn, both of you are actually," she stated.

"No shit, that's why it will never work—" I stopped talking and stared down at the pillow.

"But? There was a 'but' in there. I can see it," she said, pointing at me.

"No there's not," I snapped.

"Yes there is, and the but is that you're scared that you're never going to get over him. I get it. He took you for an emotional, sexual, exciting ride, and you're afraid no one is ever going match it."

Okay, so what if that had crossed my mind? Most people have a great love or fling that they wished would have worked out or lasted longer.

That was simply what I had to keep telling myself. Spencer was my once-in-a-lifetime, toe-curling, heart-pounding fling. The kind you tell your grandchildren about when you were old and dying. The back in my day a boy swept me off my feet. He was strong, handsome, and wealthy, then it all went to shit, and I met your granddad. *You know? The story you've heard a million times?*

"Gia, I can't keep going round and round with him. He's got issues and I'm—I'm—ah, who am I kidding? I'm so torn.

My heart is literally torn between them. I don't deserve either one, especially Simon."

Gia came over and sat her skinny little butt next to me in the chair, hugging me tightly. "You do deserve a good guy. Now whether it's Simon or Spencer, I don't know, but Simon is willing to let you decide. That's got to stand for something. Maybe you should start over with him, if you really think you are done with Spencer. Speaking from experience, don't go with one if you're not truly over the other."

Hugging her arm that was draped across my chest, I felt better. I should have talked to her earlier and avoided all this back and forth nonsense.

Twenty minutes later, Teddy came barging back through the door. "I have to go. They are having issues with the club. Spencer needs me there because he can't get a hold of Chuck and neither can I," he said, irritated.

With only a week until Christmas and then a week until the opening, Teddy was slowly getting overwhelmed. With Charles off doing God knew what, with God knew who, all the businesses they had together, including the club, were falling on Teddy's shoulders.

He stood in front of us and I couldn't help but think that he was holding something back. "What is it Teddy, spit it out," I snapped, not at him but in annoyance that Spencer must have gotten him involved in our drama.

"There's nothing to say. If there was, I'd tell you—promise." Walking over, he kissed my head then Gia's cheek. "I'll call you later," he said, looking at us both before leaving.

"Do you think Spencer said something to him?" Gia asked

"I don't know and right now I don't give a fuck. Even if he did, I don't think it would change how I feel." *Lair*! *I said to myself. You do care and it would change how you feel, but no one needs to know that.*

ℰᔆℰᔆ

Avoiding the press was, sadly, part of my routine now. I sat down on the couch in the café, thankful that they had told all the paparazzi that they weren't allowed inside. They also let me sneak in the back door.

I was one chapter into my book when the door opened and a chorus of voices called inside asking me questions. There had to be something more interesting going on than me sitting at a café, reading a book. Shaking my head in disgust, I continued reading.

"Belle?"

I froze. Simon. Simon was standing in front of me. Not only could I see his shoes, but I could smell his cologne. Closing my book, I turned to look up at him. "Hey, Simon." *Damn, he looks good.* He had spiked his hair up and it looked good on him. Unfortunately, I looked like shit in my leggings, sweat shirt, and messy bun on top of my head. My excuse for looking like shit? I was incognito.

"Is it sad that I have been coming here every day hoping to run into you?"

Every day? I smiled up at him, as I placed my book next to me. "It's a little creepy, but also cute. Do you want to sit down?" I asked, gesturing next to me.

"I'd love to," he said, placing his bag on the floor before sitting down. "I don't mean to sound forward, well maybe I do. Have you decided anything?"

Have I? Was I ready to let go of Spencer? He hadn't made any attempt to contact me whether it was through my brothers or his confusing one-liner notes. Every day it was getting easier to put him in the past. I hadn't planned on starting over with Simon when I woke up that morning, but seeing him in front of me put things in perspective. I still cared for Simon, and I did miss him. *So, what the hell? It couldn't get any worse, right?* So yes, I think I had decided.

I turned to Simon, grabbing his hands in mine clearly taking him by surprise. "Simon, if I say yes to you, that I'm willing to start over, I need you to answer a few questions."

Still in shock Simon squeezed my hands, nodding to my request.

"Did you sleep with someone while you were overseas?"

"No" he said quickly. Scooting closer he pulled my hands

towards his chest. "I haven't been with anyone but you since the night I first met you."

Well shit. Now I feel even worse.

"Why are you asking me that?" he asked.

"I just thought that if you had been with someone then maybe that's why you weren't upset when I told you about Spencer. You know? Eye for an eye."

"Beth, I cared about you. I still care about you. Don't get me wrong. I was pissed, really pissed. But how can I blame you? We were official for, what? Forty-eight hours before I left you? You're a hot commodity. What can I say? I was a fool for agreeing to leave you. Looking back now, I should have told my boss to go fuck herself and just dealt with the consequences."

Simon was a good man, and I didn't want to lose him, so I said, "Yes."

He questioned my "Yes," with scrunched eyebrows.

"Yes, I want to start over. As long as you don't leave me in the next forty-eight hours," I said, in all seriousness.

"I'm not going anywhere," he said, caressing my cheek.

I smiled. "Good."

Just like when we first came to our café months ago, the minutes slipped away turning into hours.

"Look at them," I said, pointing to the paparazzi still standing outside, waiting for me to leave.

"They love you, Beth. You're beautiful and normal. The public has latched itself on to you and they want to know more."

How the hell does he know what the public wants? "Really? And how do you know all this?" I asked, sitting back and crossing my arms.

"You're real. People can relate to you, unlike most in the spot light."

Is he saying what I think he's saying? People only like me because I'm not a stick figure? "I'm all for having better role models, but me? I don't think so." *Not this body-conscious brunette.* I hated the spotlight.

"Well, you are. All over the world, to be honest with you."

The world? "I don't want it. I don't want anything but my normal life back. I would kill to make it all go away. Don't even get me started on those Fame photographers. If I ever get my hands on one of them, they're going to need dental records to identify them!" *Ooo, I'm heated up now.*

"Killing might be a little over the top, don't you think?"

Shrugging my shoulders, I thought it over again. "I guess. Prison probably wouldn't suit me so well."

Smiling, Simon nodded in agreement. "Yeah, it wouldn't suit me either."

I laughed. *Damn, he's cheeky.* Reaching down into my bag, I pulled out my phone to check the time. "Do you think they will ever leave me alone?"

"Honestly, I don't think they are going anywhere if they still think you and Spencer are together."

I don't like that little smirk on his face. What's he getting at? "Well, what are we going to do about that?" I asked, placing my bag on my lap.

"Give them a show. Let them know you're with me and not him."

Sneaky. I see what he did there. "You think that would work?" I asked, amused at what he thought was a fool-proof plan.

"I know it will work," he said confidently.

He opened the door for me and I walked out as cameras went off all around me. Coming up behind me, Simon wrapped his arms around my waist and kissed my neck. The smile that came over my face actually hurt. I'd missed him. There was no denying that. I was falling for Simon all over again and I loved every minute of it. The paparazzi were eating it up, too.

Releasing my waist, he came to stand next to me, taking my hand securely in his. Walking hand-in-hand down the sidewalk, he leaned over and whispered in my ear, saying ridiculous things to make me laugh. I held on to his hand, reveling at how comfortable and natural it felt to have him so close, even after all that had happened. My feelings for Simon weren't a fluke. Maybe I'd made the right choice in leaving Spencer.

Not wasting any time, we hurried over to Simon's hotel room, the paparazzi still hot on our heels.

Standing outside of Simon's door, I didn't hesitate to walk over the threshold. We had a lot of missed time to make up for and I wasn't going to second guess myself about it.

Taking his shirt off and tossing it on the floor, he swept me up and into his embrace, kissing me tenderly. Resting his forehead on mine, he rubbed up and down my back.

"Thank you for choosing me. I don't deserve it, but I'm so grateful you did. I'm in love with you, and that will never change, no matter what."

I nodded up at him before pulling his face down to mine, kissing him. I didn't want to dwell on the past and the choices I had made. What I wanted to do was move on.

I pulled back from him, taking my sweat shirt off, leaving only a tank top between my skin and his. Reaching down, he grabbed the end, pulling it up and off my body. I took advantage of the moment of separation and turned around to slide my pants off, making sure to give a show as I did. He did the same, minus the show. I stood there in only my underwear, which for once wasn't boy cut, but rather a skimpy thong that I had been dying to get off, the moment I put it on. The tight leggings I had on required the thong or so Gia had so honestly informed me before I left the house.

Moving my hair to the side, he came up behind me, kissing up and down my neck, wrapping his hands around my waist. I stretched my body in what I hoped was an appealing way.

He latched his thumbs in either side of my underwear. "I like these," he breathed in my ear.

"Well, you can't have them, if that's what you're asking," I said, just as breathily.

"Oh, I don't want them, as long as you keep wearing them. They give me better access to this," he said, grabbing my ass tightly in his hands then letting go to gently smack it.

Whipping around, I saw that devilish smile of his. "You're bad, you know that?"

Leaning over, he kissed me, and I could feel the smile on his face, as the palm of his hand found my ass again.

He slapped my ass for a third time. "Hey!" I said, pushing him back.

"Don't act like you don't deserve it."

Ouch! *Guilt trip much*? Tugging me closer, he moved us to the bed. I watched in guilty pleasure as he removed his boxers and reached for his night stand. "You're lucky I have one of these," he said, returning with a condom.

"Yeah. Wouldn't want to resort to the 'Plan B' Pill." *I can't help myself.* I covered my mouth to keep from laughing, but it was useless.

"Ha, ha. Now get your ass over here," he said, grabbing my ankles and dragging me across the bed.

Crawling over me, he left a trail of kisses down my body. I threw my head back as his tongue glided over and in-between my legs. It was like coming home with him. His touch was soft and loving. When he came up and pressed into me, I expected it to feel tighter than it did. I wondered if he could tell. *Fucking Spencer and his huge cock ruined everything for me.*

Watching his large football frame move over me, I became more excited with every thrust. His hands pressed deeply into the mattress on either side of my head. I held tight on to his arms, moving my hips up to meet his.

Lowering his head to mine, he spoke softly. "I love you so much. I promise I'm never going to hurt you again."

Opening my eyes at his words, I studied his face. *What the hell was that about*? *Ahh, fuck who cares*? He moved a hand in between us, circling over my sensitive core as he continued driving into me at a steady pace.

"Oh God! Oh S—S—"*Shit, who am I with*? "S—Simon," I called to him as the walls within me pulsated in pleasure. *Holy crap that could have been so bad. Thank God, his name starts with an S, too.*

"That was worth it all," he said, as he lay next to me panting.

I nodded in agreement before turning away from him. *I can't believe I almost cried out Spencer's name.*

"Hey, are you okay?" Simon asked, turning my face back to his. "You look a little pale."

"Yeah, I'm fine. Just a little lightheaded." I tilted my head so I could kiss him.

Pulling me in close to him, he held me, rubbing my back with the tips of his fingers.

This was the start of something new between us. This was how normal people treated each other.

It doesn't get any better than this, right?

Chapter 26

The week rolled on and Simon and I acted like the past month and a half hadn't even happened. We had picked up right where we had left off, and I couldn't have been happier. I even invited him to spend Christmas with my family.

We drove from the airport to the family house in New York, with Teddy and Gia. I watched as they held hands across from us in the limo. Teddy looked so in love, but Gia—something was up with her. She stared out the window, seemingly deep in thought.

As much as I wanted my brother to be happy, I didn't want him to be with someone who wasn't equally happy with him. I couldn't help but think that maybe her feelings for Charles weren't as smothered as she once thought.

We watched as the boys carried the luggage up the front walk. Grabbing her arm, I turned Gia back toward me.

"What's up with you?" I asked her.

"Nothing, I'm fine," she said, trying to brush me off.

"Well, you seem a little off," I said, pulling her back again as she tried to twist from me.

"I'm fine."

Damn, I didn't expect the attitude. "Calm down, I'm just concerned. You haven't spoken since last night, and you kept to yourself the whole way here. It's just not like you."

Turning toe to toe with me, she took an aggressive step and got in my face. We were both tall but she had a few inches over me. "Look, I can guess where you're going with this, and you need to stop now. I'm not in some wild love triangle with your brothers. I'm not you! I can make a decision."

What the heck just happened? I can't believe her! How dare her? I'd done nothing but be there for her every time she'd needed me, and I never once had I threw it back in her face, like she was doing to me.

"Fuck you, Gia! At least I didn't sleep with every guy that walked on campus. Maybe you and Charles deserve each other." I steamrolled past her and walked toward the front door.

"At least I had a sex life the past four years!" she screamed from the walkway.

I stopped dead in my tracks. The last thing I ever wanted to do was argue with her, but here we were. Seemed whatever built-up animosity we had toward one another had just boiled over. "I'm not doing this with you, Gia. You come and talk to me when you want, and we both know you will. Until then, don't break my brothers' hearts, because as much as I care about you, I care about them more."

I continued my walk back to the house where Simon was standing in the doorway. He had to have heard it all. Smartly, he moved out of the way so I could walk by him and into the house.

ᖇᖇᖇ

"You okay?" Simon asked, standing in the doorway to my bedroom.

I had been calming down in my room for over thirty minutes, and I was okay, until he asked me.

"Ooo, she makes me so mad sometimes. And I'm the one with mood swings? Has she looked in the mirror lately?" Pacing my room, I continued to rant and rave.

"Wow, you're really pissed. Don't get mad at me, but you're really turning me on right now."

I shot daggers his way as he held his hands up in submission. "I swear if she hurts, Teddy—to be with Charles, of all people! That would kill Teddy."

Leaning against the door, Simon placed his hands in his

pockets and continued to watch me move about the room. "I didn't know she had a thing for Chuck," he commented, but I didn't really pay attention.

"She knew what I was going through. At least I wasn't sleeping with brothers!" I quickly looked at Simon. "You're not related to Salvatore in any way are you?" I asked, praying the answer was no.

"Not that I know of," he said, moving across the room to the bed. "Well, I did have a cousin—"

I pushed him and he fell back on the bed laughing.

"Not funny, Simon."

Hearing a knock at the open door, we both turned to see Gran. "Dinner is ready, wash up, so we can eat."

We both nodded and watch her turn to leave. *Okay deep breath, just get through dinner and then you and Simon can some hibernate in your room for the rest of the night.*

Luckily, dinner wasn't as bad as I expected. Gia was civil and I tried my best not to look pissed off. It was hard, but I did my best to put on a smile and laugh at jokes.

Safely back in my room, Simon and I lay in bed watching TV. Grabbing the remote, he turned the volume off and looked at me, all serious. "Beth, I need to tell you something important—"

"Simon, I can't take any more serious talk right now. Can it wait until tomorrow? I really just want to watch some TV and go to bed," I said, cutting him off. Turning the volume back up, I smiled up at him and kissed his cheek.

"Yeah, it can wait," he said, getting comfortable again.

❦❦❦

Christmas Eve was our family's big night. It was magical and we loved it. Gran had prepared a big dinner and the only thing keeping us from enjoying her wonderful cooking was Charles. He was late, as usual.

We were all sitting in the formal living room around the tree when he arrived, with Danielle. I watched Gia's reaction as the pair walked in. She immediately looked at me, and I

knew for sure this whole mess between us was because of
Charles. I smiled over at her, because I felt bad for her.
Whether she was being a bitch or not, she was my friend and I
hated seeing her so stressed.

I turned away from her and laid in on Charles. "Gran's going to have your ass for being late."

"Oh, stuff it, Beth. We got stuck in traffic. We're here now,
so drop it."

I couldn't help but chuckle. Gran was going to make
Charles do all the dishes, and I took a peek a few minutes ago.
He was going to be in there all night.

"Finally! Come on everyone before dinner gets even cold-
er," Gran said, entering the room.

"Gran, I'm sorry, we got stuck in traffic," Charles pleaded.

"Save it, Chuck," Gran said, hugging him and tuning to
Danielle. "Hello, sweetie. I'm Gran. Don't be surprised if you
don't see him all night. He has dish duty."

I knew it! *I should have bet money*!

I carried the last of the dishes into the kitchen and found
Gia and Charles standing at the sink. I wondered if I looked
that desperate whenever I was near Spencer. God I hoped not.

"Gia," I said. "Can I have a word with you?"

Nodding, she left Charles's side to follow me.

I closed us in to one of the many guest rooms in the house.
I couldn't even get a sound out before she was spilling her
guts.

"I don't know what I'm doing," she confessed.

Sitting on the edge of the perfectly made bed, I saw the
tears well up in her eyes. "Gia, I get it, I honestly do. But you
can't lead Teddy on if you still have feeling for Charles."

"I slept with Chuck the night they came over after the picture of you and Spencer at the charity event popped up. They
had both left, but Charles came back. Early the next morning,
he told me had made a mistake and to act like it never happened, so I did."

I can't take all this drama. I think I'm getting an ulcer.

"But Teddy came back to check on us that morning. We
talked until he left a few hours later, and that's who you saw

leaving. Ever since then, Teddy and I have been hanging out and—and, I fell for him."

That was a lot to process. *That jerk of a brother slept with her, even though I specifically told him not to, because of this exact reason.*

"Gia, you have to do what's right. You can't lead Teddy on." It hurt to think that my brother was going to be crushed.

"I don't want to. I think I love him. Chuck is never going to change. It does feel good to see him get jealous like he did at the club, but seeing him with someone else hurts."

I nodded in agreement because I knew all too well.

"What am I going to do?" she asked.

Honestly, I had no clue what to tell her. So I tried to wing it. "Do what your heart tells you, but let's figure it out tomorrow. It's time to open presents, and I wouldn't mind seeing Charles get jealous again. Would you be up for it?" I asked, bumping her shoulder playfully.

"Ah, hell. Whatever. Let's go make him cringe," she said, standing.

Our family had shipped all the presents to the house so everything would be there when we arrived. We sat around the tree and handed out presents. Gran got a new cookbook from Teddy. I got Charles a watch. Teddy gave Gia a pair of diamond earrings. I wish I could have taken a picture of Charles face as she kissed him. *Priceless.* I gave Simon a new camera bag since his was practically falling apart. Best of all, he surprised me with a beautiful necklace. The letter S hung on a thin silver chain, I immediately put it on. It must have cost him a fortune. There had to have been at least ten diamonds set in to the platinum S. One of them looked large enough to be in a ring.

The process went on and on until all the presents were passed out. "Well, I guess that's it," I said, sitting on the floor and crossing my legs.

"Not quiet," Gran said before standing. "There's one more. It's behind the tree, I think. It was the first present to arrive. It's for you, muffin."

Standing to meet her, I took the perfectly wrapped box

from her and sat on the couch next to Gia.

Gia saw it as soon as I did. My name was perfectly written in that signature handwriting. The wrapping was white, gold, and silver. It shimmered beautifully in the light. Placing the large box on my lap I untied the rose red ribbon. I made sure the box covered my face as I opened it. Holding the box lid to help cover my face, I thanked God that Gia and I had settled our beef before this all happened.

There on top of white tissue paper lay a note in an all too familiar handwriting.

A replacement for the one I ruined. I'm sorry I made you choose. I should have given you the time you asked for. I've been using that time to prove to you that I'm the only one who deserves your love. I'm falling apart without you. I need you. Tell me what else I can do. ~ Spencer

I took the note, after reading it, and shoved it quickly into my pocket.

"What do I say?" I asked, looking at Gia, just moving my mouth with no sound.

"Well," Gran said. "I've been looking at this box for more than two weeks trying to figure out what's inside. Spill it, muffin. What's in it and who's it from?"

I smiled over the box but quickly looked back down. Moving the tissue paper, I saw the contents within.

There, lying perfectly draped in the box, was a white dress. It was stunning. The same as the red one but even better. Small crystals were added making it shimmer against the light. I took the dress in my hands and held it up for everyone to see.

"Wow, Beth that's a really nice dress," Danielle said approvingly.

"Who's it from," Gran asked.

"It's—umm." I swallowed but my throat was too dry.

"It's from me," Gia said, wrapping an arm around me. "I saw it a couple of weeks ago and didn't want it sitting around the house so I sent it early."

I stared at her in total bewilderment. *She just saved my ass—big time.*

Quickly I put the dress back in the box and hugged her tightly. "Thank you, I owe you big time," I whispered in her ear.

Pulling back, she shook her head. "No you don't. Merry Christmas. Now come on, I want to see what it looks like on you." Grabbing my arm, she pulled me up and into a spare room.

෴

Locking the door we, stared dumbfounded at one another.

"I thought he didn't want anything to do with you?" she said, laying the dress neatly on the bed.

"I thought the same thing. What is his deal with confessing his love then leaving for a month? Does he have me on some kind of weird rinse and repeat cycle? Why is he doing this?" I asked, while I ran my hand over the perfectly beaded dress.

"You want my opinion?" Gia asked, turning to me.

"Sure," I said, sitting next to the dress in defeat.

"All right, this is what you do. You wear this dress to the club opening and make sure you look smoking hot. You find him, get him alone, and lay in on him. Tell him how he's ruining your life, tell him to leave you alone, tell him to never contact you again. That's what you should do."

I liked where she was going with this. Get him all wanton then kick him in the groin. I'd like to watch his domineering ass be on the shocked side for once. I just hopped that my stupid body didn't betray me. *Because we all know how I get around that man. Distracted, and I can't let myself get distracted.*

"Since we're here, you may as well try it on," Gia said, bringing me back into the room.

"I don't know. It's not that nice."

Ooo, bad lie. This dress is stunning, but there is no way it was going to still be stunning on me. Oh. My. God. What if he got the wrong size? How embarrassing. I probably can't even wear it to make him jealous now because my ass won't fit in it—literally.

"Oh, come on, it's a size twelve. It's got to fit."

I don't need to hear that. This was just great. The sexiest man on earth knew I was a size twelve. *No big deal, right? Not. It's a huge deal!*

"Fine, give it here. It's not going to fit. Look at this there's no way," I said, holding the dress up to my pajama-clad body.

"Go!" she said, pointing to the bathroom.

Stripping down to just my underwear, I stepped into the dress. Taking a breath, I pulled slowly and found that it hugged my hips closely. I pulled the straps up and slid my arms in.

It was stunning, but it also wasn't zipped yet. I called out to Gia to come zip it up.

"Holy shit, you're going to have him eating out the palm of your hand in this dress. There's no way he hasn't been fantasizing about you in this since the day he got it," she said, adding a high-pitched squeal on the end.

"Calm down, it's not zipped up yet."

Not even a tug to get it up. It fit perfectly. "Okay, it's zipped, it looks good, now get it off of me," I said, starting to panic.

"Come on let's show everyone first. Gran—"

"Now, Gia! I need to get this off now!" *Okay, I'm really panicking now.*

The fact that his dress fit so perfectly, like it was made just for my body—almost as if he told the person making it not only my size but every curve of my body, every mound, ever dip, just everything. It scared me to death that he could know my body so well after one night. Reaching behind me, I tried to grip the zipper and pull it.

"Hold still, I'll unzip it," Gia said, making quick work of it.

I hurried, taking my arms out, and pushed it down my hips so I could finally step out of it. Dropping to my knees in relief that I was out of it, I covered my bare chest and tried to steady my panicked breathing.

Taking a towel from the hook, Gia wrapped it around me

and knelt next to me on the floor. "Shh, Beth, it's okay. It's just a dress."

Holding the towel tightly, I looked up at her. "It's not just a dress. He's never going to stop, he's never going to stop having an effect on me."

We sat there as I calmed down, not speaking and just sitting in the silence.

"What no show?" Charles asked, smugly from his chair as we came back out.

"No, it fit fine," Gia answered for me. "You all just have to wait until the opening of the club to see it."

Staring at her as she took the heat off of me for a second time, I reflected on how much I appreciated her being here. When I first met her that freshman year when we ended up being roommates, I thought for sure it was joke. We were complete opposites, to say the least. But we worked on it and now I couldn't imagine her not being a part of my life, my family.

ᥱᴥᥱᴥ

"Come for me, Elizabeth."

I opened my eyes wearily as the sound of Spencer's voice lingered all around me. I noticed the beads of sweat on my upper lip. My heart rate was accelerated and I could feel it pounding as I placed a hand over my chest. Rotating quickly, I saw Simon sleeping peacefully, both his hands under the pillow. A faint snore was coming from his mouth. Closing my eyes, I sighed in relief that he was sleeping so soundly.

It was no use. It had been over two weeks of me being Spencer free, so free that I didn't even think about him. I rubbed my eyes harshly to get the image of his blue ones out of my mind. Somehow, he had gotten me caught up in his twisted web again.

I need a drink, a stiff one.

Wrapped in a blanket, I made my way downstairs, tiptoeing, so I wouldn't wake anyone up. Cautiously, I made my way around the corner. I was shocked to see Teddy sitting at the island counter with what looked like a glass of whiskey in his hand.

The floor creaked as I went to take a step, gaining his attention. He looked up to see me walk in.

"Can't sleep?" I asked, striding over closer.

"Yeah something like that," he said, swirling the liquid in his glass.

I held my hand out for the glass. "Do you mind?"

He let me take it from him. Downing the rest, I turned to where the bottle sat just next to him. Twisting the cap off, I filled it up again and finished that off, too. Again, I set the glass down to fill it up for a third shot.

"Whoa, slow down, sis," he said, taking the glass from me just as I went to finish it off.

"Hey!" I said, trying to grab it back. He just stared at me with disappointment on his face. "Sorry," I said. "I just wanted to clear my head."

"Salvatore have anything to do with that?"

Shit! How the hell did he know?

"Gia told me."

That little traitor.

"I had a feeling that present wasn't from her to begin with, so I questioned her and she let me in on everything."

Ah, hell, cat's out of the bag now. "So, what do you think about it all? About him?" I asked, hoping that he would give me some sort of guidance, anything to help me out.

"Honestly?" he asked, turning to catch my eye.

"Yes, honestly," I replied.

"I have no clue. I want to believe him, because he's great at what he does but then he goes off the rail and—he's one fucked up man. Don't get me wrong. He's a genius at business but everything he's telling me about his private research and developments, I just can't wrap my head around."

What the hell is he talking about? Are we even talking about the same thing here?

"Teddy, you totally lost me," I said, taking the drink from him and sipping.

"The day we came back from our weekend getaway, Spencer contacted me. He was ranting about Simon and how he was lying to you, to me, to everyone. He was trying to tell me to do my job and protect you from scum like Simon. He demanded that I come see him. So I gave in. He is the best at getting information. This all happened last week," he said, taking the glass from me and finishing it off.

"Well, what did he say about Simon? Did he actually find something?" I thought back to our last conversation—or argument was a better fit, I fell. "Spencer had told me he didn't trust Simon and that he was going to hurt me."

Could there be any real truth to it all?

"That's what he told me, too. So I checked him out and found nothing. When I finally met with Spencer again, he flipped out when I let him know my findings. Thankfully, we were in his office, because he was tossing everything he could get his hands on at the wall. His office looked like a tornado had come through. He's off the deep end, Beth. He told me he was going to keep searching until he found out the truth and proved us all wrong." Teddy shrugged his shoulders, as if it was nothing.

"Why didn't you tell me any of this?" I asked, feeling the anger build up.

"Tell you what? That Spencer was going insane? You didn't need to know that after everything. You were happy with Simon. I couldn't find anything bad on him. Why would I even bring it up? You know how I feel about you and Spencer in the first place. I figured it'd be best for everyone to just forget about it."

There was just one small problem there. Spencer hadn't forgotten and neither had I.

He was determined to prove that Simon was wrong for me, but he wasn't any better. His temper and whatever dirt Teddy had on him sure didn't make him look like Prince Charming.

"What were you blacking mailing Spencer with?" I asked in all seriousness.

He lowered his head and I could see him struggling with whether to tell me or not. "Beth, Spencer comes from a very wealthy family."

Really? So do we. That's a little hypocritical.

"I found out that they had paid a lot of money to have his slate wiped clean. I don't know what was so bad that his family went to such lengths to cover it up. I kind of bluffed. Just do me a favor and stay away from him. I'm sure they didn't seal all his files because he didn't return his library books. It must have been pretty substantial for his father to get involved."

He was bluffing. Teddy didn't even know for sure what Spencer had done, if anything. Well, I guessed he did do something. Spencer seemed to believe Teddy and backed off before. Maybe Teddy was right. I needed to just stay away and tell him to back the fuck off. In one week that was going to happen, I was going to be Spencer free for the rest of my life.

"So Gia's in love with Chuck?" he asked.

Whoa, that came out of left field. I almost want to go back to talking about Spencer. Almost. "I don't know. But I do know that she is falling in love with you. She cares about you, and I think she's willing to let her crush for Charles fade away, and that's all because of you."

I filled the glass again making sure to take a sip before I handed it to him.

"Did she sleep with him? She won't tell me."

I felt my eyes grow larger, and I was thankful I was looking at the ground. *Damn, I have to tell him. If roles were reversed, I'd want to know.* I looked up at him and knew that my face said it all.

"I should have guessed," he said, downing the drink in his hand and placing it face down next to him. "If she really cares for him, then I'm not going to keep pushing myself on her. If she doesn't care for me—"

"I do care for you."

We both turned to see Gia standing in the doorway behind us. Oh *shit. I need another drink. Is there something stronger than whiskey?*

"Teddy, how could you even think that? I care about you so much. I did sleep with Chuck, but it was before you, before us. I'm sorry. I should have told you, but I was embarrassed." She took another step toward him. "Theodor Monroe, I'm falling in love with you, and that's way better than any school girl crush I might have had on Chuck."

She took his hands in hers, holding them close to her chest.

"Gia, don't say what you think I want to hear. I'll be fine. If you and Chuck want to—"

She hushed him by a finger to his lips and shook her head. "I don't want anyone but you."

She only had to reach up a little to meet his lips. Barbie and Ken, that's what they looked like together. *Now let's all just pray that GI Joe Chuck doesn't get too jealous and ruin it all.*

"Can you come back up to bed now?" she said, tugging at the hem of his shirt seductively.

Gross, don't do it. Ah hell, now I've got a mental picture. "Please get out of here. I'm about to be sick with all the mushiness in this kitchen."

"Are you okay now?" Teddy asked

"Yeah, I'll be fine." I said, fiddling with the glass in my hand.

"Beth, be careful with Salvatore," he said before taking Gia's hand and leading them up the back staircase.

"Salvatore who?" I called behind them.

Chapter 27

S imon, do you have your camera with you?" Gran asked as we were saying our goodbyes to Charles and Danielle.

Go figure. His first time dating a girl and Danielle had him flying all the way to Main to spend the rest of the holiday weekend with her family. The look on Charles face, as he told us all they were leaving, was priceless.

"Yeah, I have it upstairs, why?" he asked.

"Would you mind taking a photo of me with all my grandbabies? I have them all here with me and I don't want to let the opportunity go to waste."

Pictures? *Really*? I quickly looked down at my yoga pants and oversized sweat shirt. It was ripped along the cuffs, the writing on the front was illegible, and I had cut the neck hole. Not really what I wanted to have a family photo taken in.

Fifteen minutes later, Simon had us all posed in front of the tree. Gran and I were in the middle with Teddy by my side and Charles on hers.

"Okay, ready? One…two…three."

Dashing from the tree, I made my way to Simon. "I blinked. I know I did. Let me look."

Of course, I hadn't blinked, I just wanted to make sure I didn't look like shit next to my gorgeous grandmother and the freaking male models.

"Eww, take it again," I said, glancing at it quickly.

"It looks great. What's the problem?" he said, confused.

"Just take it again, will ya?" I said, turning from him.

Thirty minutes and about six different poses later, I still wasn't happy.

"Beth, its fine. I have to go," Charles said.

"Just one more," I said, falling back in place behind my now sitting grandmother. I stood behind her chair as the boys stood on either side.

"I've taken over fifty shots, babe, one of them has to be good enough," Simon said

I smiled innocently. "Last one, promise."

"You said that twenty minutes ago," Gia called, looking up from her phone.

"Hey—" But I couldn't finish because a flash blinded me. "You did not just take that, did you?"

I'd been in the middle of pointing at Gia with a God only knew what kind of expression on my face. I reached for Simon's camera but he held it above his head so I couldn't get it.

"Are you kidding me?" Placing my hands on my hips, I shot daggers at him. I went to grab the camera as he lowered it. Holding it up again, he started snapping away. Immediately, I held up my hands. The bastard was using his camera as a weapon.

"Stop it, Simon." Snap. "Come on." Snap. "Okay, enough." Snap. "It's not funny anymore."

It sure as hell wasn't funny to me but that didn't stop everyone else from rolling on the floor, laughing.

Backing away from him as he moved closer and continued taking pictures of me, I turned and made a mad dash around the first floor of the house. No use. He was still chasing me with that damn camera. I headed up the steps, pausing half way when he reached the bottom.

"Simon, I swear to you. You'd better stop taking pictures of me." I tried not to smile. I tried really hard not to laugh, but I couldn't help the warm fuzzy feelings.

"Not a chance, Belle. That pretty little ass is mine and I'm not going to stop snapping until I get exactly what I want," he said with a cocky air.

Squealing, I turned and took the steps two at a time. He was hot on my ass. I ran down the hall and turned into my room.

Closing the door behind me, I barricaded myself in my closet. Thank God, it was huge. Maybe he wouldn't be able to find me.

"Come out, come out, wherever you are."

The door to the closet opened as he walked in, letting a sliver of light in with him. It didn't last long, as he closed it behind him.

"I do have night vision on this thing, just come out so I can get one picture. I promise," he called sweetly.

"Fine just one picture then you're going to put it away, right?" I asked, still huddled in the back of the closet.

"Sure," he said.

I smiled inwardly because I knew he had that smug expression on his face, even if I couldn't see it. I knew him all too well.

Stepping out, I turned on a little lamp that I used to have for keeping the boogey man away.

"Oh, intimate lighting," he said, wiggling his eyebrows.

I watched him as he raised his camera to his face. I stood maybe six feet away from him, and finally smiled for the camera.

"Hey, what happened to just one?" I asked as he pushed the button for the fourth time in a row.

"When you look this good, I can't take just one."

Shaking my head, I smiled at him, my face heating up from his compliment.

All right he wants a show, I'll give him a show. As he continued to click away, I took my sweatshirt off and tossed it on the floor. The clicking immediately stopped and he lowered his camera. I saw that sly smile fade as desire took over.

Raising my hands, I ran them through my hair and down my body. Latching them in my pants, I wiggled then stepped out of them. *I can't believe I'm doing this but the danger of him taking picture of me at my most vulnerable brings on a new excitement.* Standing in front of his camera, in only my bra and panties was liberating. Why shouldn't I feel this good? I had a man who clearly adored me and wasn't here to judge me. I felt amazing.

Plus there's a delete button. I already checked!

I flipped my head back. My hair fell perfectly around my face and body. It was long enough to reach the bottom of my back and, with its natural blonde highlights and thickness, it was by far my favorite asset.

"So is this what happens on a photo shoot?" I asked while doing my best impression of a model.

"Umm, no. I have never done this before. You're going to have to go easy on me. I'm a virgin," he said, smiling before bringing the camera back up.

"Oh, really?" I watched as he swallowed and nodded his answer. "Well, you should always make sure that the model feels comfortable," I said, rubbing hand over my hips.

"And what would make my model more comfortable?" he asked.

"Strip." That was all I said and it didn't take him long to put the camera down and drop his pants.

He rushed over, and I was all but knocked down as he knelt down before me. His arms wrapped around my ass. He kissed my stomach and gripped my hips tightly before letting go and snapping another picture up at me.

"There's really good light down here you should join me"

"Simon, there's no light down there."

Taking the lamp from the table he placed it on the floor next to him. "Look, light," he said smugly.

I knelt down on the ground with him and he kissed me. Finally letting the camera go, he used both his hands to undo the clasp on my bra.

Freed from its wires, I arched into the hand that was caressing me. His other hand wrapped around my neck, urging me to lie down. His lips felt like warm sunlight as he made his way down my neck and over my chest.

A hand ran up my leg, halting just over the edge of my underwear. Closing my eyes, I waited for him to slip a finger in but was disappointed when I felt the sudden distance between us.

I opened my eyes just in time to see the camera cover his face as he began taking pictures of me again. I wanted to be upset or disgusted, but I wasn't. I was turned on. *Like really turned on. I didn't want him to put it down.* I watched him as he took picture after picture of me. Sitting up on one elbow, I beckoned him with a finger.

"My turn," I said, reaching for the camera.

Lowering it, he raised an eyebrow at me. If I could trust him to take a picture of me basically naked, he sure as hell better let me take one of him.

"Hand it over," I said seductively.

"Okay, just push this button."

Taking the camera from him, I looked through the window and zoomed in on his perfectly sculpted face. I then zoomed out and admired his body, strong and thick and—*What the heck?* He looked shy and awkward as if he didn't know what to do with himself.

"Come on you can do better than that," I said, trying to encourage him. A few more snaps and he began to relax. "Ah that's more like it. You're a natural. Have you done this before?" I asked, moving the camera from my face.

"No, now hand it back over," he said, holding his hand out.

"Not so fun on the others side, is it?" I asked, laughing.

"Oh it's fun, but I want to fuck you right now and I'd rather both of us have our hands free."

Oh, shit! I put the camera down next to me just as he covered me with his body.

Lying on the floor of my closet, damp with sweat, I felt chilled. Sitting up, I straddled him. His hardness twitched back to life as he reached over to grab the camera again.

"Damn, you look good after sex," he said as he took a few more.

"Now you know you have to delete these," I said, covering the lens.

"Why is that?" he asked, moving me so he could turn on his side to face me.

"Because I don't need to see naked pictures of myself."

"I got bad news for you then, because I do. I need to see these naked pictures of you every night that I'm away from you." I slapped his chest, making him fall onto his back, laughing. "Seriously, we'll both go through them. I'll only keep the ones you let me."

Ha, fine by me. They will all be bad in my eyes so problem solved. Control+A+Del—done!

Sitting in bed with the covers pulled up around us, Simon loaded the memory card into his laptop and we began the easy process of deleting everything. We went through the family pictures first and there were quite a few that I thought Gran would like so that was a surprise. Placing those in a folder, he went on to the more risqué ones.

Of course, he was perfect in all of the ones I took. *Maybe I should look in to photography as a second career. Or maybe not.* I was mortified as I watched him click through my strip tease frame by frame. I might have been mortified but he sure wasn't. I didn't know what to watch—the photos or the sheet growing off his lap.

"Okay, well delete all those except for the first few where I'm fully clothed," I said, pointing to the screen.

"What are you talking about? Look at this," he said, blowing up a picture of me with my arms raised above my head. I was looking dead on into camera in only my bra and underwear, and, damn it, it looked okay. *Thank God, for soft lighting.*

Okay, on to the hard core stuff. I closed my eyes and covered them for extra resistance not to look.

"Will you put your hands down and just look. You're beautiful, just open your eyes," he said, taking my hands away from my face.

Opening my eyes slowly, I watched the pictures change every few seconds. I was amazed at what I saw. It wasn't gross, or disgusting. It was art. It was beautiful—it was *me*! First was a picture of my lips, then my eyes, my hand covering my breast, the curve of my waist, the crook of my neck where his hand caressed it. It was tasteful and stunning. There was one of my bare chest as I lay on the floor, looking up at him, and I knew that that was how he saw me.

He saw the beauty in me, the curve of my body, the roundness of my hips, the rolls on my side as I twisted beneath him.

And even though I saw those imperfections—for the first time, I didn't mind, because he didn't mind.

He had always told me the truth and I had a feeling he always would.

Okay, so they weren't all perfect. But the ones that were, I let him keep. Placing the laptop on the night stand, we settled down in the bed, looking at one another.

There was obviously something on his mind as he played with a strand of my hair.

"I want to ask you something," he finally said. I nodded for him to go on. "I've been working on opening a gallery, to showcase my work. I guess what I'm asking is, I want to use the pictures we took tonight, the ones of you."

I think my jaw just hit the mattress. He wanted to use naked pictures of me in a gallery for the world to see. *Oh the fucking paparazzi and media would have a field day with that. I can hear it now. Elizabeth Monroe turned porn star after being dumped by hottest man alive. Yeah, I don't know about all that. How do I politely say no, and tell him if he does, then I'm going to chop his balls off.*

"Simon, I don't know. I mean, what would everyone say?"

Frowning at my answer he leaned over and kissed my lips tenderly. "They'd say, 'Damn that photographer is one lucky bastard.' That's what they'd say."

Caressing his cheek, I shook my head, smiling.

"You are beautiful, those pictures are beautiful, and the world deserves to see them. Let me show the world what I see every time that I'm with you. Please."

Should I trust him? I do trust him, but these are naked pictures of me. Well, not really. I mean, there was maybe two that showed my boobs but the rest were tasteful. Ahh, what the hell? I'm sure I'm going to regret this but—

"Okay, fine. You can use them but only the ones I said. Nothing else, got it? And you better have deleted them and not just put them in a different file."

"Really? I can use them?" he said, surprised.

"You want me to change my mind?" I asked, cocking my head.

"No. No. Thank you. I will only use the ones you just approved, promise."

Chapter 28

Our few days away from reality were amazing, but here we were, back to the daily grind. Teddy and Simon had dropped us girls off at home and went on their way, both having been called into work.

There I was, once again staring at the bottom of my suitcase. Still wrapped in the delicate tissue paper, to protect the stunning bead work, sat the dress Spencer had given me. Reaching for a hanger from my closet, I carefully hung the dress up.

It's disgusting. Not the dress, the dress is gorgeous. The fact that I was so affected by him was sickening. Just when I felt that I was free, he dangled himself in front of me like a carrot to a reindeer. I was tired of it. I was tired of feeling so torn. In a few days it was going to be over. I just had to keep reminding myself that.

❦

The week went by faster than I had anticipated. I was making sure to steer clear of anything that might involve seeing or even being in the same vicinity as Spencer. I even gave up the opportunity to be in pictures with my brothers at the club. They had hired Simon to take a few for publicity purposes. Not that it needed any. Between Spencer and my break up and now Teddy and Gia's love story on blast, I was positive there wasn't a person alive who hadn't heard of us or the club.

I had been stressing about it all week, and the day had finally come. I sat anxiously on the couch, waiting for Simon to arrive. *How perfect would it be if Spencer tried to call him out or they got into some sort of 'my cocks bigger than yours' fight.* Now that I thought about it, seeing them both all hot and aggressive might have been a hell of a turn on. *Ugh what am I thinking? That would be horrible—kind of.*

"How was your day?" I tried to act nonchalant, but from the look on Simon's, face it didn't come across that way. I watched him carry our Chinese over and place it on the coffee table.

"It was good. You should have come."

Ha, I don't think so. I was not going to take the chance of being caught between the two of them—literally. "We ended up sitting around bullshitting for an hour while we waited."

"What were you waiting for? Did Gia come by? I haven't talked to her today. Was it Charles that was late? Charles is always late. He's going to be late for his own funeral, I swear it. What was his excuse?" I asked, while he sat down next to me.

"That's a lot of questions. Are you okay? Is something bothering you?" he asked.

I shook my head quickly and tried to play it off.

"It was Salvatore we were waiting for," he said, and I knew there was no color in my face.

"Oh...umm." I was speechless. "Did he—I mean was he—"

"It was fine, Beth. He didn't say anything to me, and I didn't say anything to him. Although I wanted to punch him in the face for treating you like shit, I let it roll off my shoulders, because I'm professional like that. I don't go around clocking my clients."

All I could do was nod.

"Relax, babe, it's over. I'm here and I'm not going anywhere, even Mr. Billionaire himself couldn't get me to leave you."

Smiling up at him, I kissed his lips.

"Can we eat now? Your cheap brothers didn't feed me."

Laughing, we pulled out our food and began eating out dinner.

During dinner Gia arrived back home and, by the time we had finished, she was all dressed up and getting ready to leave again.

We watched as she tied a scarf around her neck and pulled her jacket on. "Where are you going all dressed up?" I asked.

"I'm meeting up with some friends from work. We're just going to Notty's for a few drinks, very low key," she said, shrugging her shoulders.

Notty's was a local bar around the corner. It was small and only locals went.

"Well, watch out. The hounds are out to get you and Teddy. Make sure you go out the back."

Ever since our trip to New York, Gia, Teddy, and Charles had been dragged into the wonderful world of being chased down by grown men with cameras.

"Will do," she said, saluting me.

"Be careful. Call me if you need anything."

"You got it," she called back just as the door closed.

An hour later I was comfortably sleeping in Simons arms on the couch as he watched some action movie. I felt his phone vibrate before it rang. Sitting up, he reached in his pocket to answer. Checking the screen, he cursed to himself.

"Goddamn it. Can't she do anything on her own?"

I watched as he got up from the couch.

"I got to get this," he said, turning to walk in the kitchen.

This definitely wasn't something new. I had almost come to expect it. It was what he did. He was at the beck and call of his boss and, until he had saved up enough to open his gallery, he was stuck.

"I have to go," he said, sighing from the kitchen table where he was currently putting his jacket on.

I went to meet him at the door. "Simon, its fine. I'm just going to go to bed."

"I know. I just hate leaving you."

Perfect, this man is freaking perfect. "You have to work. It might not be what you want to do now, but just think about opening your gallery, and that it's all going to be worth it in the end."

He turned away from me, huffing in frustration. "I don't know, Beth, I think after the club, I'm going to quit. I just can't do it anymore. It's not who I want to be anymore. I want to be with you and, if I keep doing this, there's no way I can keep it up."

He brushed a strand of hair out of my face. There was a hurt in his warm brown eyes.

"Well, you have to do what's right for you. I'm not going anywhere." There was more to this than he was telling me, but I trusted him, and I wasn't going to let him down. I would be there for him through it all.

Kissing my lips, he turned to leave.

"Call me tomorrow," I said, holding on tightly to his thick bicep.

Kissing me again, he rested his forehead on mine. "You know I will. I love you."

That was the moment. I wanted to say it back to him. I didn't feel pressured or guilty. I loved him. After everything we'd been through, I really loved him. "I love you, too," I said with my forehead still resting on his. "Ahh!" I screamed as he lifted me up.

Holding me tightly around my waist, he spun me before placing me back on the ground and leaving a fierce kiss on my lips. "I needed that. You have no idea how good it feels to hear you say that."

It felt just as good to tell him. "All right. Well, I love you. Now get out there, go to work, and bring me that bacon," I said, laughing and pushing him away and toward the door.

"Oh, I'll bring you some bacon," he said with a wink.

"Bye, Simon, call me tomorrow."

I kissed his cheek and closed the door slowly on him. Standing there, I felt relieved, happy, giddy even. I'd just told another human being that wasn't part of my family that I loved them, and he loved me back.

Jumping in bed, I grabbed a book and tried to calm myself down. An hour later, I had drifted off to sleep.

The sound of my phone going off woke me. A new message from Simon. Immediately, I opened it.

Hey, baby. Just remember I love you.

That was weird. I never would have pegged him for someone who wasn't confident in a relationship, but throughout all of this, even before he-who-won't-be-named, Simon was fighting something inside of himself. The first few times when we hung out, he was cocky and confident. Then once we spent more time together, once he got to know me, he acted differently. I didn't know where any of this was coming from and the last thing I wanted to do was give him any reason to think that I had forgotten how he felt. I made that mistake once but I wasn't going to make it again. I texted him back. *How could I ever forget? I love you, too!*

☽☾☽

Is that hammering? I sat up in bed just as Gia came barreling through my bedroom door.

"Beth, wake up! Now!" she said, walking in and making herself comfortable on my bed. Her laptop was in her arms, the light from the screen was blinding.

"What the hell, Gia? It's 6:40 in the morning. What could possibly be that important that you have to wake me up?" I said, rubbing my eyes.

"Look at this," she said, putting the computer in my lap. I let my eyes adjust to the brightness. "Well?" she asked.

"Hold on. I can't see anything. Let my eyes focus for a minute—geeze, if this is a picture of me, I really—" I choked on my words as I realized what I was looking at. It was a picture on Fame and it wasn't me. It was Gia and Charles kissing outside of Nottys! "What the fuck is going on, Gia?" I asked, still looking through all the pictures that were posted. Scrolling down I read the caption.

> *It seems as though Ms. Monroe isn't the only one in the family stuck in a love triangle. Only three short weeks after becoming a couple, Teddy Monroe*

*has some serious competition—his younger bad boy
brother Chuck. A credible source has told us that
Gia Elliot, best friend to Elizabeth Monroe, has been
crushing on the bad boy for years. Such a scandal
for these two once-quiet entrepreneurs. New Year's
Eve will be quite a show at the grand opening of
their club 21. Make sure you get your tickets fast because I'm positive there will be plenty of fireworks
going off.*

"Gia, what the hell are you doing kissing Chuck?" I
screeched, turning to her. "You said you were meeting friends
from work, not Chuck!" I shoved my hands through my hair.
"You said you were over him, done. Oh my God, has Teddy
seen this yet?" Quickly I closed the computer and shook Gia's
frozen body.

"I—I don't think so," she said, stunned and on the verge of
tears.

"Gia, I need you to tell me the truth. Did you meet up with
Charles last night? I thought I heard you and someone else but
I assumed it was a friend from work. You didn't—" I couldn't
even say it.

"No! I didn't sleep with him. I was out with my friends, I
swear. He just happened to show up. He asked me to step outside, because he wanted to talk to me. So I did."

"Well, what the hell happened out there? Because it seriously looks like you're having some secret love affair with
him. You're kissing him, for God's sake."

Covering her face she sighed. "We talked. I swear we only
talked. He told me he cared for me. I said it was too late. That I
was with Teddy and I wasn't going to hurt him. He agreed
with me, we talked some more, then he kissed my cheek and
told me to be happy. It was innocent, I swear. I invited him to
come hang out with my friends. He joined us for the rest of the
night. I think he even got Shelly's number. He was flirting
with her all night. When everyone was leaving, he pretty much
told me he was going to walk me home. I didn't want to be a
bitch so I let him."

"So it was Charles in here last night?" I asked, trying to get the story straight.

"Yes, but he just dropped me off. He used the bathroom then left. There were no paparazzi anywhere last night, I swear. It's like they all took the night off. I didn't see anyone with a camera." She pleaded with me to understand.

"I can't believe this is happening to us," I said. "First my life, now my family. This is all Spencer's fault!" Just then we heard a knock at the door. "Who the hell is knocking on our door at seven in the morning?" I said, getting out of bed to answer the door. The pounding got louder as I reached it. "Hold on." I unlocked it and got knocked over by Charles as he barreled through the door.

"Where is she?" he asked, looking around the condo.

"Charles! What are you doing here? And please tell me you came in through the back," I said, closing the door.

"What? I came in the front like a normal person."

Oh shit! I know there will be another picture posted soon. I can already see the caption. Bad boy Monroe rushing to console a weeping Gia.

"Did they see you?" I asked

"Did who see me? I wasn't really checking my surroundings," he said, getting ready to walk down the hall to our bedrooms. He was stopped by the presence of Gia, standing in the doorway.

"Chuck, what are you doing here?" she asked in just her oversized T-shirt.

Really? She couldn't put some pants on?

"Gia, I'm so sorry, I swear I didn't know," he said, walking toward her.

"How could you have known?" she said, reassuring him that she didn't blame him for this.

"I'm going to call Salvatore and get him to pull whatever strings he did before to get it taken down, I promise." *Great, just what I needed to be thinking about at seven in the morning—Spencer the knight in shining armor, taking naughty photos down with the swipe of his hand.* We were all standing around, complaining about the hounds and their ruthless ways.

Charles had taken his jacket off and sat down next to Gia on the couch like he owned the place, in his pajamas no less.

The door handle turned and swung open just and the three of us watched as Teddy walked through.

Oh, this just keeps on getting better and better. All we need now is for Spencer and Simon to show up and we'd have ourselves a fucking Jerry Springer episode.

"What the hell is going on here?" Teddy asked, looking at the couch where Gia and Charles sat next to one another in their pajamas.

"Teddy, it's not what you think," Gia said, standing from the couch.

But as she went to move toward him Charles grabbed her hand and pulled her back down. Standing, he looked at Gia then Teddy. "It's my fault. I saw her at a bar and I was being selfish. She put me in my place, though," he said, turning to smile down at her.

"That's fine and dandy," Teddy said. "But why are you over here sitting on her couch at seven in the morning in you fucking pajamas?"

Wow. Teddy angry was not a common occurrence. I'd seen him angry with Spencer but this was a whole new level.

"Wait, haven't you seen it?" I asked, butting in.

"Seen what?' he asked, turning to me.

"Hold on." I retrieved the lap top from my room and showed Teddy the pictures.

He simply stared at the two of them.

"It's nothing. It was nothing," Gia called to him.

"I told you I would back off if you still had feelings for him. I will not stand here and take this from my own family. If you wanted to be with Chuck, you should have just told me. I have to go." Turning, he headed for the door. "Beth, I'll talk to you later."

Before I could process what had just happened, he was gone, the door closed. The tree of us sat there in disbelief. *This day was starting off great.*

"Chuck! Get up and go after him, tell him everything. Jesus, he probably thinks you slept with her again."

Hearing my phone buzz from my room, I walked out and checked it. I checked the caller ID but didn't recognize it. Hitting the end button, I shoved it in my bra, since my pajamas didn't have any pockets. I didn't have time for unknown numbers. My brothers needed me on damage control. I wasn't going to let the media ruin my family.

I walked back to the living room and saw that neither one of them had moved. Just as I got back into the room, Gia was crying and heading for her room, locking the door after she slammed it shut.

"Will you do something besides sitting there and sulking? Go talk to her. I'll deal with Teddy and, for Christ's sake, keep your hands to your damn self!"

Nodding up at me, he walked toward Gia's locked door.

I made it to the elevator, hitting the down button. As the doors opened, Teddy was standing at the back, his hands in his pockets, deep in thought.

"I thought you left?" I said, stepping inside.

"We're surrounded. They're everywhere," he said, looking up at me.

"Oh, Teddy, it's not what you think. Those people are just trying to make you paranoid. She loves you. Don't let them win.

Wrapping an arm around me he pulled me in close. "I want to, but you saw that picture. What am I supposed to think? You can't fake that or play it off. He was holding her and kissing her, and it didn't look like a brotherly kiss to me."

I had to get through to him. It was clear he was hurting bad. "Teddy, he ran into her, she told him she was in love with you, that whatever was between them was gone, over. You have to believe me—believe them—not the paparazzi."

As the elevator came to a stop, we walked out. *Fuck, he wasn't kidding. We were surrounded. I had never seen so many people outside our home before.* Things were getting out of control. "Just come back upstairs and talk to her, please," I begged, looking up at him. "Wait a minute. Why were you even over here this early if you didn't know about the picture?" I asked curiously.

"I was coming to surprise her, take her out for the day."

He was totally defeated, and my heart hurt for him. I hated seeing my brother like this. "You can still do that. Just go up there and talk to her, take her away from here. This is all just a big mistake." I was trying my best, but it was obvious he had already made a decision, and that didn't involve him coming back upstairs with me.

"Beth, you're right. This was a big mistake. Who was I trying to kid? She is always going to have feelings for Chuck. Just like you're always going to have feelings for Spencer."

Oh no, he didn't just go there. It's too early for this.

"Wait a minute, this is nothing like that," I said, getting defensive.

"Listen, Beth. I'm hurt that I let myself fall too fast for Gia, but I think this was bound to happen. There are too many things stacked up against us. She's so much younger, she's your best friend, and she's always dreamed of Chuck. I think it was doomed from the start."

Why is he giving up? He isn't even fighting.

"Don't talk like that. I won't let you give up."

"I appreciate you trying, but I think we should all just concentrate on the club opening and get back to our normal lives."

Always taking the high road, this brother of mine.

"Do me a favor and tell them I'm not upset. Tell Gia—tell her I'm sorry and I that I'll call her later once I have time to think everything through." With his hand on the door, he began to open it.

"What about Charles?" I asked.

"Tell him I love him, and that will never change. He's my brother and I won't jeopardize our relationship for anything." Relieved that he was at least going to call Gia and didn't have any ill will toward Charles, I figured there was really nothing else I could do.

"Teddy, wait up," Charles yelled, running over from the elevators.

Taking his hand off the door Teddy stepped back.

"Please, let me explain," Charles begged, breathing heavily from running over.

"Chuck, its fine. You don't have to explain anything. I'm just going to back off. I love you too much to let this come between us."

Clasping his shoulder, Teddy squeezed it comfortingly.

"Teddy she really likes you," Charles said, looking up into his face.

"Well, not that long ago she 'really liked' you, too. It's just not going to work for us. I still care for her, and I will do anything in my power to take care of her, but I think we should take a step back from the intimate stuff."

He was such a peace keeper.

"I think it's going to be best if I just go. Tell Gia I'll call her later." Teddy squeezed Charles's shoulder one last time before exiting through the door.

Shoving his foot in to stop the door from closing, Charles opened it and walked out behind him.

"Teddy," he called. "If you leave, I can't promise you I won't step in and comfort her."

He didn't. He did. And cameras went off like crazy.

"I know, Charles," Teddy said, smiling at him "I know." Nodding one last time, he opened the car door and left.

Chapter 29

As we rode the elevator back up, my phone began ringing again. Unknown number for the second time this morning and no message. Ending the call, I brought up Fame's web page. Just as I figured there was a picture of Charles and Teddy, damn they were getting fast at posting this shit.

"He's making a huge mistake," Charles said, breaking the silence.

"I don't know. Maybe he has a point. You know him. He doesn't like drama and, let's be honest, Gia brings drama wherever she goes."

Nodding in agreement, Charles placed his arm around my shoulders. I stared up at him surprised at his maturity about the whole situation. Maybe he was finally getting it, growing up, getting out of his "me" stage of life. It had been a long one and I believed the world was ready for it to be over. He could do so much good if he wasn't so worried about impressing women.

"Gia locked herself in the bathroom. I couldn't get her to come out. Maybe you'll have better luck," he said.

"Gia?" I knocked lightly on the bathroom door. "Please come out here."

"I can't, not right now, just leave me to wallow, please," she said through a sob.

I think a different approach is needed here. "Gia, you open this door, I'm not playing around." *No more mister nice guy.*

"Go away, Beth!" she yelled back.

Oh hell no, she's not going to talk to me like that. "Gia, get your ass out here or I'm going to let Charles kick the door in. You know he will. One...two—Ah, thank you," I said snidely as she opened the door.

Her face red and splotchy, she stood in the door way looking at me.

"I'm so sorry, Gia, if I could go back, I'd never—" Charles said, pausing mid-sentence.

"Chuck, it is what it is. Would you mind just giving me some time?" Gia asked, straightening from the doorway.

"Yeah, of course, I'll just go," he said, defeated and worn out.

"Come on, bro. I'll walk you out. Gia, go get in my bed. I'll be there in a minute."

Opening the door to let him out, I heard my phone buzz again, from the inside of my bra where I had stashed it. *Who the hell is this*? It was a different number than before, but I still didn't know who the hell was blowing up my phone. *Fine, you win. I'll answer.*

"Hello?" I said, lacing my voice with disgust.

"Miss. Monroe?" the male voice asked.

"Yes, this is her. How can I possibly help you at seven-thirty in the morning?" I snapped.

"Would you like to comment on the recent discovery of your brothers and the fact that they are both dating your so-called best friend?"

All I saw was red. "No, you fucking asshole. How the hell did you get this number? Don't you have any kind of respect for anyone you motherfu—"

The phone was ripped from my hands. Charles immediately hung up for me.

"Baby sis, I don't think that's the best way to deal with the bastards," he said, flipping my phone over in his hand.

"How dare they? I can't believe they are calling me now! How did they even find my number? I feel so dirty, eww," I said, shaking my body as a chill ran down it.

"I'll take it with me and get you a secure line. I'll bring it by tonight for you."

This was usually the stuff Teddy would take care of. It was

beyond strange to see Charles stepping up, acting responsible—outside of work that was.

"Thank you, Chuck."

"No problem, baby girl. Make sure she's okay for me? I'll call Spencer and see if he can help me get this taken care of, although he's been pretty hard to get a hold of lately. I bet if I called from your phone he'd pick right up," he said with a sly grin.

Okay, so he hasn't totally changed. "Go ahead and try. But he doesn't have my number. He won't answer."

Charles was going through my phone while I talked. "Who are you trying to fool? His number is right here? He called you like ten minutes ago."

He showed me the missed call. The two calls that I hadn't answered because I didn't know who it was.

"I didn't know that was him," I said, looking at the phone like it was diseased.

"Here, you want to call him back?" he asked, handing my phone back.

I can't call him, not now. What would I even say?

Clearly he had something to say to me. Did I really want to listen to anything he had to say? *Yes—no! What am I thinking?* You would have thought I'd learned my lesson by now.

"No, I don't want to call him back, not now, not ever," I said, pushing the phone back toward my brother.

Laughing at me, he slid the phone in his pocket. "You are so stubborn. I don't know what happened between the two of you, and I don't care but—ugh, God help me for saying this, but maybe you should give him a chance. He's not as bad as Teddy makes him out to be."

I stared dumbfounded at him. "Thanks, but no thanks. Spencer had his chance and he blew it—twice," I said, crossing my arms.

"Well, you know what they say. Third time's a charm," he said, winking devilishly at me.

I hit his shoulder. "Bye, Charles. Go fix my phone and go to work." Opening the door I pushed him out.

"Bye, baby sis. Love you."

I couldn't help but return his smile. "I'm not a baby, now scoot!" I said, kicking him out the door.

I walked into my room to find Gia curled up on my bed, fast asleep. Joining her, I settled in under the cozy covers and waited for sleep to take me over. Just as I was drifting off, Spencer's face came to the forefront of my mind—his smiling sexy, carefree face, the one that always seemed to get me in trouble. As much as I tried to deny it, my subconscious wanted him—bad.

⌘⌘⌘

We woke up to the house phone ringing. I answered sluggishly. "Hello?" Sitting up, I rubbed my eyes, waiting for a response from the other end.

"Beth, its Teddy. Put Gia on the phone for me."

I kicked Gia's butt. She rolled over and looked at me.

"Teddy," I said, pointing to the phone.

Sitting bolt upright, she took the phone from my hand. "Hey," she said getting out of bed and walking into her room for some privacy. Walking back in only a few short moments later, she sat back down on the bed.

"Well?" I asked

"He wants to talk in person. He's meeting me out back in fifteen minutes."

She should sound happy. Why doesn't she sound happy?

"Did he say anything else?' I asked.

"No, nothing," she said pathetically.

I wished her good luck and told her to really listen to what Teddy was telling her. Laying back down in bed, I wanted to scream in frustration. The media was ruining my life. Worst of all, now they were ruining my family's lives. I wanted to blame Spencer for all of this, but I knew that I was just as much to blame. If I could have been stronger around him, not let him affect me like he did, then none of this would have happened.

Grabbing my phone, I called Simon to fill him in on all that had happened. "Can you believe they are going after them now? I mean like really going after them? I hope it doesn't hurt the opening of the club."

"I'm so sorry. Hopefully that will be the worst of it." The sincerity in his voice was comforting and just what I needed to hear. "I'm sure it's not going to affect the club opening at all," he continued. "It will probably hype it up even more, believe it or not."

I didn't want to believe it but I knew he was right. As much as this was hurting my family, it was probably the best thing that could happen right before they opened.

"I can come over if you want me to?" he asked.

"Nah, I think Gia will be in need of a girl's night once she gets back. I should give my undivided attention to her."

I did want him there but I thought Gia and I both needed to hype ourselves for tomorrow night's opening.

"Okay, I can find some work to keep me busy. Oh I'm going to meet you at 21 tomorrow. I have to get a few shots early on, so if you don't mind, I'll just find you inside."

Anxiety took over. I needed him next to me. I didn't want to be sucked in Spencer's web. I needed Simon. I needed his presence next to me.

"What do you mean? When are you getting there?" I asked anxiously

"Relax, babe. I'll be there. I'm just not going to ride with you. I have to get there early. Soon as I see you, I'm dropping the camera and I'll be all yours."

Oh, thank God.

※

The house was spotless. I had the wine chilled and ready for consumption. All I needed now was for Gia to get back. Finally, the door opened and Gia walked in. Red eyed and defeated.

"That good?" I asked

"It's over. He said he needed some space. He thinks we rushed into it too fast." Sitting next to me, she covered her face with a pillow.

"I'm sorry, Gia. This is all my fault."

Moving the pillow, she stared at me. "How could this possibly be your fault?"

"If I had never been with Spencer, the media wouldn't be hanging around. They wouldn't have touched you guys if I hadn't been so stupid. I knew being with Salvatore was too good to be true, but I didn't think—well, I did think. I just thought with the wrong part of my anatomy."

Laughing, we settled into the couch. "That all might be true, but you slept with the sexiest man alive. Own it, scars and all."

"I think this conversation needs wine. Lots of wine," I said, smiling across at her.

"Agreed."

One pizza, two bottles of wine, three shots of tequila, and four spoonfuls of Ben and Jerry's later, Gia and I were feeling damn good.

"I'm going to march right up to him and slap him then tell him to leave me the hell alone," I said, slurring my words.

"You march right up to his fine ass and do that. Just get all up in there and—and—hey, do you mind if I try to...you know?" she said, wiggling her eyebrows at me. "You know once you're finished kicking him up and down the street?"

Why the hell does she keep moving? Oh wait, I'm swaying back and forth. Glaring at her, I placed my hands on my hips. "Hell no! You can't have sex with him! I can't—you can't—no one is having sex with him tomorrow night!" I said, slashing my arms about.

Pouting, Gia sat down, or fell down. I couldn't tell.

Hearing a knock at the door, our eyes got huge.

"Who the hell could that be?" Stumbling to the door, I reached up on my tiptoes and peered through the peep hole.

"Well, who is it?" Gia asked, taking a bite of cold pizza.

Drunkenly turning around, I leaned against the door. "It's Teddy," I said, like a kid getting caught. "Clean that shit up. Put the alcohol in the kitchen!"

Running around, we quickly cleaned up the living room, tossing pillows back on the couch and removing the pizza box, melted ice cream, and bag of chips. Neither one of us wanted to show weakness in front of my brothers.

Laughing hysterically, I almost peed my pants as we ran around. Gia plopped on the couch as I took a breath to gain whatever composure I could, which wasn't much right now. I unlocked the door and let Teddy in. Still chuckling silently, we tried not to make eye contact with him. Walking in, he took in the room, no doubt noticing the mess we had attempted to clean up.

Eyeing Gia up on the couch, he then turned toward me. "Beth?" he asked

"What?" I answered back as I closed the door.

"Been drinking?"

"What's it matter to you?" Gia said snidely.

He turned back to me with his disapproving face on. "Really, Beth, this is how you are helping her deal with all of this?"

I do not need the disapproving parent talk right now. "Don't blame me. You're the idiot who told her you needed space."

I glanced at Gia who nodded her head in agreement.

"Well, now neither one of you are getting any 'space,'" he said, taking his jacket off and laying it over one of the chairs. "Now I have to stay here and make sure neither one of you do anything stupid. Oh, here's your phone. Charles set it all up," he said, tossing me my new phone.

"Whatever, Teddy." I rolled my eyes at him. If he was going to act like a parent, then I was going to be a bratty teenager.

Walking over to the couch where Gia was seated, he began to sit down.

"Umm, you can sit over there. I need my 'space,'" she said nastily.

Go, Gia!

Shaking his head, he moved over to a chair and sat down, pulled his phone out, and started typing something. He ignored us for the rest of the night.

Chapter 30

"Spencer, is that you?" I could hear the loud music pounding through the walls. I was at the club, in a dimly lit office. There was a desk and a man sitting behind it. His back was to me, and all I could make out was the tall swivel chair and the top of someone's head.

"You wore it," the mystery man said.

Turning slowly, I saw Spencer's haunting blue eyes examining my body. The closer I stepped toward the desk the faster my heart raced.

"It's stunning on you," he said while his predatory gaze undressed me.

I ran my shaking hands over the bead work. "I guess you remembered every curve of my body."

Standing from the desk, he made his way from behind it. Less than three feet separated us. His hands rested casually in his pockets, his hair slicked back, but still lose. Our eyes met and the air was sucked out of me. I couldn't breathe. Removing his hands from his pockets, he reached for my hips, pulling me closer to him with a roughness I hadn't realized I'd been craving. I melted at his touch, giving into what my body desired.

"I couldn't forget if I tried," he crooned.

I was held tightly between his legs as he ran his hands over my body. His lips hovered over mine. The warmth of his breath chilled me. The room spun and I lost myself in his eyes, his arms, in all of him. Closing my eyes, I let his smell flood my senses. I was savoring this moment, never wanting it to end. Opening my eyes again, I expected to see his face, but all I saw was my ceiling.

I clutched at my chest, my heart pounding furiously within me. *Fuck, these dreams of Spencer are getting out of control. I can even smell him, like really smell him. Oh my God, I'm in his shirt.* Grabbing at my chest I held out his white shirt and looked down at it. *How the hell—alcohol. I'm never drinking again.*

I should rip it off, toss it in the trash. But it smelled too good. Making a deal with myself, I left it on for five minutes then tossed it back into the depths of my closet, this time, making sure to bury it in a pile of old ratty clothes.

☙❧☙

Eight hours later, I was standing face to face with the dress Spencer had given me. I had delayed putting it on until the last minute. My hair and make-up were done, the necklace Simon had given me was securely around my neck, and the limo my brothers had sent over to get us was waiting outside, with them in it.

"Beth? Are you ready?" Gia asked from the other side of my door.

Here goes nothing. Taking the dress off the hanger, I stepped in and slid my arms through their designated holes. "Yeah, can you come zip me up?"

Zipping it up effortlessly she stepped back to get a good look. "Damn, Spencer can pick 'em," she said, eyeing me up.

Checking the mirror for lines or unwanted bulges, I admired myself for the first time. The fabric was tight but manageable. My chest was snug and my cleavage was amazing.

"Yeah, Spencer the personal shopper. Maybe he turned gay in the last three weeks."

Laughing, we both took in our images in the mirror, Gia in a lacey navy blue cocktail dress, and me in all white. Gia was going to get over my brother, or brothers, and I was going to rid myself of Spencer. We had our missions for the night, and nothing was going to get in our way.

Charles jumped out of the limo, dressed in his nice suit. Helping us in, he then climbed back in and closed the door.

"Hey, Teddy." I said, scooting closer to him.

"You look lovely, Beth," he said, leaning over and kissing my cheek.

"Thanks, and thanks for putting me to bed last night. I really appreciate it." I did. As much as I hated when he was over protective, I still needed him to tuck me in when I was drunk.

"It's not a problem. I was just watching out for my girls."

At that he glanced at Gia, who was trying not to pay attention but failing miserably. "Yeah, thanks, Teddy," she said, trying to act like she didn't care.

There was nothing I hated more than awkward silence.

"Well, damn, baby girl, you trying to break some hearts tonight?" Charles asked, finally breaking the silence.

"Just one," I said, smiling wickedly. "Oh, let's lose the whole baby girl thing tonight. Please."

"What's wrong with it? You're my sister and you act like a tantrum-throwing baby. I'd say it's rather fitting."

He was so pleased with himself. But I wasn't going to give in to temptation and throw a "tantrum" as he put it. So I simply huffed and looked out the window.

"Ooo, that's pretty good self-control there, but I still see a little tantrum," he said, pointing at my face.

Leaning across the limo, I hit his arm roughly. We all seemed to relax and make small talk the rest of the way. The awkward tension gone, my family was back—*kind of.*

We pulled up to the front, where the press was camped out. Teddy and Charles exited first then Gia. As she stepped out, Charles held her hand to escort her out of the limo. The cameras went off like crazy. The three of them stood side by side, as a sea of flashes went off.

Sitting by myself, I closed the door not ready to exit just yet. I wanted to yell to the driver to drive and get me as far away from that club as possible. My stomach began to turn like it did that first night at mood. *What the hell am I doing here? Why am I wearing this dress, his dress? This was all a big mistake. I can still escape, right? Wrong.*

The door opened back up and a hand reached in to help me out. The chill from the night's air sent a shiver down my spine as I looked at the out stretched hand. I reached for it, simultaneously stepping out. I squeezed tighter, assuming it was Teddy's. The cameras went off, and I knew the moment the hand squeezed back that it wasn't my brother.

I looked up into Spencer's blue eyes as I stood up straight from the limo. I watched numbly as he held my hand. Bringing it up to his lips, he kissed the back of it. The cameras erupted as he gently left a kiss on my hand then led me over to where my brothers and Gia stood.

Catching my gaze, Gia widened her eyes, indicating for me to stay strong. I nodded back weakly. We stood in a line—Charles, Gia, Teddy, myself, and Spencer on the end as people took our pictures. I wanted to look up at him, but not with all these people around. Although I couldn't see his face, I could feel him staring down at me. I held my ground, smiling pretty for what seemed like hundreds of cameras.

I held on to Teddy for dear life as we stood there. Spencer's hand began to move to the small of my back. His thumb caressed me slowly and, each time, I weakened a little more. Before I knew what I was doing, I turned to look up into those blue eyes which were thankfully focusing on the cameras. *Shit!* *He looked sexy as hell. Oh fuck. He's looking at me.* I was frozen. His eyes cast a spell over me. The rest of the world faded around us.

"Let's get one of just the owners," someone called.

"Beth," Teddy whispered in my ear and I was finally free from the trance I had been in.

Turning from Spencer, I saw Gia back away. We bee-lined for the open doors, pausing once we reached them to watch the boys get their pictures taken.

"Goddamn, they look hot. I think I'd do any one of them at this point," she said.

"Gross, Gia. Considering that you've already done two of them, I'd say cool your jets. Come on, it's cold and I need a drink," I said, taking her arm and dragging her inside.

I was blown away by the transformation of the place. The

space didn't even resemble the once-abandoned restaurant. Spinning round, I took in all the changes. Spencer's description from moths ago came to mind. It was exactly as he described it back then.

It was manly but still soft—warm browns and soft leather with wood furnishings. The décor had an old-world feel, yet remained updated and modern enough for those who didn't appreciate old-world charm.

The music was loud and there was already a ton of people dancing. The tables were filled with celebrities and socialites alike. Charles had made sure to rub it in that Spencer had pulled as many stings as he could to get movie stars and musicians to show up for the opening.

Gia and I made our way to the bar where the bartender had our drinks ready and waiting for us, even though there was a line waiting to be served. *Maybe this brothers owning a club wasn't going to be so bad,* I thought as I sipped on the cold liquid. Even the glasses were beautiful. We stood there, admiring all the hard work my brothers had put into the place.

"Ladies, I don't believe we have ever been introduced. I'm Kyle."

Kyle Foster is talking to us. A class-A movie star is actually talking to us.

Gia and I looked at one another, and then scanned the stranger up and down. His movie-star good looks were just as hot in person as they were on the big screen. His perfectly quaffed blond hair and green eyes were breathtaking. This man was famous, like legit famous, and he was standing in front of me. Another actor stood next to him. I couldn't put my finger on who he was, but I knew I had seen him in something. His features were dark and masculine. They both eyed up Gia. *Great. Here I am again, the frumpy sidekick.*

"Hey, I'm Gia," she said, placing a delicate hand on herself. "And this is—"

"Elizabeth Monroe," Kyle said, taking the words out of her mouth. Prowling eyes ran up and down my body, and suddenly I didn't feel like the frumpy sidekick any more. Taking my hand in his, he kissed the top of it.

A freaking movie star just kissed my hand. This is so surreal. "How do you know my name? I think I would have remembered meeting you." I couldn't help saying it as a smile pulled one side of my lips up.

Pulling my hand and me closer, he whispered in my ear so only I could hear. "I've heard a lot about you. Word travels," he said, leaving a tender kiss upon my neck.

"Oh, and pray tell what words have been traveling about me? Huh? Cat got your tongue?" *What the hell is he smirking at?*

"Come dance with me?" he asked, trying to reach for the hand I had pulled out of his moments before.

Slapping his hand away, I shrieked. "No! I don't think so," I said, crossing my arms.

"He wasn't kidding when he said you were a stubborn woman, but damn it's sexy," Kyle said, chuckling and scratching the scruff that grew on his perfect movie-star face.

Peeking over his tall body, I watched as Gia and the other guy start dancing. *Damn that girl, she left me again.* Bringing my attention back to the man standing in front of me, I eyed him up and down.

"Who told you I was stubborn? Was it Charles?" *That jerk of a brother.*

"No, I've never meet your brother until tonight. Salvatore let it slip one drunken night," he stated.

Snapping my mouth shut, I ground my teeth together. This was just perfect. Spencer was running around, telling movie stars that I was stubborn. *Doesn't he have anything else to talk about with these people? This is good. Keep fueling my fire, Salvatore.*

"So will you dance with me?" Kyle asked again.

I scanned the room, looking for Simon to come save me but he wasn't there. I decided to take Kyle's hand. When, if any other time but tonight, would I get to dance with a movie star? *Who thinks I'm sexy, for Christ's sake.* Simon was just going to have to get over it.

A few songs later, I was done. Walking back to the bar, I glanced back to see both men dancing with Gia. She looked like she was on cloud nine. I was happy for her. Leaning against the bar, I was given another drink without even asking. *Yeah, I could get use to this.*

I scanned the crowd again for Simon, still nothing. A flash caught my eye and I glanced up. The second level was dimly lit by the chandeliers that hung all around. Their soft glow set a calm tranquil tone. Standing, I stepped away from the bar. I felt him before I saw him. Spencer stood at the railing, staring down at me.

His dark hair was raked loosely off his face and the light blue of his eyes seemed to glow. His fitted suit jacket was unbuttoned and moved to the sides, his hands placed securely in his pockets. I stood there, hopelessly staring up at him. My heart raced and my breath hitched. I couldn't get my lungs to fully expand. The tightness of the dress made it impossible to take in a full gulp of oxygen.

One moment he was standing there, watching me. The next he disappeared into the darkness of the hallway behind him. Backing up toward the bar, I gained the attention of the bartender.

"What can I get you Miss. Monroe?" he asked, leaning over.

"How do you get up there?" I said, pointing at the second level.

"Go through those doors," he said, pointing, "The stairs are on the right. Just let the bouncer know who you are and he'll let you up."

I smiled my thanks before making my way to the door.

Opening it, I was greeted by the bouncer. "Good evening, Miss. Monroe, you enjoying yourself?" he asked, as if we were friends.

"So far so good," I said.

It dawned on me that this was the same man who once prevented me from entering the VIP section in Mood. I inwardly cringed at the way I'd acted when he wouldn't let me in. Clearly, he knew who I was now, as he stepped aside and let me walk up the stairs.

Taking hold of the railing, I felt the vibrations of my phone from within my bag. Ignoring it, I continued my way up the stairs. Spencer was up there, and I was determined to end this for good.

Chapter 31

There were three doors, two were closed and one was cracked open. Taking my chances, I stepped toward the middle door that was open. A faint light made the doorframe seem aglow. Pushing it open with a shaking hand, I stepped inside.

A large desk sat opposite the door. Two large leather high-backed chairs faced it. A sense of déjà vu washed across my mind.

"Spencer?"

I didn't know if I had vocalized it or simply thought I had. The chair at the desk turned revealing him sitting there, attentively watching me as I moved closer.

"You wore it," he said, leaning toward the desk, his elbows resting upon it. His hands folded over one another as he brought his mouth to his knuckles.

Okay, this is freaky. Straightening, I held my ground unwaveringly.

"It's stunning on you."

I knew he was going to say that. This was more than déjà vu, it was *Groundhog's Day*. Taking another step, I looked down at the stunning dress.

"Yes. Yes, it is Thank you," I said, not breaking a smile.

This was where the déjà vu stopped and reality took over. He didn't stand, or take me in his arms. He sat there unmoving, his eyes never leaving mine. "It was the least I could do," he said, still staring at me.

"Since you ruined my last one, I'd say that's about right."

Finally standing from his desk, he walked around to the front of it. His hands by his sides, he took another step closer to me.

"Stop," I said, taking a step back to keep him at arm's length. "Just stay there."

The closer he got to me the more I forgot the real reason why I was there.

"I just need to know something," he said, leaning back against the desk.

"What could you possibly need to know? You're Spencer Salvatore Don't you know everything?" I snapped.

Placing his hands back in his pockets, he hung his head, before looking up at me with a wicked grin on his face. The kind of grin that could make a woman drop her panties. *But not me! I'm not falling for it, not tonight.*

"I do make it a priority to know everything, but there's one thing that I can never figure out, and that's you. Are you happy with him?" he asked, standing upright from the desk. His large muscular frame stood over me as I stared up into his blue eyes.

"Yes." I threw the word maliciously in his face. His scent drifted under my nose at that exact moment. My body wanted me to give in, but I wasn't going to let it. "He won, and you lost. You walked away, he stayed. I asked you for one day and you wouldn't even give me that. I would have chosen you, but you let your stupid pride get in the way, and you lost." I poked my finger at his chest. The force behind it bent my finger back, but he just stood there like a statue taking in all I had said.

"You're lying to yourself, if you actually believe that. He didn't win, he was just conveniently there. If you were happy, you wouldn't be here right now. You wouldn't have gone out of your way to come find me. This isn't remotely close to being over," he said smugly.

Damn him and his confidence. I was there to end it all with him, bury him in my past. *Fuck me, he's a jerk.*

"I only came up here to tell you to leave me the hell alone. Stop sending me notes, stop leaving me presents, just leave me alone."

Narrowing my eyes up at him, I saw his anger was starting

to take over. His jaw clenched, his hands fisted noticeably by his side. He shook his head, which only made me angrier.

"No, not a chance, Monroe."

"You don't have a choice, Spencer. I'm done. I'm finished with you, and it's over."

Turning on my heel, I went to take a step.

His tight grip held my arm as he spun me back around. "I should have run after you. You're right. I let my pride take over."

"Well, it's too late now." I tried to move my hand from his grasp. My efforts were useless.

"I can't stop," he confessed. "I see you everywhere. I close my eyes and your face is all I see. When I sleep, you're all I dream about. I hear your stubborn-ass voice in my head. I can't stop it."

Letting me go, he raked his hands through his hair.

Hearing him confess everything, I understood. I got it. "Spencer." Letting my guard down for a brief moment, I re-laxed. "I get it. I know exactly how you feel but—"*Shouldn't have let that guard down so easily.*

"How the hell do you know how it feels? You're happy," he roared.

"I know because all I see is your fucking, perfect face! I know because I dream about you every fucking night! I get it. So don't stand here and preach to me about how miserable you are. I hate myself for thinking about you when I'm with him. But you're always there. Are you happy? You were right all along, I'm with him and I'm constantly thinking about you!"

On the verge of tears, I covered my face with my hands. *Damn him for doing this.* I wanted to run away, run into Si-mon's arms, and forget all of this, but my feet were firmly planted beneath me.

"What are we doing, Spencer? We can't keep going around on this crazy carousel."

He stood there not saying a word.

"Spencer! Answer me!" I yelled at him, my arms out-stretched.

Forcefully he stepped closer. Holding my ground inches

from his body, I could feel the tension that radiated between us. He wasn't touching me, but he was all over me.

"What do you want me to say?" Face to face with me, he leaned closer. His hot breath danced on my neck as he spoke. "I'll do whatever you want."

His words were breathy and desperate. Men like Spencer didn't submit, yet here he was doing just that. I took deep breaths, my chest rising and falling heavily. I watched as his hand hovered near my cheek. He held back, making a fist, then quickly releasing it. Wetting his lips he stared at mine. The seductive way he did it made my body weak with want. I looked into his eyes and felt a tear roll down my face, landing on the bare skin of my chest.

"Don't let me leave," I said, weakly giving into my body, my heart. I couldn't have stopped the words from coming out it if I wanted to.

His hand gripped the back of my neck. Our lips crashed onto one another's. Sparks were everywhere. My body throbbed like it never had before. Holding me tightly, he turned me, pushing me against the edge of the desk. His other hand held my face as the desire we had both been holding back finally spilled over.

I gripped the edge of the desk, afraid that if I let it go, it would all end and I'd wake up. I had given into my desires and it felt amazing. His lips left mine, but I selfishly reached out to find them again. Gazing up at him, I noted the serious expression on his face.

"I will not let you go again," he said, running his thumb over my bottom lip.

The intensity in his voice was everything I needed to hear. I believed him. I believed that he would never leave me again.

I managed to nod up at him before he kissed me again. His strong hand ran down the front of my neck and over my collar bone. Reveling in his touch, I realized just how much I missed his dominate ways. Grasping the strap of the dress, he tried to pull it down and off my arm, but settled for letting it go and caressing my arm, instead. Grabbing my waist, he backed up, bringing me with him. Sitting in one of the high-backed chairs, he tugged me between his legs. I stood there, watching him watch me. His fingers grazed my leg. I marveled at the way he touched me, the way he could make the simple act of running his fingers along the hem of my dress the sexiest thing I had ever seen.

He gripped the bottom of the dress, tugging it up to reveal more of my leg. The hem of the dress rested at the under-curve of my ass and both of his hands wrapped around the back of my thighs. He tugged me down. I straddled his lap and held on tightly to the back of his neck for balance. My fingers went up the back of his head, getting lost in his dark hair.

I pulled him roughly toward my neck, needing him to devour me. His nose ran across my skin. I arched toward him. He left a trail of soft kisses down my neck and over the top of my cleavage. The tight fabric added to the ecstasy of it all. My nipples tingled beneath it, begging for him to release them and use his mouth more thoroughly.

Feeling the necklace around my throat move, I sat back and watched him take it between his fingers.

"I'm going to pretend that S is for me," he said, tugging on it lightly.

The thin chain dug blissfully into the back of my neck as I nodded in agreement. I wasn't going to fight it. That S had stood for him all along, whether Simon had given it to me or not.

Releasing the S of the necklace, his hand came up to cup my face tenderly. I held it with my own. Pulling it away from my face, I left a kiss in the palm of his hand before I stood. Blue eyes never left mine.

Sitting back in the chair, he wet his lips then rested his elbows on the armrests of the chair as he intertwined his fingers. I took a second to get my thoughts straight. If we were going to do this, there were a few things that I needed to get off my chest.

Exhaling and moving the hem of my dress down slightly, I began. "I don't care what happens anymore or what people say. I'm done fighting this—fighting you. I'll give you all of me, but don't break me," I said sternly, pointing a finger at him. "I won't survive it again." I needed him to know that. I needed him to know that one more heartbreak from him would destroy me beyond repair.

Standing there a second, I waited for a response. He stood and reached for my hand. I placed it fully in his. Toe to toe, we searched each other's faces before he spoke.

"I won't survive either," he said, caressing my face. "I need you, right here with me. I'm not letting go. Ever."

He rested his forehead on mine. I reached up to kiss his full lips. My heart had never healed from him. He broke it and it hurt more than I cared to admit, but I'd do it all again to be in his arms just as I was now. Maybe it refused to heal because it knew where it truly belonged, which was in his hands, mended, and open only to him.

"Get your fucking hands off her!"

Chapter 32

Simon's lion-like growl bounced off the walls. My head was telling me to back up and explain to him what was going on, but my body wasn't listening to my head at that exact moment. I took a chance and glanced up at Simon. When I looked back at Spencer, his eyes had gone from a cool blue to straight fire.

"I said get you motherfucking hands off her, you son of a bitch,"

Caressing my face, Spencer turned to face the intruder. Seeing Simon in the room with us brought reality crashing down around me. I had never seen Simon mad. It was a little frightening. His usual calm, carefree demeanor was gone. What stood before me was not the man I had thought I was in love with.

Even though I wasn't sure if I was in love with Simon, I still cared about him. Seeing him like this was horrible. I was horrible. I had done this to us all. Taking a step in his direction I attempted to explain. "Simon—I—let me—"

"Save it, Elizabeth." His words were laced with rage.

"Don't talk to her like that," Spencer said, moving next to me.

"Hell, no, you don't get to talk. I watched you hurt her time and time again. I watched you pull her into your mess of a life then spit her out one too many times. I'm not going to sit back and let you drag her into your twisted web of lies again. You don't deserve her," he said, pointing at Spencer.

What the hell is Simon talking about? I've never been in the same room with both of them. I never told him—"Simon, what the fuck is going on?" I asked, needing answers fast.

Simon froze. His face fell as if realizing that he had said too much.

"Oh come on, Sullivan, don't play the poor pathetic boy next door now," Spencer said with a cocky grin.

I turned to Spencer and glared. "One of you better start talking now, or I'm going to lose it," I said, crossing my arms in frustration.

I looked between the two of them before Simon spoke up. "Elizabeth, I've been trying to tell you for a long time," he said then paused.

"Tell me what?" Feeling Spencer's body next to mine, I turned back to him.

"Oh, please let me tell her," Spencer said. "You see, Elizabeth, Simon isn't who he says he is."

My heart pounded even harder within my chest as I continued watching both men. Spencer was arrogant and determined to make Simon squirm under his thumb. Simon, on the other hand, seemed defeated and overwhelmed.

Smiling across at him, Spencer gloated. Standing behind me, he leaned next to my head and spoke. "Those pictures of you—of us, they were taken by him, every last one of them."

I took a step away from Spencer. I needed space, and I needed air. "Is this some sort of sick game between the two of you? Are you trying to pull me until I snap?"

"It's a fake, he's a fake. It was all a lie. He's been using you this whole time. That's what I've been doing these past weeks. I had to find out the truth, and I was right. He's working for Fame! Hell, he probably owns Fame! Think about it, Elizabeth, he was always calling you when we were together. He knew where you were the whole time because he was there, too. He never left to go overseas. It was a cover story. He's nothing but scum beneath your feet."

I stared at Simon during Spencer's entire speech. With each word, I was convinced that Spencer was telling the truth. It was written all over Simon's face.

"I do love you. It was easier to lie than tell the truth. I didn't want to hurt you," Simon said, stepping toward me.

"Was any of it real?" I asked, sitting down in one of the chairs.

"Yes, it was all real. It might have started out as something else, but I fell in love with you, I'm still in love with you. It killed me to watch him hurt you. I wanted to tell you so many times, but I couldn't. I didn't want you to look at me the way you're looking at me now," he said, coming to kneel before me and taking my hands in his. "Please, I didn't have a choice."

It felt like a stranger had touched me. I sat back, jerking my hands from his. I didn't know the man who was pleading with me. Simon wasn't who I thought he was. *Is his name even Simon?*

"I think you should leave." My words were cold as ice, freezing even my lips as they left them.

"Please, let's talk about it," he begged as he rose from the floor.

"Get out, Simon. I can't even look at you right now. You brought the media into my life, into my family's lives. You knew how much I hated it, yet you were able to lie to my face and send in pictures that you knew would destroy me. You're a beast, an ugly beast."

"If that's what you want, then I'll go, but I'm not giving up on you. I do love you. That's the truth. If there's one thing I want you to believe, it's that I love you. I made a mistake, but you, of all people, should be able to forgive me." I watched as he went toe to toe with Spencer. "I hope you're happy," Simon snapped at him.

They stood there, eyeing the other up. This was definitely not the way my fantasy of these two men in the same room had played out in my mind. In fact, it was the complete opposite. They were too busy intimidating each other to even notice that I had stood up.

"Don't get too comfortable, Salvatore. I'm not going anywhere and there are some pretty nasty people out to get you. I'd watch your back. I'll give you what you ask for, Beth. I'll step down, back off, but don't be surprised when he breaks your heart again. I'll be there to pick the pieces up. I'll be there to help mend your broken heart, and you can count on that." Taking a step back, Simon glanced my way one last time before leaving.

We watched as he left the room slamming the door behind him. Instantly, I turned on Spencer. "How long have you known?" I asked, keeping my distance.

"Thursday morning. I tried to call you the moment I had figured it out but you didn't answer," he said, tilting his head.

"Who else knows?" I asked, pacing the room.

"No one. I wanted to tell you first."

I can't believe this is really my life. If you would have told me five months ago that I'd be standing here dealing with this, I'd have laughed in your face. Sitting down again, I looked up at Spencer. The emotions that I had been holding in finally took over and a tsunami of tears ran freely down my face. The only man that I had ever said "I love you" to had betrayed me, used me. I should feel relieved, happy that I didn't have the burden of choosing one man over the other. *So why does it feel so dirty, so wrong?*

Kneeling, Spencer rubbed my back consolingly while I took it all in. Wiping my eyes, I began to reel in my emotions.

"I want you to know that I'd never lie to you. I'll always tell you the truth," he said, helping me wipe my tears away. He leaned closer and kissed me softly on the cheek. "Do you want me to get your brothers?"

I nodded silently and squeezed his hand. I was grateful he had figured it all out. Who knew what would have happened if Spencer had given up on his mission to figure out Simon, or if he had given up on us?

Kissing the tops of my hands, he rose and walked over to grab the phone. Punching in a few numbers, he held the receiver to his ear.

"Yes, it's Salvatore, can you find Teddy and Chuck and send them up to my office?…Yes…I don't care. Tell them that their sister is up here and she needs them, now!"

Chapter 33

It only took a few minutes before Teddy came crashing through the door. Still sitting, Spencer and I turned simultaneously as he barged in. Although I wasn't a blubbering mess, I was sure my face bore the evidence that I had been crying.

Teddy stood in the doorway, glancing between Spencer—who had moved the other chair closer to me—and me. Spencer sat on the edge, his hands folded and holding up his chin. I was sure I looked like a weeping child huddled in the large high-backed chair.

"What the hell is going on, Salvatore?" Teddy asked, briskly coming across the room,

Spencer stood, straightening his tie.

"I swear to God if you touched her—"

Teddy wasn't waiting for an answer from him. He was going to punch Spencer first. I stood quickly, placing my hand on his chest to impede his very clear intentions.

"Teddy, stop, he didn't do anything," I said, trying to shake his jacket and bring him back from the edge of manslaughter.

Finally noticing me, Teddy took my hands from his chest and leaned down to look in my puffy and red face, wiping his thumb over my cheek. "What's going on?"

As I fought to find the right way to tell him everything, Charles came striding into the room. "This better be good, because I just left a Victoria Secret model for this." Assessing the situation, he saw Teddy holding me. "Baby girl, what's with the tears?" he asked, coming over to us.

It was obvious the wheels in his head started turning as he watched Spencer back away.

"You son of a bitch, what did you do to her?" Charles growled, rushing over, grabbing Spencer's suit jacket, and pushing him forcefully into his desk.

"Chuck!" I screamed from Teddy's arms.

Breaking free, I tried to pull him off of Spencer. Although Spencer was taller than Charles, my brother could have easily done some serious damage if he wanted to.

"Chuck, let him go," I pleaded, still trying to tug at his arm.

Releasing him, I quickly stood in front of Spencer. My back was flush against him. His hands hovered over my hips, but he didn't say anything to defend himself.

"Start talking, Beth," Charles demanded, fixing his suit jacket.

"It's not Spencer. It's Simon. He's not who he says he is at all."

"What are you talking about?" Teddy asked. "I checked him out. I didn't find anything."

"Well, you didn't look hard enough," Spencer said from behind me, the weight of his hands pressed protectively against my hips.

Turning around, I looked up at him. I didn't need him being spiteful or arrogant right now, so I shot him a warning glare to back off. Shaking his head at me in obvious frustration, he held his hands up before folding his arms across his chest.

Why do I get so turned on when we fight? I don't get it, but the thought of arguing with him then making up is a nice distraction from all that had just happened. Stay focused, Beth.

"Spencer figured out that it was Simon who had been taking the pictures for Fame and leaking information about all of us," I said, turning back to my brothers.

"How the hell did you figure that out?" Charles asked skeptically.

Honestly, I wanted to hear that as much as they did.

We all turned to Spencer, waiting to hear how he did it. "I was skeptical from the first night when I met you at Mood. I brushed it off, but I couldn't keep ignoring that every time we were together, he'd know about it and call you. When I got the picture removed from Fame, the IT guys traced it back to the hotel he was staying at. The day you hurt your ankle, I could have sworn I saw him in the crowd, and now I know that I did. The weekend you were in New York, I thought I saw him in my lobby, after you left."

"All right, we get it you had your suspicions," Teddy challenged. "How do you know for sure?"

"Wednesday night, I was out and saw Gia and Charles, so I called in an anonymous tip, to see if my suspicions were right. You were a hot topic in the media and I took advantage. I didn't tell them where I saw them just that I had. Twenty minutes later, he showed up at the exact spot where Gia and Charles were. I watched him hide in the bushes and wait. When Charles leaned in to kiss Gia, he took the picture. Simple as that.

"Oh, and he didn't deny any of it when I confronted him twenty minutes ago. That was the clincher," he said, leaning back on his desk, clearly pleased with himself.

"You set me up?" Charles was seeing red again.

"I didn't set you up. I didn't make you kiss her. That was all you."

"Shut the hell up, Salvatore." Charles said, turning away from him, clearly not wanting to hear the truth he was saying. "Where is he? Where is the little bastard?"

The door opened again and Gia walked in. "Umm, private party and no one invited me?" she said, clearly tipsy.

"Gia, I…umm…"*Shit she is going to be pissed once I tell her this.*

"Spit it out, Beth. What's going on? I thought you were coming up here to dump his ass, not rub up all over him," she said, gesturing at Spencer.

"I was, but—" I caught Spencer's wolfish grin and lost my train of thought.

"But—oh God, you had sex with him again, didn't you? Why are you're brothers here? That's a little twisted," she said, swaying slightly.

"Gia." Walking over to her, I held her shoulder so she

stopped swaying. "Simon's been lying to me, to all of us," I said, looking around the room.

"What do you mean lying to all of us?" she said, finally sobering up a little.

"Gia…" I went on to fill her in on all that had taken place. But as I wrapped up, her focus was solely on Spencer.

"You? You were the one that told them about me and Chuck?" Walking away from me, she stood before Spencer. He nodded at her, saying nothing. The room was silent until the sound of skin being slapped filled it. "You ruined everything for me," she seethed

"Gia!" I shouted as she pondered slapping him again.

"Beth, don't you dare make excesses for him. He put you through hell, remember that? As far as I'm concerned, he's just as bad as Simon is. You deserve better." Eyeing him with disgust, she turned to me. "Let's go." Taking my arm, she tried to make me leave. I stopped immediately, taking my arm out of her hand. "Don't be stupid, Beth, he's not worth it."

Why is she doing this? It wasn't his fault. She let Charles kiss her. She had a choice, she made the wrong one, and she has to deal with her own consequences. Spencer didn't deserve to be treated like the criminal here.

"I'm not leaving, this isn't his fault," I said, defending him

"You're acting like a crazy person." I simply shook my head. "Beth, he ruined me and Teddy!" she shouted out in frustration.

"I'm sorry that you got caught up in all of this," Spencer's said, walking to stand next to me. "But I wouldn't take it back if I could. He kept us a part for long enough and I'm not letting anyone come between us again."

Reaching for his hand, I held on tightly. We had fought what felt right, given in to our own pride, and let others come between us, but not anymore.

"You've got to be kidding," she said shaking her head as we stared at one another amorously. "Ya know what? Do whatever you want Beth, but when he leaves you again and hurts you, I don't want to be around to watch it, because we all know he's going to do it again, mark my words."

This had to be the alcohol talking. She's just not thinking clearly. We all watched as she stormed off.

"Gia, hold up. I'll go with you," Charles called to her just before she was gone.

The three of us were left standing silently, before Teddy spoke up. "Spencer, I think I owe you an apology. I should have listened to what you were saying. I've always been against you being with my sister, but maybe I made a hasty decision about you. Don't get me wrong. If you hurt her, I won't have a choice but to ruin you," he said, holding his hand out.

Spencer's took it in a firm hand shake. "I'm not going to let anything happen to her. You have my word."

Teddy kissed my forehead and I held on tightly to my brother, my stand-in father. "Thank you, Teddy," I said into his chest.

"I love you, baby girl. All right, I have a club full of people to entertain," he said, sighing. "Best not keep them wondering where I am. I'll call you tomorrow."

He left, closing the door behind him. Spencer and I were alone.

Sitting back down in the chair, I took my heels off. "These Goddamn things are going to kill me," I said, dropping them to the floor.

Hearing a chuckle come from Spencer, I watched as he sat in the opposite chair. Leaning over, he grabbed my foot and placed it on his lap. "Give me the other one, too," he said, tapping his leg.

So here we are, coming full circle. Placing my other foot on his lap, he began rubbing my feet. As I watched the man that I thought would never show a girl like me the time of day, I almost didn't believe it.

How was it possible that this man—who challenged me at every turn, who had secrets, who could make me weak in the knees with just the sound of his voice, a man who could have any woman in the world—chose me? Could we make something real out of all of this? Were we fooling ourselves in thinking that we could? Just because Simon was out of the picture, that didn't mean there weren't a million other things that could keep us apart. Was a gut feeling, fate, an undeniable attraction enough? I had no idea, but I sure as hell wasn't going down without a fight.

Epilogue

Simon

Whathat do you mean you quit?" Natasha yelled at me from across her desk.

Her short fashionable hair was swept off her face. For someone who was old enough to be my mother, she was stunning and didn't look a day over thirty-five. She kept her figure healthy and lean. I'd be lying if I said I hadn't had a Mrs. Robinson moment when she first hired me on.

She was the face behind Fame. She could make or break the rich and famous and sometimes the unknown and average. I was her protégé, her shining star pupil. At first, I took the job simply because I needed the money. My parents had cut me off and I had nothing until she swooped in and took me under her wing.

I had never had the problem of keeping my personal life separate from my work. I was there strictly to get dirt on Spencer plain and simple. I saw an opportunity to use Elizabeth as a means of getting to Spencer. I had it all figured out, but the one thing that I hadn't counted on was falling for the one person I had to hurt to get the job done.

"I can't do it anymore, I won't."

The image of Beth's face, when she realized it was me, was still fresh in my mind and it stung like a bitch.

"You know what will happen if you walk out now?" she said, threatening me for the millionth time.

"It's too late, Natasha. She knows. Your threats mean nothing now."

Sitting back in her chair, she wiggled a pen through her fingers, unfazed. "So she left you?" she asked, moving to the edge of her seat.

"What do you think, Natasha? Of course, she left me."

"Well, you know how I feel about you. I think you're making a big mistake. However, if you're interested I do have a proposition for you."

Ever the business woman. "I'm done Natasha, I'm out for good." Reaching for my bag, I stood from her desk.

"You know, it really is a shame. I know you care for this girl. You've done this how many countless times and you fall for this one girl. She must be 'the one,' if you're willing to give this all up," she said, gesturing to the lush office.

Mine was across the hall and just as extravagant as hers.

I watched as she shifted the papers on her desk haphazardly. "What's your point, Natasha?"

"You wouldn't want the love of your life in the arms of a murderer, would you?"

My body froze while her lips curved into a wicked grin.

"That's what I thought. Have a seat, Nickolas."

The End

About the Author

M.E. Gordon, was born and raised in Maryland, where she still resides with her husband. She is a stay-at-home mom to four children, three boys and one very, spoiled, little girl, all under the age of five. Growing up Gordon was an avid journal writer. She wrote her first romance novel at the age of 14, and it was pretty bad, but over the years and through all the kids she honed her craft. When Gordon doesn't have her mom hat on, you can find her reading, working on her next story, or watching guilty pleasure television.